A FORTUNE
WORTH
KILLING
FOR.

DESTINY

"My real mother was a whore," Valerie said again. "And my real father, he was probably even worse."

"Don't do this to yourself, Valerie," said Victor, running his hand through his hair, looking pained.

Slowly, Valerie pulled open the cashmere robe, unbuttoned the top of the white silk pajamas, and pulled them away from her shoulders, her breasts. Leaning forward, she tried to take his hand. "I know you don't want to marry me now, Victor," she whispered. "But I want us to make love. I've always wanted that. I want you to touch me, Victor. All over. Please."

Victor's eyes met hers, dropped to her neck, her white shoulders, her breasts. Met her eyes again.

"Do you love me, Valerie?" he asked.

Valerie felt her cheeks go hot, then cold. Her whole body trembled. With emotion. The champagne.

"Yes," she said hoarsely.

BARBARA WILKINS

ELEMENTS OF CHANCE

Harper Paperbacks

Harper & Row, Publishers, New York
Grand Rapids, Philadelphia, St. Louis, San Francisco
London, Singapore, Sydney, Tokyo, Toronto

This is a work of fiction. The characters, incidents, and
dialogues are products of the author's imagination and are not
to be construed as real. Any resemblance to actual events or
persons, living or dead, is entirely coincidental.

Harper Paperbacks a division of Harper & Row, Publishers, Inc.
10 East 53rd Street, New York, N.Y. 10022

This book is published by arrangement with Contemporary
Books, Inc.

Cover photography by Herman Estevez

First Harper Paperbacks printing: August, 1990

Printed in the United States of America

HARPER PAPERBACKS and colophon are trademarks of
Harper & Row, Publishers, Inc.

10 9 8 7 6 5 4 3 2 1

For David Marriott,
with my love and gratitude

ELEMENTS OF CHANCE

1

The traffic on the San Diego Freeway was backed up as far as Valerie could see in the rearview mirror of her red Ferrari. Five miles ahead, maybe more, the private planes landed at the southernmost part of Los Angeles International Airport. She turned up the classical music station. Vladimir Horowitz was playing Rachmaninoff.

Sitting, stalled in traffic, she watched the temperature gauge on the dashboard quiver upward. Her gauzy white dress clung to the leather of the seat. The engine was making strange popping noises, as if it were about to die.

Valerie glanced at the dashboard clock and checked it against her Piaget watch. The timepiece, with its loose, wide band and tiny diamonds at each number, had been a present from Victor when he returned from Paris several weeks ago. It was nearly three o'clock now, and the company's 727 jet would be landing. Valerie felt a twinge of anxiety at the thought of being late. She was never late when it came to Victor. She was always there, waiting.

"I'm flattered," she remembered Victor saying on the phone that morning when Valerie insisted on picking him up. "How long have I been gone? Two days? It must be love."

"It is love," she whispered, holding the receiver

close to her lips as she pictured the living room of their penthouse in New York City. She visualized the signed antiques, the magnificent Sarouk carpet, the new Renoir already in its ornately carved gilt frame over the mantelpiece, the view of Central Park below. "I start to miss you when I even think you're going to be out of my sight."

"After twelve years of marriage?" he gently mocked in his soft, English-accented voice. "That's quite a testimonial from a former child bride. I miss you, too. So much, darling."

"We have that benefit tonight at the Beverly Wilshire Hotel."

"I know, I know," he laughed. "We always have a benefit at the Beverly Wilshire. What's the disease of the evening?"

"Cystic fibrosis," she said, "and I have a new dress."

"I can't wait to see you in it. I can't wait to touch you. What time is this thing?"

"The usual. Seven o'clock for cocktails."

"That will give us a few hours alone, darling. I can't wait to have you in my arms, to be inside you. I'm barely alive when I'm not with you, Valerie. You know that. I love you."

A thrill went through her the way it always did when Victor, so proper, so formal, talked about making love to her. Even over the phone he could make her nipples harden, make her ready for him. Newspapers and magazines called theirs a great love affair; they were the perfect couple. Both were tall and slim; elegant and proud. Their colorings complemented each other perfectly. Victor's hair was dark brown with just a bit of gray at the temples, his eyes a pale blue. Valerie's hair was so blond it was almost white, cut to perfection like a cap on her small, well-shaped head. Her long, dark lashes framed large eyes that changed from hazel to green, following her moods or the clothes she wore.

When they were sensuously, erotically together, Valerie became so lost in Victor's pleasure that she felt herself disappear into him. When he was finally spent, lying across her, it was always with a tiny shock that she found herself once again to be a separate body and mind. At those moments, Valerie would stroke his thick, dark hair, run her tongue along the nape of his neck, and think that never could there be another love so perfect, that no woman could feel as tender, trusting toward any man.

Well, Victor would love the way she would look to-night in her new gown, Valerie thought with a smile, remembering her reflection in the huge mirrored dressing room off her bedroom. The gown was glorious, in black silk chiffon with spaghetti straps that showed off her white shoulders, the white swell of her breasts. Below the waist, slight flares flowed in two tiers to the floor.

"It's perfect," Mary di Stefano, Valerie's personal shopper, had breathed. "I knew it would be."

"I love it," said Valerie, spinning around. "Victor will love it. Nobody has taste like yours, Mary."

"I think the emerald earrings surrounded with the diamonds," Mary suggested. "Maybe nothing around the neck."

"I thought the pear-shaped diamond drop earrings and the diamond necklace," Valerie said.

"Which one?"

"The one that hits just below the collarbone, the ten-carat, pear-shaped diamond."

"Oh, right. The one Victor gave you one week 'just because it was Tuesday.' "

"*That* one."

"Your basic black and white?" said Mary doubtfully. "Well, maybe. But I still like the emeralds."

"I guess it doesn't matter," Valerie smiled. "They're all paste anyway."

"But great paste," Mary grinned.

Valerie was still smiling at the thought of the conversation when the Horowitz piece ended and the cultured voice on the radio announced the news.

"A jet has crashed in Mexico in the last half hour," the newscaster said. "From eyewitness reports, it is believed to have gone down approximately a hundred miles northeast of Acapulco." Now, as Valerie cut across the lanes of the freeway, the speedometer climbing to sixty-five, seventy, the palms of her hands on the leather steering wheel were damp and her mouth was dry. But it was Acapulco, she told herself firmly, and it couldn't be Victor.

The roar of a silver jet overhead cut off the newscaster's words. That would be Victor's plane, Valerie thought, relieved. She jammed the gears back into second and heard the tires squeal as she hit the off ramp. How she loved to drive. In the cossetted world that Victor had created for her, driving the Ferrari was about the only thing she did in which there was any element of chance.

"None of the airlines with regularly scheduled routes in the Acapulco area is missing an aircraft," the newscaster continued. "Early reports indicate that the plane may have been illegally transporting drugs from South America." Drug smugglers, Valerie thought, as the car crept up to the gates of the private section of the airport. Well, you could feel only so sorry for drug smugglers.

As she parked, all she could see were a few corporate Learjets off to the left of the terminal that serviced private planes. On the ground in the distance was a shimmer of silver as Victor's plane made its final turn to taxi up to the entrance. Members of the ground crew, in orange overalls, waited beside the aluminum stairs. On the field, two chauffeurs in black stood chatting between two white stretch limousines.

Valerie expertly applied a pink lipstick as she studied her reflection in the rearview mirror. Her face was flushed, she saw, which gave her a healthy glow. She looked close enough to the image of the elegant international beauty, Mrs. Victor Penn, to bring that look of pride and even lust to his face. As the jet cut its engines and the ground crew wheeled the aluminum stairs into place, Valerie could almost feel Victor's arms around her, his cheek pressed against her own.

It took her an instant to comprehend that the plane that had just landed was a DC-9, and that the legend painted on its side read Air Am rather than the familiar Penn International.

So Victor's plane was a little late, Valerie thought with disappointment as she pushed open the door of the terminal building. Behind a long counter, two men huddled together over the screen of a computer.

"Is anybody home?" Valerie asked brightly, leaning against the counter.

The two men turned.

"Hi, Mrs. Penn," said the shorter, stocky man.

"Hi, Mike, Kevin. I see Mr. Penn's plane is late. How soon will it be here?"

"We don't really know," Mike said. "There's some kind of mix-up. We're working it out with the control tower. The computers have been down and we don't know where we're at." He ran one of his big hands through his hair. "Look, why don't you come around the counter and sit down. I'll get you a cup of coffee."

Valerie felt her stomach muscles tighten, her mouth go dry again. Her dress suddenly felt wet against her body. "Mike, what seems to be going on?"

Mike was at her side, his hand on her arm, as he led her around the counter and guided her into a chair.

"Maybe you'd better call somebody to come be with you, Mrs. Penn. A relative. Maybe your mother. Is your whole family in England?"

"I'm American," Valerie said, hearing her voice rise. "I don't have any family. Just Victor. Mr. Penn, that is. He's my family. He's my life."

"Maybe a friend. Your doctor," Mike said, pouring her a cup of coffee from an automatic coffee maker. "Surely your doctor would come."

"Has Victor's plane crashed?" she asked. "Is that it?"

"I don't know. I just don't know what to tell you."

"Well, what *do* you know? Tell me what you know."

"Okay," he sighed. "Everything was just the same as always. A flight plan was filed this morning by the pilot. La Guardia to LAX. The plane took off. And that was that. It just vanished. We haven't heard from it since. And we're not talking a Piper Cub here. It's pretty hard to lose a 727."

"Could they have been hijacked?" Valerie asked, panicking.

"You know how it is when they board at La Guardia. You do it all the time. The limousine pulls up right next to the plane. The ground crew didn't notice anything unusual. It was the pilot, the copilot, the flight engineer, the stewardess, Mr. Penn, and that guy he always travels with. The bodyguard, I guess. It was the same as always. Of course, there could have been somebody hiding on the plane, but there's always a guard posted at the Penn International plane when it's on the ground."

"Sometimes the plane stops to pick someone up in Chicago," Valerie said.

"We'd know about that," Mike said. "The plane didn't land in Chicago. It didn't land anywhere." He ran his hand through his hair again. "Look, Mrs. Penn. I really think you should call someone. What about one of your girlfriends?"

"There has to be some explanation," Valerie insisted.

Mike shook his head.

"Call someone, Mrs. Penn. Please. We've got a jet that just went down in Mexico, and we've got the only plane missing in the world. Maybe it's just a coincidence. Maybe it isn't."

Someone had switched on the radio to the news. "Sources have confirmed that a 727 belonging to Penn International, the conglomerate that includes banks and real estate holdings in Europe, South America, and the United States, has not been heard from since it left La Guardia Airport in New York City at ten o'clock this morning after filing a flight plan for Los Angeles. It is believed that Victor Penn, the chairman of the board and chief executive officer of the conglomerate, was on the plane, as well as a four-person crew and a man thought to be Penn's bodyguard. Authorities at this point refuse to conjecture whether there is any connection between the missing Penn International jet and the plane that crashed within the last hour northeast of Acapulco in Mexico."

With shaking hands, Valerie picked up the phone on the desk in front of her and sat for a moment, wondering whom to call. The obvious person was Victor's brother, Raymond. Calling Raymond wouldn't do her any good right now, she realized. He was in London. It wouldn't get her home where she could wait for Victor to turn up to straighten out all this nonsense. A friend? She had no friends. There was only Victor, and the people they paid to attend to their needs.

Finally, Valerie called Mary di Stefano at her apartment in Beverly Hills. She felt weak with relief when Mary answered on the fourth ring.

"Mary," she whispered.

"Oh, God, sweetie. I've been hearing it on the news. Where are you?"

"I'm at the airport. I brought the Ferrari, and I don't think I can make it home."

"I'll be right there."

"Maybe it would be a good idea to call Daniel and have him pick you up in the Rolls," suggested Valerie. "I hope this isn't too inconvenient, Mary. I really don't know who else to call."

"You try to stay calm, and we'll be there in about a half hour."

"Thank you, Mary." It was all a tempest in a teapot, she thought calmly, as she replaced the receiver, then leaned forward to let the blood rush to her head. It was just a computer error of some kind. Sitting up, Valerie looked through the window into the bright, sunny sky, willing the speck of silver on the horizon to be Victor's plane.

Instead, the speck turned into a bulging 747 beginning its descent into LAX, two miles to the north.

2

The Rolls was a ten-year-old, custom-made, maroon limousine that Victor liked because it gave him room to stretch his long legs. A nineteen-inch color television set had been built into the back of the front seat. The fully equipped bar was for the convenience of guests rather than for Victor and Valerie, who drank only wine or champagne.

Valerie sat stiffly behind Daniel, the chauffeur, her hands folded in her lap, her legs crossed demurely at the ankles. The images on the television screen floated in front of her eyes as if underwater. Regular programming had been interrupted to concentrate on the Victor Penn story. It was as if a president had been assassinated. Valerie felt embarrassed at the thought.

"I'm going to fix us a drink," Mary said. Without makeup, her hair in a ponytail, wearing a pair of tight jeans and a striped shirt with the sleeves rolled up, Mary looked more Valerie's age than her own. Tentatively, she put one tanned hand on Valerie's arm. It was rigid. She's like a block of stone, Mary thought.

"I don't drink."

"Well, you're going to make an exception this time, sweetie." Mary pressed the button that opened the bar and fixed two scotch and waters, heavy on the scotch.

Valerie took the glass from Mary's hand and made a face as she sipped. "Oh, I'm so sorry," she said graciously. "I forgot to thank you."

Shock, thought Mary, mentally giving herself a pat on the back for calling Valerie's doctor to meet them at the estate. He could give Valerie a shot and put her out of all of this until tomorrow.

On the television screen, the anchorman discussed the Victor Penn story with the station's financial analyst.

"What do you think all of this is going to mean to the financial community, Jim? Where does Victor Penn stand?"

"Well, some say he's one of the two or three richest men in the world," said the financial analyst. "The Penn operation is international, with banks in London, Paris, New York, the Bahamas, Luxembourg. They've diversified into mining in South Africa, cattle ranches in Argentina, fish canneries in Alaska, all sorts of things. Since it's a privately held company, there's no way to know for certain."

"But he's certainly very much on the scene here in Los Angeles, wouldn't you say?"

"Oh, yes. Victor Penn is a prominent philanthropist. He supports a dozen charities, and it's said that he's even more active anonymously, behind the scenes."

"So if it's true that Victor Penn has been killed in a plane crash, it would be a real loss."

"Well," the analyst said, hesitating, "there have been some ugly rumors in recent months about Penn International. There's been talk in the financial community that federal bank examiners are about to step in to take a look at the whole operation. It's also said that they are asking foreign governments to cooperate."

"What sort of rumors?" the anchorman prompted.

"The talk is that the Penn International banks have been lending vast sums to its other companies, sums that run as much as a thousand percent more than their assets, for example," he replied. "Once this sort of thing starts, there's a snowball effect. For instance, some of the uglier rumors are that the Penn bank in the Bahamas has been used not only to launder drug money, but also to launder money paid as ransom in terrorist kidnappings all over the world."

"The disappearance of the plane carrying Victor Penn sounds like more than a coincidence then, wouldn't you say?" asked the anchorman.

"It certainly seems suspicious."

"Just who is Victor Penn? We'll be right back after these messages."

"How dare they talk about Victor like that," Valerie said in a low voice, her eyes blazing. "Victor is the sweetest, dearest, most open man in the world. His integrity is more important to him than anything else. They're a bunch of hyenas."

"It happens every time, sweetie," said Mary, between sips of her drink. She wondered if this meant the end of her hefty yearly salary, the end of all those delicious kickbacks from the stores where she shopped to dress the wife of Victor Penn. "They'll always get you when you're down. Nobody knows that better than I do."

"Victor's lawyers are going to have a field day with the slander suits," said Valerie, her jaw tight.

"Did you know about this? That the government is sending the bank examiners in?"

"It's a lie," Valerie said firmly. "Victor is above reproach."

On the screen, the visuals profiling Victor Penn began with file footage of Victor and Valerie at various charity events. Valerie in a white, beaded Givenchy, her diamonds glittering at her throat, with a tall, handsome Victor, his hand possessively on her arm, bending down to whisper in her ear. Valerie in a flame red Galanos, with Victor smiling dazzlingly into the camera and running a hand through his hair. Valerie, draped in full-length Russian sables, reaching up to kiss Victor on the cheek, his expression both proud and embarrassed. Then came the earlier films, of the brief time they had lived in their New York penthouse, of the many years in London. Victor and Valerie, each holding one of their newborn twins, beaming as they stepped off the aluminum stairs leading down from the Penn International jet. Valerie as a bride in a white gown with a cathedral-length train, a white veil covering her pale hair. She and Victor were on the steps of Saint-Ange in Paris, the first couple to be married there since well before the French Revolution. It had been Victor's decision, of course. Victor had always wanted to be married at Saint-Ange.

The commentator resumed his voice-over. "Ever since Victor Penn appeared on the banking scene in the mid-fifties, he has been a man of mystery in international financial circles. Starting in London, Penn gained an impressive reputation in the community, entertaining lavishly at his Regent's Park estate, or at his country estate in Sussex where the cream of London society often enjoyed hunt weekends, and where musical evenings featured such stars as Maria Callas, Arthur Rubinstein, and Jascha Heifetz among others. In 1973, Victor Penn married eighteen-year-old Valerie Hemion, a music student and the American-born niece of Lady Anne Hallowell, in a sumptuous, internationally celebrated ceremony at Saint-Ange in Paris. The couple has nine-year-old twins, a boy and a girl."

On the television screen, the glorious teenage bride gazed into the face of her handsome husband, her eyes dazed with love. Victor was leaning down, gently kissing Valerie's lips, touching her cheek with his.

"Great wedding gown," Mary murmured. "Nobody can touch Givenchy."

"Victor loves Givenchy," Valerie replied automatically, remembering as if it were a moment ago the touch of Victor's lips on her own.

"Still," the narrator continued, "as visible as Victor Penn has always been, his origins remain unknown. Although it is thought that he is English, there is no record that he ever attended any public school or university in England. His acceptance into the banking and social circles of London seems to have been on the basis of his own personal charm and lavish entertaining. Once he had established his contacts, Victor Penn moved quickly to consolidate his position in the banking world."

"This is absurd," Valerie said indignantly. "Of course Victor is English. He was educated in Switzerland, just like the children."

"Oh, they'll probably figure that out by tomorrow,"

said Mary, hoping that would turn out to be the least of their worries.

"Penn International, the umbrella for the vast international Penn empire, has never released a biography of its dashing chairman of the board, who also holds the title of chief executive officer. Nor has Penn ever agreed to be interviewed unless it has been in connection with one of the charities he supports. In short, Victor Penn has pulled off the impossible: simultaneously becoming the most visible of men and, at the same time, shielding himself in secrecy much like the late Howard Hughes."

The narrator spoke briefly of the move Victor and Valerie Penn had made some years earlier to New York City before finally settling on their hundred-acre estate in Beverly Hills. "Raymond Penn, older brother and, it is believed, second in command after Victor Penn, is refusing comment through his public relations spokesman in London." The limousine turned into the entrance of the estate as reporters, correspondents, and television crews surrounded the car, pressing against its fenders, thrusting microphones against the bulletproof glass windows. The chauffeur pressed the buzzer that opened the huge wrought-iron gates, and in a moment the car was gliding through the short underground tunnel with the electronic monitoring system screening all entering vehicles for weapons or explosives. Then it was onto the long winding drive that led to the graceful mansion itself.

Inside the usually tranquil house was pandemonium. Gregson, the impeccable butler who ran the house and its staff of twelve, hurried down the hall toward them. "Dr. Feldman and Mr. O'Farrell are in the music room, madam," he said to Valerie. "I do hope none of this turns out to be true."

"Thank you, Gregson," said Valerie. "It *is* untrue. All of it."

In the music room, with its framed, autographed scores and letters signed by Beethoven, Brahms, Mozart, and Chopin, a six-foot television screen displayed the mob scene outside the estate. Valerie's doctor, Elliott Feldman, a tall, muscular, fair-skinned man in his early forties, sat in one of the lounge chairs. John O'Farrell, Victor's attorney, was there, too, in his lawyer's uniform of dark gray suit, blue shirt with a white collar, and a red patterned tie. Kyle Jones, Valerie's live-in piano teacher, was perched on the piano bench in front of the Steinway. The two visitors leaped to their feet as Valerie and Mary entered the room. Kyle, looking exhausted, lifted a languorous hand.

"Valerie," said the doctor, as he took her hand and led her to an overstuffed, chintz-covered chair, "what a shock for you."

"We're all praying this isn't true," John O'Farrell added. "I'm sorry you're going through this."

"Thank you," Valerie said in a small voice, her chin high.

"Where does everything stand?" asked Mary, casting a sympathetic glance toward Valerie.

"We don't know any more than you do." John O'Farrell shrugged. "The public relations departments in the various cities are dealing with the press. Raymond has called several times."

"To talk to me?" Valerie asked with a shudder.

"No, to talk to me," said John. "We're to talk to nobody, and he'll be in touch."

"Do the children know?" Valerie asked suddenly. "Did Raymond say anything about the children?"

"Only that the children are not to be called until there's something more definite."

"But they'll have heard. Why can't I talk to my own children?"

"It's the middle of the night in Switzerland," the attorney said kindly. "I'd say it's probably better to do what Mr. Raymond Penn wants, at least for the moment."

"But . . . what do I do now?" Valerie asked.

"I guess what everybody else in Los Angeles is doing," said the attorney. "We just sit here in front of the television set and see what happens."

It was another hour before the next news update.

A disembodied voice was heard as the screen showed a blur of green. "We've just been able to confirm that the plane that crashed in Mexico this afternoon is the 727 belonging to Penn International. The Penn International logo is clearly visible on the side of the plane, according to the reports we are just receiving. As far as we can see, there are no signs of life."

With a little sigh, Valerie crumpled to the floor.

Elliott Feldman was instantly at her side, leaning over to pull her up. Valerie's eyes opened vacantly.

"We'll get her up to bed and I'll give her a shot," he said. "I have the feeling it's going to get worse."

"You have no idea," John O'Farrell said gloomily. "I better get on the phone to Raymond and see what he wants us to do."

At the piano, Kyle picked out a few bars of Chopin, his long white fingers with their bitten nails as tentative on the keys as if playing for the first time.

3

Valerie leaned against Mary as the two women walked slowly up the staircase, which had never seemed so long and winding.

"Just a few more steps," Mary said, her arm around Valerie's waist.

"I'm going to call the children anyway." Valerie panted. "If they've heard anything, they'll panic."

"Let's get you into bed," Mary said, pushing open the door that led into Valerie's suite.

The living room was large, its dimensions extended by mirrored walls at each end. Fine Louis XVI pieces, a gilt-wood table and four fauteuils upholstered in pink silk formed a seating arrangement, while a Chinese tortoise-shell-inlaid lacquer cabinet and a Louis XV chinoiserie silk screen further ornamented the magnificent room. A huge Bonnard hung over a marble fireplace. Silk draperies of a pink so pale it was almost white covered the doorway that led to Valerie's bedroom. On the nine-foot concert grand, the twin to the Steinway in the music room downstairs, a crystal vase displayed a vast spray of pink-throated cymbidia. In an alcove with a view of the grounds from its curving windows were a table and two chairs where Victor and Valerie had their morning orange juice and coffee following the nights Victor stayed with her.

For her bedroom, Victor had selected white carpeting, with white silk upholstered walls. The chairs and sofa in the sitting area were upholstered in pale peach moiré. On the coffee table in front of the sofa was a small sculpture by Rodin and two newly acquired Fabergé eggs. Later, they would join the main collection in the drawing room downstairs. The bedspread was the pale peach of the upholstered furniture, and over the headboard was a large Degas painting of a ballerina tying a shoe. Victor had surprised Valerie with the painting, a gift, he said, because the dancer reminded him of her. The fireplace chimneypiece was white marble tinged with peach.

In Valerie's bathroom next door, a room almost as big as some of the living rooms in Beverly Hills, was a sink of shimmering white marble, with a matching white marble floor. Victor and Valerie occasionally drank champagne in the big Jacuzzi, or made slow, exacting love while they watched themselves in the mirrored walls. The fluffy towels and washcloths were all white, the monograms on everything *VPV.*

The different cosmetics in the drawers of the makeup table, with its large mirror framed with lights, were all for Valerie's public face. When the two of them were alone, Valerie's face was scrubbed and clean the way Victor wanted it.

She stood in the middle of the bathroom as Mary helped her out of her dress.

"It doesn't look good, does it, Mary?"

"You wash your face," Mary said soothingly. "I'll go find you a nightgown."

"I don't think Victor was on that plane," Valerie continued. "I think he's been kidnapped by some terrorist group. It happens everywhere in the world, Mary.

Why not New York? There'll be a phone call, asking for ransom. I just know it."

"You wash your face," Mary repeated. "I'll be right back."

Yes, kidnapping was a possibility, Mary thought, opening the closet in which Valerie's nightgowns hung. Anything was a possibility when it involved somebody as rich as Victor Penn. Rich people. God, it seemed that she had spent her entire life catering to them.

First there was the count. Mary had been a showroom model in New York when fat little Enrique had come in to pick out a few things for another girl. Each of the models, herself included, was after a rich man. Mary hadn't been able to believe her good luck when Enrique picked her out of all of them. On the second night he took her out, he gave her a diamond bracelet. He had money, and a title, too. They drove up to Connecticut and married the next weekend, which made all the papers, of course.

Mary loved what the money would buy. The trouble was that the money came attached to Enrique, who, it turned out, drank too much and who, after two months, didn't seem to remember that he had gotten married. Mary began to play around, too. Quietly at first, and then blatantly. Enrique was enraged, but relieved that he had an excuse to divorce her. What little money she had was soon gone. She became a floating houseguest, kissing up to the lady of the house and fending off the passes made by most of the husbands. With her blond hair in a pageboy showing streaks of gray even though she was only in her mid-thirties, and a taste for simple clothes and very expensive walking shoes, Mary always looked as if she had come straight from a stroll with the queen and her corgis. And she was so helpful, arranging parties and shopping trips, dealing with difficult guests and the household details, that she never wore out her welcome. But it was a precarious life. Awful, until Victor had hired her. Now she toadied to Valerie, but at least she went home to her own apartment, to her own life.

Mary regarded Valerie as a demanding, spoiled little girl. A toy who didn't even know she was a toy. A collectible, like Victor's many other collectibles. She was a magnificent musician, though. She could have gone on to become a top professional. But no. As soon as Victor had appeared in her life, that, essentially, was that. True, she practiced all those hours every day, and she had her lessons with Kyle. But the music was just for Victor, who of course had to have a wife who was more than just beautiful, chic, and charming. She had to be accomplished, too.

Reaching into the closet among the flowing peignoirs in whites, ivories, lavenders, and lilacs, the nightgowns in either black, white, or ivory that Valerie wore depending on Victor's mood, Mary picked out a white cotton nightgown, cut low, with lace at the bodice. What would happen to Valerie if Victor were dead? Mary wondered, walking back toward the bathroom. Valerie had a few shocks coming, that was for sure. More important, what would happen to her? Oh, God, she thought suddenly, let Victor be alive.

Valerie was standing in front of the sink where Mary had left her. "I'll just be a minute," Valerie said, taking the nightgown from Mary's hand. "Would you mind closing the door?"

That little-girl thing, Mary thought, as she waited for Valerie to reappear. So oddly shy. In all of the years

Mary had worked for Valerie, she had never seen her nude.

After changing, Valerie went to the phone beside the bed. In a moment, Mary heard her. "No, no. Daddy isn't on the plane, Raymond. He's been kidnapped, darling. And when they get their ransom money, they'll let him go."

Valerie was silent for a moment, leaning against the silken pillows. "But darling, they *have* to let him go. Don't you see? If they did anything to him, it wouldn't work the next time. Now, how's Alexandra? Is she terribly upset? Give her a hug for me. Darling, I'll call you as soon as I know anything more. No, there's no reason for you to come home. Everything will be fine, just fine. Good-bye sweetheart. I love you very, very much. Good-bye, Raymond, darling."

Dr. Feldman, carrying his bag, came through the door. Impulsively, Mary leaned over and kissed Valerie on the forehead before she left him to tend to his patient.

When Mary returned to the music room, she saw that John O'Farrell was on the phone in a corner, while Kyle had moved to the chintz-covered sofa in front of the television set. He sat smoking, nervously swinging one crossed leg.

"Anything new?" she asked.

"You mean has Victor walked out of the jungle?" said Kyle. "No, that hasn't happened."

"He'd better walk out of the jungle." Mary walked over to the tea caddy and poured herself a stiff scotch and water.

"I'll second that," Kyle said. "I'm too old and too spoiled to go to work."

"Perish the thought."

"Perish is the right word."

"Well, it's not over until it's over," Mary said. "Valerie thinks he's been kidnapped."

"How is she?"

"Shaken, but Elliott is giving her a shot. She called the children and told them everything is going to be fine."

"If that's what Elliott's shots do for you," Kyle said, "maybe I should get one, too."

John hung up the phone. "That was Raymond," he said. "He's on his way to Acapulco."

"Better there than here," Kyle breathed.

"What does he think?" Mary asked.

"Well, he's taking Victor's dental records." John shrugged. "I'm going to stay here, at least for tonight."

"Maybe I'd better stay, too," Mary said. "Valerie may need me. Isn't it funny? I can't think of one friend Valerie has to call."

"Just us, the loyal employees," Kyle said. "Kind of sad."

"I'm going to send Daniel over to my place to pick up my shaving things," John said.

"Maybe he could stop and get some things for me, too," Mary said, reaching for her handbag to make a list.

"And a copy of the classifieds," Kyle added. "Or maybe I should just get on the phone to a publisher with the real story of Victor Penn."

"And what would that be?" John asked.

"Aren't you supposed to read me my rights or something?" Kyle asked. "It's a joke, John. Lighten up."

Elliott popped his head in the door to say that Valerie was asleep and he would stop by again in the morning.

"What I can't figure out is how that plane got to Mexico," Mary said after he was gone.

"Simple," Kyle said. "Victor knew the feds and the bank examiners and the IRS were moving in, so he picked up a billion dollars or so, threw it on the plane, and split."

"Without Valerie?" asked Mary.

"Well, as Valerie is here, obviously without Valerie," Kyle said. "He was on his way to Brazil—no extradition, you know—and voilà, the plane crashed. What they're going to find when they get to that plane is a whole lot of money."

"Going through Acapulco from New York to get to Brazil seems a little out of the way," John said.

"Not a direct route," Kyle agreed. "That's to throw everybody off."

"Maybe Valerie is right and Victor was kidnapped," Mary said thoughtfully.

"Okay," said Kyle. "With that scenario, the bad guys were waiting for Victor on the plane. Why not? So, what they're going to find is Victor, the crew, the bodyguard, and some mucho dead hijackers. But let's turn to our legal expert, Mr. John O'Farrell, to hear what he has to say."

"I don't know," said John, leaning back on the sofa. "It doesn't make any sense."

"What I want to know is what you meant when you said we had no idea how much worse things were going to get," Mary said.

"It is true, then, that the feds and everybody are sniffing around?" Kyle prompted.

"Well, there's been some talk," John said cautiously.

"Which would be reason enough for Victor to take the money and run," said Kyle.

"I just don't think he would leave Valerie," insisted Mary.

"Maybe he was going to send for her later," Kyle suggested.

"Maybe we should just stop all this," John interjected. "We're all in shock and it isn't getting us anywhere."

He smiled ruefully at Mary and Kyle. Everybody here was owned to some degree, he thought. And every one of them was being paid the highest price. Funny, he thought, how one changed. Managing Victor Penn's estate certainly wasn't the future he had seen for himself when he was editor of the *Law Review* at Harvard. His dream then had been to sit on the United States Supreme Court. But after he had graduated with honors, he had been courted by some of the country's leading law firms. The Supreme Court could wait a few years, he'd decided. First, get some bucks in the bank.

He accepted an offer from the firm that handled the affairs of Penn International in New York. He was already a partner when he met Victor, who liked him at once. When Victor decided to make the Beverly Hills estate his main residence, John was reassigned to the firm's Los Angeles office to handle Victor's affairs. As he became more involved with them, John found that his principles were being compromised in direct proportion to his raises, bonuses, and other perks, which came often and in gratifyingly large amounts.

Thinking about his early idealism, which he described to himself as his early pomposity, made him smile these days. What counted, he often told himself in the mirror as he shaved in the bathroom of his half-million-dollar condominium in Beverly Hills, was the bucks. Oh, he was in good shape, with investments, a stock portfolio, and the condominium at Aspen. But it still wasn't big, big money. Kyle and Mary and pretty Valerie weren't the only ones who were praying that Victor was alive.

4

Valerie awoke slowly at three o'clock that morning. Fighting her way out of her drugged sleep, she instinctively reached out for Victor. The bed beside her was empty, the Porthault sheet soft and smooth to her touch, its scent only her own perfume. She lay there for a moment and looked around the huge, silent room faintly illuminated by the moonlight filtering through the curtains. Unconsciously, she ran her hands over her small, firm breasts, her flat stomach, before the horror of the day before flashed through her mind.

Oh, God, Valerie thought. My darling. My love. I'm barely alive when I'm not with you. Those had been Victor's words to her on the phone from New York only the morning before. Dear God . . . I have to be strong. Victor would want me to be strong, Valerie thought, pulling herself out of bed. In the bathroom, she took a hot shower, wondering how her body could feel so bruised. Then, dressed in a caftan, she walked slowly down the winding staircase and into the music room.

Two hours later, as the first rays of sun crept into the room, Mary found Valerie huddled in the corner of the sofa, an old black-and-white movie flickering on the television set.

"Mary, I didn't know you were here," said Valerie.

"I thought I should stay in case you needed some company." Mary covered a yawn with her hand.

"That's really very nice of you," Valerie said shyly.

The words "You'd do it for me" were almost out of Mary's mouth when she stopped herself. It wasn't true, of course. She and Valerie weren't friends, and Valerie wouldn't do it for her. She was a paid employee. Staying overnight in an emergency was just the same as staying late at the office. Part of the job.

"Is there news?" Mary gestured toward the television set.

"Just what they were showing yesterday," Valerie said, shaking her head.

"How do you feel?"

"As well as can be expected, I guess."

"Is anybody up yet? Do you think we could get some coffee?"

"Nobody's up, but we can make some coffee. I just didn't think about it."

"Do you think we can find the kitchen?" Mary asked.

"Well, I saw it once," Valerie smiled. "I think it's somewhere around the dining room."

"John stayed too," Mary said. "He's upstairs in one of the guest rooms. He's in the command post. Raymond's orders."

"Raymond," said Valerie, her voice filled with contempt and fear. "I suppose he's on his way."

"He's going right to Acapulco."

"I don't see why. Victor wasn't on the plane."

"Valerie, you'd better be prepared," Mary said as they walked through the dining room and pushed open the swinging door leading into the hotel-sized kitchen. "Even if you're right and Victor was kidnapped, he still could have been on the plane."

"He can't be dead, Mary. He's my life."

"I don't think that comes into it," Mary said gently.

The two women were on their second pot of coffee when John, wearing a pair of chinos and a blue polo shirt, came into the room.

"How do you feel?" he asked Valerie, then nodded to Mary.

"Better. It was just the initial shock."

"Has there been anything yet?" he asked, thinking how pretty she was, how natural and young she looked without makeup, like a girl.

"Not yet."

An hour passed before there was a news brief at five minutes to nine. "Ladies and gentlemen," began the anchorman, "there have been sensational developments in the ongoing Victor Penn story. Five badly burned bodies, one a woman's, are just being removed from the plane belonging to Penn International which crashed yesterday in the rugged jungle a hundred miles northeast of Acapulco. The rear door of the 727 was open, with the stairs extended, according to reports from the scene. Although six people were assumed to have boarded the aircraft at its point of origin, five bodies—I repeat, five bodies—were found. Raymond Penn, the brother of Victor Penn, chairman of the board and chief executive officer of the corporation, has just arrived by chartered jet at the Acapulco airport. He declined to be interviewed before being driven away, with his aides, to meet with authorities.''

"Holy Jesus,'' somebody whispered.

Everybody in the room turned to look at Gregson.

5

Mary and John, just off the tennis court, sat at a table under a yellow and white striped umbrella sipping iced tea from frosted glasses. It was a sunny morning and the clear blue sky was punctuated only by one of the television station's helicopters hovering overhead.

"You play well,'' John said, wiping the sweat from his tanned face with a towel.

"Just another social skill.'' Mary smiled. "It's just like making polite chitchat at a dinner party, or holding your own at backgammon.''

"Yeah, engaging the attention of the rich. I guess we all do it in our own way.''

"Your way is more profitable,'' Mary laughed.

"What about your way?''

"Well, it's a good living. I'm sure you have some idea of what Victor pays me.''

"And I'm sure you receive finder's fees, shall we say, from the stores and the jewelers.''

"That's unkind,'' she protested, running her hand through her blond hair.

"But true?''

"Of course," she said. "Every single time anybody who works for Victor buys anything from anybody, there's a finder's fee."

"What's the justification?"

"We're agents." Mary shrugged. "We're hired because we're the best at what we do."

"What's your bottom line?" he asked between sips of his iced tea.

"What's yours?" she asked.

"Well, money," he admitted. "I'm sure you can imagine what having control of this account does for me. No matter what happens in this situation, though, I'm fine. Just fine."

"I can't say the same," Mary said. "When I started all this, I knew what I wanted. The contacts. Another rich man. Getting married again. Security."

"Well, why not?" he asked, looking at her critically. "You're one of the most elegant women in this town, or any other, I would think. I'm sure you've met everybody there is to meet."

"Yes, but now I really wonder if marrying rich is what it's about. Look at little Valerie. She works for Victor twenty-four hours a day. That's quite a price, even for all of this."

"But Valerie is in love with Victor."

"Maybe she is," Mary conceded.

"She really thinks he's all right," John mused. "Incredible."

"What do you think?"

"I sure can't see Victor parachuting from a 727," John laughed.

"Are things bad enough that Victor would go on the run?" Mary asked casually.

"No you don't," John said, his voice lazy. "I'm a lawyer, remember? I keep my own counsel."

"And you cover your own ass."

"That too," he agreed, thinking that she was really attractive in an understated way.

Across the lawn, Valerie came toward them, followed by her personal trainer. Both of them wore workout sweats. Strange, Mary thought, all of them pretending that it was business as usual.

As Valerie approached them, Mary realized she looked strained. "I wish that thing would go away," Valerie said, gesturing toward the helicopter. "Why can't they leave us alone?"

"How was your workout?" Mary asked.

"Oh, it's better to be doing something than just sitting and wringing my hands," she said. "Didn't you say that Elliott was going to come by?"

"What do you want Elliott for?" John asked. "Do you feel all right?"

"Oh, I'm fine. I'm just exhausted, that's all."

The intercom on the telephone sitting on the table buzzed insistently, and John reached over to answer it.

"It's Kyle," he said. "There's going to be some news in five minutes."

Quickly, they walked to the mansion's music room, where Valerie had spent many hours, either practicing or taking lessons from Kyle. The room's focal point was the magnificent nine-foot concert grand Steinway piano. The yellows, greens, and reds of the sofa and chairs picked up the colors in the priceless Aubusson carpet, which covered most of the floor. The marble fireplace was deep enough to roast a boar. Even the sunlight usually caught the room in a way that made it warm, welcoming. On the screen, a network correspondent stood in front of a government building in Acapulco. "The five bodies recovered this morning from the Penn International jet have all been identified through dental records flown to the scene, although those names will not be released pending notification of next of kin. To repeat, four of the bodies, including that of the woman on the plane, died as a result of bullet wounds to the head. Tentatively, the fifth body is believed to have succumbed from smoke inhalation."

"What did he say?" Valerie asked incredulously.

"They were shot," Kyle said. "All but one man."

The ringing of the phone cut through the shocked silence. Five times, six. Seven times. Finally, John picked up.

"Valerie," he called from across the room. "It's for you. It's Raymond."

She crossed the room and took the receiver from John's hands. "Yes, Raymond?" she said stiffly.

"I'm sorry," he said abruptly. "The dental records have confirmed that Victor is dead."

"He can't be," Valerie whispered.

"Stop being a fool for once," he said icily. "I'm not here to play your little games with you."

For a moment, Valerie held the phone, unable to collect herself to speak.

"You did this," she hissed into the receiver. "I don't know why, or how. But you did this. I know you did."

"I've decided that the funeral will be in London," he continued, as if she hadn't spoken. "I've already spoken to Miss Furst, and she's starting to make the arrangements." He paused for a moment, and then he said, "It seems to me that if you plan to arrive in London two days hence, it should be soon enough."

"Why can't it be here?" she wailed. "I want Victor to be buried here." The words seemed absurd, even as she spoke them. She didn't want Victor buried anywhere, didn't want Victor dead at all. He couldn't be dead.

"This is a difficult situation," Raymond said. "If you manage to pull yourself together, it will be somewhat less difficult. Now, let me talk to Mr. O'Farrell."

"What about my children?"

"Miss Furst is arranging for them to fly to London immediately. The staff at the Regent's Park house has been informed to expect all of you."

"This isn't what I want, Raymond."

"Nobody cares what you want," he said savagely. "I'm trying to be civil."

"You don't know what civil is," she whispered before handing the phone to John.

"Victor is dead," she said aloud to those in the room, "and it was Raymond who did it." Her voice rose to a scream. "I know it was Raymond!"

"Valerie, dear," Mary said, rushing to her side. "Come and sit down." Putting her arms around the younger woman, she helped her to a chair where Valerie collapsed, sobbing, her face in her hands.

In a minute, John hung up the phone.

"Valerie," he said tentatively.

She looked up at him, her eyes red, her cheeks wet with tears.

"Now, I want you to listen to me. Can you do that?"

She nodded slowly.

"I don't know if this is going to be harder on you.

Maybe it will be easier. Victor wasn't shot. He was the one who died of smoke inhalation."

She nodded again.

"Now, as soon as the identification is released, the bank examiners and the IRS will be moving into the banks and all the companies. Do you understand that?"

"I understand," she said in a tremulous voice.

"And I'm afraid the marshals will be moving in here."

"But this is our home," she protested.

"Well, yes and no," John said. "The house is actually in the name of Penn International. So is everything in it. To the feds, all of this is just another asset of the corporation."

"Do you mean I own nothing?"

"It'll all have to be straightened out. It could take a long, long time. Years, even."

"Is this what you meant when you said that things were going to get worse?" asked Mary.

"Yeah," he said, glancing at her. "This is it."

"And how bad are things?"

"Pretty bad."

The jewelry, Mary thought, locked away in that safe-deposit box in a bank in Beverly Hills in Valerie's name and her own, so that either of them could get to it if Valerie wanted to wear the real thing. Quickly, Mary ran a mental tape of what was there. Ten million dollars, easy, she calculated. And the jewelry, at least, was not a corporate asset. She realized she wasn't going to mention the jewelry to John. She looked up at him. He was so handsome in his tennis whites, with his dark curly hair, his well-muscled arms, his long tanned legs. Still, Mary knew that John would go where the money was. To Raymond, not Valerie.

"None of this adds up," Kyle said suddenly, as if he had been thinking about it for a long time. "Maybe Raymond engineered it, or maybe it was Victor. Or maybe it was both of them, and Raymond double-crossed Victor. But whatever, I've got to tell you, I agree with Valerie. Victor is alive."

"What about the dental records?" John reminded him.

"With Raymond's money and power, you think he couldn't come up with some phony dental records?" Kyle asked incredulously.

"Oh, look," John said. "Victor has been going to the same dentist in London for years. His dental chart checked out. What do you think happened, Kyle? Do you think Raymond got down to Acapulco and bribed somebody in the coroner's office?"

"Come on," said Kyle. "Raymond and Victor are two of a kind when it comes to money and power. Both of them know it can buy anything and anyone."

Except for me, Valerie thought, feeling battered and miserable as she sat huddled in her chair. I'm the one who's here for love.

Valerie was grateful when Dr. Feldman stopped by that evening to give her a shot. She lay in her bed in the silent room, her thoughts jumbled, as the doctor's face loomed above her. She felt the almost imperceptible sting of a needle in her arm. Elliott's face gradually drifted away, and she heard the soft click of her bedroom door as he closed it behind him.

How strange life is, Valerie thought, feeling herself slipping into a drugged sleep. Penn International is in ruins, and marshals will be in this house. And where will I be? How will I take care of myself? How will I take care of my children? Why has Raymond done this? It had always seemed impossible to her that Raymond could be Victor's brother. Suddenly, everything seemed impossible, even her relationship with Victor. How could a seventeen-year-old music student from Los Angeles ever have met and married one of the world's richest, most attractive men?

An image of herself at fourteen flickered through Valerie's fogged mind. It was the summer of 1968, and she was an usher at the Hollywood Bowl. She stood in the aisles handing out programs while in the boxes, picnic baskets were opened and bottles of wine and champagne were pulled from ice coolers. Concertgoers draped white tablecloths over folding tables, and candles burned steadily in the still night. She glanced at the stage, where the orchestra was already tuning up for that night's program of Debussy, Chopin, and Rachmaninoff. Zubin Mehta was conducting, and the guest artist was Maria Obolensko, the pianist, making her first appearance in southern California.

Valerie, working at the Bowl for the second summer season in a row, handed programs to a couple hurrying to their seats, and to the tall man who sauntered along after them.

"Thank you," he said, his English perfect but still with something faintly European in his voice. "You're a very pretty girl. Your hair is extraordinary."

Valerie felt the blood rush to her face, and she averted her eyes. A line, Valerie thought, handing programs to the next couple. She felt she was too skinny, with barely formed breasts. But she had always been secretly vain about her hazel eyes, sometimes green with flecks of yellow. She liked her shiny blond hair that was almost white, pulled back tonight in a ponytail.

"I understand all the ushers are music students," the man said.

"Yes, most of us, anyway," she replied, looking up at him. His intent brown eyes scrutinized her almost as if he recognized her from somewhere. Out of the corner of her eye, she saw the couple he had come with waiting impatiently for him. The Talbots. They were a handsome middle-aged pair, very social and very rich, whose pictures were always in the society pages.

"What do you play?" he asked.

"The piano."

"Like Maria Obolensko?" he asked, quirking an eyebrow.

"Well, no," Valerie said, unconsciously taking a step back. "Not yet."

"I can introduce you to her," the man said. "I'm Claude Vilgran, and I've known her for years. Perhaps you can play for her, my dear."

"Claude, come along," the woman called.

"What is your name?" said the man called Claude, his voice low, insinuating, as he leaned toward her.

"I don't know you," Valerie replied, as she felt her heart beating faster, her face flushing.

"You think about it," he said, giving her shoulder a little pat as he turned to join his friends. Valerie looked after his well-tailored back as he strolled away, wondering why she felt so confused, so frightened. After all, he was a friend of the Talbots. Everybody knew them. But she had the oddest feeling that he had recognized her. Did she remind him of somebody else?

She put it out of her mind at the scattered applause that swelled in volume as Zubin Mehta, dark and handsome, dressed in white tie and tails, strode to the podium. Turning, he made a deep bow to the audience, his black curls cascading dramatically over his forehead. Straightening, he shot out a hand, smiling broadly. Maria Obolensko appeared out of the wings, wearing a low-cut red gown that was like a blaze of fire against her pale skin. Her black hair was pulled into a chignon at the nape of her neck, and her mouth was a bright slash of scarlet. Diamonds glittered in her ears, at her throat.

Valerie caught her breath. Someday, she thought, her eyes sparkling. Someday I'll be standing there.

The crowd was quiet as the maestro raised his baton, and Maria Obolensko bent over the keys of the Steinway. Usually, Valerie would close her eyes and let the music sweep over her. Tonight, though, she found herself surreptitiously searching the boxes for Claude Vilgran.

As the lights came up for intermission, Valerie felt her body tense. Any minute now, she thought, there would be a tap on her shoulder, a card slipped into her hand. Claude Vilgran. It took her a few minutes to spot him in the crowd drifting toward the bar. He was deep in conversation with one of the other ushers, a tall girl of sixteen or so with flowing, curly dark hair. Even from the distance that separated them, Valerie saw the same insinuating stance, the intimacy with which he leaned toward her.

Just some lecher with a taste for young girls, she thought, feeling like a fool. How did anybody ever learn what was real and what wasn't?

The concert was a triumph for Maria Obolensko. A standing ovation, the beautiful sheaf of long-stemmed roses cradled in her arms. Two encores, and then, impossibly, a third. When the applause subsided, and Valerie was making her way up the aisle, she saw Claude Vilgran again. He was standing with the older couple in their box. Their eyes met as Valerie was caught up in the milling crowd.

She joined the passengers pushing onto one of the buses waiting in front of the Hollywood Bowl, keenly aware of her disappointment. It would have been wonderful to play for Maria Obolensko, really wonderful to meet such a great artist. It had only been a line, she reminded herself. Next time she would recognize a line for what it was.

At Sunset Boulevard, she transferred onto another bus, that took her west to Crescent Heights, in the middle of the Sunset Strip. Looming over the strip as far as her eye could see were huge painted billboards advertising Smirnoff vodka, Marlboros, movies. A new Beatles album. The Rolling Stones.

As Valerie stepped into the crosswalk, a boy sitting on the back of a convertible, his hair to his shoulders, his fingers spread in the sign of peace shouted, "Make love, not war." Umm, he's cute, she thought, smiling.

I wonder what my life would be like if I didn't have my music? I'd probably be marching against the war in Vietnam, listening to the Beatles and the Stones, going out on dates. But there's no time for that. She sighed as she walked past Schwab's Drugstore. There isn't time for anything, really, except my lessons, my practicing, getting ready for competitions.

Valerie saw that the lights in her family's apartment were still burning. Even before she put her key in the ⌐or, Valerie could hear Muffin, her mother's miniature apricot French poodle, panting and scratching on the other side.

Valerie scooped the little dog into her arms as it licked her face, wild with joy. On the flowered couch, her mother lay asleep, her bleached blond hair in blue rollers and her coarse face lathered with the latest rejuvenating night cream. Her voluptuous body was wrapped in a tired yellow terrycloth robe.

With the little dog cradled in her arms, Valerie crept across the room to her bedroom. She kicked off her shoes as she turned on the light. Her twin bed was covered by a white chenille bedspread. A nightstand with a reading lamp stood in the corner, next to the desk where she did her homework. The shelves were filled with Story Book dolls dressed in costumes from different countries.

Her father wouldn't be home for a few hours. He was working as a bartender at a restaurant with a piano bar a couple of blocks away, he said, from the place where Nat King Cole had been discovered in the forties. He knew all about things like that. Al Hemion usually worked as an agent, booking dates in clubs and at piano bars. His clients were either the ones who tried for the big time and should have made it, or the ones who had just been kidding themselves from the beginning. When things were slow in the business, it was back to bartending. At least it paid the bills—or some of them, anyway. But sometimes, Valerie would lie in her bed, the pillow over her head, trying not to hear the ugly fights her parents had about money.

The big issue of the moment was the Cadillac El Dorado that Al had just bought. It was red, with a real leather interior that smelled wonderful.

"How are we going to pay for it, Al?" Vicki said

the day he drove it home. "It'll be repossessed like the last one. Isn't it bad enough we have every bill collector in town after us?"

"You gotta keep up appearances in this town. You know that," Al shouted.

"God, I never should have married you," Vicki went on. "You've never been anything. You never will be."

"You dumb cunt!" he finally yelled, storming out of the apartment. Valerie and Vicki sat there, looking at each other for a moment. Then, with a little sigh, Vicki turned on the television set and went into the tiny kitchen to get herself a beer.

At one time Valerie's mother had been a contract player for Twentieth Century-Fox. When one of her old movies came on television, she would scream for Valerie to come and watch it with her. Vicki Drew was the gum-chewing waitress, the girl behind the counter in a department store, the moll sitting beside the gangster who was just about to be blown away. In those faded movies of the early fifties, Vicki was blond and luscious, with her big sensuous mouth that always looked as if she had just run her tongue over it.

"Sorry about that scene, baby," Vicki sighed, sipping her beer. "God, he never learns. Marry a rich guy, baby, so you'll have beautiful things."

"Mom, I don't even have time to date. I love my music. That's enough for me."

"You're fourteen," Vicki replied, patting Valerie's arm. "Wait a few years."

Some evenings when Al was working, she and Vale-
ie would go through Vicki's old scrapbooks. Vicki
ld cry at the sight of herself in a black-and-white pub-

licity still, fair and pouting, looking over her bare shoulder to seduce the camera's eye. Or, she would be in a two-piece bathing suit, her shoulders thrown back, her big breasts thrust forward, her long, pretty legs demurely crossed at the ankles, as she leaned against a palm tree. And there were snapshots of Vicki holding Valerie in her arms, her brassy blondness overwhelming the tiny, pale infant who looked at the camera with pleading eyes.

These days, Vicki worked as an extra, or as a manicurist at a beauty salon on the Sunset Strip.

Valerie remembered how frightening her parents had seemed to her when she was a baby. Their largeness, their loudness, had seemed to take up all the space available. When Valerie was a young child she pretended she was really a princess who had been kidnapped from the castle and her real parents, the king and queen, would find her one day. The fantasy made her feel guilty until a couple of her girlfriends happened to say that they had the same fantasy.

Valerie had been picking out little tunes on Al's upright piano since she was old enough to scramble onto the bench. One of Al's clients convinced Al and Vicki that Valerie should have lessons from a qualified teacher. Valerie remembered the tears of frustration as she spent hours practicing basic exercises and hating her demanding teacher, Nancy Carroll. By the time she was five, though, all of the hard work had started to pay off. She was playing Bach, Chopin, and Mozart with a technique that was precise and elegant.

That year, she was one of the children selected to perform for the Southwestern Musical Society. She stood in the wings, waiting her turn, wearing a white organdy dress embroidered with yellow daisies, and a yellow bo in her pale hair. There were butterflies in her stomach as she heard, for the first time, her name announced by the mistress of ceremonies and hesitantly walked onto the stage to polite applause. As she made a little bow to the audience, she heard the cheering from the middle of the second row, and smiled gratefully as she saw Al and Vicki, beaming with pride. After that, it was easy.

6

Max Perlstein, the brilliant composer and studio musician, occasionally took on a promising piano student, and when Valerie was ten, Nancy Carroll arranged for her to audition for him. Valerie had been terrified, not knowing what to expect. He was very nice, though. He was very casual. Tall and thin, he had long blond hair down to his shoulders. He wore jeans, a shirt, and loafers with no socks.

His house in Bel-Air sat on a half acre of land. It was low and rambling, vaguely Spanish, with light hardwood floors and very little furniture in the living room. Sofas flanked the stone fireplace, and a chunk of glass on a base served as a coffee table. The Steinway, of course. Several good oriental rugs. A few large expressionist
~~~~~gs. Hundreds of books. Two German shepherds.
~~~~rie sat stiffly on the edge of one of the sofas as
~~~~~Nancy bantered and laughed about mutual
~~~~~king around the huge room, she realized the

only times she had ever seen a house like this was in movies or in magazines.

She performed what she had rehearsed for months with Nancy, remembering her teacher's words. "Feel the music." She played a Beethoven sonata, part of a Mozart concerto, and finally a Bach fugue. Finishing, she turned toward Max. He was leaning forward, the expression on his face interested.

"Your technique's pretty good," he said, smiling. "Let's try it out for a couple of weeks to see how we work together."

"You did it," said Nancy as they left, hugging her. "You're on your way now."

Valerie soon learned the routine of the house. A maid came in twice a week, and occasionally one of Max's girlfriends would sun herself by the pool while Valerie had her lesson. Max pushed her into the master's program at UCLA, and she played for Zubin Mehta, for Georg Solti, and for other conductors and musicians passing through Los Angeles. She even played for Vladimir Horowitz one heady afternoon, and dreamed for days of his kind words for her performance.

At fourteen, Valerie looked like a twelve-year-old. When she made any kind of public appearance, Max had her dress in little Peter Pan collars and pleated skirts, her shining blond hair in a ponytail.

"Musicians, mathematicians, and poets all hit when they're young, kiddo," Max told her. He prepared her for the Young Musicians Foundation competition, in which two hundred contestants from all over the country competed for the prize of fifteen hundred dollars and a concert tour with guaranteed publicity.

Valerie played her way through the series of eliminations at UCLA's Royce Hall. Her interpretation of Beethoven's *Appassionata* in the finals brought her a standing ovation and first place.

The concert tour included appearances throughout California. "Fire . . . poetry of sound . . . vibrant," said the *Los Angeles Times,* who called Max to arrange an interview with her. There was another interview with the *Herald-Examiner,* and others with the classical music stations.

"Great news, kiddo," said Max, waving a piece of paper at Valerie as she arrived for her lesson. "You've been offered a scholarship to the London Conservatory of Music. A grant's been established by Penn International. They're a world-wide banking outfit. It's recognition, Valerie. It's the next step. You win every competition, you got some press when you won the Young Musicians Foundation award, the concert tour got you some more. It's all building. It's the next step."

"I can't do it, Max," she said. "I'm not ready to leave you."

"Don't count on me, kiddo. I've always been straight with you about why I took you on. Somebody did it for me when I was at that point in my own career, and it's my way of paying my dues. We couldn't have gone on forever. You're going to need a manager soon, and I can't do it. I have my own life, and my own career. Now that I'm scoring films, I don't have a lot of teaching time."

"But my mom and dad, they'd never let me go."

"et serious," Max chided. "You'll be staying with named Anne Hallowell. She's a lady, with a big patron of the arts, and mucho bucks."

." Valerie breathed, and the fantasies she'd

had of herself as a kidnapped princess flooded her mind. Lady Anne Hallowell. She savored the titled name in her mind.

By the time Valerie walked the three blocks to Sunset Boulevard to catch the bus home, her mind was buzzing. London. Lady Anne Hallowell. Maybe there was even a castle. Oh, she could hardly wait to get home to tell her parents.

Vicki was strangely subdued. "That's wonderful, baby," she said. "It's a great opportunity for you. You'll need some clothes, I guess. I suppose Max can take you shopping. He'll know what you need. God knows where we'll get the money, though."

"Don't you want me to go?" Valerie knew from the tone in Vicki's voice that something was wrong.

Al, when he got home, barely acknowledged her news. The next day was no better. Valerie felt as if she had done something vaguely shameful.

"Max is going to take me down to get my passport tomorrow," Valerie said as she arrived home one evening. She saw what seemed to be fear in Vicki's eyes. "Mom, is there something wrong?"

"No, no. Nothing," said Vicki, sipping her beer.

"Anyway, we have to go to the Federal Building down on Wilshire. There's a place across the street where Max says I can get my picture taken. I'll need my birth certificate."

"Oh, God," Vicki sighed.

"What's the matter, Mom? Are you okay?"

"I'm okay," Vicki said sadly.

"You haven't lost my birth certificate, have you? Is that it?"

"No, it isn't that," Vicki said, pulling herself to her feet. "You sit down. I'll get it."

A wave of panic washed over Valerie as she watched her mother walk down the hall on her way to the bedroom. In a moment, she returned with a manila envelope. Her face was white.

"I've been thinking and thinking about this, baby, and I don't think there's any easy way to do it. It's been driving Al and me nuts, I'll tell you that. Believe me, I never wanted this day to come."

Valerie took the manila envelope from Vicki's outstretched hand and removed the document inside.

A female infant had been born on January 21, 1954, at 7:20 in the morning. The weight was seven pounds, eight ounces, the length twenty inches. Under "Name of mother" was Cynthia Schuyler. The father was unknown. The infant was named Valerie Jane Schuyler. The hospital was Saint John's in Portland, Oregon, and not in Santa Monica, where Valerie had always been told she was born.

"What is this?" Valerie asked, her voice shaking.

"It's your birth certificate, baby," Vicki sighed.

"It can't be," Valerie said, bewildered.

"It's why Al and I have been so upset about you going to England. Because we knew you'd have to get a passport, and you'd have to see your birth certificate."

"I'm adopted," Valerie said, wondering why her voice sounded so strange. Adopted. Impossible. She felt sudd-ly lost.

"ll, not really," said Vicki. "We've never really u. Cini would call, but we never had a number uld reach her. She never even told us what using, so we couldn't find her to sign the papers. Then we were afraid the records could be traced. So we just let it go. Of course, we knew all along it couldn't be kept a secret forever."

"I don't understand. What do you mean you were afraid the records could be traced?"

"Oh, baby, I'm sorry," Vicki said, shaking her head. "Cini was a good friend of mine, a real party girl. She was hanging around with a guy from out of town, a very dangerous guy. She got pregnant, and when she finally told him, he said she was blackmailing him and he was going to kill her. By that time it was way too late for an abortion, so she split. She thought nobody would ever find her in Portland. I went up to be with her for a few months until you were born. When I brought you back, Al and I played it like you were our own. The only time we had to show your birth certificate was when you started kindergarten. We said we were in the process of adopting you, and we were filing papers. We just stalled and stalled. Finally, they got a new secretary at the school, and it just never came up again."

"Where is she? What happened to her? Who was my father?"

"Cini stayed in Portland for a couple of months. She'd call. But that was just for those two months. She called me once from Dallas, about six years ago, but she didn't call me anymore after that. Maybe the guy found her after all. He was very powerful, nobody to fool with. She miscalculated, that was all. She was in over her head."

"Who was he?"

"She never told me," Vicki sighed. "She said it would be better if I didn't know. I always thought he was from Las Vegas. Maybe with the mob. Cini liked those guys . . . the more dangerous, the more exciting. That was how she looked at things. This guy, well, he gave her some beautiful jewelry, and one of those little red Thunderbirds. And money, of course. What we cared about then was having a good time, guys, and what we could get from them. Or where we had been the night before, and clothes . . ." Her voice trailed off as she remembered.

"She was a prostitute," Valerie said slowly.

"Well, not exactly. Cini was from a good family back East somewhere. She just liked to have a good time. She was gorgeous, baby, a showstopper. All delicate and fragile. But the way she walked . . . the way she looked at a guy. They couldn't keep away from her. And fun. God, Cini was more fun than anyone." Vicki paused, and the expression on her face was compassionate and loving.

"Are you okay, baby?" She touched Valerie's hand.

"I'm fine," she whispered numbly. "I'm just, well, surprised is all."

"I've got some pictures of her. Do you want to see them?"

"No," Valerie cried, wanting to run out of the apartment, run and run, until all this went away.

"I'll get them," Vicki said, jumping up, seemingly energized by relief. In a moment she returned with a bulging brown envelope.

"Here, come on. Sit with me on the couch." Vicki pulled Valerie next to her and scattered dozens of snapshots over the magazines, newspapers, and ashtrays on the coffee table.

Gingerly, Valerie picked up a large black-and-white head shot of a face that could be her own in a few years' time. Her hair was as fair as Valerie's, her eyes pale, her cheekbones high. My mother, Valerie thought, with a thrill of recognition that took her breath away. The next snapshot, out of focus, showed Vicki, Al, her mother, and another man, all smiling for a nightclub photographer. There were drinks on the table in front of them, ashtrays, a little lamp with a metal shade.

"That was just after Al and I started going together," Vicki said. "And Cini. Isn't she gorgeous? I can't remember who that guy was."

Vicki picked up another picture and handed it to Valerie. It was a long shot in color of her mother sitting on the fender of a red Thunderbird, one of the little ones from the fifties that Valerie still saw driving around town.

"That was the car," Vicki said. "Look at that dress. Her clothes were great."

Photograph followed photograph. Cini, tall and slender, wearing a one-piece bathing suit on a beach, the ocean and blue sky behind her. Her legs were spread, her hands on her hips, and the look on her face seemed to dare the world to show her how good it was. "That was the weekend a couple of guys flew us down to Rosarito Beach in their private plane," Vicki said. "We landed right in front of the hotel on the landing strip there, and went in for lunch. Everybody used to do that. And this is at a Jimmy Durante show in Las Vegas. What was that hotel?" Vicki paused to sip her beer. "Well, I can't remember, but we had a ball. Here we were at Romanoff's. Everybody used to go there. Bogart. Bacall. This is at the Coconut Grove. That's in the Ambassador Hotel, down on Wilshire. We used to go there to see Lena Horne, Harry Belafonte. And here . . ."

Later that night, as she lay in bed, too exhausted to sleep, Valerie felt that nothing would ever be right again.

7

Terminal Two at London's Heathrow Airport was jammed. All around her, Valerie heard the unfamiliar buzz of what seemed to be a hundred different languages as the crowd pushed her along to the line in front of the table marked Immigration. The name inside her passport was Valerie Jane Schuyler.

"Purpose of your visit?" the man asked.

"I'm a student," Valerie said, thinking that he, at least, had a reassuring English accent. "I have a scholarship to the London Conservatory of Music."

"Oh, jolly good," he smiled. "We'll be seeing you in the Albert Hall, I suppose, playing for the queen."

"I don't think so," she said shyly. "I'm only going to be here a year."

"Well, if you work hard, you never know what might happen," he said. He stamped her passport and handed it back to her. "Welcome to London, then. Now, you fetch your luggage right over there. If you've anything to declare, get in the red line. If you don't, it's the green line."

"Thank you," she murmured, moving toward the baggage claim area. There was the big black and green plaid suitcase Max had given her as a going-away present, the matching two-suiter, its bottom stuffed with shoes and handbags, the little brown weekender, and the big beige canvas suitcase Vicki had borrowed from one of her girlfriends. Well, it took a lot of luggage to hold enough clothes for a year, Valerie thought, wondering if she needed to declare the new clothes inside the suitcases. Not the clothes, she decided, but maybe the money. She had five hundred dollars in an envelope Al had pressed into her hand as he and Vicki said good-bye to her at the airport. "And when this runs out," he had told her, "you just write home for more."

"Thanks, Daddy," she had said, giving him a big hug, feeling touched when she saw the tears in his eyes. Vicki had cried too, but Vicki was sentimental. Valerie had expected Vicki to cry.

"Can I help you with your suitcases, miss?" asked a voice, and Valerie turned to see a tall man in the gray uniform of a porter.

"Oh, please," she said gratefully, wondering how much she should tip him. She had never felt quite so confused in her life.

"Do you have anything to declare?" he asked.

"I don't know." She shook her head.

"Well, you just follow me," he said, piling her luggage onto the cart and pushing it into the crowd, past the customs tables. Valerie followed the porter until they finally trudged up the ramp leading into the arrivals area. People in all sorts of clothes leaned over the rail above, waving at the travelers they were meeting. Nobody, though, was peering over the rail and trying to catch her eye. Suddenly a man's voice with an English accent said, "Miss?"

"Yes?" She turned to see a tall slender man in his

mid-thirties, wearing a black suit, black tie, white shirt, a black cap. Lady Anne had sent her chauffeur. Of course.

"Did you have a nice flight, miss?" he asked, taking Valerie's elbow as he helped her into the huge black limousine.

"Oh, it was wonderful," Valerie said enthusiastically. I'm finally here, she thought gleefully, leaning back against the leather seat. I'm in England, taking my first ride in a beautiful limousine.

The highway was wet from a recent rain, and overhead, bright blue patches peeked through ominous gray clouds. When the car glided onto a long overpass, Valerie looked down on row after row of adjoining brick houses, their blue-black slate roofs glistening. Behind each house was a small fenced garden blooming with flowers and neat rows of vegetables.

Soon they were passing multi-storied hotels, tall office buildings, and expensive-looking shops. The morning rush hour traffic was heavy with the ubiquitous black taxis, red double-decker buses, a sprinkling of Rolls-Royces, and small European cars that Valerie had never seen before. Motorcyclists and uniformed messenger boys on bicycles darted in and out of traffic.

"We're almost there, miss," the chauffeur said into the speaking tube, as he made a left turn off Park Lane onto Green Street. Valerie sensed an air of quiet luxury as she noticed equestrians trotting along a bridle path rimming a huge green park. Valerie's pulse quickened as she wondered what Lady Anne would be like.

The limousine came to a stop in front of an impressive house. Seven stories, Valerie counted, as she waited for the chauffeur to gather her luggage. Her heart raced as she followed him up the stairs to the front door.

"Oh, it's you, Bernard," said the portly maid who answered his ring. She wore a black uniform with a little white apron, her gray hair twisted into a bun at the base of her neck. Her blue eyes twinkled. "You've collected Miss Hemion." She smiled as she turned to Valerie. "My name is Janet, Miss Valerie. You come right in."

"How do you do," Valerie said shyly as she stepped into the entry hall. It was as large as many living rooms she had been in, with a black-and-white marble floor and a high ceiling with intricate molding. On an antique table against one wall stood an arrangement of flowering branches and a silver tray, probably for the mail, Valerie thought. The gilt-framed mirror above the table reflected the muted rose and pink drawing room through partly open doors.

"I hope you had a nice trip, miss," Janet said, looking Valerie up and down. "So, you come from Los Angeles, where all the movie stars live. Do you know any of them?"

"Well, no," Valerie admitted. "But my mom used to be in movies."

"Isn't that nice," Janet beamed. "Well, I suppose you're tired, and you'd like a nice cup of tea. Maybe something to eat. Does that sound good to you?"

"It really does," Valerie said gratefully.

"Well, Her Ladyship is out shopping. She said she'd be back in time for tea. That's five o'clock sharp in this house. Why don't you come down to the kitchen with me, and we'll fix you up. Then you can go to your room and freshen up a bit, maybe take a little nap. You're on the fourth floor. Her Ladyship's suite is on the third."

Sitting at the round table in the comfortable, old-fashioned kitchen in the basement, Valerie devoured the fried eggs and bacon that Janet made for her on the eight-burner stove.

"How long have you worked for Lady Anne?" she asked between gulps.

"Only a few months," said Janet, leaning against a counter. "Lady Anne has been mostly in the south of France. She's just opened up this house. Wanted to be in London for the season. Well, they're like that, you know."

"What's she like?"

"Oh, she's very nice, very refined. She's quite well-known in society circles, of course. There's a lot of entertaining done here in the house."

"I can't wait to meet her."

"Well, she's been looking forward to your coming," Janet said. "We all have. Maggie, though, is off today. She's the cook. Then there's Bridget. She helps me out." She gestured toward a closed door. "Our rooms are back through there, behind the butler's pantry. We have a nice little sitting room and telly." She paused to pour more tea into Valerie's cup. "Bernard lives in the mews house out in back, at the end of the garden. You know how chauffeurs are. They're always with the motor cars."

Four servants, Valerie thought, impressed. At home, she and Vicki did the housework, and even Max's cleaning woman came in only a couple of days a week.

After Valerie finished breakfast, Janet took her on a tour of the house. Above the kitchen was the dining room, with tall windows and a gleaming mahogany table and chairs. Across the hall was the library, where a grand piano stood in front of a curving window. Valerie ran her fingers over its keys. The tone was pure. Wonderful, really. On the next level was the entry hall, and next to it the drawing room, running the length of the house, a blur of pinks and roses, fine antiques, handsome screens, and paintings of haughty aristocrats. There was a round mahogany table surrounded by four chairs. A crystal chandelier and bowls of flowers accented the room. Logs had been laid for a fire in the marble fireplace.

"It's here you'll be having your tea," Janet said, flicking a bit of imaginary dust off one of the tables. "Sometimes Her Ladyship has her breakfast here, too, at that little round table."

The room that Valerie had been given was just above Lady Anne's suite. She peeped in to see a fire burning brightly in the fireplace, and a double bed with a white spread, a pile of lacy white pillows, and a white canopy. Nightstands with pretty lamps stood on either side of the bed, and an oriental rug in white and blue covered most of the dark wood floor. A matching chaise longue was bathed in sunlight that filtered through the sheer curtains covering the tall window behind it. On a table sat a tall crystal vase filled with white and yellow chrysanthemums. Valerie's clothes had been hung in the walk-in closet in her dressing room. Her bathroom was all in blue and white, with fluffy white towels on the towel racks.

"It's so beautiful," Valerie whispered.

"Well, it's comfortable, I will say that," said Janet. "I think Her Ladyship enjoyed fixing it up for you. She kept asking, 'Will a young girl like this?' 'Will a young girl like that?' " Janet bustled around the room, plumping up the pillows on the bed. "I expect you'll want a hot bath, Miss Valerie. And you can have your lie-down. There's a little clock there on your nightstand, but don't you bother about setting the alarm. I'll come and wake you around four o'clock. Is that all right?''

"Yes, thank you," said Valerie, hardly able to believe that this lovely room was to be hers for a year.

After Janet had closed the door behind her, Valerie ran a bath as hot as she could stand. When she had dried her body, still tanned from the hours she had spent at Max's swimming pool, she put on the new white terry-cloth robe hanging in her closet.

She crept into the bed and looked around the graceful room. Sunlight streamed through the curtains. The fire crackled cheerfully in the fireplace. All of this for me, Valerie thought. Suddenly she felt more tired than she ever had before as she drifted off to sleep.

When she awoke, the room was dark, and pale moonlight filtered through the airy curtains. Somebody had covered her with a down comforter. Valerie changed to a nightgown, and crawled in between the soft white sheets. The next time she awoke, it was to Janet's voice.

"Time to get up," Janet called. "It's a fine morning, and Her Ladyship is waiting to have breakfast with you."

When Valerie walked into the drawing room fifteen minutes later, Lady Anne Hallowell was sitting at the round mahogany table reading a newspaper. In front of her was a silver tea service, china cups, and saucers patterned with pale flowers. She was in her late forties, Valerie saw, with shining brown hair in a loose pageboy. Her face was long, with high cheekbones and a generous mouth. She was dressed simply in a pale blue sweater set, a tweed skirt, and pearls. Reading glasses perched on her aristocratic nose. She glanced up from her newspaper as Valerie stepped tentatively into the room.

"Well, my dear," Lady Anne smiled, rising and taking Valerie's hands in her own. "I'm so glad you're finally here. Come and sit down." She led Valerie to the table and tinkled a little bell. "Now, you must tell me all about yourself. First, what would you like for breakfast? Eggs? Bacon? I know how it is to be a growing girl. It was a long time ago, but I remember. Let's start with some tea," she said briskly, pouring the tea as Janet appeared. "Bring this young lady some bacon and eggs. And maybe several patties of sausage. Toast, of course, and that wonderful strawberry jam."

"Yes, Your Ladyship," Janet murmured.

"You'll love the London Conservatory of Music," she continued when Janet was gone. "I'm sure you know its reputation. They've turned out some of the finest musicians. And you know about the pianists. Simply the most brilliant. Maria Obolensko, for one. I jumped at the chance when I was asked to be a patron there," she said. "I always wished for talent, but I'm afraid it was just the usual piano lessons. But, my dear, all those competitions you've won. The concert tour. And your reviews. My heavens! Fire and passion, they say. And you're such a delicate little thing."

"Perhaps I could . . . ," Valerie began.

"Give me lessons? Oh, no," Lady Anne said, waving a finger. "It's enough for me that the house will be filled with beautiful music. You're here to work, young lady, and I'm here to make it as easy as possible for you. Why, we're a little family, the two of us. I want you to think of me as your aunt. And I'll think of you as my niece. In fact, I already do. That's just what I'm going to tell my friends. 'This is Valerie Hemion, my American-born niece.'"

"Thank you," Valerie said.

"Isn't it nice that your classes don't start for another week?" Lady Anne asked brightly. "I'll have plenty of time to show you around London. I think we'll have a dinner party so that everybody can meet you."

Valerie gave a silent prayer of thanks as she managed to sip her tea without spilling it all over the damask flowered tablecloth. She didn't know what she would do when breakfast came. Just watch Lady Anne, she decided, to make sure she was using the right fork. The right knife. The right everything.

In front of the vast expanse of Buckingham Palace, a throng of tourists watched the soldiers in their red tunics, black pants, and towering bearskins, marching past them in the ceremonial changing of the queen's guard.

"Look, dear," Lady Anne said, sitting next to Valerie in the back seat of the limousine. "Do you see the flag? That means the queen is in residence."

Obediently, Valerie directed her attention to the roof of the palace, where the queen's own standard fluttered in the breeze. With its row after row of windows, its great stone pillars, and its balconies, the palace almost took her breath away.

Lady Anne took Valerie to tea at Brown's Hotel, where they ate cucumber and watercress sandwiches in its frumpy, paneled dining room. "This is my little American niece," Lady Anne would say when she ran into a friend. "Valerie Hemion. She's studying here for a year at the London Conservatory of Music."

"How lovely," they would murmur in their well-bred voices, as Valerie smiled shyly.

Lady Anne's conversation was a bewildering litany of helpful hints. "Well-brought-up young ladies cross their legs at the ankles, dear," she pointed out. "Put your napkin in your lap as soon as you sit down, dear." And, looking at her critically, "You know, Valerie, you're such a pretty girl. You're going to be quite the raving beauty. But those teeth. I do think we should see about them, don't you?"

Valerie nodded in agreement.

One day, they were out driving and the big Daimler turned into the section of London called the City, where every other pedestrian on the street was a businessman in a bowler, striped trousers, or a dark suit. "This is the financial hub of London," Lady Anne proclaimed. "And look, my dear. There's Penn International."

Valerie turned her attention to a glass prism soaring into the sky. She stared up at the name of the corporation that had made her trip to London possible.

At seven o'clock that night, Lady Anne sent Janet up to help Valerie fix her hair for the dinner party she was giving to introduce her to some of her friends.

"I've just finished putting the place cards on the table," Janet said, as she stood pulling Valerie's hair into a ballerina's knot. "You're right in the middle of the table, miss. You've got a Mr. Ronald Fox on one side. He's escorting his mother, and I think the family is in shipbuilding." She gazed critically at Valerie's reflection in the gilt-edged mirror, and reached into the little crystal jar of hairpins that sat on the dressing table. "And on the other side, you have a Mr. Harold Carrington. I don't know who he is." Looking into the mirror again, she said, "There. What do you think, miss?"

Valerie looked at herself in the mirror and saw Cini's face. The shiny pale hair, the cheekbones, the narrow nose, the mouth surprisingly full with even a hint of sensuality. The wide-set hazel eyes, hinting at green, with their yellow flecks. Only the expression on her face, in her eyes, was different.

"It's perfect, Janet," she said.

"I'm glad you're pleased, miss," Janet said. "I've helped my ladies with their hair for, well, it's going on four decades now." She looked through the door of the dressing room to the bedroom where Valerie's dress was carefully laid across the bed. It was beige crepe, with antique beige lace at the throat and the cuffs of its long sleeves. New shoes, also beige, with a two-inch heel, were on the soft carpet. "You might want to start thinking about getting out of that robe, miss. I think a little pink lipstick might cheer you up a bit. I'd rub a bit of it into my cheeks, too."

"I'll be down right at seven-thirty," Valerie said.

———

Standing shyly in the entrance to the drawing room, Valerie gasped. There were flowers everywhere, and the fire in the fireplace seemed almost to be dancing. The lights from the lamps, the crystal sconces on the wall, the chandelier overhead set the room aglow. The evening was alive with the hum of conversation and an occasional throaty laugh from the men in dinner jackets, the women in evening gowns. And there was Lady Anne, her hair swept up, diamonds glittering at her ears and on one gesticulating wrist. She wore a low-cut black gown with puffy sleeves that just covered her shoulders. How pretty Lady Anne looked, thought Valerie admiringly.

"Over here, dear," Lady Anne called, her smile so reassuring, Valerie thought gratefully, as she moved stiffly across the room. Lady Anne took her hand as she began her introductions.

Somehow, Valerie managed a strangled, "How do you do?" for each of them. In their gorgeous gowns and jewelry, the titled women were intimidating, and the men, emanating power and money, were overwhelming.

I'll never get the hang of this, Valerie thought, although she had to admit that it was worth almost anything to be sitting at such a pretty table. The china and silver were gorgeous, and there were low bowls filled with roses from the garden. The flickering candles made all of the women look beautiful and the men not quite so scary.

After the sumptuous meal of roasted veal loin medallions with wild rice risotto, dessert was a chocolate mousse pie with caramel sauce. Every course was served with a different wine or champagne.

The gentlemen stayed at the table to smoke their cigars and drink their port and, while the ladies retreated with Lady Anne to her suite upstairs, Valerie hurried up the stairs to her own room to splash some water on her face and make sure she looked all right.

———

The guests were all sitting on chairs in a semicircle near the piano in the library when Valerie appeared in the doorway. She took a deep breath and forced herself to walk slowly across the room to the piano.

The expectation in the room was palpable. Her hands shook a bit as she raced through the scales a couple of times, warming up.

Valerie started, as she always did, with a Scarlatti sonata. She was aware of her audience relaxing, of legs being crossed and uncrossed, of chairs being slightly moved. She decided to dazzle them with Beethoven's *Appassionata*, the piece that had won her the Young Musicians Foundation award. Everything in the room faded from her consciousness, and there were just the two of them—Ludwig van Beethoven, who had something to say, and Valerie Hemion, who was trying not to get in his way as she said it for him. With her mind, her body, she lost herself in his music.

When Valerie finished playing, the room was still for a moment and the applause, when it came, was loud and ringing with cries of, "Bravo."

"Ladies and gentlemen," said Lady Anne, her voice filled with pride. "My niece, Valerie Hemion."

Late the next afternoon, after she and Lady Anne had finished with their tea in the drawing room, Valerie sat at her little rosewood desk and thought about her parents—well, Al and Vicki—and all the money they had spent to get her ready for the year in London. It was funny how she thought about them now. All the time she was growing up, there had been a feeling of not belonging, of being an outsider. Now, when she had found out that it was all true, that she was an outsider, she suddenly felt closer to Al and Vicki than she ever had before. In fact, she consciously felt that they were her real parents after all. They had raised her. They had sacrificed for her and her music. That was what parents did. And they would have adopted her, too, if they had ever been able to find Cini. Cini. Oh, she thought of Cini all right. Whenever she wanted to, Valerie could conjure up Cini's face in her mind. That beautiful, fragile face with the wonderful bones, the wide-set eyes with their long, curly lashes just like Valerie's. Valerie was secretly pleased that she had a good chance of growing up to be as beautiful as Cini. Seeing those pictures was like a preview of coming attractions.

"Dear Mom and Dad," she wrote on a postcard depicting Buckingham Palace. "Here I am in London. Lady Anne is really nice. She has a beautiful house, and a limousine. I love London." It was true, Valerie realized, as she signed the postcard with her love. "P.S.," she added, "I miss you both, and Muffin, too. I'm going to be a great artist, and I'll make you proud of me."

9

Valerie woke to the buzz of her alarm clock on the morning she was to start her classes, and even before she pushed back the covers she realized she had finally gotten her first period.

Janet was already tapping on the door with her breakfast as Valerie made a dash for the bathroom.

"Come in," she called, closing the bathroom door behind her. Well, Vicki would be glad to hear she had finally started to menstruate, Valerie thought, swabbing at the insides of her thighs with a wet washcloth. Suddenly, an image of Cini flashed through her mind as she looked at her naked body in the mirror. Her breasts were certainly larger, with their pale pink nipples. Her stomach seemed rounded, even womanly. Her pubic hair was pale gold, almost white, like the hair on her head.

The blue box of tampons she had brought with her all the way from Los Angeles was in the bathroom drawer. By the time Valerie was dressed, Janet had already changed the sheets and made her bed.

On the little table in her blue and white bedroom, with a pale London sun filtering through the curtains, was a sterling silver tray with a tea service, a linen napkin in its napkin ring, silver utensils. Her toast was kept warm with a silver cover. There were miniature urns of jam and butter.

Life in Los Angeles seemed very far away.

The familiar sounds of cellos and violins tuning up filled the halls as Valerie walked into the London Conservatory of Music for the first time.

Her own classes this first semester were in music history, music theory, and whatever repertory her piano teacher, the celebrated Leon Stern, decided.

Leon Stern was tall and imperious, with thick white hair and rimless glasses. His students, among them Maria Obolensko, were among the world's top classical pianists. Stern wore a white carnation in his buttonhole and, old as he was, was quite a romantic figure.

"Your tapes are good, very good," he said in his heavily accented voice as they sat in a studio containing a grand piano and a few chairs. "It's quite astonishing that you play with so much power. You are very small and delicate to be able to do that."

"Thank you," Valerie murmured, flushing at his praise.

"I'll hear you now," he said, gesturing toward the piano.

Valerie played part of a Mozart concerto she had been practicing for the past week. When she finished, she kept her eyes on the keys waiting for his judgment.

"Excellent, excellent," he said, and from the back of the room she heard applause. Looking up, she saw a boy who was perhaps a couple of years older than she was. He was tall and slender, with brown curls that fell to the shoulders of his old suede coat. On a chair next to him was a violin case.

"Bravo," he said, his eyes meeting hers.

"Oh, here's Julian Unwin," said her teacher, looking around. "He's one of our stars here. She's good, eh?"

"She's marvelous," the boy said, and as her teacher introduced the two of them, she felt his hand closing around her own.

"Yes," said Leon Stern, "if we work hard, this young lady will be ready for the Van Cliburn Competition in Paris next spring." He counted the months on his long, slender fingers. "We're going to be very, very busy."

The Van Cliburn Competition, Valerie thought with alarm. Competing with pianists from all over the world. Along with the Tchaikovsky Competition, it was the toughest in the world. When she'd asked Max when she'd be ready for either of them, he'd just shrugged.

It seemed to Valerie that her schedule at the conservatory was going to take all of her time, but Lady Anne wasn't impressed.

"Your classes are over at noon," she pointed out.

"And the car will be there to bring you home. There's no reason why you can't work with tutors in the afternoon in French, philosophy, English literature, history. And, my dear, you should have at least a smattering of the sciences."

"But when will I practice?"

"Let's give it a try," Lady Anne said in a soothing voice. "A well-brought-up young lady needs to know about more than just one subject."

Valerie was up at dawn each morning to practice. When she got to the conservatory, Julian was usually waiting to walk her to class; often he met her to chat in the hall during the five-minute break before the bell rang for the next one. Julian had been performing since he was five years old. He had been preparing all summer for his upcoming appearance with the London Philharmonic Orchestra. Valerie would often find herself remembering Julian's handsome pale face, his brown eyes, the brown hair curling on his shoulders just before she drifted off to sleep.

Every couple of weeks there would be a letter from Vicki telling her all about what she and Al had been doing, and how they couldn't wait for her to come home because the apartment was so empty without her. Once she sent a color snapshot of the two of them. Al was smiling, and he had his arm around Vicki, who was holding Muffin in her arms. Janet found a little silver frame, and Valerie kept the picture on the nightstand next to her bed. Once in a while, there was a letter from Max, along with the current *Doonesbury* and *Peanuts* strips, and news about movies he was scoring. A couple of the girls she knew from junior high school wrote occasionally, too.

Valerie sighed, reading the letters. She was so busy she didn't even have time to think about Los Angeles.

One afternoon as Valerie and Lady Anne sat comfortably in front of the crackling fire in the sitting room after tea, Lady Anne remarked that none of Valerie's clothes fit her anymore. Time was found for a flurry of shopping for new dresses, sweaters, skirts, a beautiful rabbit fur coat, and, finally, a stop in a fashionable boutique for lacy panties, brassieres.

Valerie's pale hair was trimmed and shaped by Lady Anne's hairdresser. A makeup artist showed her how to subtly accent her eyes, her cheeks, her mouth. Looking into the mirror at the salon, Valerie realized suddenly that she was really pretty, even at fourteen. She thought of Cini for the first time in weeks.

———

Julian noticed the difference at once. "I've been thinking about you," he said, looking at her admiringly as he took her arm and drew her aside.

Valerie's stomach fluttered. Her cheeks felt hot.

"I thought maybe we could get together," he said, "maybe work on a duet. Just for fun, really."

Valerie nodded as she realized he was asking her for a date. A little shiver of excitement shot up her spine.

"I don't know." She hesitated. "I have so much work to do for the Van Cliburn Competition. It's only a few months away."

"Hey, you're looking at a chap who's going to solo with the London Philharmonic," he said, "and that's only a few weeks away." He met her gaze, his dark eyes imploring. "Oh, do say yes," he insisted. "Let's have a spot of lunch tomorrow and talk about it. Pick out what we want to play and all. We could wander over to Carnaby Street and look at all the crazies. Or we could go to Soho.''

The next morning, when Bernard opened the door of the car for her in front of the conservatory, Valerie said to him, "You don't have to fetch me today, Bernard. I'm having lunch with friends. And I remembered to tell Janet.''

"Very good, miss," Bernard replied, looking perplexed.

"What's the matter?" Valerie asked.

"Well, miss," he said, "Her Ladyship specifically mentioned to me last night that I was to be quick about getting you directly home today. She said that she was expecting you for lunch with someone she is anxious for you to meet.''

"Her Ladyship didn't say anything about it to me," she said.

"Maybe it was something she arranged when she was at the theater last night, miss," Bernard suggested. "You always come straight home, so she wouldn't have any reason to think you'd made other plans.''

"That must be it," Valerie said slowly. "Well, okay, I'll see you here at noon, Bernard. As usual.''

Valerie had never felt so disappointed as she plodded glumly up the steps of the conservatory. She had imagined every detail of her date with Julian. She had almost been able to see the two of them milling along Carnaby Street with the rest of the kids, maybe even holding hands. When Valerie told Julian she had to be home for lunch, she could see the disappointment in his face.

"Maybe I can work it out for Monday," she said.

"Will you telephone me when you know?" he asked.

"Well, sure," she said bashfully. "Okay."

Julian tore a piece of paper out of his notebook and scribbled down his telephone number.

During her next class, she looked surreptitiously at Julian's name and phone number on the paper. He had the most beautiful handwriting, thought Valerie. Valerie Unwin. Mrs. Julian Unwin. Julian and Valerie Unwin. The most famous piano and violin duo in the world.

If I were in Los Angeles, Valerie thought, I might have written our initials on my notebook, and enclosed them in a heart.

10

Pedestrians hurrying down Park Lane in the driving rain fought the wind with their umbrellas. The denuded trees reached spidery black branches toward the gray sky. Tourists bundled up in furs and overcoats huddled in the entrances of all the grand hotels as doormen frantically whistled for taxis that never came.

Valerie felt chilled to the bone as she ran up the steps of the house in Green Street; her teeth chattered as she fumbled with her key in the door. Upstairs in her room, she took off her wet shoes and her stockings. After she had changed, she ran a comb through her hair and applied some pink lipstick, ready to join Lady Anne and her guest in the drawing room for a sherry before lunch.

A man's hearty laugh echoed along the winding staircase as Valerie walked down the stairs.

In the drawing room, Lady Anne sat across from her guest in front of the fireplace, a glass in her hand. The man who rose was tall, with intent brown eyes. His face was tanned, and he wore a well-cut dark suit. There was something familiar about him, something soft and mean, around his mouth. The Hollywood Bowl, a glowing half shell of light, flashed into Valerie's mind. She recalled handing programs to a couple hurrying to their seats for the concert that night, and the tall man sauntering after them who had stopped to speak to her in a low insinuating voice.

"Valerie," Lady Anne was saying, "may I present Monsieur Claude Vilgran. He's just back from Palm Beach, the lucky man. And this is my niece from America, Claude. Valerie Hemion."

"How do you do," Valerie stuttered, almost recoiling as she felt his dry hand engulfing hers, his appraising eyes fastened on her own.

"You're a very pretty girl," he said, and as she snatched her hand away, Valerie wondered if he remembered saying that to her before. "I understand you're a brilliant pianist," he continued. "Your aunt tells me you've won a scholarship to the conservatory."

"Let's all sit down and finish our sherry," suggested Lady Anne. "I'll ring for Janet to bring you something warm to drink, dear."

"Yes," said Valerie, averting her eyes from his gaze, which seemed locked on her face. "I'm preparing for the Van Cliburn Competition. It's in Paris this year. In March."

"Oh, yes," he said thoughtfully. "I have a friend

who is one of the great concert pianists of the world. Maria Obolensko. She won that competition. It was the beginning of her career."

"She lives near here, doesn't she, Claude?" asked Lady Anne.

"In Eaton Square," he said in his perfect English that hinted at somewhere foreign. France, Valerie knew now. Monsieur Claude Vilgran. "She's on tour at the moment," he continued. "Berlin. Rome. Vienna. She leads quite an exciting life."

"Your life is quite exciting, too," said Lady Anne.

"Oh, it's nothing," he laughed.

"Claude is too modest," Lady Anne said to Valerie. "He roams the world collecting beautiful things. Paintings, tapestries, furniture, *objets d'art.* Anything at all as long as it's perfect."

Valerie thought about that as they went in to lunch. Either he was very, very rich, or he was an art dealer, in which case he was just rich. She didn't dare to ask.

At the dining room table, Valerie saw that even though Lady Anne was smiling and animated, her face looked tense. She seemed to be uneasy with Monsieur Vilgran, too.

"I suppose Lady Anne has been showing you around," he said to Valerie.

"Oh, yes," Valerie said, squirming under his gaze. "She's been wonderful."

"You must find it very different from Los Angeles," he said. "When I first started to go there, Wilshire Boulevard was mainly vacant lots. There was nothing. Now you have skyscrapers, the new museum. The Music Center downtown. There's some magnificent art, too. The first truly American city, really. I have several good friends there, in Beverly Hills and Bel-Air."

"The Talbots," blurted Valerie.

"Why yes," Claude said, looking at her with amazement. "How would you know that?"

"I saw you with them," Valerie said. "At the Hollywood Bowl. I was ushering there."

"But how could you possibly remember me?"

"You spoke to me."

"Oh, no," he laughed. "If I had spoken to you, I would never have forgotten you. I could never forget a girl as pretty as you are."

Valerie saw the corners of Lady Anne's mouth tighten at his words, felt her own discomfort at his eyes that never left her face, that seemed to bore into her soul.

Later, she stood beside Lady Anne in the entry hall as they said good-bye to Claude. Janet helped him on with his black overcoat, brought him his bowler and his umbrella.

"Good-bye," Claude said as he took Lady Anne's hand and brought it to his lips. "It's always wonderful to see you, my dear." As he turned to say good-bye to Valerie, he added, "I don't know when Maria returns to London. She always calls me, though, as soon as she gets over her jet lag. I can introduce you, if you like. Perhaps you can play for her."

When the door had closed behind him, it seemed to Valerie that Lady Anne was as relieved as she was to have him gone.

"Why don't you come up to my suite with me for a moment, dear," Lady Anne said, a distracted look on her face.

Valerie took her place on a chintz-covered love seat

across from Lady Anne and waited for her to begin. "When you made luncheon plans for today," Lady Anne said, "did you think about your classes this afternoon?"

"I guess I forgot," Valerie admitted, flushing.

"My dear, I know girls your age are starting to be interested in boys," Lady Anne said, her voice weary. "It's natural for you to want to go to lunch with a boy, or even a girlfriend your age. But you're an artist, Valerie, and all of your time has to be devoted to just one thing. Your career."

"Well, Julian—he's the boy I was going to have lunch with—he's an artist, too," she mumbled. "He's been performing since he was five years old. He's going to be a guest soloist with the London Philharmonic in a few weeks. He has time for lunch. We were going to talk about working on a duet. For fun."

Valerie felt her stomach muscles tighten as Lady Anne looked into the fireplace. It was as if she thought she might find the words she wanted to say written in the dancing flames.

"Let me put it this way," she finally began in a gentle voice. "You're a brilliant talent with a great career ahead of you. But talent is only a part of it, don't you see? You have to be able to handle yourself, my dear, in the very best circles. You have to be able to hold your own when the people around you are talking about paintings, or where they've been on holiday. Whatever they're talking about." Lady Anne paused and smiled at Valerie, begging comprehension. "I know how much you love your parents," she continued. "But with their backgrounds, they couldn't possibly give you the social graces you're going to need. I feel it is my responsibility to help you, to teach you."

How could somebody who was so good to her also make her feel so small? Valerie wondered. It wasn't fair. She fought hard to keep back the tears.

"Do you see my point, dear?" asked Lady Anne. "Do you see why it's to your advantage to make some sacrifices at this time in your life?"

At Valerie's nod, Lady Anne glanced at the ornate clock standing on the mantelpiece. "I see we've kept your French teacher waiting," she noticed. "Why don't you run along, Valerie. I'm dining out this evening, but we'll be able to chat tomorrow morning."

Lady Anne's voice stopped Valerie just as she put her hand on the handle to open the door of the suite. She turned to look back at her.

"I'm sorry if I hurt your feelings, dear. I just thought it would be a good idea if you understood what we're all trying to do for you. It's for your own good, Valerie. You'll be thankful when you're older."

Valerie just looked at her for an instant before she rushed out.

Later that week, Lady Anne herself opened the door when Valerie returned from the conservatory. In her hand she held a stack of mail.

"I met the postman coming in," she said, brushing Valerie's cheek with her own. "All bills, except for this one." She held out to Valerie a letter she had sent to her parents two weeks earlier. "It's been returned. Is the address wrong?"

Valerie saw that the address was right. Al and Vicki must have pulled their usual trick, moving in the middle of the night when they were behind in the rent, leaving no forwarding address.

"They must have moved," she said.

"But wouldn't they have told you?" Lady Anne asked, her eyes worried. "Shouldn't we phone?"

"Oh, I'll hear from my mom when they're settled," Valerie said.

A week later when she still hadn't heard from Vicki, Valerie asked Lady Anne if it would be all right if she tried to call them. All she managed to reach was a recording telling her the number was no longer in service. Confused and frightened now, she dialed Max Perlstein's number.

"Well, hi, kiddo," Max said when he heard her voice. "How's my little genius?"

"I'm fine, Max," she said. "I really miss Los Angeles. I miss you, too. I can't wait to come home."

"Well, your letters sound as if you're doing okay," he said, and Valerie could almost see him grinning. "Limousines and fancy houses. Studying with Leon Stern for the Van Cliburn Competition. I wouldn't have let you go for the Van Cliburn for another couple of years."

Valerie sensed Max waiting for her to get to the point.

"What's wrong, Valerie?" he said at last.

"I can't find my mom and dad," she said, beginning to cry. "They've moved, and their number is disconnected."

"Well, they've moved before," he said, his voice kind. "It's probably just the mail, kid. But look, let me see what I can do. I'll check it out. If you hear anything, you call me right away."

"Okay, Max," she said, stifling her sobs. If anybody could find them, Valerie thought with relief as she hung up the phone, Max would be the one. He had sounded so glad to hear from her. She wished she were back in

Los Angeles with all its sunshine, with her parents and friends, instead of in this house in cold and gloomy London where it rained all the time.

The call from Max came a couple of afternoons later just as Valerie was sitting down to tea with Lady Anne in the drawing room. She caught Lady Anne's eye for an instant and saw her concern before she hurried from the room to answer Janet's summons. She was panting by the time she picked up the extension in the library and heard Max's voice.

"Kiddo, I don't know how to tell you this. I called every one of Al's clients, but nobody knows a thing. I called the places where Al tended bar. No one's heard from him either. I stopped by the beauty salon on Sunset Strip where Vicki worked, and talked to the owner, the other employees, some of Vicki's clients. Nobody has seen or heard from her.

"I asked them how she had seemed the last time they saw her, which was about a month ago," he said. "They said she was just the same, bragging about you in London, talking about Al's business opportunities.

"I checked the police, the hospitals, the morgue, even the animal shelter to ask if they'd seen an apricot poodle that fit Muffin's description. I ran Al's name and address and a description of his car through a friend who works at the Department of Motor Vehicles. The Cadillac was repossessed a couple of months ago."

With a sinking feeling, Valerie knew why the Cadillac had been repossessed, knew why they had moved. The money they had spent to get her to England had wiped them out. It was her fault, pure and simple.

"Are you okay, kiddo?" he asked. "Do you need anything? Can I send you some money?"

"I'm fine," she whispered into the receiver.

"You know how flaky Al is," said Max in an unnaturally hearty voice. "Don't worry too much about it. You'll hear from them."

When she went back to the drawing room, Lady Anne was pacing back and forth, wringing her hands. When she saw Valerie in the doorway, she stood still.

Valerie just shook her head.

"Two people can't just disappear from the face of the earth," Lady Anne said tensely, one pale hand at her throat. "What could have become of them?"

"I don't know," Valerie sobbed, her whole body heaving. "I don't know."

11

"I think the first thing to do is meet with Mr. Carrington," said Lady Anne, sipping the sherry she had asked Janet to bring her. "It was Mr. Carrington who handled the details of your scholarship with the Penn International people. He's certainly in contact with people on the proper level there."

"What can they do?" Valerie asked, her tone hopeless.

"Penn International is a huge international banking organization," Lady Anne pointed out. "Surely they'll realize your dilemma, and do whatever they can to help. After all, if it weren't for them, you wouldn't be here."

Valerie didn't think Penn International would be

able to help. She didn't think anybody could help after all of Max's efforts had led nowhere. Where could Vicki and Al be? she asked herself over and over again, too stunned even to cry.

———

"Surely, Mr. Carrington, you can do something," Lady Anne said the next morning. "It seems to me Valerie's welfare is as much the responsibility of the conservatory as it is mine." Valerie tried to make herself as inconspicuous as possible in her high-backed chair.

"What would you suggest, Your Ladyship?" he asked.

"I should think the very least you can do is try to reach someone at Penn International and explain the problem," she said firmly.

"Yes, of course," he murmured. "I believe the music scholarship is handled by a Mr. George Bothwell in the public relations department there."

"Well, try him," Lady Anne commanded.

Bothwell was sympathetic, Mr. Carrington reported as he hung up the telephone. He would make some calls and get back to Carrington as soon as he could.

"Thank you for your time, Mr. Carrington," said Lady Anne, pulling on her full-length mink coat as she rose and held out her hand to him. "I suppose that's all we can do for now."

"I'm sorry about all of this, Lady Anne," Valerie said as they left Carrington's office.

"Oh, don't be," Lady Anne said, smiling sympathetically. "If there's one person who isn't to blame in all of this, it's you."

As Valerie watched Lady Anne's limousine slide

away into the heavy traffic, she wondered what she had meant. How could Valerie be the one person who wasn't to blame in all of this? After all, her parents were the ones who had disappeared. If anything, she was the only person who could be blamed.

Walking up the stairs to her music theory class, Valerie felt a small shock of pleasure as she saw Julian.

"That was your aunt, wasn't it?" he asked, falling into step beside her. "She's attractive, don't you think? Better than her pictures in the papers."

"She's very nice, too," Valerie said as she hurried up the narrow stairs.

"How come she's here?" Julian asked. "Is there something the matter?" He took two steps at a time, trying to keep up with her.

"Everything's fine, Julian," she said. "But I've already missed one class, and I'm late for the next one."

"You haven't seemed yourself the last few days," he said, ignoring what she had said. "You've been all white and strained. You're going to work yourself into a nervous breakdown if you don't watch it."

"The work's fine," she assured him.

"What class do you have now?"

"Music theory."

"Oh, don't go, Valerie," said Julian. "As long as it's not old Stern who's waiting for you, let's go get a cup of tea somewhere."

"I can't, Julian," she said, trying to get by him as he blocked her way on the landing.

"Yes, you can," he said, putting his hands on her shoulders. "I'm your friend. All I have to do is look at you to see something's upsetting you."

He really was concerned, Valerie saw when she

looked into his dark eyes. She almost burst into tears right there on the stairs.

"Come on then," he said, taking her hand as he led her back downstairs. "A nice cup of tea will do you the world of good."

A few minutes later they sat in a coffee bar near the conservatory.

"I've never cut a class before," she said, shrugging out of her coat.

"Then it's time you did," he said, reaching across the table to take her hand. "Now, tell me what's going on."

Ten minutes later Valerie was brushing away the tears with the back of her hand after she had told Julian the whole strange sequence of events, starting with the letter to Vicki and Al that had been returned to her several weeks earlier.

"There's one thing you can do," Julian said. "You can go to the American embassy. You're an American citizen."

The American embassy, Valerie thought. Of course. How silly she and Lady Anne had been not to think of it.

"That's a great idea."

"I'll go with you if you want."

"Oh, I don't know how I could work that out," Valerie said. "There's always somebody around. Lady Anne. Bernard."

"What we could do is this," Julian said. "I'll wait for you tomorrow just inside the front door of the conservatory. When the chauffeur drops you off, you come inside. We'll wait until he's gone, and then we'll just nip over to the embassy. It's just over in Mayfair, in Grosvenor Square." He looked at her anxiously, a frown on his face. "How does that sound to you?"

Valerie looked across the table at him, at his dark eyes, the pale skin. She felt safe with Julian. He would take care of her.

"Okay," she said.

The next day, Julian was waiting inside the front door. Together they looked outside and saw the long black limousine pulling away from the curb. Then they raced down the stairs to the bus stop on the corner. Valerie felt almost giddy with freedom as they crowded aboard the big red double-decker bus. Just sitting next to Julian on the second deck was like breaking out of prison, she decided.

Inside the light, airy reception room of the American embassy, Valerie felt almost as if she were back in California. It was so cheerful, so open, so American somehow.

"This is a first," said the middle-level embassy employee who was sitting across the desk from them. "What we always get are calls from parents in America trying to find their missing children."

"But you can do something, can't you?" Julian asked. "She is an American."

"We can advance you the money for a ticket home," he said, turning to Valerie.

"That's all?" she asked, her eyes wide.

"I'll contact the State Department and make a few other calls. Anyway, I've got your address and phone number, Miss Hemion. I'll call you with anything I find out." Reaching into one of the drawers of his desk, the man handed Valerie one of his business cards. "Are you all right for money?" he asked.

"She's fine," Julian answered for her. "She lives with her aunt, Lady Anne Hallowell."

The man quirked an eyebrow as he shook hands with her and Julian, then showed them out.

"Which one of your parents is related to Her Ladyship?" Julian asked as they hurried along to the bus stop.

"My mother," Valerie mumbled, remembering what Lady Anne had told her to say if anybody ever asked.

"So, your mother is Lady Anne's sister," Julian continued. "Was your father rich when they got married?"

"No, he wasn't rich," said Valerie, thinking about what the expression on Julian's face would be if he ever met Vicki and Al.

"The family must have been terribly upset," he said.

Valerie was trying to find a way to change the subject when Julian said, "Oh, look. There's our bus. We can make it if we run for it."

They were both panting as they climbed the spiral staircase and found a couple of seats together in the rear of the second deck.

Valerie was sure Julian was going to start asking her about her mother again, but what he said was, why didn't the two of them go to a movie some night.

"Oh, Lady Anne would never let me," Valerie said.

"Well, doesn't your aunt go out?" asked Julian.

"Oh, sure. All the time."

"Well, if you waited until after she left, and you were back home before she was, how would she ever know you'd been gone?"

"I could never do that," said Valerie, realizing that she was really shocked at Julian's suggestion. "I can't leave the house at night without Lady Anne's permission." But then, she'd cut classes this morning to go to the American embassy without telling her. When she thought about it, one was as bad as the other.

"Would you at least ask her?" Julian pleaded.

"Okay," Valerie said. "I'll ask her."

12

"You're very quiet today, dear," said Lady Anne between sips of tea.

"I'm sorry, Your Ladyship," Valerie murmured, as she gathered her courage to tell Lady Anne about her visit to the American embassy with Julian, to ask her if it would be all right if she went to a film with him one evening.

"You're worried about your parents, of course," Lady Anne mused. "Well, I'm sure Mr. Carrington will call us as soon as he hears from that public relations person at Penn International."

"I went to the American embassy today," Valerie blurted.

"You did what?" asked Lady Anne, horrified.

"Well, I was talking to Julian about it," Valerie explained, "and he said I was an American citizen, and it seemed to him it would make sense if I went to the American embassy."

"When did you go?" Lady Anne asked. "You were at the conservatory all morning, weren't you?"

"It was all very spur-of-the-moment," Valerie lied,

her eyes averted as she concentrated on her cucumber and cream cheese sandwich. "Julian said, why didn't we just go right then, and so we did. The man at the embassy thought it was kind of funny. He said that usually it was parents in America trying to find their kids."

"You cut a class," said Lady Anne, her voice like ice. "And you discussed a matter that concerns only the two of us with a stranger."

Valerie looked imploringly at Lady Anne, trying to make her understand. "The man at the embassy said he would contact the State Department in Washington, D.C.," she said. "He told me that they would know if my parents had applied for passports."

"Valerie, I would like you to explain to me how you rationalize cutting a class," said Lady Anne. "We won't even go into what bad form it was for you to go to the American embassy without me. After all, I am responsible for you while you're here in London."

"I'm sorry, Lady Anne," said Valerie, feeling the tears in her eyes. "I'm really sorry."

"It would be best if you went to your room," Lady Anne ordered in an awful, cold voice Valerie had never heard before.

———

Julian was waiting for her the next morning when Bernard dropped her off at the conservatory, and Valerie had to gather up her courage to tell him that she hadn't asked Lady Anne if she could go out with him.

"Just do me a favor," said Valerie, "and don't pressure me."

"I'm sorry," he said, and he looked so hurt that it made Valerie feel just awful.

Over the next few days, Julian was always waiting, with that same hurt look on his face, to walk her to class. Sometimes, they even held hands. After a few days, Julian seemed to realize that Valerie wasn't going to ask Lady Anne if she could go out with him at night, so he started to push her about cutting class and just going to the little coffee bar in the next block where all the kids from the conservatory hung out.

Lady Anne didn't even like it when Julian called her at home.

"You're far too young for that sort of thing, dear," Lady Anne would say vaguely.

The man from the American embassy called to report that no passport had ever been issued to Al or Vicki Hemion.

Valerie felt as if she were in limbo, right back where she started, which was nowhere. There was one lone flicker of hope, though, and that was Christmas. If she was ever going to hear from Vicki, decided Valerie, it would be at Christmas.

Bernard carried a tall, bushy tree into the drawing room, and when it was set up in front of one of the tall windows overlooking the street, Valerie helped Janet decorate it.

On Christmas morning, Valerie and Lady Anne opened presents before the roaring fireplace. Lady Anne's special present to Valerie was genuine pearl earrings. The little package Julian had pressed into her hand just before the Christmas break was a sketch of her he had drawn, framed in silver filigree.

There was nothing from Vicki, though.

Lady Anne sat pensively in a wing chair in the drawing room. "I remember the first day you walked into this

room. You were so pretty, as delicate as a little fawn."
She held her teacup with both hands as she smiled at
Valerie, who sat in the matching chair across from her.
"And oh so very frightened," she continued. "My heart
went out to you, dear. That's why I told you I wanted
you to think of me as your aunt, and to think of yourself
as my little American niece. I wanted you to feel secure,
loved."

Valerie felt tears in her eyes.

"And, of course, I've been thinking about your
dreadful predicament almost as much as you have." Lady
Anne put her teacup on the little Chippendale table next
to her, and reached out her arms. "Come here, dear,"
she said as she stood.

As Valerie moved into the circle of Lady Anne's
arms, she felt the older woman's body trembling. "I'm
going to make an appointment with my solicitor to see
about becoming your legal guardian. This is our home
now," Lady Anne said, her voice husky with tears. "The
two of us."

She cares for me, Valerie realized. She really does.
"Oh thank you, Lady Anne," she whispered, tears of relief welling in her eyes. And then the anger, the bitter-
ness again.

"How could they do this to me?" Valerie whispered, her own arms tentative around Lady Anne's waist.
"How could they leave me like this?"

"But we don't know that, do we?" Lady Anne said.
"We don't know that they left you, dear. Something may
have happened to them, something they couldn't control."

"Well, I don't care," said Valerie stubbornly. "I'll
never forgive them. Never."

"You mustn't say that," Lady Anne admonished.

"But they're my parents," she sobbed, realizing she could never trust anyone, not even Lady Anne, to be there when she needed them.

13

When Valerie got back to the conservatory after the Christmas break, there was an announcement on the bulletin board about Julian's upcoming appearance with the London Philharmonic Orchestra. She was bursting with excitement as she walked into the drawing room that afternoon to tell Lady Anne about it.

"That's a bad night for me, dear," said Lady Anne, looking through her reading glasses at her date book. "I have dinner at Lady Dartmouth's. We're only ten, and she would never forgive me if I canceled."

"Oh, that's all right," Valerie said. "I'll just go with some of the other kids." She paused for a moment, savoring the thought. "Julian's going to perform the Mendelssohn E-Minor Concerto," she bubbled. "And Andre Previn's conducting."

"It's out of the question," Lady Anne murmured.

"But all of the other kids are going." Valerie's voice wavered as she fought to keep back the tears.

"I'm sorry, dear," said Lady Anne.

"Why not?" asked Valerie. "It's not as if I'll be alone or anything. I'm sure somebody's parents would come and pick me up, and bring me home."

"That will do," Lady Anne said, her voice sharp.

Suddenly, Valerie's aching loneliness for a friend her own age made her break into sobs, and she fled from the room.

The next day Valerie told Julian that Lady Anne wouldn't let her go to the concert.

"Everybody comes, you know," he said, sounding hurt. "It's a family kind of thing. Scream for the team, and all."

"I know," Valerie sighed. "I know."

On the night of the concert two weeks later, Valerie stood, her ear against her bedroom door, until she heard Lady Anne's footsteps as she hurried down the stairway. The front door clicked shut.

A few minutes later, it was Valerie who was standing in the entry hall, fumbling with the buttons on her rabbit coat. "You have a good time, miss," Janet said. "I'll be waiting to let you in at nine o'clock." Her glance fell on Valerie, and she added, "You look very pretty tonight, miss. You always do when you put on a little rouge and lipstick. Perks you right up."

Valerie's steps were cautious as she picked her way down the front steps of the Green Street house. The street was empty, and lights dotted the windows of the houses across the way. She broke into a run, feeling the exquisite pain of the icy London air filling her lungs, exhilarated with the sheer joy of being out on her own. The taxi she caught dropped her a few minutes later in front of the Royal Albert Hall, where the concert was to take place.

Her seat was in a row with the other conservatory students. The boys were all in dark suits, shirts, and ties, the girls in party dresses. Valerie slipped off the rabbit coat. She wore her green calf-length taffeta dress, and around her neck was a pearl necklace on loan from Lady Anne. Her pale hair was pulled up in a ballerina's bun, and in her newly pierced ears she wore the pearl earrings Lady Anne had given her for Christmas.

She looked up at the boxes, hoping none of Lady Anne's friends had a pair of opera glasses trained on her. Behind the red velvet curtain, Valerie could hear the cellos, the violins tuning up. A French horn played a fragment of a melody.

The house lights dimmed, and those in the audience were still, anticipating. To the swell of applause, Andre Previn strode purposefully onstage in front of the eighty-piece orchestra. There was more applause, then cheers, especially from the rows around her, when the maestro introduced Julian Unwin.

Valerie caught her breath.

Julian looked so handsome, so impossibly romantic in his tails, his white tie, with his shiny brown hair cascading to his shoulders. His eyes met hers as he made his bow to the audience. His eyes were closed as he addressed his bow to his violin. The first bars of the Mendelssohn E-Minor Concerto sang through the jammed hall as Julian's bow danced across his instrument, his body swaying to the music. The bow went faster, faster, as Valerie watched it fly, hypnotized. His playing was seamless, soaring, as the concerto came to an end. There was an instant of silence, and then wild applause, cheers, and cries of "Bravo" as Julian made a deep bow to the audience.

If only she could have stayed for the second half, she thought, still dazed by Julian's playing as she scurried through the crowd that had broken for the intermission. But no. She had to get home.

Promptly at nine o'clock, Valerie's taxi pulled up in front of the Green Street house. The front door was opened by Janet the moment Valerie tapped on it with the knocker.

"Did you have a nice time, miss?" asked Janet, closing the door behind her and helping her off with her coat.

"Oh, it was wonderful," Valerie breathed, thinking again how handsome Julian had looked, how rapturously he had played. "He was wonderful."

"Shall I bring a snack up to your room, miss?" Janet asked. "How about a nice cup of cocoa? It's a cold night, that's for sure."

"That would be wonderful," Valerie said. Everything was wonderful, she added to herself. Julian, and his masterful performance. The Albert Hall itself. Just being out alone, riding in a taxi.

"I'm happy you had a nice time, miss," said Janet, moving off in the direction of the kitchen. "A young girl like you, well, you should be able to see your friends. All work and no play makes Jill a dull girl."

So, she had done it. Valerie smiled to herself as she snuggled in her new robe, sipping the cocoa that Janet had brought her on a silver tray. She had gotten out of the house, heard Julian play, and gotten home with Lady Anne none the wiser.

All of the reviews in the London papers the next day were ecstatic raves. Julian was waiting with the papers at the front door of the conservatory when Valerie arrived. She had already seen the one in the *Times,* of course.

"We've got to go out and celebrate," he pressed.

She looked up at him, recalling how handsome he had looked on the stage of the Albert Hall the night before. Then she remembered Lady Anne's icy voice.

"Oh, I don't think so," she said. "There's a lot going on at home."

"The next time your aunt goes somewhere without you," he said. "That's when we'll have our celebration."

"Well, I guess I can let you know," she said hesitantly.

14

Julian and Valerie celebrated a few nights later when they went to a film in the West End. Another night, when Lady Anne was at a dinner party, there was only time for a walk on Carnaby Street and a cup of coffee. The next time, Julian picked Valerie up in his father's Rover a couple of blocks from Lady Anne's house. He drove to the embankment on the Thames at the foot of the Albert Bridge, which was illuminated against the murky gray evening. A sliver of pale moon hung over the Houses of Parliament across the river as the minute hand on the big round face of Big Ben jerked forward. In the backseat of the car, Valerie, in a panic, realized that it was tolling nine o'clock.

Julian's body was heavy on top of hers. His hands were everywhere, under her rabbit coat, as he tried to fondle her breasts, her thighs. Valerie, struggling under his weight, averted her tightly closed mouth from his wet kisses.

"Why not, Val?" Julian whispered in her ear. "I love you. You love me. We'll be married. I'm going to take care of you. Forever." He was panting, and his breath was hot. The insides of the car windows were steamily opaque. "Nothing will happen," he pleaded. "You don't have to worry. I've got something with me."

"I've got to get home," she panted as she pushed his hands away. He was overwhelming her, compelling her to surrender. Oh, I do love you, Julian, I do, she thought to herself. All she wanted was to stop the struggle, feel the thrill of him as he kissed her.

"Touch me, Val," begged Julian, trying to force her hand onto his penis, swollen in his jeans.

Gathering all of her strength, Valerie shoved him away and sat up, her breath coming fast.

"Don't you love me, Val?" he asked in a quiet voice.

"Oh, yes," she sighed.

"I love you," he said, looking at her. "You do know that, don't you?"

"Please, Julian, I've got to get home," she insisted.

She felt his exasperation as they climbed into the front seat and he started the car, saw the set of his mouth as he drove. "Please, don't be upset," she begged.

"Let's just forget it."

His words stung as if he had slapped her, and she gazed morosely out of the window of the car. She had never felt so alone as he stopped the car a block away from the house on Green Street. She sat, with her head bowed, while he came around and opened the door for her.

"Julian," she began, but she was talking to his back

as he hurried around to the driver's seat of the Rover, shoved it into gear, and, with squealing tires, drove away.

Janet's face was white as she opened the front door before Valerie even had a chance to lift the brass knocker.

"Her Ladyship's just gone up," said Janet, a worried frown on her face, her voice hushed. "She asked if you were still awake, and I said I didn't know."

Valerie looked up at the wide, winding staircase, at the dark wood stairs gleaming with highly polished wax. There was no way in the world, she realized, that she could get to her room without Lady Anne knowing she had just come in.

"Maybe if you took off your shoes, miss," said Janet, her voice anxious.

Valerie shook her head.

"Do you want me to bring you anything, miss?" asked Janet, nervously wiping her hands on her apron.

"No thanks, Janet," said Valerie, giving the maid a little pat on one plump shoulder. "If there's still a light under Her Ladyship's door, I'll just say good night to her."

"I'm sorry, miss," whispered Janet. "I'll see you in the morning, then, with your breakfast."

There was no light under the door, and Lady Anne didn't call out, but Valerie knew that she had been found out.

———

By the time she got home from the conservatory the next day, Valerie was practically out of her mind with anxiety. She lay stiffly on her bed, trying to take a nap, but sleep would not come. When she glanced at the little clock on the nightstand and saw that it was nearly five o'clock, she went downstairs.

Lady Anne had already poured herself a cup of tea, Valerie saw when she walked into the drawing room. There was a pretty arrangement of sandwiches and tea cakes on a silver tray. A fire in the fireplace crackled a welcome. The lamps were all on, as usual, and the chandelier was a brilliant blaze of crystal. Through the tall windows came the pale light hinting at lengthening days.

Lady Anne put the magazine she was reading on the table next to her and looked up at Valerie through the reading glasses perched on the bridge of her nose. Her face was composed, her dark eyes reflective.

Valerie sat down stiffly in the wing chair across from her. Her mouth was dry; her hands, and even her legs, were trembling. Still, it would be a relief to get it over with.

"I'm sorry, Your Ladyship," she began in a strange voice she hardly recognized.

"It's that boy, of course," said Lady Anne, her tone mournful. "You've been leaving the house to meet him. Julian, isn't it? Julian Unwin?"

Valerie nodded miserably, feeling the heat in her face, the racing of her heart.

"Has it been going on for long?" she asked.

"A few weeks," Valerie mumbled. "I went to his concert. And a few times after that."

"I should have taken you to his concert," Lady Anne mused. "That was terribly insensitive of me. I should have realized how important it was to you to be there with all your friends."

Valerie sat in silence, waiting for her punishment to be pronounced.

"Where else did you go?" she asked.

"To the movies once. To Carnaby Street. Last night, we just drove around."

"He has an automobile?"

"It's his father's."

"Dear, I have a terribly important question to ask you," Lady Anne said, her tone suddenly urgent. "And it's imperative that you tell me the truth. Do you understand?"

"Yes, Your Ladyship," Valerie whispered.

"Did he do anything to you?"

"I don't know what you mean," Valerie said.

"I think you do, young lady."

Valerie shook her head, wishing she were dead.

"All right," said Lady Anne. "I want to know if you had sexual intercourse with him. I don't know how much more plainly I can say it."

"Oh, no," Valerie said. "I didn't let him."

"Is that the truth?" she asked.

"Yes, Your Ladyship. I swear it. I swear it's the truth."

"But you kissed him," she continued. "You let him fondle you. Did he touch your breasts? Did he put his hand between your legs?"

"He tried, Your Ladyship," Valerie said, shaking her head. "I wouldn't let him do that. I wouldn't even open my mouth when he kissed me." It wouldn't matter to Lady Anne, she thought wildly, that the reason was because she was embarrassed about her braces. All that metal all over her teeth.

"When do you want me to leave?" Valerie whispered, realizing she couldn't take another moment of the conversation.

"When I told you this was our home, Valerie," said Lady Anne, looking surprised, "I didn't mean conditionally. If you were my own niece, I wouldn't ask you to leave, no matter what the circumstances. As I've told you from the beginning, I do think of you as my niece." She paused for a moment and smiled warmly at Valerie, who was trying to absorb the words. "But I certainly don't countenance your behavior," she added. "You obviously can't go sneaking around the moment my back is turned."

"Oh, I won't, Your Ladyship," Valerie promised, close to tears.

"I feel I'm to blame," Lady Anne said reflectively. "I've concentrated so thoroughly on educating you so you'll be comfortable on the highest social level, I just didn't think you might need guidance in other areas as well, or that you need to socialize with friends your own age." She took a sip of her tea, and then she gave a start. "My dear," she said brightly. "You haven't had your tea."

Valerie took the cup of tea, realizing that not only was she to stay, but Lady Anne was going to take her even more firmly in hand. Valerie felt so drained by relief that all she wanted to do was crawl up the stairs and sleep.

———

Valerie was humiliated when Lady Anne dragged her off to a gynecologist in Harley Street several days later. Valerie didn't understand why Lady Anne needed the reassurance that she was a virgin, but it seemed to clear the air.

Julian stopped speaking to her, ignored her whenever they happened to pass in the hall, looked away whenever her eyes caught his in class. Why had he changed? All she could remember was what Vicki had once told her about men. They would say anything to get the one thing they wanted, which was sex.

15

"Now, you mustn't let Maria frighten you," said Monsieur Vilgran to Valerie as they sat in the backseat of his Rolls-Royce limousine. Lady Anne, on his other side, was looking very smart in a gray wool suit and a creamy satin blouse. An olive green hat covered her dark hair; pearls adorned her blouse, her ears. "She's a Czech, as you may know. A volatile people, the Czechs." When he patted Valerie's arm, it was all she could do not to pull it away.

Sitting in the back of the Rolls-Royce with Monsieur Vilgran and Lady Anne, on her way to play for Maria Obolensko, seemed strangely right to Valerie. Inevitable, in fact. Talk of it had begun so long ago on that night at the Hollywood Bowl.

"I don't know how Weyburn puts up with her, actually," Monsieur Vilgran said, almost to himself. "Why, the woman actually throws things at him. She's tried to kill him."

"The duke of Weyburn?" asked Lady Anne, looking out the window.

"Yes, Weyburn," Monsieur Vilgran acknowledged. "Her lover, you know. Her patron. It isn't a state secret that there isn't a fortune in classical music. Every classical artist needs a patron. Weyburn underwrites her concerts, and her recordings. And, of course, the jewels he has given her are legendary. The diamonds, the sapphires. There is a ruby and diamond necklace, with earrings to match, that are the finest I have ever seen. Oh, those diamonds. Their clarity, their perfection." Monsieur Vilgran seemed lost in thought for an instant, savoring his memory of their magnificence. "She has wonderful art, too, if you like the Impressionists," he continued. "And with all of it, she treats Weyburn like a dog. She humiliates him in public."

"And he's so attractive," Lady Anne murmured.

"So many people are," observed Monsieur Vilgran. "It doesn't save one, unfortunately, from obsession." Picking up the speaking tube, he said, "Allen, my good man, it's a miracle. There is a parking space right in front of Madame Obolensko's house."

Claude's knock on Maria Obolensko's front door elicited a cacophony of hoarse, frantic barking and then silence.

The butler who opened the door was in gray striped trousers and a black coat. Panting as they sat on either side of him were two large black Doberman pinschers. The entry hall and all of the rooms that could be glimpsed from it were in black, white, and blazing red. In the distance, Valerie heard a woman's voice shrieking what sounded like obscenities in Italian.

"Madame is on the telephone," said the butler. "She

asked me to tell you that she will join you shortly in the drawing room."

Its floor was a geometric sea of black-and-white marble, the walls upholstered in red silk, matching the curtains on the tall windows that faced Eaton Square. The sofas, the chairs were all in white. There was only one painting in the room, of Christ dying on the cross, a crown of thorns on his head, his palms bloodied.

"Have you ever seen such a magnificent El Greco?" sighed Monsieur Vilgran reverently. "It was stolen, of course, from the Prado. I've told Maria a thousand times that she's a fool to have it hanging on a wall in her drawing room where everybody can see it. Some public-spirited soul is going to call the police one of these days. I've advised her to announce that it has come into her possession and give it back. She would be a heroine. The publicity would be marvelous, and the Spanish people would love her. But she won't do it. She is the most selfish, greedy person I've ever met," he concluded. There was admiration in his voice.

And then Maria Obolensko was standing in a beam of sunlight at the door of the drawing room, making her entrance. Her black hair was pulled back in her signature chignon; her black eyes glittered. She wore a silk tunic to her knees and matching silk trousers in a red so intense it seemed that flames were licking at her tall, thin body. Her toes, their tips crimson, peeped from high-heeled sandals.

"You're slandering me again, you bastard," she said, kissing Claude fondly on either cheek. "I should have you arrested for what you say about me. I should have your knees broken for you."

There was a broad smile on her red lips as she turned to Lady Anne and put out both her hands.

"Lady Anne," she said. "You honor my humble home."

"This is Valerie Hemion," said Claude. "She is Lady Anne's niece. She comes from Los Angeles."

"How many times are you going to tell me that, you bloody fool?" Maria asked crossly. "Do you think I can't remember from one day to the next what you've told me?" Taking Valerie's two hands in her own, she continued, "Welcome, my dear. I hear you're brilliant, absolutely brilliant. Claude tells me you're to play in the Van Cliburn this year. It's a ridiculous idea. You're much too young, and you'll lose. You'll make a fool of yourself. But what can you expect from Leon Stern, that tyrant, that Attila the Hun? All he thinks about is his own glory, his own triumphs. Pianists? We're nothing to him. Dirt. Scum. Every day in all the years I studied with him, I woke up every morning hoping he was dead. A heart attack. Run over by a bus. Anything. We're machines to him, interpreting his visions."

She lapsed into a moody silence at the thought of Leon Stern until the butler announced that luncheon was served.

"That was Weyburn on the phone just now," Maria said to Claude in a confidential voice, as Valerie strained to hear her words from across the table. "He was begging to see me tonight, begging." The butler poured the white wine that was to accompany lunch into the crystal glass in front of her. "I could kill you for introducing me to that fool," she continued. "You only did it to drive me to an early grave. It was a spiteful, terrible thing. I would rather have your slander, your back stabbing, than Weyburn in my life."

"Don't see him," Claude suggested, his tone amused.

"And give up all of this?" Maria asked, gesturing with her fork. "You're crazy, you know?"

After lunch, sitting at the concert grand piano in the music room, Valerie played the Mozart concerto she was preparing for the Van Cliburn. When she finished, Valerie kept her fingers on the keys, her head down.

"You're a genius!" Maria screamed, rushing over to Valerie. "You've thrilled me, thrilled me."

She nearly wrestled Valerie off the piano bench, covering her cheeks with wet kisses.

"I have it," she said, her black eyes snapping. "We can play together, a duct, after the Van Cliburn. We will start to prepare a program. It will be at Wigmore Hall."

"But Madame Obolensko, I'm not ready," Valerie stammered in amazement.

"Oh yes you are, my dear. Of course, I will be the draw to fill the hall, but you, my darling Valerie, you will complement me." She was pacing the room, muttering to herself. "An orchestra? Forty? Sixty?" Her black eyes narrowed as she saw the stage in her mind. "No. No orchestra," she said. "Just the pianos. The two Steinways. Maria Obolensko and her protégé, Valerie Hemion."

Later, in the drawing room as the butler poured coffee, Maria said to Valerie, "You're a pretty little thing, you know. Oh, you blonds are always washed out, but you'll be all right. I can see it from your beautiful cheekbones. And you're how old? Fifteen?" She sipped her coffee and reached down to pet one of the Dobermans that lay at her feet. "I always knew that I would be beautiful, too," she murmured. "I knew it back when I was a tiny girl in Prague, studying at the feet of my dear papa. I knew it because of the cheekbones."

"Well, this has been charming," Claude said, glancing at his watch. "But I have an appointment that I'm already a bit late in getting to."

As Maria stood with the three of them in the doorway, she put her arms around Valerie and said, "We'll make a good team. We'll show that bastard Leon, won't we?"

All Valerie could do was nod.

The Wigmore Hall concert was a major triumph for Maria, and it also netted Valerie critical praise. A lengthy interview with Maria in the *Times* of London reported her heartfelt interest in helping younger artists with their careers. A recording Maria's label made of the concert was released to excellent reviews. The duke of Weyburn partially underwrote the record's release by purchasing five thousand copies at a discount and distributing them to music classes in the grammar schools.

"You're wonderful, Maria," said Valerie, gazing at her with the sense of wonder she always felt in Maria's presence. "You can do anything."

"That's true," Maria said. "There's no point to being falsely modest. It isn't attractive." She glanced at the diamond-studded watch on her slender wrist. "Bernard will be knocking on the door in exactly one minute," she said. "He is always on time. You had better get home or your aunt will be worried, and she won't let you come to see me anymore."

As Valerie started to rise, Maria asked, "Do you know Victor Penn?"

"No," said Valerie, shaking her head. "I've seen

him, though." Lady Anne had pointed him out to Valerie when they were at the opera, at the theater, and once at the Ritz when they had been there for dinner. Victor Penn was always with a different beautiful woman. "He's very handsome, isn't he?" Valerie asked.

"And, he's very rich," Maria said. "Very, very rich and very, very generous."

———

Penn International renewed Valerie's scholarship for a second year, and then a third. Valerie's blossoming career seemed to become even more important to Lady Anne. When Valerie thought about it, it seemed to her that attending to its details had replaced whatever life Lady Anne had been leading before she came along.

16

Backstage in her dressing room at the Albert Hall, Valerie sat in front of the bright lights of the makeup mirror. She examined her face, the wide forehead, the pale hair swept up into a bun on top of her head, the high cheekbones. She had coaxed her eyes to their most vivid green with shadow, and darkened her long, sweeping lashes with mascara. After applying blusher to the hollow under her cheekbones, she dabbed some on the tip of her nose, on her chin, all to create a vivid face to be seen from the audience, the way Maria had taught her. She smiled, admiring her straight white teeth, and applied a glossy pink lipstick.

Valerie's eyes were reflective, cool despite her dry mouth and her perspiring hands as she fumbled with the clasp of Lady Anne's pearl necklace.

The swell of her breasts was nearly as white as the chiffon of her gown, which fell to her narrow feet in their white satin slippers. "Always wear white when you perform," Maria had insisted. "White makes you look like a Grecian goddess, a wood nymph. White is good theater!"

Maria's white roses were arranged in a tall crystal vase on a little table next to one of the flowered, chintz-covered chairs that decorated the pretty dressing room. As always, there were white cattleya orchids from Leon Stern, long-stemmed pink roses from Lady Anne. An extravagant spray of pale green cymbidia from Claude Vilgran. Red roses from Max in Los Angeles. Charming bouquets from conservatory friends and the staff of the house in Green Street, who would be cheering from the audience later. There were the usual long-stemmed red roses from Penn International, and an array of daisies with no card.

Valerie started at a tap on the door.

"Come in," she called as she glanced at the clock. Fifteen minutes.

"You look beautiful, dear," said Lady Anne, closing the door behind her. "How do you feel?"

Lady Anne, in a two-piece black evening suit, its jacket beaded, its skirt to the floor, wore her hair in a chignon, diamonds glittering in her earlobes, but she looked strained and tired. Perhaps she was ill, Valerie worried, remembering how radiant Lady Anne had looked when Valerie had first come to London three years before. "The usual nerves," smiled Valerie, adding, "You look beautiful, too, Your Ladyship."

"Thank you, dear," said Lady Anne, looking over Valerie's shoulder at her own reflection in the mirror. "There's a full house," she added. "You'll have another triumph, and we'll all have a lovely supper at Claridge's to celebrate your performance and your seventeenth birthday. Happy birthday, dear Valerie."

"Thank you, Your Ladyship," smiled Valerie.

There was a tap on the door, a man's voice calling, "Five minutes, Miss Hemion."

Valerie sighed as she slowly rose from her chair, smoothing the chiffon dress over her hips. "Wish me luck, Lady Anne. My first solo appearance with the London Philharmonic. Another step along the way. I might be a star at the conservatory, but I'm less than a glimmer in the world of classical music."

She smiled at Lady Anne as their eyes met in the mirror.

Lady Anne was smiling too. "Good luck, my dear."

Applause filled the hall as Valerie swept onto the stage, took Georg Solti's outstretched hand. They made little bows to one another, then, turning, bowed to the audience. Valerie glanced at the ornately carved boxes, their occupants a blur of color. In the Queen's box was an elegant gathering. The orchestra was a sea of bare shoulders, of throats glittering with diamonds, rubies, of black dinner jackets, white shirts.

Sitting at the piano, the eighty-piece London Philharmonic Orchestra behind her, Valerie watched the baton in Georg Solti's raised hand, heard the crystal tones of Mozart swelling through the hall. Her fingertips were resting on the piano keys.

The maestro gestured toward her with his baton.

Valerie bent her pale blond head over the keys, all anxiety gone as the music flowed from her fingertips, filling her with a wild exaltation. The performance. All of the grueling hours shading each phrase, each measure, sent the notes soaring. There was only the music, transporting her higher and higher.

When she had finished, Valerie stood, remembering nothing except her own rapture, her hand in Georg Solti's as they bowed to wild applause. The maestro stepped back, and Valerie bowed alone, to cheers and cries of "Bravo." Her friends were on their feet. Here and there in the audience, others joined them. A sheaf of long-stemmed red roses was thrust into her arms. She bowed once more, and hurried off the stage into Lady Anne's arms.

"You were magnificent, dear," said Lady Anne, her eyes sparkling. "You were superb. Utterly superb."

"I can't remember any of it," Valerie admitted, leaning against the wall next to the open door of her dressing room, pushing her nose into the red petals. "Oh, I'm so glad I didn't faint, or fall down," she said gratefully. "Was I really good?" she asked everybody who crowded into the dressing room to congratulate her. "Was I really good?"

"You were perfection," said a voice. "Absolute perfection." It was a man's voice. Soft, like a caress, the English accent, upper-class.

Valerie turned. He stood in the doorway holding a bouquet of long-stemmed red roses. He was tall and slender, with thick brown hair and pale blue eyes. He wore tails, a white shirt, a white tie. Over his arm he carried a black evening overcoat.

He was very handsome, much better looking than when she had seen him at the opera, the theater, from across a restaurant.

"I'm Victor Penn," he said, looking down into her eyes. "These are for the young woman who is turning into one of our greatest corporate assets," he smiled, presenting the roses to her.

Accepting the roses, she put one hand against the wall behind her for support before tentatively clasping the hand he offered, feeling its power, its strength.

Lady Anne swept up to welcome him.

"We're all very pleased with Valerie," he said, taking the hand Lady Anne held out to him. "It's so nice, Your Ladyship, to finally meet you. I grew up hearing about your late husband's exploits during the war. He was something of an idol of mine."

"How very kind of you, Mr. Penn," said Lady Anne, taken aback. "How very, very kind."

What a charming thing to say, Valerie thought. The dressing room was warm with the body heat of those crowded into it. There was the buzz of conversation and excited laughter. A couple of the boys from the conservatory came up to Valerie and congratulated her again and said goodnight. Others, too, were drifting through the door.

"Mr. Penn wants to take you to supper, dear," Lady Anne murmured in her ear.

"But the party at Claridge's . . ."

"That's all right, Valerie. You run along. Everybody will understand."

Victor helped Valerie on with the full-length, pale

mink cape that Maria had loaned her, then put on his own coat. Then it was just the two of them, hurrying down the street toward Victor's automobile.

He stopped beside a vintage Bentley convertible and fumbled with the key as he opened the door for her. It was British racing green and gleamed under the street-light. Valerie thought it was the most beautiful car she had ever seen.

"It's exquisite," she gasped as he took her elbow and helped her into the car.

"It's really for Daniel, my chauffeur," he said with a little laugh. "He gets so bored with the Rolls. I got it so he would have something to tinker with."

"Where shall we go?" he asked as the engine roared to life. "Do you like Rules, in Maiden Lane? Or would you prefer someplace else?" She could feel his smile. "It's your celebration, after all."

"Rules is fine," she said shyly. "I've never been there."

"Oh, that's splendid," he said, his voice excited. "I can show you something new."

The sommelier bowed in front of them, pouring Roederer Cristal champagne into fluted crystal glasses. "To you, and your brilliant career," toasted Victor, touching his glass to hers.

A few minutes later, the waiter served fluffy om-elettes filled with caviar. It took only that long for Valerie to realize she felt as if she had known this man all her life.

"The music, well, it's something I have to do," she said, amazed that she didn't feel shy. "You see, it's not like being the composer himself. It's not like actually being Beethoven. Or Mozart. But it's being chosen, in a way. Being blessed with talent, well, you have to carry it out. You have to see it through to whatever it can be. If you don't, you're denying your own humanity.''

"That must be a wonderful thing," Victor said slowly. "To have a gift like that, and to be encouraged to follow it. Your aunt must be so proud of you."

"Oh, she is," Valerie agreed, wanting to touch his arm. "It's almost as if my music has become her life since I've been here in London." She looked away for a moment, remembering where her music had really started, in a little apartment where, as a toddler, she had picked out tunes on the upright piano.

"Well, it all paid off this evening," he smiled. "You were brilliant."

"It was a wonderful evening," Valerie said somberly. "The only thing wrong was that my parents weren't there to see me play."

"They live in Los Angeles?" he asked, his expression showing he was eager to hear anything at all that she wanted to say.

"They did," she said.

"Tell me what happened," he said gently.

Her words were halting as she told Victor Penn about the disappearance of Al and Vicki nearly three years earlier. He understands, Valerie thought. He cares.

When Rules closed, Victor drove to an embankment where they could look across the Thames at the Houses of Parliament, at the illuminated face of Big Ben in the clock tower. Valerie didn't even notice that its hands pointed at two o'clock.

Valerie stared at Victor, fascinated, as he told her about his lonely childhood.

"My parents were killed in a plane crash when I was

just learning to walk," he said. "There was an immense fortune, and guardians who took care of everything. There wasn't love, of course, or even affection."

Valerie wanted to put her arms around him, to make up for everything he had been denied. Instead, she sat still, her hands folded in her lap.

"I don't know why I'm telling you all of this," he smiled. "I've never told anybody else."

"I want to know," she said. "I want to know everything about you."

"There was a castle, a tutor. But the only family I had was my brother, Raymond."

"I've heard of him," Valerie said.

"Yes, a lot of people have heard of Raymond," said Victor thoughtfully. "He keeps to himself, though."

"Are you close, the two of you?" she asked.

"Oh, yes," he said with a little laugh. "Raymond doesn't quite approve of me."

"How could he not approve of you?" Valerie asked indignantly.

"Now, now," he said, patting her hand, sending a little thrill through her. "It's the way I live. The mansion, the paintings, all the glorious things I enjoy having around me."

"I don't see why that's any of his business," Valerie murmured.

Idly, he reached out one hand, put a finger on Valerie's chin, and turned her face toward him.

"He thinks I'm very, very extravagant," he said, laughter in his eyes. "And, do you know something? He's quite right."

Valerie looked into Victor Penn's face, felt her whole body opening toward him like a flower toward the sun. She waited for his arms to encircle her, draw her to him. Waited for his kiss on her mouth.

The black night softened to the gray of dawn, to a smoky pink. The occasional car driving over Westminster Bridge near where they were parked turned into a steady stream of buses, trucks, taxis. All around them, London was waking, preparing for the day.

Victor dropped his hand into his lap.

"I had better take you home," he said. "It's dawn. We've talked all night."

With a guilty start, Valerie looked across the bridge at Big Ben's face and saw, as Victor started the car, that it was nearly six o'clock in the morning.

The Bentley drew up to the curb in front of the house on Green Street. Will he kiss me now? Valerie wondered as she turned to face him. Surely he will kiss me now.

"I had a lovely time." She smiled.

"So did I," he said, opening his door. "I'll just come around and let you out."

"It was really nice of you to come to my concert," she said a moment later as he took her elbow and helped her out of the car.

"You were wonderful," he said, making a gallant little bow to her. "We had a good notion when we came up with the arts endowment program. And you, of course, are the jewel in its crown."

"Thank you again," she said shyly, taking a step toward the house, wanting to beg him to take her wherever he was going.

He waited patiently for a moment, until Valerie realized she was to walk up the stairs, give him permission to leave. After walking up to the front door and raising the knocker, she turned for a moment. He was standing beside the door of the beautiful green Bentley, which gleamed in the early-morning sun. He gave a little wave, a smile as he got into it and drove away.

"Good morning, miss," whispered Janet as she opened the door. She was already dressed in her uniform, her gray hair in a neat bun at the base of her neck. "You played like an angel last night. It was wonderful."

"Thank you, Janet," murmured Valerie, looking tentatively up the stairway, toward the door to Lady Anne's suite.

"You'd better go up, miss," whispered Janet. "Take off your shoes, and hurry as fast as you can. Her Ladyship won't hear from me that you've been out all night. And that's a promise I'm making you."

It wasn't until Valerie leaned against the closed door of her bedroom that she realized how desperately tired she was.

Sighing, she threw Maria's mink cape over the chaise longue, slipped out of her gown. She kicked off the white satin slippers and wiggled out of her panty hose. In the dressing room, she stood in front of the mirror. Golden strands of hair straggled out of the bun on top of her head. Her white shoulders sloped with fatigue as she touched her chin where Victor Penn had touched it. Reaching behind her neck, she unclasped the pearl necklace, took the matching earrings from her ears.

She ran a steaming bath, then lay there, her eyes closed. All she could see was Victor Penn standing in the doorway of her dressing room. "He toasted me with champagne and he made me feel as if I were the only other person on the face of the earth," she said to herself with a smile.

Lady Anne was in the entry hall, shrugging off her dark mink coat into Janet's waiting hands when Valerie finally came downstairs just before teatime.

"Well, good afternoon, sleepyhead," said Lady Anne, taking her arm. Together they walked into the drawing room, where a fire crackled in the fireplace and every table held flower arrangements that Valerie had received the night before.

"Janet is bringing tea directly," Lady Anne said as she puffed up a pillow on one of the sofas, moved a vase. "Aren't all these flowers glorious?" she asked. "Perhaps you should give a concert every week, dear, and then we'll always have these marvelous roses, the orchids. Wouldn't that be nice?"

Valerie sat gingerly on the edge of her chair, trying to find a way to tell Lady Anne she hadn't gotten home until dawn.

"Did you have a nice supper with Mr. Penn?" Lady Anne asked brightly. "He's certainly handsome, isn't he?"

"He's the most handsome man I've ever seen."

"Where did he take you?"

"Rules, in Maiden Lane."

"Oh, yes," said Lady Anne. "They get a younger crowd there, of course." She smiled her thanks to Janet, who was setting the silver tea service on the table. "What's he like?" she asked, her dark eyes alive with curiosity.

"He's so easy to talk to," Valerie said. "I feel as if I've known him forever."

"Yes, people say that," Lady Anne nodded. "He's supposed to be very charming."

"Lady Anne, I have something to tell you," said Valerie with a burst of courage. "I didn't get home until six o'clock. I couldn't help it. I just didn't realize what time it was. After Rules closed, we went to a place where we could look across the river at the Houses of Parliament. We talked all night." She paused, catching her breath. "I'm really, really sorry. It won't happen again."

Lady Anne sat silently for a moment, sipping her tea.

"I'm sure it was just the excitement of your triumph last night, dear," Lady Anne said, smiling. "And, after all, Mr. Penn is the man behind your scholarship. Did he ask to see you again?"

"No, he didn't," said Valerie, slowly shaking her head. "What would he want with me? I'm only seventeen."

"Well, dear, you're a very beautiful and talented seventeen," said Lady Anne, offering Valerie the platter of cakes. "But six in the morning won't do, as you know. We must keep to our standards."

As Valerie reached her hand toward the platter, Lady Anne added, "Try one of the lemon ones, dear. They're quite good today."

Her voice was cheerful and bright.

Valerie dutifully took one of the lemon cakes. The standards of the house changed, she concluded, when the male in question was one of the richest and most powerful in the world.

17

Reviews of Valerie's performance appeared in the London papers over the next few days. All raved over her tone, her technique, and the intensity of her passion. Even her fragile blond beauty was noted. One reviewer waxed lyrical as he wrote of his anticipation of the mature artist unfolding in the pretty child who looked like a Degas painting.

"Valerie, my angel," said Maria when she called from San Francisco, where she was on tour. "I'm so thrilled that your reviews are magnificent. One of these days, you'll be nearly as good as I am."

"Thank you, Maria," said Valerie, flushing with pleasure.

"That bastard Leon must be happy," she said, and Valerie could almost see the dark look on her face six thousand miles away.

"Victor Penn took me to supper afterwards," Valerie said.

"Oh, yes?" said Maria, at the other end of the line. "Has he called?"

"He didn't even ask for my telephone number," sighed Valerie. "I'm sure that by now he doesn't even remember who I am."

"It isn't up to him to remember you," said Maria. "It is up to you to remind him."

"But Maria," said Valerie, an incredulous tone in her voice, "how do I do that?"

"We'll talk about it when I get back to London," said Maria, her tone imperious. "Men are all such imbeciles. Babies. The most idiotic woman can wrap them around her little finger."

"Well, I don't know about that," said Valerie slowly.

"You'll see, my little one," said Maria. "Now, a million kisses for your cheeks, and all my love."

In the drawing room of the Green Street house, Victor Penn's long-stemmed red roses, along with all the other flowers sent to Valerie the night of her concert, faded and were replaced with fresh ones by the maids.

"You haven't been concentrating the last three times," Leon Stern said after her next lesson. "Go to a movie. Read a book." As she gathered up her notebooks, he patted her shoulder. "It's always like this after a concert," he reassured her. "You're tired. It's natural."

But Valerie knew it wasn't fatigue. It was Victor Penn. She couldn't get him out of her mind.

———

He was waiting for her when she walked down the front steps of the conservatory, her notebooks pressed against her breasts. His arms were crossed in front of him as he leaned against the green Bentley convertible, which shone in the pale sun of the winter day. Its top was down.

"Hello," he called, taking a few steps forward as he saw her. "I thought we could drive to the country and have a bit of lunch." The look on Victor Penn's face was boyish, imploring.

Valerie looked up and down the street, expecting to see Bernard turning the corner in the Daimler.

"I'd love to," she stammered, "but I have to be home for lunch. Her Ladyship, my aunt—"

"Oh, I called Her Ladyship as soon as I saw that I had a few hours free this afternoon," he said, taking her elbow and guiding her into the passenger seat of the car. "She gave us her permission after I promised faithfully I would have you home in plenty of time for tea."

Victor threw the big Bentley into gear and guided it into the flow of traffic. Valerie glanced at his profile, watched his left hand pushing the shift through its gears.

The outskirts of London melted into the countryside with its rolling green fields dotted with black-and-white cows, the occasional horse, the villages with their clusters of thatched-roof cottages, gray smoke curling from their tall round brick chimneys. The icy wind slapped color into Valerie's cheeks, the tip of her nose, and she was shivering with the cold when Victor, an hour or so later, guided the automobile into a nearly full parking lot next to a charming old country inn framed by graceful trees.

Valerie was uncomfortably aware of her schoolgirl blouse and sweater, the pleated plaid skirt, her knee socks, as the tuxedoed maître d'hôtel pulled out her chair at their table in a window alcove that looked out at miles of green acres, stands of trees. Victor, she saw when the maître d' took his overcoat, was dressed for the country in a corduroy jacket, casual trousers. The collar of a tattersall shirt peeked from his crewneck sweater.

"What would you like?" Victor asked in an intimate voice, glancing up from the menu to look at her. "The stew is superb," he said. "It's perfect for a cold day like this one."

"Oh, the stew," she breathed, unable to comprehend that she was actually sitting there with him. "I love stew. I really do."

"I rather hoped you would," he said, smiling. His teeth were straight, and very white.

"What about a red wine?" he suggested, beckoning for the maître d'. "A Montrachet?"

"Anything," she said. "Anything at all."

———

Lights were on all over the neighborhood when, promptly at five o'clock, Victor drew up in front of Lady Anne's house and hurried around the car to help Valerie out.

"Wasn't it wonderful to get away?" he asked, his eyes bright and excited, as they stood facing each other.

"Oh, yes, Victor," Valerie agreed, putting out her hand to him, thinking that she hadn't really gotten away at all. That she had been just where she wanted to be all the time, which was with Victor Penn.

"Thank you very much for playing hooky with me," he said, taking her hand.

"I enjoyed it." She smiled. "It was the best time I've ever had. I felt so free."

"You know," he said suddenly, "you have the most beautiful voice. I can hear your music in it."

"Well, thank you," she said, feeling a sudden flush of pleasure. "I love your voice, too. It's like, well, it's like . . ."

"Give my regards to Her Ladyship," he said, dropping her hand.

"Oh, I will," said Valerie, taking her cue and starting up the stairs. She turned at the door and waved goodbye to him as he got into the car and drove away.

Everything has been so orderly, so routine, thought Valerie, all of the years since I've been in London.

Except today.

With one phone call to Lady Anne, there was no Bernard, no hurried lunch before the cadre of tutors. Victor Penn has set me free.

The next day, when Valerie got home from the conservatory, there was a large white box addressed to her sitting on the console in the black-and-white marble entry hall.

"A chauffeur just brought it, miss," said Janet, closing the door behind her and helping her off with her coat. "The car was one of those long Rolls limousines. It was very fancy, miss."

Flowers from Victor, thought Valerie, feeling a rush of pleasure.

"Aren't you going to open it, miss?" asked Janet. "I'm near dying with curiosity."

Tentatively, Valerie opened the card, read it, and handed it to Janet.

" 'She reminds me of you,' " read Janet aloud. "And it's signed, 'Victor.' Do you know anybody named Victor?"

"Victor Penn," said Valerie, nodding her head.

"Well, that's wonderful, miss," said Janet, looking at her with new respect.

Inside the package was a small sculpture of a ballerina, her hands clasped behind her back, her chin tilted upward. Her hair was in a chignon at the base of her neck.

"It's Degas," said Lady Anne later, looking through her reading glasses at the little sculpture she turned in her hands.

"I thought it was," Valerie said. "Isn't she beautiful? It's the most perfect thing I've ever seen."

"Ummmm," murmured Lady Anne, turning it again. "It's museum quality. It would be, of course." The look she gave Valerie was searching, contemplative. After a moment of silence, she added, "You must have had a very pleasant day in the country."

"He was a perfect gentleman," Valerie protested, shifting uncomfortably in her chair.

"I'm sure he was," said Lady Anne, setting the little sculpture on the table next to her chair. Flames from the fire in the fireplace danced on its burnished surface. "Of course, you can't accept it." Her gaze was steadfast as she met Valerie's eyes. "You do realize that, don't you?"

"Yes, I do," Valerie sighed.

"Well, Bernard can run it back," Lady Anne pronounced. "Still, it can wait until tomorrow, I think. At least we can have the pleasure of its company for a few hours."

They smiled at each other over the tea things in the pretty drawing room, made cheerful on the gray winter day by the lamps on each table and by the brilliance from the huge crystal chandelier in the dome in the middle of the room.

———

"Victor Penn has invited us to a little dinner party," said Lady Anne a few days later. "His secretary just telephoned."

"Oh, where is it going to be?" asked Valerie, feeling a pleasurable little shudder.

"At his home," said Lady Anne. "I'm quite thrilled, actually. The house is supposed to be a masterpiece. And there will be bridge after dinner. Two tables, the secretary said."

"My bridge isn't very good," said Valerie doubtfully.

"I don't think that's the point," Lady Anne mused, looking at Valerie sitting next to her at the dining room table. "And you know, dear, I do think it's time we did something about your hair and your clothes. You're growing up, you know."

———

As the big Daimler coursed its way through the heavy traffic on Friday night, Valerie, in the back seat next to Lady Anne, wore a new gown in sea-foam green chiffon. Her pale gold hair had been cut into a cap that followed the shape of her head. When she had looked at herself in the full-length mirror in her dressing room, she felt as though she had made a great leap into adulthood. She looked twenty at least, and very poised. She pirouetted in front of the mirror, loving the way she looked, loving the way she felt about herself.

———

After the security guard buzzed open the gates, it seemed to Valerie they must have driven for more than a mile on the wide, winding road flanked by ancient oak trees before Victor Penn's Regent's Park mansion loomed into view, silhouetted against the full moon. A butler opened the massive arched doors; a footman was there to take their wraps as the two of them looked around. The entry hall was as large as the drawing room in the Green Street house, its gleaming dark floor partially covered by a massive oriental rug in reds, greens, and blues. The framed tapestries on the walls reminded Valerie of those she had seen in the British Museum. The bas-reliefs on the ceiling depicted Greek gods, goddesses.

"Oh, there you are," said Victor Penn, coming forward to take Lady Anne's hand and nodding to Valerie. "We're all having a cocktail in the drawing room."

A hundred people could have been assembled with comfort in the huge room. Instead, there were only six, the men, like Victor, in dinner jackets, the women in long gowns. They sat chatting in chairs gathered around a crackling fire.

Valerie noted how the gold of the pilasters and ceiling brought together the richness of green brocade on the walls and the deep crimson and gold of the carpet. A massive gilt-framed mirror over the fireplace reflected some of the masterpieces in the room. Paintings by Rembrandt, Van Dyck, Tiepolo.

"What a beautiful room," Valerie exclaimed.

"Do you like it?" asked Victor. "I'm so pleased."

The men pulled themselves to their feet, the women looked up expectantly, as Victor led the two new arrivals to the cozy little group.

"Here is Lady Anne Hallowell," he said, "and her niece, Valerie Hemion." Turning to the group, he added, "This is Roscoe Danforth, and his wife, Caroline. Sir Edward Winston, Lady Winston." The women were handsome, aristocratic in pale satins, jewels; the men lean, emanating power, money. "And this is my brother," Victor continued, "Raymond Penn."

Everybody was shaking hands, murmuring, "How do you do," "So nice, finally, to meet you," when Valerie's hand was briefly touched by that of Raymond Penn, and he, too, was uttering appropriate pleasantries.

So, this is the mysterious Raymond Penn, Valerie thought, as she looked up into his face, which was very much like Victor's. "How do you do, Mr. Penn," smiled Valerie, her hand clasping his. Her smile froze as she saw the contempt etched on his face, the expression of utter loathing in his pale, cold eyes. He pulled his hand away from hers as if the mere touch of it made him ill. She stood bewildered, startled by the hatred flowing toward her. Shaken, she averted her eyes from Raymond Penn, trying instead to concentrate on the conversation.

Dinner in the magnificent dining room, with its two dramatic chandeliers illuminating paintings on the walls, was superb, and later Valerie was Victor's partner, Raymond was Lady Anne's, as they played bridge for several hours in the library over coffee and brandy. Valerie, watching Victor's face, played fairly well. Every time their eyes met he seemed to be asking her something. For approval, she decided, when it was finally time to leave. Victor Penn was asking for her approval. Was that the reason for the disdain on his brother's face?

By the time Valerie and Lady Anne were in the back seat of the Daimler, plans had been made for a weekend at Victor Penn's country estate.

"Well, what did you think? What did you think?" Valerie asked excitedly, her eyes shining.

With an imperceptible motion of her head toward Bernard in the front seat, Lady Anne put one gloved finger to her lips.

"What a delightful evening," Lady Anne said. "And the mansion, well, it's quite beyond belief."

"What about Raymond Penn?" said Valerie. "He's—"

"What a marvelous bridge player," said Lady Anne, cutting her off. "Quite the best I've ever played with, really."

"I can't wait to go to the country," Valerie said. "Imagine, Victor said Arthur Rubinstein will be there."

"Yes, dear," said Lady Anne, absently patting her hand. "It should be a divine weekend. I'm looking forward to it, too."

Valerie lay on the blue and white chaise longue in her bedroom, a blanket over her legs, gazing at the picture of herself and Victor Penn in the latest issue of *Country Life*. It had been taken during the weekend Lady Anne and Valerie had spent at Victor's country estate. Their heads were together, smiling into the camera. Victor wore a corduroy jacket over a crewneck sweater. There was a hint of a shirt collar. Valerie wore her camel hair coat, a sweater under it, pearls. He looked boyish, and proud. She looked soft, beautiful, a little dazed.

She remembered lying in the four-poster bed in the bedroom of her suite at the estate, which was a castle, really, bought from some ancient royal family, restored and decorated with treasures Victor's agents had collected around the world. As the moonlight streamed in the tall windows, Valerie had fantasized a tap on the door. Victor, coming to her, taking her. She imagined herself swooning in his arms, imagined him entering her.

Instead, she had seen him the next morning at breakfast, along with all the other guests. Victor's eyes had been bright, solicitous, as he asked if she had slept well, hoped that she had been comfortable. He always seemed to want something from her. But whatever it was, he didn't seem to want her. Valerie put a finger to her chin where Victor had touched her after her concert at the Royal Albert Hall the night they met. Other than taking her elbow to help her into the car, or up a stairway, or to shake hands with her when he said good night at the front door of Lady Anne's house, he had never touched her again.

Several times, Victor was waiting for her when she got out of the conservatory at noon, and they went off for lunch, chatting, laughing, and flirting. Coming home at night after attending some performance or other, and the supper that invariably followed, Valerie would sit next to Victor in the car, willing him to touch her, take her in his arms, kiss her. Anything.

When Marie came home, triumphant, from her American tour, Valerie talked with her about Victor for hours.

"He is playing games with you," Maria pronounced. "He is like a cat, waiting for the right time to pounce on the mouse."

Maria's words consoled her for a while.

A quiet knock on her bedroom door brought Valerie back to the present.

"Valerie?" called Lady Anne.

"Come in, Your Ladyship," she said.

"Victor rang up this morning, dear," Lady Anne

said as she crossed the room. "He has to run over to Paris to look at some tapestries he's thinking of buying. He thought it might amuse you to go along, but, of course, he wanted my permission before he asked you."

Paris with Victor Penn. Valerie jumped up excitedly. "Would it be all right, Your Ladyship? Please? May I go?"

"Well, it's just for the day. You would leave in the morning, see a bit of the city. Victor can look at whatever he's thinking of buying. Then, dinner and home." She paused for a moment, and then asked, "Do you think Victor is courting you, dear?"

"I don't know," said Valerie, shaking her head. "Oh, Lady Anne, I've never dated anyone but Julian. . . . I feel so confused. . . ."

"Well, how do you feel about Victor?"

"I'm not sure," Valerie answered. "I can't figure out what he wants with me."

A few days later, Valerie sat on the Penn International jet at Heathrow. Victor sat at a round oak table, going over some papers with Brian Graham, his secretary. As the jet's engines revved the instant before takeoff, sending a vibration of power through the cabin of the plane, Victor glanced over at her and smiled. He was so attractive, Valerie thought, clutching the arms of her seat. She smiled back at him. And, oh, he made her feel so good. But why me? That was finally it, she decided. The unanswered question that kept everything from falling into place.

Threatening storm clouds buffeted the jet as it bumped its way up to its cruising altitude, leveled off, its engines so silent it seemed barely to be moving in the sullen morning sky. A stewardess served breakfast and, an hour later, the plane descended through the ominous gray clouds. Below, Valerie saw the Seine, the spidery black Eiffel Tower reaching into the gray morning, the centuries-old buildings. Paris lay before her eyes. What would a day in Paris bring to her and Victor Penn?

At immigration, Valerie was careful not to let Victor see her passport. Then they were through with customs and Victor helped Valerie into the backseat of the waiting limousine. As they drove along, Victor leaned across her, pointing out the sights of Paris, the Arc de Triomphe, the wide, beautiful Champs-Elysées.

Looking at his watch, Victor said, "I'm going to drop you off at the hotel for an hour while I go to see those tapestries. Then we'll have a bit of lunch, do a little more sight-seeing." He looked moodily out the window of the car, and added, "I'm sorry it's such a gloomy day."

"I'm not," said Valerie, smiling radiantly. "Just being here is wonderful."

In the bustling, elegant lobby of the hotel, Valerie watched Victor at the reception area as he chatted with the man behind the desk. As she stood beside him a few minutes later, waiting for him to open the door to the suite, she felt almost faint with desire.

Valerie caught her breath as she heard the click of the door behind her. There was a fire burning in the marble fireplace, vases of flowers on the tables. There was an antique sofa, antique chairs. She waited stiffly, looking out the window at the gray street below, the pedestrians hurrying under their umbrellas, the cars streaming past under the sodden sky. Waited for Victor's arms to circle her waist, for his cheek next to her hair. For his whispered words.

He moved past her, opening a door to one of the bedrooms.

"If you want a little rest," he said in his soft voice, "I think you'll be comfortable in here."

Valerie glanced beyond him, saw pale blue walls, a carved four-poster bed, a chaise, a desk.

"I won't be long," he said, glancing again at his watch. "I told the concierge you were here. If you want anything, just ring down for it."

He smiled at her as he slipped out the door.

An hour later, they hurried through the rain, their heads down, to Laurent, just a few steps from the Crillon on the Champs-Elysées. Laurent was in a lovely old house with gardens out in front. Inside, a pianist played. There were flowers in vases on the white tablecloths, maîtres d'hôtel, bevies of captains, waiters. When they finished lunch, the car was waiting for them at the entrance to the restaurant.

———

They drove through the Tuileries, desolate and forlorn in the rain. They wandered through the Jeu de Paume as Victor commented on the Impressionist paintings, all so familiar to Valerie from countless reproductions she had seen of them. Later, they dashed into the Louvre for a few minutes, and Valerie's head swam as she tried to grasp the magnificence of the Winged Victory of Samothrace, reflecting the ages as it stood at the head of the wide stone stairway.

When they got back to the hotel, there was a message from the pilot saying that the weather was going to prevent them from leaving Paris, very possibly until the next afternoon. Victor placed a call to Lady Anne, explaining the situation with his apologies and laughing assurances that he would take good care of her niece.

"I think I'll make a dinner reservation at La Tour d'Argent," said Victor as he hung up the phone. "It's so much fun for me to show you places, Valerie. Your sense of wonder, your understanding of what you're seeing. It's as if I'm seeing it for the first time myself." He slipped out of his coat, loosened his tie, and sat down in one of the chairs facing the fireplace. "You'll love La Tour d'Argent, I know. It's across the street from Notre Dame, with all its lights. Even in this weather, it's one of the most beautiful sights in all of Paris."

Valerie slipped off Lady Anne's mink coat, folded it over the back of a chair, and sat opposite Victor, looking into the fireplace.

"Victor," she said slowly, "what are you planning to do with me?"

"I thought you knew," he said softly, his voice like a caress. "If you'll have me, I'm going to marry you."

"Why?" she asked, turning to meet his gaze. "Why do you want to marry me?"

"Because you're adorable," he said. "Because you enchant me." Then his voice dropped almost to a whisper as he added, "Because I love you, my darling." He waited, his eyes on her.

"Do you love me, Valerie?" he asked.

She looked at him silently, seeing the hope, the bright expectation in his eyes, realizing she was going to have to tell him the truth about her past.

"Do you think we could have dinner here, in the suite?" she asked him finally. "There's something I have to tell you."

"Of course, my darling," he said hastily. "Whatever you want."

In the closet of the bedroom, she found a pair of men's white silk pajamas, a navy cashmere robe. She undressed, then showered, and put them on. She checked her reflection in the mirror wondering what Victor's reaction would be.

They sat across from each other at the table sipping champagne. Slowly, painfully, Valerie revealed her past to Victor. The bottle of Roederer Cristal was chilling in its ice bucket. There were candles on the table, and flames reflected from the fireplace danced across the red silk walls of the room. Outside, the rain beat against the windows, the doors that opened onto the balcony overlooking the Place de la Concorde.

"My dear child," murmured Victor when she finished, "what difference does it make?"

"My real mother was a whore," Valerie said again. "And my real father, he was probably even worse."

"Don't do this to yourself, Valerie," said Victor, running his hand through his hair, looking pained.

Slowly, Valerie pulled open the cashmere robe, unbuttoned the top of the white silk pajamas, and pulled them away from her shoulders, her breasts. Leaning forward, she tried to take his hand. "I know you don't want to marry me now, Victor," she whispered. "But I want us to make love. I've always wanted that. I want you to touch me, Victor. All over. Please."

Victor's eyes met hers, dropped to her neck, her white shoulders, her breasts. Met her eyes again.

"Do you love me, Valerie?" he asked.

Valerie felt her cheeks go hot, then cold. Her whole body trembled. With emotion. The champagne.

"Yes," she said hoarsely.

"Then marry me."

Abruptly, Valerie lurched to her feet and took the few steps around the table, where she leaned over Victor, trying to put her arms around his shoulders. He was stiff in her embrace, pushing her arms away.

"Don't you want me, Victor?" asked Valerie, stepping back. "Aren't you even going to kiss me?"

"Not yet," he said, shaking his head. "Not like this."

Disappointed, Valerie slumped into her chair, sipped the last of her champagne. She reached out her glass for Victor to refill.

"To us, my exquisite girl," he said, touching his glass to hers. "Tomorrow I'm going to take you to Saint-Ange. It's the most beautiful structure in Paris, in the world, actually. That's where we're going to be married next year. In June, I think."

Valerie could see his mind racing as he grinned at her across the table. "Won't it be wonderful?" he asked. "It will be the most fabulous wedding of the century.

"Now it's time for bed. I'll leave a call for ten. Is that all right?"

Valerie nodded, expecting an embrace. A kiss.

"Go to bed, little one," he said. "I'll see you in the morning." As she rose, he added, "You have beautiful breasts, my darling. I knew you would."

Valerie closed her bedroom door behind her and crawled into the four-poster bed. All her thoughts merged into a few words. Mr. and Mrs. Victor Penn. Mrs. Victor Penn. Valerie Penn.

19

The wedding of Victor Penn and Valerie Hemion was scheduled for the end of May in Paris at Saint-Ange, opposite Notre Dame, when the trees along the Champs-Elysées would be dressed in lacy green, the Tuileries would be alive with strollers, and the sunsets over the bridges of the Seine and over the Louvre would be alternating bands of pink and baby blue.

Lady Anne, looking better than she had in years, Valerie thought, became the general of a vast army of party planners, stationers, florists, travel agents, and the entire public relations department of Penn International, which was to coordinate guest lists, party reservations for the four-day celebration, couturier showings for the women who would be coming, arrangements with the orchestra that would be performing at a Friday night concert in Saint-Ange before the wedding. The ceremony itself would be held the following afternoon at four o'clock, when the light would still be good for the international press. The reception was to be at the Crillon. There would be fittings for Valerie's wedding gown, which Victor decided would be designed by Hubert De Givenchy, fittings for the rest of her trousseau, which would come from Givenchy, Yves Saint Laurent, and Valentino, all of which required several trips to Paris and Rome. Her own gown, Lady Anne decided, would be made by the House of Chanel.

Whenever Valerie came home from the conservatory, it seemed Lady Anne was on the phone to George Bothwell in the public relations department of Penn International, or to Victor himself.

"George, the minister of culture says it's impossible to have the wedding itself at Saint-Ange. Nobody has been married there since before the French Revolution, and that, after all, was in 1789." Valerie watched Lady Anne as she listened intently to what George Bothwell was saying. "No, no, George. You know Victor. It has to be Saint-Ange, and there's no reason, logically, why it can't be done. It's been deconsecrated. It's only a public building, no more, no less.

"Yes, yes. The concert the night before is fine. They've agreed to that. But, George, I have to get busy with the invitations. The wedding is only a year away. I think this is something that Victor should deal with himself. Have him call Georges Pompidou, for heaven's sake."

Only Victor knew how much he had donated to which French charity, Valerie thought as Bernard drove her, as usual, to the conservatory. But it got done, and Lady Anne was able to order the four hundred invitations on white-kid-finish stock, blind-embossed with the Saint-Ange altar on the outer flap of the first announcement and the transverse section of the apse on the actual invitation.

Lady Anne spent an entire week at Penn International, working on a tentative guest list with George Bothwell for Victor's approval. Heads of state. The Rockefellers, Mellons, and all of the other banking interests from New York. The Rothchilds from Paris, England. The governor general and his lady from the Bahamas, newly independent from Britain, where Penn

International was negotiating to set up a branch. The cream of society from New York, Palm Beach, Detroit. Victor's friends from Los Angeles, film stars, and members of old California families with whom he had played polo over the years. Royalty from England, France, and Germany, the rich and celebrated from every walk of life, the glittering luminaries from the worlds of music, art, theater, and film.

Leonard Bernstein was booked as conductor for the concert at Saint-Ange with the London Philharmonic Orchestra. Maria Obolensko and Valerie Hemion would perform a duet on matching Steinway grand pianos.

———

Valerie stood in front of the three-way mirror in the huge dressing room at the House of Givenchy, with its silk upholstered walls, its silk-covered chairs. Lady Anne, sitting on one of them, nodded approvingly as Hubert De Givenchy, tall and handsome, a frown creasing his forehead, draped white peau de soie over her slender shoulders, held up samples of handmade white lace. The gown would be simple. The peau de soie, long sleeves. The skirt flowing into a long train. The lace from its round collar framing her jaw, her chin. A fingertip-length veil cascading from its crown of dried country flowers. A tiny, delicate bouquet of country flowers to match it.

———

"Victor, he makes you happy in bed?" asked Maria, as the two of them sat at lunch at Victor's favorite table in a corner of the dining room at Claridge's.

"Oh, Maria," said Valerie, her cheeks burning.

"It makes no difference," said Maria, her black eyes reflective. "He's one of the richest men in the world. He gives you everything. With Victor and his money behind you, you can become one of the major concert pianists in the world. Nothing can stop you." She waved across the room at somebody she knew. "I knew he would marry you," she said in a low voice. "It would have to be a young girl for Victor, somebody he can mold to his liking."

Valerie heard her own voice in her memories of her evenings with Victor. "Please, Victor. Please make love to me. Why not, my darling love? We're engaged. I want you so much."

"We'll wait until we're married, my exquisite girl," he would soothe. "I want it to be perfect between the two of us. I want to know you belong to me."

"Well, kiss me, then. Hold me."

And he would look at her with that thoughtful look in his eyes, and slowly shake his head.

Valerie would lie in her bed in the blue and white bedroom in the Green Street house after an evening with Victor, wondering if they would ever have a physical life together. It wasn't as if he wasn't interested in her physically. Valerie could almost feel his effort not to touch her. Maybe something was wrong. Would that matter to her? she worried. No, no. It wouldn't matter at all. She loved Victor, loved him with all her heart and soul. There would be their spiritual life together. That would be enough.

"The only problem will be the babies," Maria said thoughtfully. "Babies don't work in the life of a great artist. But then, there are always nursemaids for the babies of the very rich."

⸻

"What should I do about birth control?" Valerie asked Victor. "Should I go on the pill?"

"No," Victor said, his voice sharp. "I don't believe in putting all of those chemicals into the body."

"A diaphragm? Foam?"

"No. No."

"Victor, are you telling me that you want me to get pregnant at once?" she asked, thinking of her high, beautiful breasts swelling, her flat stomach protruding, heavy with Victor's son. It thrilled her.

"We don't have to talk about it now, my darling child," he said, with that quick smile that always touched her heart.

So, maybe there *was* something wrong, she thought night after night as she lay unable to sleep in her blue and white bedroom in the Green Street house. But it was all right. They could kiss, hold each other. Fondle each other.

"I'm going to be the most beautiful woman at your wedding," Maria said. "I am not wearing red, of course, since it is a wedding. Beige silk. I fly to Paris for my final fitting next week."

⸻

Valerie looked at herself in the three-way mirror in the huge dressing room at the House of Givenchy, saw her tall, slender figure in the peau de soie gown, tight through the bodice, billowing from the waist into its long her golden cap of hair, her veil, set in place of dried country flowers, cascaded behind ed her face to her chin. Her green eyes were excited, her color high. Unconsciously, she licked her lower lip as she turned to Lady Anne for approval.

"Exquisite," smiled Lady Anne, swinging one crossed leg, as she sat in her furs, her black suit. "Magnificent."

"Just a little bit right here," said Hubert De Givenchy, putting two straight pins in one of the shoulders of the gown.

On his handsome face reflected behind her own in the three-way mirror, Valerie saw his look of satisfaction.

"Are you pleased?" he asked.

"It's perfect," she said.

———

The beginning of the last week of May, the Penn International 727 was almost always in the air, bringing in contingents of guests from California, Palm Beach, New York. Other guests arrived in their own private jets, or first-class on commercial flights, paid for by Victor Penn. There were parties every night, luncheons every day, trips to the country estates belonging to Victor's friends, the couturier showings. On the night of the concert, the fifty-foot stained-glass windows of Saint-Ange arching to its dome, the ornately carved statues, the banks of magnolia bushes, the eight hundred guests on their red and gilt chairs, the orchestra, the conductor, and the soloists were bathed in an other-worldly light generated by the powerful floodlights that had been hoisted into place outside by huge cranes.

Sitting across from each other at the two Steinway concert grands, Valerie and Maria watched the baton in Leonard Bernstein's hand, listened to the swell of the London Philharmonic Orchestra, saw the maestro his leonine head toward them. They bent their heads over their pianos, lowered their hands to the keys.

Max Perlstein had flown in from Madrid, where he was scoring a film.

"You were superb, kiddo," Max smiled after the concert. "I'm amazed how far you've come. You've really been putting in the work."

"Thank you, Max," said Valerie, surprised at how young he still was. When she had started to work with him at his house in Bel-Air eight years earlier, he had seemed so mature, so adult. Now, as she looked at his bright blue eyes, his tanned, unlined face, his blond hair curling to his shoulders, she saw that he was no more than thirty years old, if that.

"You can go all the way," he said, giving her hand a little squeeze. "Now you have it all, plus the talent. Don't blow it."

"I won't, Max," she said. "Don't worry. Victor is behind me all the way."

He raised his eyebrows and gave her shoulder a pat before disappearing into the crowd surging around her, a crowd that was offering congratulations, shaking her hands, exchanging little social kisses.

Afterwards, Valerie and Victor slipped away to have supper alone in the suite in the Crillon. There was a fire burning in the marble fireplace, vases of flowers on the tables. Valerie went into the bedroom to slip on the pajamas and cashmere dressing gown she had worn the night Vi had asked her to marry him. By the time she re- he was already closing the door behind the had wheeled in their supper, brought the ling in a silver ice bucket.

had finished supper, Victor pushed the

table out into the hallway. He opened the champagne and poured each of them a glass. Seated next to each other on the antique sofa, they silently watched the flames in the fireplace.

"Here's to us, my exquisite girl," said Victor, raising his glass.

Somberly, Valerie faced him, and raised her glass to touch his.

"I had hoped to be able to give you the best wedding present of all," he said a few minutes later, breaking their silence.

"You're the best wedding present of all," Valerie murmured. "All I want is you, darling."

"I want to tell you what I tried to do," he said. "For months now, I've had private investigators working for me, darling. I've had them combing records, looking everywhere. Trying to find the Hemions. Trying, even, to find your mother."

Valerie stared at him, amazed.

"Don't you see, darling?" he said. "I wanted to give you the present of your own past. I wanted to be able to repair the break, restore the continuity." His look was unhappy, his eyes troubled. "But it didn't work. They couldn't find anything. Nothing."

He shook his head, his shoulders bowed with the weight of failure. "I guess there are some things that even I can't do," he said with a wry smile.

Valerie sat staring at him for a moment, trying to grasp the magnitude of what he had tried to do for her.

"You're my past, darling," she said, fighting tears. "You're my continuity."

"I'm sorry this is all I have to offer you i‑

he said as he handed her a large, flat box wrapped in white, tied with silver ribbons.

Inside was a diamond and pearl necklace, matching diamond and pearl earrings.

He led her over to a huge mirror, stood behind her as he fastened the clasp of the necklace. She saw the pleasure on his face in his reflection in the mirror as she placed the earrings into her earlobes.

"You're so beautiful," he said, looking at her reflection in the mirror, at her pale hair, her face with the wide-set green eyes, the ears where the diamonds and pearls glittered, the necklace incongruous over Valerie's dressing gown. "I've never wanted anything in my life as much as I want you, darling," he murmured, standing very close to her. "But hasn't it been exquisite, this waiting?"

And, as Valerie met his eyes in the mirror, she realized for the first time exactly what Victor had been doing.

"You'd better get dressed and get back to the Georges Cinq," he said abruptly. "Her Ladyship is probably waiting up for you. And, it's bad luck for the groom to see the bride before the wedding."

Valerie dressed quickly, and Victor's arm was around her waist as he walked with her to the door.

"I think I won't come back with you," he said. "The car is right downstairs, waiting."

"All right, darling," she said.

"And don't forget our date tomorrow," he smiled. "⸺ ⸺ ᴼclock. Saint-Ange. There will be a lot of televi-⸺ ⸺s around. You can't miss it."

⸺ the back of the limousine, Valerie thought ⸺rds. The exquisite waiting. She thought ⸺ had pleaded with him to make love to her, and how he had pushed her away. She remembered Maria's words on one of the days they had lunched in London. That it would have to be a young girl for Victor, somebody he could mold to his liking. All of these many months, she realized, had been just that. He had been molding her. Training her.

Valerie relaxed, no longer worried that she and Victor would never have a sexual life. A shiver went through her as she wondered just what that sexual life would be.

20

Valerie looked up at Victor as he gingerly pushed back her wedding veil. His eyes held hers for an instant, on his mouth was a fleeting smile. Then, his arms were pulling her to him, and his mouth, for the first time, was open, wet, on her own. Valerie opened her mouth in response, and felt his tongue on her lower lip. For a moment, he held her away from him, his hands on her shoulders, hers at his waist, as he looked into her eyes.

"I love you," he whispered.

As the organ in the pulpit of Saint-Ange boomed Mendelssohn's "Wedding March," his arm slid around her waist, and Valerie and Victor Penn turned, smiling broadly, to face their eight hundred guests, who were already rising from their red and gilt chairs as late-afternoon sunlight streamed through stained glass windows.

Valerie picked out Maria, elegant in beige, stan

between the duke of Weyburn and Claude Vilgran. President and Madame Georges Pompidou. Mrs. Gerald Ford. The shah of Iran in his white uniform with its epaulets and gold braid. Various members of the royal families of England, Sweden, Denmark, Greece. The governor general of the Bahamas. King Hussein. The Aga Khan. Rockefellers. Rothschilds. Mellons. Gettys. Agnellis. A sprinkling of film stars from Victor's polo-playing days in Los Angeles and Santa Barbara. Mr. and Mrs. Leonard Bernstein. The Arthur Rubinsteins. Others from the world of music, theater, dance. Victor's secretary, Brian Graham. George Bothwell, and some of the key members of his public relations staff. Leon Stern, Harold Carrington, and some of Valerie's friends from the London Conservatory of Music. Raymond Penn had sent regrets, claiming a temporary indisposition. Janet, in tears, and the others on the staff at the Green Street house. Gregson from the Regent's Park estate.

Lady Anne, Valerie's only attendant, in her rose chiffon gown and her wide-brimmed matching hat, started her measured retreat down the aisle toward the high arched doors of the cathedral. Outside, a fleet of limousines, chauffeurs, and bodyguards waited to take the wedding party to the Crillon, where the reception was to be held. As far as the eye could see on the perfect afternoon were journalists, television camera crews, hordes of curious onlookers controlled by what seemed to be a battalion of French police in their tall visored hats ringing capes.

"kiss her, kiss her," the crowd chanted as Valerie stood outside on the steps of Saint-Ange.

gazed up into the face of her handsome husdazed with excitement and love. Victor leaned down. She felt his lips on hers again, gentle, caressing. She felt his cheek touching her own. To the applause and laughter of the crowd, Valerie gathered up her train and, on her husband's arm, hurried down the stairs where Daniel was waiting by the open door of the long black Rolls-Royce limousine.

——

Hours later, Valerie, still in her wedding dress at Victor's request, nestled in the crook of his arm, her golden head against his shoulder, in the backseat of the car as it sped silently through the French countryside. She twisted her gold wedding ring as thoughts of the reception tumbled through her mind. The brilliantly gowned guests, some of the men in sashes and medals, the orchestra playing Cole Porter, Rodgers and Hart, Vernon Duke. The massed cymbidia in creamy white and pale green, individual sprays in crystal vases on the sea of pale green tablecloths. The cadres of captains, waiters. The pop of champagne corks. The laughter, the buzz of excited conversations. Security guards everywhere, glowering, in their dark suits. The cheers and applause when, together, Victor and Valerie plunged the knife into the towering wedding cake, and fed each other bites of the first piece.

"I love you, darling," Valerie murmured drowsily, feeling safe, content in Victor's arms.

"We're almost there," Victor said, his lips brushing her hair. "I love you, too."

A wall twelve feet high loomed ahead, the turrets on top of an old château outlined in the moonlight. The car drove through the gates, wended its way up a long drive fringed by tall cypress trees until it stopped in front of a pair of high arched doors.

At Daniel's knock, the doors creaked open. Standing there was Gregson. "Good evening, madame, good evening, sir," he said.

Victor swept Valerie into his arms, and nuzzled her neck as he carried her across the threshold. He stood, holding her in his arms, in the great stone entry hall of the old château.

"I've laid a little supper upstairs, sir," said Gregson, as the chauffeur carried the luggage past him and up the stairs. "There is quite a nice bottle of champagne, as well."

"Thank you, Gregson," grinned Victor.

"And, may I wish both of you my heartfelt congratulations, sir," the butler beamed.

Valerie felt like a princess as Victor carried her up the stairs and through an open door into a large room with white, watered-silk walls and an oriental carpet nearly covering the gleaming dark floor. Victor, with a flourish, placed her gently on the white quilted satin cover of the huge bed.

"This is the only room in the whole château that's finished," he said. "The decorators have been working on it for weeks."

Valerie propped herself up on the mound of lacy pillows and looked around the room. There was a table, plates with silver covers. A couple of pretty little side chairs with needlepoint seats. There were crystal vases filled with sprays of white cattleya orchids. A fire crackled in the white marble fireplace carved with Greek goddesses, gods.

"It's beautiful, darling," she whispered.

"I wanted it to be just right," he said, untying his tie. "I didn't want a bridal suite anywhere, and not my suite at the Crillon. No, it had to be somewhere new for both of us." He looked at her, his eyes looking into her soul. "Only for us, my darling."

"Oh, Victor," she said. "I love you."

Valerie watched him as he took off his coat, threw it over the back of a chair. He unbuttoned his waistcoat. She looked at his back, the broad shoulders, the slim torso, the long legs, as he silently opened the champagne.

Then, as turned toward her, a smile on his face, a glass of champagne in either hand, Valerie shrank against the pillows heaped at the head of the bed, torn by overwhelming desire for Victor, but fearing what was about to happen.

Victor was sitting next to her on the bed, handing her a glass of champagne. Touching her glass with his own.

"I love you, Mrs. Penn," he said.

"I love you, Victor," said Valerie, her voice weak with longing.

"I'm going to undress you now, darling," he said, putting his glass on the table next to the bed. Valerie watched as he took off each satin slipper, reached under the yards of white peau de soie and peeled the sheer panty hose over her hips, her legs. He dropped them on the floor, while Valerie fought back the panic she felt at being naked under her gown, vulnerable.

Valerie breathed the lemony scent of his shaving lotion as he pulled her toward him, ran his tongue over her lips, and kissed her hard. His other hand was under the skirt of her wedding dress, caressing her pubic hair, gently fingering the folds of her vagina.

"I can't wait to see you, my exquisite girl," he whispered, his mouth against her lips.

Valerie felt her breath coming faster, her pulse racing, the moisture between her legs as he unfastened each peau de soie button on the back of her gown, kissing the back of her neck, licking her spine. Then he was pulling the gown off her shoulders, down her arms. Valerie sat, nude above the waist except for the lacy white brassiere. The yards and yards of skirt, the cathedral-length train trailed over the bottom of the bed, onto the floor.

"You really are beautiful," said Victor, running his hand over the white swell of her breasts. "Remember the night I asked you to marry me, darling? Remember when you showed me your lovely breasts?" He kissed her softly, ran his tongue over her eyelids, her ears, followed the line of her cheekbones. "I wanted you so much that night," he whispered.

"I wanted you, too," Valerie sighed, her whole body trembling.

"But wasn't it better to wait, dearest?" he said. "We're married now. We belong to each other. Forever."

"Oh, yes, Victor," she whispered. "Oh, yes."

He unfastened her brassiere, dropped it to the floor, and looked at her as she sat, nude to the waist. Valerie saw that his eyes were glazed with wanting her as he took a breast in each of his hands, leaned forward to suck each pink nipple. She held his head in both hands, ran her fingers through his thick, wavy brown hair, kissed it, ran her tongue along the outline of his ears.

One arm was under her buttocks, and he was lifting her, pulling away the dress, the skirt, the train. It looked like a parachute billowing all over the carpet, Valerie thought, as she lay back, involuntarily covering her pubic area with both hands.

Victor took one of her hands and guided it to the swelling in his trousers.

"This is for you, my darling," he murmured in her ear. "This is what you've wanted all this time, isn't it?"

"Yes, darling, yes," she whispered.

Victor scooped her up in his arms and carried her into the bathroom, where he sat her on the marble counter next to the wash basin. He spread her legs and, as Valerie watched incredulously, he lathered the hair in her pubic area, the fine golden hair of which she was so proud, and she felt the scrape of a razor on her mound of Venus, on the outer lip of her vagina.

"Victor," she protested hoarsely.

"It's all right, darling girl," he crooned. "I don't want anything about you hidden from me." She saw the top of his head, felt his fingers prodding her, felt them pulling open the folds covering the secret place that only she had touched until now.

"You're beautiful," he said, a note of satisfaction in his voice. "You're the softest pink, darling, like the most perfect seashell."

Then she felt his lips, his tongue, saw his head forcing her legs apart. Her arms were propped behind her on the counter, her head was thrown back, and she fought for consciousness.

Abruptly, he stood and, reaching out a hand to her, helped her down. Putting his arm around her, he led her back to bed and turned back the bedcovers.

"Are you all right, darling?" he asked as he started to unbutton his shirt.

Trembling, Valerie nodded.

"Here, let me help you," he said, taking her arm as she fell onto the bed. "Let me get you some more champagne."

Valerie watched him as he crossed the room, watched his concentration as he poured the champagne. She looked down at her own breasts, her flat stomach, the naked pubis, her long white legs. She looked at Victor, so tall and slim and handsome, as he walked back across the room, smiling, a glass of champagne in his hand.

She sipped the champagne as he sat, undressing, on the bed next to her. Her face was hot, her head swimming. The insides of her thighs felt wet, sticky.

Victor stood to take off his trousers and, in the candlelight, Valerie saw his broad, naked shoulders, the sparse hair on his chest, his muscled arms. The white of his flat buttocks, his huge penis engorged with blood, his long, well-muscled legs.

And then she was in his arms, his mouth was hot on hers. He touched her everywhere, tasted her. He sucked on her fingers, her toes. Outlined her underarms with his tongue. Outlined her breasts, her nipples. Thrust his tongue into her navel. Then he drew her legs apart, and she felt his tongue on the inner folds of her vagina, on her clitoris.

He finally whispered, "Put your legs around my waist, darling. That's right. That's my good girl."

And Valerie felt his hand between her legs, felt the head of his penis as he guided it to the mouth of her vagina.

He moaned with satisfaction at her scream of pain as he pushed into her. Held her tightly as he pushed, and pushed. Covered her face, her mouth with kisses as Valerie's brutalized body shrieked with pain. And then, Victor was moving faster and faster inside her, riding her, and he screamed, too, as she felt his fluid spurting inside her body. His chest was wet on hers, his heart racing, as he fell against her.

Later, he held her, kissing her face, her breasts. Whispering his love for her. For her perfection. He leaned down and licked the insides of her bloodied thighs, the bruised and bloodied lips of her vagina. He stroked her golden hair, ran a finger over her closed eyelids. Over her parted lips.

Valerie lay, panting and drained, in his arms, her body drenched with perspiration, her mouth tasting of him.

Twenty minutes later, he was ready to take her again.

It was nearly dawn before Victor, next to her, finally fell asleep. Valerie looked over at him as he slept on his side, one fist curled at his cheek, like a child. Tentatively, she reached out and touched the smooth skin of his back, his soft, thick brown hair.

She crawled out of bed and hobbled to the bathroom, where she stood for a moment looking at her reflection in the full-length mirror, at her white face, her hazel eyes glazed, her mouth swollen from Victor's kisses. Her breasts seemed full, the nipples red. She almost cried at the sight of her naked pubis, suddenly so vulnerable. At the blood streaking the insides of her thighs.

Penetrated. Violated. Used.

Valerie sighed. Then she remembered how hot she had felt when Victor was making love to her, the feeling that every blood vessel in her body was contracting and expanding, the throbbing contractions of her womb when he had brought her to orgasm, his fingers on her clitoris while his penis was deep inside her.

Valerie smiled at herself in the mirror as she whispered the words, "Mrs. Victor Penn. Valerie Penn."

When she climbed back into bed, she put her arms around her husband as he slept, barely seeming to breathe. She snuggled up against his back, fit her legs into the curve of his. She brushed his shoulders with her lips, the back of his neck. Drifting off to sleep, she found herself hoping, praying even, that Victor would want her again when he woke up. Want her even before a shower, or the tap on the door when Gregson brought breakfast. She was his forever, and he could do what he wanted with her. Always.

21

By the time the wheels of the Penn International jet bringing Mr. and Mrs. Victor Penn home to London after their month-long honeymoon in the Bahamas kissed the runway at Heathrow Airport, Valerie's suite in the Regent's Park mansion, a connecting door away from Victor's, was ready for her.

Her sitting room was in pale yellows and greens, the walls upholstered in pale green watered silk. An ornate gilt-framed mirror over the elaborately carved marble fireplace reflected the furnishings, all Louis XV and Louis XVI signed pieces, the Steinway grand piano, the vast expanse of the priceless carpet. A marquetry bureau on one wall was inlaid with mother-of-pearl. In their gilt frames were a Turner seascape, a Gainsborough, and a magnificent Corot. The bedroom's focal point was a huge four-poster bed, its canopy and bedspread a flower-strewn French chintz. Beside a chinoiserie drop-front secretary was a Louis XV armchair upholstered in a silk brocade. Sprays of ivory cymbidia from the greenhouse on the estate filled crystal vases.

Huge, mirrored closets held daytime dresses, evening dresses, furs, shoes, sweaters, skirts, the trousseau she and Lady Anne had bought on their many trips to Paris and Rome. In the bathroom was a large, sunken, white marble tub, a marble floor, mirrored walls. Valerie looked at her reflection in the mirrors, at her hair bleached white, her skin colored a rosy beige by the Caribbean sun, knowing that she and Victor would make love in this room, watching themselves in these mirrors. Her legs would be spread wide apart for him, and he would want her to be very still, almost lifeless. Silent. She would feel him gushing into her, watch her own face with its dazed eyes, its wanton expression so like her mother's. She could understand Cini now. It seemed to Valerie that all she and Victor had done for the entire month was make love. All she wanted was Victor, touching her, tasting her, making every nerve end in her body scream for him. Valerie had never imagined that anything could feel so exquisite as the moment when she and Victor became one. She thought of the rapture she felt with her music, but it paled compared to making love hour after hour with Victor.

Outside the sanctuary of her suite were the other forty rooms of the mansion, each of them filled with

treasures from around the world. In addition to the fourteen servants inside the house was the new personal maid
Lady Anne had hired for her, and the social secretary
who would help her to write the thank-you notes for the
hundreds of wedding presents still arriving from all over
the world, and to tend to the invitations from the cream
of London society, all curious about Victor Penn's
charming new bride. Before too long, Valerie thought,
the decorators would arrive to do a nursery for the baby
she hoped she was pregnant with. A little boy, she
dreamed, with his father's bright blue eyes and quick
smile. There would be a proper English nanny and, in
time, the tutors. Unconsciously, she ran a hand over her
flat stomach as she wondered how Victor would deal
with her as her breasts swelled, her stomach protruded
in front of her. He would be repelled, she knew. All im-
perfections repelled him. Well, she would just have to
deal with his reactions when her body started to change,
to become voluptuous with their child. Their son.

There was a tap on the connecting door to Victor's
suite.

"Come in," she called, her voice gloomy.

Victor looked tanned and fresh in gray trousers, a
white shirt, a patterned cravat, a blue blazer.

"What's the matter, darling?" he asked, his voice
anxious, as he saw her slumped in the chair.

"Nothing," she mumbled.

"Aren't you glad to be home?" he asked.

"Yes," she said, looking up at him with tragic eyes.

"Oh, my poor little girl," he said, ruffling her hair.
"Don't worry, darling. Our honeymoon will never be
over. I promise you that."

Then she was in his arms, the only place in the world

she wanted to be. He was holding her, stroking her, as he kissed the tears from her cheeks. Picking her up, he carried her into the bedroom and placed her gently in the middle of the vast canopied bed. He undressed her slowly, pulling the silk shirt over her head, the silk skirt down over her hips, until she was lying there wearing only the garter belt and stockings she now wore instead of panty hose. "So I can touch you any time I want," Victor had said. "So that I can think of you nude under an evening gown, always available. It excites me so, darling."

Then he was nude, outlined in the sun of the dying afternoon. His brown arms were around her, his mouth crushing hers. His hand was on her smooth, bare pubis, his fingers tentative on the folds of her vagina.

"Turn over, darling," he whispered.

He grabbed each of her buttocks hard, spread them apart, and Valerie gasped in pain as he entered her vaginally from the rear. And, then it wasn't pain anymore but fabulous, exquisite, as he pushed into her, coming together with her, as she panted under him. Hours later, she lay in Victor's arms, her eyes closed, as he kissed her lips, her eyelids.

"Welcome home, Mrs. Penn," he whispered, as Valerie looked at him gratefully, knowing he understood that making love with him centered her. She drifted off to sleep, safe in his arms.

When she awoke, it was dusk, and she was alone in the tangle of sheets.

The phone on the nightstand next to the bed buzzed, and when Valerie picked it up, she heard Victor's voice.

"Have I told you lately that I love you, Mrs. Penn?"

"Oh, Victor, I love you. I love you, darling."

"What are you wearing?" he asked, a little laugh in his voice.

"Well, let's see," she said. "Stockings, a garter belt."

"Ummm, sounds very sexy," he said.

"Earrings, a wedding ring."

"Oh, you're a married lady. Who's the lucky chap?"

"Well, he's very handsome, and very smart, and his name is Victor Penn."

"He doesn't deserve you, darling," he whispered. "He'll never be good enough to deserve you."

"Oh, Victor," she said. "You're always with me, darling. Do you know that? I can smell your shaving lotion now, right in my bed."

"What a sweet girl you are," he said. "I have some news, though, darling. Your aunt called. She wants to hear all about the honeymoon, so I've asked her to supper."

"Oh, Victor. What will we tell her?"

"We'll make something up," he laughed. "We can say we went swimming, dining under a tropical moon. We went for walks. You get up now, my exquisite girl. She'll be here in an hour."

———

That evening, Valerie stood in the entrance to the drawing room and thought how well Victor and Lady Anne looked together as they sat, laughing, their heads together, drinks in their hands.

"My dear child," said Lady Anne, getting up to put her arms around Valerie, to kiss her cheek. "How well you look. You're so tan. It's becoming."

"You look wonderful, too," said Valerie, hugging the older woman. And she really did, Valerie thought, as they all sat down and Gregson brought her a glass of white wine. Lady Anne looked ten years younger than she had looked only a month before, on Valerie's wedding day. All of the little tension lines around her mouth were gone. Her eyes were bright and clear, and even her hair seemed shinier, more healthy.

Later, at supper in the small dining room, Lady Anne was beaming as she announced that she was giving up the Green Street house and moving back to Cap Ferrat in the south of France.

"That's wonderful," said Valerie, waves of sadness sweeping over her.

"It's a tiny villa," said Lady Anne, "with a divine view of the Mediterranean."

"What about the staff?" asked Valerie, thinking about Janet, who had been her co-conspirator, her friend.

"Oh, my friends are standing in line for them, my dear," said Lady Anne. "I always have the most perfectly trained servants."

"When are you leaving?" she asked.

"Well, actually, in two weeks," said Lady Anne. "It's the season now, as you know. Everything is very festive."

"I'll take that Daimler off your hands," said Victor. "Valerie needs a car. And that chauffeur of yours, too."

"Oh, marvelous," said Lady Anne. "I was wondering what to do with the car. And Bernard does take such good care of it."

Victor tapped on the connecting door between their suites that night as Valerie lay waiting for him, wearing an ivory silk nightgown with handmade lace at its high neck and at the wrists of its long sleeves. Silently, she watched him as he removed his beige cashmere robe and slipped out of his beige silk pajamas. He stood for a moment, outlined by the pale moonlight that filtered through the gossamer curtains before he slipped into bed beside her and pulled her into his arms.

Softly, he kissed her unresponsive lips.

"You looked beautiful tonight, dearest," he said as he pulled the nightgown down over her shoulders to her waist and caressed her breasts. "I was so proud of you. And, so is Lady Anne. She just glows when she looks at you."

"All of those years that she had to put up with me," Valerie said softly. "All of that time when I was taking up all that room in her life." She sighed as she turned her head away from Victor. "She's so happy to be leaving, Victor. She's so happy to be leaving me."

"Oh, that isn't true, darling," he soothed, reaching under the nightgown and running his hand over her thigh. "All you have to do is watch her face when she looks at you to see how fond she is of you."

"No, no, Victor," said Valerie, wanting to push away his prodding fingers. "She's happy to be rid of me, finally, just like everyone else."

"Darling, she loves you," said Victor, taking her hand, guiding it to his stiff penis. "But you're a married woman now, the time came for her to let go. Nice is only an hour or so away. You can visit her whenever you want to."

"She won't want me to visit her," said Valerie, lost in thought. "I just know it."

"You know what your problem is, my angel?" said Victor. "You're just having post wedding blues. After all, it's been such a busy time, and now that part of our life is over. It's time for us to get on with our married life. As for Lady Anne, well, it's time for her to get on with the next phase of her life, too. That doesn't mean that the years you spent together didn't mean as much to her as they did to you."

Despite herself, Valerie felt her breath coming faster as he caressed her clitoris, the folds of her vagina, felt her nipples taut under his lips, his tongue. Finally, she opened her mouth to his kiss, felt his thrusting tongue. She spread her legs wide apart so that it would be easier for him to touch her, to taste her, as she lay there silently. Immobile.

Victor placed a pillow under her buttocks. "Touch yourself, my darling," he whispered, "open yourself to me."

Valerie felt the perspiration on her forehead, her neck, the curve under her breasts, her stomach, the wetness between her legs.

"Victor," she whispered as she felt the head of his penis prodding, ready to enter her, "please don't leave me. Please."

"I'll never leave you, my exquisite girl," he said, and Valerie felt pain shoot through her at the second he penetrated her, and then the ecstasy, the euphoria, as she wound her long white legs tightly around his waist.

"Oh, I love you, Victor," she moaned. "I'll love you forever. Just don't leave me. Just don't leave me."

"Never, never, never, my darling. You're home. With me, finally, you're home."

———

After her mornings at the conservatory, Valerie spent the afternoons dreaming of Victor even as she practiced hour after hour at the Steinway in her sitting room.

"And the amazing thing is that it's never enough," Valerie said to Maria one day as they sat over lunch in the dining room of Maria's Eaton Square town house. "I feel alive only when Victor is making love to me."

"You're a very lucky girl," said Maria, petting one of the Dobermans that lay at her feet under the table. "If you can only keep him interested until you're of age. Then, I'll take you off to my solicitor, and you can start making arrangements to have him transfer property to your name. Stocks and bonds, office buildings, maybe a couple of businesses."

"I think of him all the time, Maria. On the nights when he doesn't come to me, I'm awake all night, waiting for him. All I want to do is beat on his door until he lets me in."

"The jewels, of course, are yours," said Maria. "Only a cad would ask for the jewels back."

"He won't come near me when I'm having my period, either," said Valerie.

"You're using birth control, of course," said Maria.

"Victor doesn't want me to," said Valerie, shaking her head. "He wants me to get pregnant right away."

"That's all right," said Maria, her dark eyes thoughtful. "A baby will set you up for life. All it will mean is a few months off from the career."

"And, Maria," whispered Valerie. "He shaves me. Between my legs, I mean."

"Rich men." Maria shrugged. "They get to do what they want. Take that imbecile Weyburn, for example. He likes me to whip him like a dog."

"What?" blurted Valerie, her eyes wide.

"Oh, it's nothing," she said, with a dismissive wave of her hand. "It all goes back to public school, he says. A lot of these English are like that."

"But, how do you feel about it?" asked Valerie, shuddering.

"Oh, I like it," smiled Maria. "Weyburn is an idiot, and when he acts like one, which is usually, he deserves to be punished."

"But Maria, he's so good to you," said Valerie.

"Yes, he's good to me," replied Maria, "and so I am good to him back. He gives me what I want, and I give him what he wants." She looked around the dramatic dining room, a satisfied smile on her wide mouth. "Who cares about any of them, anyway?" she said with a shrug. "For us, it is the music, the career. Anything else is just a means to the end." She tossed back the last of her wine. "Now, are we in agreement on the Mozart we will play, my friend, or are you going to fight with me about it?"

That night, curled up in Victor's arms after making love, Valerie giggled as she told him about Weyburn and how he liked Maria to whip him, expecting him to be amused, or shocked.

For a moment, he was silent, idly stroking her hair, brushing it with kisses.

"I've been wanting to talk to you about Maria, my darling," he said finally. "I know how much she means to you, professionally and as a friend. But I don't think the relationship is good for your reputation, or mine either."

"What do you mean, darling?" Valerie protested. "Look what she's done for me."

"I don't know that it's worth the gossip about the two of you," he said. "It makes me uncomfortable."

"Victor, what are you talking about?" demanded Valerie.

"Well, Maria doesn't exactly make a secret of the fact that she's the most notorious lesbian in Europe," he said. "And, obviously, since the two of you are so close, people are talking."

Stiff with shock in Victor's arms, Valerie thought over every moment of every meeting she had ever had with Maria. There had been nothing, not a hint. Maria was dramatic, theatrical, with her huge wet kisses on everybody's cheeks.

"I don't believe it," Valerie said, her voice firm.

"Why don't you ask her, darling?" Victor suggested in a gentle voice. "See what she says. I'll go along with anything you decide to do."

It was days, nearly a week, of rehearsing with Maria before Valerie got up the nerve to confront her with Victor's shocking words.

"But of course, darling," Maria said calmly. "Everybody knows about it."

"But you've never been that way with me, Maria," said Valerie in a small, bewildered voice.

"You ask yourself why that is," advised Maria, her black eyes glittering. "Maybe the answer will tell you something."

"You tell me, Maria," said Valerie.

"I don't seduce children," said Maria. "That is beneath me."

"Well, thank you for that, Maria," said Valerie. "I'll always be grateful to you for that."

Valerie was glad that Victor was in Paris on business for a couple of days so that she could think it out. Maria and her talent, her vitality, had been so much a part of her life for so long. But how could she continue a friendship that embarrassed Victor? It just wasn't possible. She would have to give it up. With the friendship would go the tour, the next step in her career. But all she could think about, finally, was that she was Victor's wife, and Mrs. Victor Penn had to be above reproach.

Victor smiled when she told him, and he said that he was sure she had made the right decision.

"I have to go to New York for a couple of weeks," Victor said one night when the two of them were having dinner alone in the small dining room.

"Oh, darling," whispered Valerie. "Two whole weeks. I'll die without you."

"I want you to come along." He smiled. "We'll have a wonderful time. The theater season is just starting, and everybody will be back in town." He leaned over and gave her a quick kiss on the cheek. "And while I'm starting negotiations to open a branch there, we should start to meet with real estate agents. We'll be moving there before too long, darling. New York is the center of the financial world, and Penn International has to be there too."

"But my lessons with Leon," said Valerie doubtfully.

"Bring him along," said Victor. "I want you to be part of every decision about where we live, darling, and how we live. It's your responsibility, you know. You can't leave everything to Gregson the way you've been doing. It isn't fair to him."

"I'm sorry," she said, feeling her cheeks burning. "It's just that everything runs so smoothly, and I don't want to be in the way."

"How could you be in the way?" he asked, amused. "You're my wife."

Victor Penn's wife, she thought later, after they had made love and Victor was asleep in her bed beside her. It had never occurred to her that it would be a full-time job, absorbing everything that mattered to her—her music, her career, and sometimes, it seemed, her soul. She knew that marriage brought change. But to this extent? It seemed to Valerie that she was disappearing. Victor should have married somebody like Lady Anne, somebody like all those titled, beautiful women he used to see who had been raised to marry a rich and powerful man like Victor, and to run his many residences. She couldn't even manage to get pregnant. Month after month she would feel her bloated breasts, her bloated stomach, the vague discomfort, but, inevitably, also the sticky feeling between her legs, the sinking feeling of failure.

She could hardly even look Leon in the face the next day when she told him that she wouldn't be there for the next two weeks because her husband wanted her to be in New York with him. She was, in a way, selling out her music. Selling out herself.

22

"All right, Mrs. Penn," the doctor said. "You can get dressed now."

"Does everything seem to be all right?" Valerie asked anxiously, pulling her feet out of the stirrups, as she sat up on the examining table.

"Well, I'm going to have to run some tests," he said vaguely. "One can tell only so much from an examination alone."

"But how does it look?" Valerie begged. "Am I normal?"

"You seem to be, Mrs. Penn," he said, his voice guarded. "But, as I said, we'll have to take blood, run some other tests. There may be a hormone problem. Have you heard from Lady Anne?" he asked, turning toward her. "Is she well?"

"She's fine," said Valerie. "She was staying with us in the Bahamas over the Christmas holidays."

"Well, come into my office when you're dressed, Mrs. Penn," he said. "I'm going to make an appointment for you at a laboratory to have some tests made."

At least I seem to be normal, Valerie reassured herself as she stood in the tiny dressing room, attaching her sheer silk stockings to the lacy white garter belt, pulling the little white silk chemise with its narrow straps over her head. She had half expected something magical when she turned nineteen. But that birthday had passed, perfectly celebrated and marked by Victor's gift of a diamond and emerald bracelet that had belonged to Marie Antoinette.

Then their first anniversary, which had been a perfect day until Valerie opened her present, a thirty-carat canary yellow diamond on a golden chain, and burst into tears.

"You don't like it," Victor had said, his voice disappointed. "I thought, with your pale hair, your pale skin, that you would love it, darling." He ran his hand through his thick brown hair, his look thoughtful. "I'll find you something else."

"It isn't that," she sobbed.

"Well, what's the matter, my little one?" he asked, pulling her onto his lap, kissing the tears on her cheeks.

"I should be pregnant, Victor," she wailed.

"It will happen, darling," he soothed. "We'll have our little son."

"It's been a year," she said, gasping out the words as she tried to catch her breath. "A whole year."

"You're just a child yourself, darling," he said. "We have plenty of time."

"I feel like I'm being punished because I'm so happy," she whispered into his neck.

"Oh, you sweet little thing," he said, kissing her hair, running his hands over her breasts, her hips. "How I adore you, my exquisite girl."

———

The news was as bad as it could be, Valerie realized as she sat across the table from Victor. They had been having supper in the sitting room of her suite in the Regent's Park mansion.

"There's blockage in the Fallopian tubes," said Victor, not looking at her, and Valerie felt the blood drain from her face. With both hands, she clung to the edge of the table, steadying herself.

"Both of them?" she asked faintly.

"Yes," he nodded.

"What does that mean?" she asked.

"Darling, it doesn't matter. We have each other. That's what counts."

"I can't get pregnant," she said flatly. "I can't give you a child."

"Oh, my sweet girl," he said. "You're my child, and my lover, my wife. You're all I need."

Valerie leaned back against her chair, unconsciously glancing down at her useless, barren body. She would have to divorce him, of course. A man like Victor Penn was head of a dynasty, in need of an heir. Valerie thought of life without Victor. She would never hear that soft voice again. Never feel his arms around her. Never feel him deep inside her as she gasped for breath. Never feel his pride as they walked into a room together, with her on his arm. Losing Victor was her punishment for all she was not, for coming from nowhere.

"I'm sorry, Victor," she whispered, her tragic eyes meeting his. "I'm so sorry."

"I think you need to be alone," he said, standing.

Silently, she nodded, half expecting him to take her in his arms before he left, to console her, at least, with a kiss. But as he opened the door connecting her suite to his own, all Victor had for her was a tight, embarrassed smile, a helpless wave of his hand.

Valerie watched the door close behind him, heard the click of the lock shutting her away from him.

She wandered through her bedroom, where the

covers on the bed had been turned down by her maid, through the huge dressing room, into the bathroom, with its mirrored walls shooting back her pale reflection.

She quickly dressed and went downstairs to the music room in the north wing of the mansion. At dawn she was still sitting at the Steinway, her fingers flying over the keys. Bach. Chopin. Stravinsky's *The Rite of Spring.*

"Are you all right?" said a voice, and with a start, Valerie turned to see Victor framed in the doorway. He was dressed in an impeccable charcoal gray, pin-striped suit.

"Victor," she said.

He walked over to her, and looked down to where she sat on the piano bench.

"Are you all right?" he repeated, concern in his blue eyes.

"I'm going to see a solicitor today," she said in a weary voice. "I'm going to file for divorce."

"That's not what I want, Valerie," he said. "I told you my position last night."

"It isn't fair, don't you see?" she said, looking up at him. "We don't mean anything if I can't give you a child."

"Does it really mean this much to you?" he asked.

"It was the only thing I could bring to you," she murmured, trying not to cry.

Awkwardly, he petted her shoulder as she sat huddled on the piano bench.

"There must be a way, darling," he said finally. "There's work being done all the time. Let me see what I can find out."

"Do you mean it, Victor?" she whispered.

"Of course I mean it," he said, with a hint of his old

grin. "If money is a factor, we'll have our son. Now, come here," he added, pulling her up. "I hate to leave you, darling, but I'll take a kiss before I go to my board meeting."

———

Valerie dragged herself off to her classes at the conservatory. When Bernard brought her home, she told Gregson she was going upstairs for a nap. Told her social secretary she would see her later in the afternoon. She slept for hours, tossing and turning as she dreamed of nursing their infant son cradled in her arms. His eyes were tightly closed, and his mouth greedily sucked the milk from her swollen breasts. She saw herself on her own, a virtually unknown concert pianist, in dreary hotel rooms.

Valerie woke at dusk, bathed with perspiration, aware of Victor's arms around her, one of his hands grasping her buttock, hurting her. His mouth was on hers, hard. She could taste the blood in her mouth as she felt his fingers between her legs, his hands pushing her legs apart.

"You're not going to leave me, darling," he said softly, on his knees between her legs. "We'll find a way. I promise you that we'll find a way."

———

Victor came along with Valerie to her first appointment a few weeks later with Gordon Lerner, who was doing experimental work in infertility at his clinic.

Her mouth was dry, her pulse racing as she sat, tightly clutching Victor's hand, across the gleaming expanse of desk from Dr. Lerner, who was studying the records that had been sent to him by Lady Anne's gynecologist. She tried to swallow as she looked at diploma after diploma framed on the walls. At the bookshelves crammed with leather-bound medical books.

"You're nineteen years old, Mrs. Penn," he said, glancing up. He had an angular face, sandy hair, ears close to his head. He wore a white coat, a pale blue shirt, an old Etonian tie.

Valerie nodded, her nails digging into Victor's hand.

"Well, the procedure we're working on is called *in vitro* fertilization," he said to Victor. "I see from Mrs. Penn's records that her body does manufacture eggs, that the problem is with blockage in both the Fallopian tubes." He paused, looking, Valerie thought, for the simple words that would let her understand. "Our theory involves harvesting the eggs from the mother's body, fertilizing them with the father's sperm, and trying to effect a pregnancy by planting the fertilized eggs in the mother's womb."

"And your success rate?" asked Victor, leaning forward.

"We have no success rate," the doctor said with a grim smile. "And I see from Mrs. Penn's records that there is a hormone problem, as well. If we managed to effect a pregnancy, it would terminate at the end of the second month."

"You're saying that you've never made this work," said Victor.

"That's right," said the doctor.

"And you're also saying that my wife couldn't carry to term even if there were a pregnancy."

"That's also right," he agreed.

"Well," sighed Victor, leaning back in his chair, "where do we go from here?"

"Theoretically a surrogate could work," the doctor said, shrugging narrow shoulders. "It's worked in animals for years."

"You mean another woman would carry our child?" asked Valerie, her eyes wide. "But, nobody would do a thing like that. It's horrible."

"This is all theory, as I pointed out," the doctor said to Victor. "We do know, though, that we're getting close." He permitted himself another tight little smile. "That, of course, is why you're here, Mr. Penn."

"What exactly happens, Dr. Lerner, if everything goes the way it should?" asked Victor.

"In a normal situation," the doctor began, "one egg is released each month during ovulation. If the egg is fertilized, of course, a pregnancy is effected. Now, in the work we're doing, the woman is given hormones to increase her egg production. Instead of one egg, four, five, as many as twelve are produced. We harvest them, and they are mixed with the father's sperm."

"When you say you harvest them, what do you mean?" asked Valerie.

"A small incision is made in the woman's abdomen," he said. "The eggs are harvested before they would normally enter the Fallopian tube."

"And then?" asked Victor.

"Then, the fertilized eggs are implanted in the woman's uterus."

"All of them?" asked Victor.

"No," said the doctor, shaking his head. "Four is the maximum for the safety of the mother. Our theory is that out of four possibilities, one embryo might start to develop.''

"But it never has," Victor reiterated.

"Oh, we've had embryos that have started to develop. The mother has always miscarried, usually at the end of two months.''

"And what about the surrogate you mentioned?" said Victor. "Are women actually available for this purpose?''

"Mr. Penn," the doctor smiled. "I'm sure you're well aware that, for a price, anything can be accomplished.''

"Would there be any danger to Mrs. Penn?" asked Victor.

"None at all," said the doctor. "The surgical procedure is quite simple, even though it does require a general anesthetic. All that would remain would be a small scar on Mrs. Penn's abdomen.''

"But that could be corrected by plastic surgery," Victor said quickly.

"Certainly," said the doctor, raising his eyebrows.

"My main concern, of course, is that there would be no danger to Mrs. Penn," said Victor.

"What we're trying to do here, Mr. Penn," said the doctor, "will revolutionize the whole future of conception. Do you realize what our work will mean? We can monitor the fertilized eggs, the embryos as they develop. There will be no more genetic errors, no more birth defects. Every child born will be a perfect child, capable of becoming the best he can be. And, it's all starting here, Mr. Penn, in this building, in our facility in the country where we do actual surgical procedures.''

"You'll have the Nobel Prize in medicine one day," mused Victor.

"The Nobel Prize doesn't matter," said the doctor, his voice tinged with scorn. "The work is what matters. The success of the work. That's all that matters."

Valerie wet her bottom lip with her tongue as she saw the fervor in the doctor's pale eyes. She had once felt that way about her music. Now, all that mattered to her was to give Victor Penn his son.

That night, Valerie lay in Victor's arms as he ran his hand over her small breasts, her flat stomach, the swell of her hips.

"It won't work," he said, his voice pensive. "It never has."

"It's our only chance," she said.

"It will have to be discreet," he said. "You'll have to go away. To Switzerland, I think. I'll come and see you, of course, whenever I can."

"Do you think Lady Anne would come to stay with me?" Valerie asked.

"No. No Lady Anne. Nobody. Just you and the surrogate. She can be monitored at the clinic. The birth will take place there."

The birth. The birth of their baby. It was thrilling even to think about it. Valerie stirred in Victor's arms. She kissed his shoulder.

"This is the first time that I'm happy you're very, very rich, Victor," she whispered.

"You're going to have to be very brave, darling," he said, kissing her hair. "You know I won't be able to stand seeing you cut, seeing you scarred. You're going to have to go through that part of it alone."

"I can do it, Victor," she vowed, and she drifted into sleep, the face of their son a fuzzy outline in her mind.

23

In the box at Covent Garden, Valerie sat leaning forward, looking through her opera glasses at acquaintances filing into their seats in the orchestra. She wore the canary yellow diamond pendant Victor had given her on their first anniversary, and her full breasts seemed to be bursting out of her low-cut pale gold gown. She glanced at Caroline Danforth, who sat next to her, elegant in black with diamonds and rubies at her throat, her own opera glasses trained on the audience down below. Behind the two of them, Victor and Roscoe Danforth were talking about the stock market that day.

"Well, everybody seems to have turned out to hear Joan Sutherland," said Caroline Danforth, smiling at Valerie. "It was so nice of you and Victor to ask us to join you, my dear. I always have such a time trying to get Roscoe to leave the house, unless it's Ascot, of course, or Wimbledon."

"We're so glad you were free," Valerie smiled.

"I must say you're looking very well," said Caroline. "That's the most glorious diamond I've ever seen."

"Thank you," said Valerie. "It was a present from Victor."

"Roscoe never gives me a thing," Caroline sighed. "If I want something, I always have to buy it myself. We've been married for thirty years, and he has yet to remember my birthday."

"Oh, Victor remembers everything," said Valerie,

with a quick, shy smile. "He buys me presents to celebrate the night we met, the day he first took me to lunch.
Everything."

"Well, he must be utterly thrilled," said Caroline.
"I'm sure you both hope the first one is a boy. Men always want their sons, don't they? And then, of course,
they all fall in love with their daughters. Why, Roscoe
could hardly wait until little Edward was born, and then
Charles. But it's Sarah he really cares about." Caroline
paused, and trained her glasses on a nearby box. "Oh,
my heavens," she murmured. "It's the duke of Weyburn
with Maria Obolensko."

Valerie looked over at the other box, where Weyburn was helping Maria with her furs. Maria was beautiful in low-cut black satin, her hair pulled back in a
chignon. Valerie looked away, feeling a pang of guilt.

"At any rate," said Caroline, turning back to Valerie, "your aunt must be so happy about the baby.
We certainly miss her. Is she coming to be with you during the pregnancy?"

"How did you know I was pregnant?" asked Valerie
slowly.

"Oh, we women can always tell," said Caroline.
"You've always been such a slender little thing, and now
you're quite voluptuous. And radiant, too. I'm so happy
for the two of you."

Valerie knew her body had changed since she had
started to take the hormone shots twice a week at Gordon
Lerner's clinic. Her breasts were full and womanly, laced
with barely visible blue veins. Her stomach was rounded,
too, and even her hips seemed wider, more feminine.

At the clinic just the day before, the nurse who gave
her the hormone shot had told Valerie that Gordon Ler-

ner wanted her to stop by his office for a minute when she was finished.

A little pang of fear shot through her as she tapped on his door.

"Come in," he called.

Cautiously, Valerie pushed open the door and saw him sitting behind his desk. In one of the chairs across from him was a girl who seemed to be a couple of years older than Valerie. She was tall and slim, with the build of an athlete. Her hair was blond, hanging down the middle of her powerful back. Her eyes were a deep blue, her face wide, with a strong chin, a wide mouth.

"Oh, Mrs. Penn," said Gordon Lerner, rising from his chair. "Here is somebody I want you to meet."

He introduced Valerie to Engvy Erickson, Engvy Erickson was introduced to her, and, as she realized who Engvy Erickson was, the whole thing seemed so improbable that she had to sit down while she caught her breath.

———

"Do you feel well?" asked Caroline. "No morning sickness or anything?"

"No, no morning sickness," Valerie replied.

"I would imagine you might have rather a hard time of it," clucked Caroline sympathetically. "You're so fine-boned."

———

Engvy Erickson, on the other hand, was bursting with good health. She had come to Gordon Lerner in response to advertisements he had placed in newspapers in Sweden and Denmark. And that was probably Victor's doing, Valerie realized, with his insistence on secrecy as he conjectured about the circus the world press would make of the situation if, against all odds, the pregnancy worked. Engvy was already staying at Gordon Lerner's hospital in the country, a thirty-minute drive from London. She had done well on the battery of tests the psychiatrist had given her. The money she was to be paid would be used to further her studies. She was planning to become a doctor herself when she returned to Sweden.

Still, it made Valerie a little sick when she thought of Engvy at Gordon Lerner's hospital in the country, eating nutritious foods, going to bed early, taking long walks, all to prepare her body to be implanted with another woman's fertilized eggs.

"Oh, look," said Caroline Danforth, her opera glasses directed at a tall, thin man in white tie and tails, a black opera cape, who was just helping a tall woman with a silver chignon out of her fur coat. "There's Raymond Penn. What a surprise to see him out and about. Well, I suppose even Raymond Penn needs to see life at first hand once in a while."

Valerie felt a shiver of fear as she turned her glasses on Raymond Penn, saw the pale, austere face, the thin, cruel mouth, the rigid posture. She hadn't seen Raymond since the night they had first met at supper and bridge, and Victor never mentioned him. She knew, of course, that Victor telephoned Raymond at his gloomy old house behind the high gates in Belgravia many times a day. Valerie knew Raymond hated her. She would never forget the look on his face the night they had been introduced.

"Victor," said Caroline Danforth, turning around in her chair. "There's dear Raymond, with that assistant of his. What's her name? Miss Furst?"

"So it is," said Victor, training his glasses on the two standing figures in the center of the sixth row. "I wondered if Joan Sutherland would get him out."

"Perhaps he'll join us later for supper at Claridge's," said Caroline. "I can hardly believe the change in him over all the years we've known him. He used to be just everywhere, and now it's an age since I've seen him."

"Oh, Raymond is quite happy to be alone with his books and his records," Victor grinned. "He's quite a serious chap, you know. Not at all the way I am."

"Well, I'm sure he's just delighted about the baby," said Caroline. "That brings out the warmth in anyone, don't you think? Even Raymond Penn must be pleased that he's going to be an uncle, that the line will continue."

"Oh, you told Caroline about the baby, darling," Victor said with a smile, putting one hand on Valerie's bare shoulder.

"Not really," Valerie said, her cheeks burning.

"She didn't have to tell me, Victor," said Caroline smugly. "We women always know."

"Yes, Raymond is pleased," said Victor with a laugh. "If it's a boy, of course, it will be named for him." He ran his hand over Valerie's back.

"If it's a girl, Valerie will pick the name, won't you, darling?" said Victor.

"When is the baby due?" Caroline asked.

"You're not going to start counting on your fingers, are you, Caroline?" laughed Victor. "After all, we've been married for more than a year."

"Oh, Victor," said Caroline. "You are so amusing. Such fun that you asked us to join you tonight."

The house lights dimmed, and the conductor of the

orchestra in the pit below the stage raised his baton, a single light illuminating the score on the podium in front of him. As Valerie applauded along with the rest of the audience, her eyes strayed to the row below them, where Raymond Penn sat with Miss Furst. Victor couldn't have meant it when he said the baby was to be named for Raymond if it were a boy. He just couldn't have meant it.

———

Later that evening, in the backseat of the Rolls, Victor put an arm around Valerie's shoulder and reached under the skirt of her dress to caress her calves, her thighs, between her legs. He ran the tip of his tongue over the swell of her breasts. "It won't be long, my angel," he murmured, his lips against hers. "I can't wait to make love to you again."

"But Victor, why not now?" Valerie breathed. "Please . . ."

"I can't, not now. You know that. I want my son, Valerie."

Her legs were trembling as Daniel helped her out of the car in front of Claridge's, and Victor's hand on her elbow was firm as he escorted her to the front door. Somehow Valerie managed to smile, to extend her hand to Caroline Danforth, who, with Roscoe, was already waiting for them at the entrance to the paneled dining room.

———

Every morning, Valerie stood in front of the mirror in her marble bathroom shaking the mercury down in the thermometer, taking her temperature at Gordon Lerner's direction. She shivered when she saw that her temperature was elevated, that she was ovulating. When she called Dr. Lerner at the clinic, he told her, as they had planned, to check into the hospital in the country no later than one o'clock that afternoon.

"We'll do the surgery first thing in the morning," said Gordon Lerner, his voice excited. "I'll stop by to see you early this evening."

"Thank you, Dr. Lerner," she said, slowly replacing the receiver. She would have her maid pack a few things, a couple of nightgowns, her toiletries, some books, magazines. And, of course, she had to tell Victor at once.

He wasn't in his suite next door, and when she buzzed Gregson, the butler told her that Mr. Penn had already left for an early meeting. When Valerie called him at the office, Brian Graham told her that the meeting was elsewhere.

"Is there something I can do, Mrs. Penn?" he asked.

"You might tell Mr. Penn that I'm off to the country for a few days, Brian. He knows about it, of course, and he has the number there. I just wanted to say good-bye."

"I'll tell him, Mrs. Penn."

Valerie felt alone and frightened as she hung up the telephone.

———

The hospital itself was in a beautiful old Victorian house that sat in the midst of several acres of rolling lawn. The room into which the nurse led Valerie was large and pleasant.

"Someone will be along shortly to take urine and blood samples, Mrs. Penn," said the nurse, the hint of a Scottish burr in her voice. "I'm sure you'll be comfortable here. You'll be getting some juice at teatime, but no food. Surgery is scheduled for seven o'clock tomorrow morning. Dr. Lerner will be in to take a peek at you this evening."

"He told me," said Valerie.

"Will your husband be wanting supper when he comes this evening?" asked the nurse as she stood in the doorway. "We can arrange something for him if he wants it."

"He's away on business," Valerie said abruptly.

"Well, if you need anything," said the nurse, "the buzzer is right there, next to your bed." As she left the room, the door closed automatically behind her.

Engvy dropped by for a moment, her slender, athletic body radiating health. And then, at around nine o'clock in the evening, a nurse with a tranquilizer to help her sleep.

Valerie slept fitfully on the narrow bed, thoughts of Al and Vicki vivid in her mind for the first time in years. She was only nineteen years old, little more than a child, and her husband wasn't there when she needed him. Nobody was there.

Hours later, in the recovery room, Valerie opened her eyes, feeling nauseated and ill, aware of a vague pain on the left side of her abdomen. A nurse wiped her face with a warm, damp washcloth, patted her hair. Then she slept again. Later, she found herself back in her own room. By the next afternoon when Gordon Lerner stopped by on his rounds, Valerie was sitting up in the narrow white bed, drinking a cup of tea and eating soft-boiled eggs, a milky pudding.

"How do you feel?" he asked.

"I'm fine," she said. "I think the anesthetic was worse than the operation."

"Yes, it always seems to be," he agreed, coming over to the bed. "Let's take a look at the incision."

Valerie lay back against the pillows as he turned down the sheet that covered her, raised the hospital gown. She felt adhesive tape tearing off her skin, and she saw the look of satisfaction on Gordon Lerner's face.

"Very neat," he said.

"May I see it?" she asked.

"Certainly," he said.

Valerie felt a sinking feeling as she looked at the stitches, the angry welt scarring her abdomen.

"The stitches will come out the middle of next week," he said.

"What about the plastic surgeon?" asked Valerie, pushing down the hospital gown, trying to erase the thought of the ugly red welt from her mind.

"Oh, in a couple of months, I would imagine," he said. "It has to heal completely."

"Did it go well?" she asked.

"Perfectly," he assured her, absently patting her shoulder. "The surrogate will be inseminated tomorrow. With any luck, Mr. Penn will have his son."

"What about me?" blurted Valerie. "Who am I in all of this?"

"Technically, you're the donor," he said. "But, obviously, it is also your child. You are its mother."

"What about Engvy?" she asked. "Isn't it her child, too?"

"The genes are yours and Mr. Penn's," he said with a shrug. "How could it be her child?"

"But she will be carrying it, nurturing it," said Valerie. "It's her body that will give it life."

"I wouldn't worry about it, Mrs. Penn. Once you

hold the child in your arms, you won't even remember how it got there." He smiled again, then looked at his watch. "And when I spoke with Mr. Penn, he was very pleased to hear that everything had gone so well."

Her dreams that night were confused.

She awoke the next morning before dawn to the ringing of the telephone.

"Oh, Victor," she whispered. "I'm so happy to hear from you."

"It's all over now, my darling. I'll have my son. Go back to sleep."

"Oh, yes, Victor. Yes."

The flowers came that afternoon, dozens and dozens of long-stemmed red roses, baskets of white orchids. Around teatime, one of the nurses bustled into the room, a broad smile on her face, as she handed Valerie a flat white box tied with blue ribbons, just delivered by Mr. Penn's chauffeur. Inside were a diamond and sapphire necklace and matching earrings. "Blue is for a boy. I love you." Victor's writing, jagged, strong.

"It's beautiful," the nurse gasped.

"Yes, isn't it," said Valerie, knowing that everything was all right now between her and Victor, and wondering just what conclusions he had reached on his own. "I want my son, Valerie," he had told her so many weeks ago, and this morning he had said, "I'll have my son." He had sounded so satisfied, so sure.

As if there had been some test she had passed.

24

The Essleblad Clinic was high in the Alps, an hour's drive above Montreux, Switzerland. It was nearly dawn when the limousine pulled through the heavily guarded gates leading into the grounds and, finally, came to a stop in front of one of the chalets.

A uniformed maid opened the front door and offered Valerie coffee while the chauffeur carried in her twenty-seven pieces of matching luggage. Valerie found a chair at a little table in the living room with a window that looked onto rolling lawns dotted with white daisies, and the snow-capped mountains already shimmering in the morning sun. It would be many weeks before Engvy would join her to wait out the pregnancy together, if there was going to be a pregnancy. Victor would visit when he could, probably every weekend, but she would wait until her body returned to normal, and the plastic surgeon at the clinic had removed the scar that, even now, was fading on her abdomen.

Meantime, there was working with the personal trainer who came every morning, appointments with the hairdresser and manicurist, with the masseuse who prodded her into shape. Waiters brought elegant little meals three times a day. There was the grand piano that Victor had ordered, standing in front of a curving bay window with its glorious view of the Alps.

Gradually, Valerie's breasts returned to their normal size. Her stomach was flat again, her hips lithe. Her plastic surgery was performed under local anesthetic, and two weeks later there wasn't even a trace of a scar. She told Victor when he phoned from Los Angeles.

"I'll be there tomorrow, darling," he said. "I can't wait to hold you in my arms, darling. I love you."

———

It had been so long since they had been together, Valerie thought, as she carefully shaved her pubis before she stepped into her steaming tub. She could almost feel Victor's arms around her, smell his lemony fragrance. When she was through with her bath, she dried herself with the thick white towel, pulled a satin nightgown over her pale hair, wrapped herself in a matching kimono.

The sky above the Alps was twinkling with stars when Valerie heard a car pull up outside. Then there were voices for a moment. A door closed.

Valerie was in Victor's arms, his mouth crushing hers. He carried Valerie down the wide hallway and into the master bedroom with its wall of glass.

As they sank onto the bed together, he was pushing up her nightgown, she was fumbling with the buttons on his trousers. And then, finally, he was inside her, holding her tightly against his shirt, tie, the coat he still wore.

It was over in seconds.

They lay, gasping, Valerie's hands in Victor's thick brown hair. His face was buried in the curve of her neck. His eyes never left her face as he sat up, helped her out of the peignoir, pulled the matching nightgown over her golden head.

"You're beautiful, you know," he said as he took off his coat, tie. Shirt. Threw them on the floor. She gazed at him as he stood up to take off his shoes, socks.

Trousers. Strip away his shorts. His penis was already hard again.

She raised her outstretched arms to him, closed them around his back as she felt his chest pressing against her breasts, felt his tongue thrusting between her lips. Unconsciously, she spread her legs for his hand, his fingers.

It was nearly dawn, the gray sky over the Alps brushed with pink, when Valerie awoke, feeling his fingers between her legs as he prepared her so that he could take her again.

They were dozing in each other's arms when Valerie heard the buzz of the doorbell. Through the glass wall of the bedroom, with its view of the swimming pool, rolling lawns, the Alps in the distance, Valerie saw that it was dusk again, and dinner had arrived.

She was still glowing two mornings later as she closed the door behind Victor, who was being driven to Geneva where the Penn International jet was waiting. The surrogate, he had told her, was at the crucial two-month point in the pregnancy. If all went well, she would be joining Valerie at the clinic in a few weeks.

"The pregnancy has worked," he said on the telephone when he called her one night from the mansion in Regent's Park. His voice was electric with excitement. "It's going to be twins. A boy and a girl."

"Oh, darling," said Valerie, feeling faint. She dropped into a chair next to the table that held the phone, unable to comprehend his words.

"The doctor is beside himself," he said. "All of his dreams are coming true."

"All of our dreams are coming true, too," she said.

"The surrogate will be joining you tomorrow," he said.

"I love you, Victor," said Valerie, realizing that her hands were shaking to the point where she needed both of them to hold the phone. "Thank you, darling."

"No, it is I who should thank you, my exquisite girl," he said softly. "Thank you for my son. And my daughter."

When Valerie answered the buzz of the doorbell to see Engvy Erickson looking so healthy and radiant, enveloped in a navy blue wool coat against the chill of the autumn evening, she had to fight down the impulse to throw her arms around her.

"Hello, Engvy," she said, then turned to show the chauffeur where to take the suitcases. "How do you feel?"

"Very well, thank you," Engvy said, following Valerie toward the stairs. "Dr. Lerner is very pleased." She looked around the entry hall, the vast expanse of drawing room that lay beyond it. "This is a very pretty place," she added.

"Yes, it's lovely," said Valerie. "The Alps are beautiful during the day, and the grounds here are superb. There are still flowers everywhere, and there is a lake where people swim, or go boating. We can go for walks."

Valerie led Engvy into the room she was to occupy. It looked very pretty, Valerie thought, with the yellow chrysanthemums she had ordered in their vases. The double bed had a green and white chintz spread, and bolsters and pillows in the same fabric. There was a thick carpet patterned in greens, whites, and yellow over the parquetry floor, a chaise upholstered in a forest green with tufted edges.

"I am so happy," said Engvy, looking around the room.

"Do you want me to send the maid to unpack for you, madame?" the chauffeur asked the young woman.

"No, I'll do it myself," she said, taking off her coat and walking heavily toward the dressing room to hang it in the closet.

Valerie felt a pang of guilt as she noted Engvy's thickening waist, her widening hips.

In the days that passed, Valerie quizzed Engvy endlessly about her life, her parents—a housewife in Stockholm and a pharmacist—her brothers and sisters, even the family pets. She asked Engvy about the house where they lived, what she did with her time, about her studies, her decision to become a doctor. About her boyfriend, Lars, who was already a medical student, and the boyfriends who had come before him.

She went along with Engvy to the clinic for her first examination and sat waiting for her, with slippery palms and a racing pulse, until Engvy reappeared with the doctor, who said that everything was wonderful. Perfect. The two of them went for long walks on the clinic's grounds. They ambled to the pretty lake, where Engvy swam, nude, while Valerie, fascinated, memorized her swollen breasts with their brown nipples the size of silver dollars, her bulging belly, the thick bush of light brown pubic hair, as she thought of her son and her daughter metamorphosing from embryos to fetuses in that strong, athletic body.

When Victor arrived for the weekend, he treated Engvy with the gallant politeness he always showed to members of their household staffs. At dinner, he seemed uncomfortable when he realized that the young woman would be dining with them, but he was deferential to her, and boyishly charming.

=====

"You seem preoccupied, darling," said Victor, leaning on one elbow and looking down at her while with one finger he idly outlined the curve of her jaw. "What are you thinking about?"

"I'm thinking about Engvy," she said. "All I think about is Engvy, and the babies. I want my babies growing in my own body."

"Oh, but you mustn't think about Engvy, darling," he said thoughtfully. "She's a servant, being well paid to fulfill one of our needs."

"But, Victor," insisted Valerie. "Bearing our children isn't like running a house, or altering a gown."

"I want you to stop thinking like this, darling," Victor said gently. "The only thing you are to think about is me. Now. Tomorrow. Forever."

Victor's fingers were like butterflies dancing on her shoulders, touching her breasts, her stomach. Valerie turned her face for his kiss, and felt her breath coming faster as he explored her body, rested one hand on her naked pubis, while with the fingers of the other he stroked the inner lips of her vagina.

"Oh, I love you, Victor," she gasped as he entered her. "I love you."

Valerie realized, as she sat beside Engvy in the electric golf cart, that she had felt relieved when Victor left. She glanced over at the other girl, bundled up in the mink coat Valerie had given her the night before.

"Such a beautiful day, Mrs. Penn," she said.

"Valerie," corrected Valerie. "Please call me Valerie."

"I don't think Mr. Penn would like that," smiled the other girl, turning the cart onto a wide road rimmed with wild flowers that led to the edge of the clinic's grounds.

"Mr. Penn isn't here," said Valerie.

"All right," said Engvy. "It is a beautiful day, Valerie."

Valerie decided one gift she could give Engvy was to teach her to play the piano. In return, Engvy offered to teach Valerie how to drive, using one of the automobiles available to the patients.

During the first few lessons, Valerie sat in the passenger's seat of the gray Peugeot as Engvy expertly negotiated the narrow mountain road that wound down to the sprawling city of Montreux. Then Valerie would slip behind the wheel and, tentatively responding to Engvy's instructions, head the powerful Peugeot toward Geneva.

Within two weeks, Valerie was negotiating the hairpin turns leading down the mountain, then swinging the wheel of the Peugeot toward Geneva, her foot pressing the gas pedal nearly to the floor.

"Oh, Engvy," she said, with a dazzling smile, "it's so wonderful to know how to drive. It's so exhilarating to sit here behind the wheel, to feel the car respond. I feel as if I could almost fly. I feel free."

Engvy smiled shyly, and patted Valerie's shoulder.

In Geneva, Valerie, in dark glasses and with a scarf tied over her hair, would sit with Engvy at lunch in a restaurant overlooking Lake Geneva, watching the fountain in its center spray hundreds of feet into the air. The two girls combed the boutiques, and Valerie bombarded

Engvy with gifts—maternity dresses, sweaters, skirts, beautiful, expensive leather shoes, evening gowns to be worn after the babies were born, a diamond pin, earrings—all paid for with cash advances taken from the administration office at the clinic. Valerie knew that the accounting department at Penn International in London, which paid the bills, would never bring it to Victor's attention.

One early evening, as the two sped through the crisp winter night on their way back to the clinic, Engvy took one of Valerie's hands from the steering wheel and silently placed it on her swollen belly. Valerie felt a surge of movement under her hand as one of her babies turned, or kicked. She blindly guided the Peugeot to a halt on the side of the road, where she lay her head on the steering wheel. Her hands were shaking, and her heart pounded. She traded places with Engvy, who had to drive them home.

"I felt one of the babies kick tonight," Valerie told Victor when he called that evening. "It was so wonderful. I've never felt anything like that before. Never."

"That's wonderful, darling. Really wonderful." He paused for a moment, and then he said, "I tried to reach you for hours today."

"Oh, yes," she said, with a pang of guilt. "We went for a long, long walk. The doctors want Engvy to walk."

"I was worried," he said. "I don't want anything to happen to my exquisite girl. You're my life, darling. I love you."

"Oh, Victor," she sighed. "I'm so happy. I love you, too."

Valerie watched Victor's expression at dinner as he looked at Engvy, saw his eyes drop to the full breasts, the round belly.

"It's kicking," Engvy said, with an embarrassed little laugh.

"Touch it, Victor," said Valerie encouragingly.

"Do you mind, Engvy?" he asked, his voice tentative.

"Go ahead, Mr. Penn," she said.

Gingerly, Victor put one hand on Engvy's belly, and Valerie glowed as she saw the look of amazement, of reverence, on his face before he pulled his hand abruptly away.

Later, Valerie lay awake listening to Victor's quiet breathing as he slept beside her, his arms wrapped around her. She thought again of Engvy, the look on Victor's face as he felt the movement in her belly.

"Victor," she said to him the next morning as they had breakfast together in their suite, "do you think that Engvy could come back with us to London?"

"As what?" he asked, looking surprised.

"Well, as my friend," she said. "She could go to medical school there."

"Oh, darling," he said, shaking his head. "It's impossible, don't you see? Think of the twins. She can't be in their lives."

"I suppose not," said Valerie.

"I know how fond you are of Engvy," he said. "But it will be better for her, too. She'll go back to her own young man and have children of her own."

"I guess I'm being selfish," Valerie admitted. "I was just thinking about how much I will miss her."

"The only one I want you to miss is me, my darling," Victor said. "The only one I want you to feel close with is me."

Slowly, he rose and came around the table, where he leaned over her, pulled her robe down over her breasts as he stroked her golden hair. He led her back to the crumpled bed, where he undressed her as she lay waiting for him. When he was next to her, he guided her hand to his half-erect penis as he sucked at her nipples. Valerie thought of her babies sucking at Engvy's massive breasts, nourished by Engvy's mother's milk.

25

For several days, the chalet swarmed with technicians setting up the huge screen where, on closed-circuit television, Victor had decided he and Valerie would watch the birth of the twins in the delivery room. He had arranged his business appointments so that he would be with them in the chalet during the final two weeks of pregnancy.

Even Engvy had fear in her blue eyes as she found Valerie, reading by the swimming pool on the beautiful spring afternoon, and told her that her water had broken, and that the contractions were coming five minutes apart.

Within minutes, a limousine was at the door of the chalet, and a chauffeur helped Engvy into the backseat. It was all Valerie could do to keep from jumping into the car with Engvy, to be with her, to hold her hand, to soothe her. Victor took Valerie's arm and pulled her back into the chalet, where he closed the door behind them.

In the little sitting room, Valerie stood at one of the curving bay windows and looked at the snow-topped Alps sparkling in the sun, her mouth dry with anxiety for her friend and for her babies. Twenty minutes later, the phone rang.

"They're prepping her now," Victor said, replacing the receiver. "Everything looks fine. The contractions are four minutes apart. It should take three hours, perhaps four."

"Oh, Victor," she said. "I'm so scared for her."

He took her into his arms and held her, petting her hair, comforting her. Then he led her up the winding stairs to the master suite where, in the bedroom, the huge television screen covered an entire wall, and champagne chilled in a silver bucket.

When the message that Engvy was to deliver finally arrived, Valerie was sitting up in bed, propped against her pillows and wearing a nightgown of white silk with spaghetti straps. Delicate handmade lace covered the pale nipples on her small, firm breasts. Victor, lying nude beside her, clicked on the remote control just as Engvy, on a gurney with a sheet covering her huge belly, her thick blond hair pushed into a sterile cap, was being wheeled into the cool green delivery room. For a moment, she turned her head toward the camera, and at the sight of Engvy's pale face, the blue eyes dazed with fear and pain, Valerie buried her own face in the pillow, wishing that it were she lying there in that green room, feeling Engvy's pain, paying the physical price to bring her children into the world.

Under the silken fall of her nightgown, Valerie felt Victor's hand resting on her flat stomach, felt his fingers tracing the lines of her hipbones. Unconsciously, she spread her legs, primed for his touch.

On the television screen, Engvy's feet were in the stirrups at either end of the delivery table. Then there was the surgeon's head in its green covering, the green mask. Valerie felt Victor's fingers between her legs, her own wetness as he pushed apart the inner lips of her vagina, rubbed her clitoris. Slowly, he pushed down the straps of her nightgown, brought his head down to her breast. His tongue was on one erect nipple, then on the other.

"Push, mother," said the surgeon on the screen as Engvy sobbed in pain.

Victor guided Valerie's hand to his stiff penis.

"Harder, harder," the doctor on the screen commanded.

The baby was coming now, Valerie could see the top of its head. Valerie was awed by the little face, the eyes tightly closed, a rosebud mouth. Shoulders, arms, little hands clenched into fists. A penis, testicles, the legs and feet. The cunning little toes. The baby was streaked with blood as the doctor held him up by his tiny feet, slapped his bottom. He wailed as the doctor laid him on Engvy's stomach.

"My son," said Victor, his voice reverent. "My son, Raymond." Drawing Valerie into his arms, he kissed her lips and removed her nightgown. Valerie lay, looking up into Victor's blue eyes, her legs apart, as he pushed a pillow under her buttocks, guided his penis to the mouth of her vagina.

"Put your legs around my waist," he whispered hoarsely, and she gasped as he entered her. "Hold me, my darling. Hold me."

Thirty minutes later they lay panting, still coupled, dripping with perspiration, their mouths tasting of each other, watching the television screen as the second baby wailed in protest at the doctor's slap on her bottom. Their daughter. Alexandra. The doctor placed her on Engvy's stomach for a moment before one of the nurses picked her up, cradling her in her arms as she gently cleaned the baby, wiping away the streaks of blood.

Engvy still lay on the delivery table, her feet in the stirrups, eyes closed, her forehead wet with exhaustion.

The nurse, with one perfect baby in each arm, walked toward the camera and held them up. They were beautiful, magnificent.

"Oh, Victor," Valerie sighed, her arms tightening around him. "Our babies. Oh, I can't believe it. Oh, I love them."

He was moving again, faster and faster, as he held her buttocks with his hands. With a few final thrusts, Valerie felt him spurt into her. He lay, his cheek against hers, her legs wrapped around him, as the television screen went black.

===

The brilliant morning sun streamed through the filmy curtains in the bedroom the next morning as Valerie, lying nude in a tangle of sheets, tried to fight her way out of sleep. There was a bitter taste in her mouth, and she felt drugged. Perhaps she had drunk too much champagne, or maybe there had been something wrong with one of the bottles. She smiled to herself at the thought of their two perfect babies. Alexandra and Raymond.

She would hurry over in the golf cart to see them as soon as she was dressed. Oh, she just couldn't wait to hold them in her arms, to touch them. She couldn't wait to see Engvy. Wonderful, marvelous Engvy, her friend who had given them the greatest gift on earth. Valerie glanced at the little clock on the nightstand and saw, with surprise, that it was nearly ten o'clock.

Trying to sit up, she realized that she felt numb between her legs. Her head swam, and she fell back against the pillow. With a trembling hand, she reached between her legs, touched the inner lips of her numb vagina. There was something metallic there, a stud of some sort, piercing one of the lips. Valerie gasped as she half stumbled, half crawled to the bathroom. On her hands and knees, she reached up to the counter and felt around for the hand mirror with the long silver handle that she knew to be there. She pulled it off the countertop and crumpled to the floor, panting with exhaustion and disbelief.

Her eyes widened as she examined her genitalia in the mirror. There, in the soft pink fold on one of the inner lips of her vagina, was a gold stud. The area was caked with dried blood. Valerie fell back on the cold marble floor and tightly closed her eyes. Her head was clouded with panic, her thoughts foggy.

She awoke again in her bed between soft, clean sheets. Pale moonlight outlined the bureau, the chaise longue, the writing desk, the chairs, tables. There was a bitter taste in her mouth, and she felt strange, drugged. There was a dull ache between her legs. When she reached down, she felt again the cold metal of the stud.

She slept again.

Victor was sitting on the side of the bed, petting her golden hair. His eyes were bright with concern. Slowly, Valerie opened her eyes, remembering the perverse thrill she had felt making love while their babies were being born. Or had that been a dream? Then she remembered the hard, metallic object between her legs. Her hand shot down to find it as she realized it wouldn't be there, that the whole thing had been an awful nightmare. It was with a swell of panic that she realized the stud had been replaced by a ring exactly the same width as her wedding ring.

Victor's lips brushed her forehead.

"Why, Victor?" she whispered, exhausted.

"Don't you see, darling?" he said softly, his lips against her forehead. "The birth of our babies symbolizes our perfect love. Every time you move, take a step, you'll think of me, of us. Of what our love for each other has created."

"Our babies, Victor," she said, leaning against his chest as he held her in his arms.

"They're perfect, darling," he said as he kissed her hair, fondled her. "They're screaming their heads off. All of the nurses at the clinic are crazy about them."

"And Engvy?"

"She's fine," he said. "She's as healthy as a horse. She was walking around an hour after the delivery. And her milk came right on schedule."

"I want to see our babies, Victor," she said, tears of self-pity filling her eyes.

"Oh, my exquisite girl," said Victor, kissing her wet cheeks. "You will. You will."

Then he was quickly undressing, tossing his clothes

on the floor next to the bed. Gently, he turned her over, pushed up her nightgown, pushed a pillow under her stomach before he started to play with her. He took her, finally, vaginally from the rear, and as Valerie felt him rubbing against the hard metal of the golden ring, she acknowledged that she had never had a more sensual experience in her life.

Valerie sat on the terrace next to the swimming pool, breathing the warm mountain air, closing her eyes against the rays of the sun. In the distance, the rolling lawns were dotted with white daisies, and beyond them loomed the Alps, white topped and somehow benevolent. Brushing the inside of her thighs were the ribbons Victor had looped through the golden ring. When he came for weekends these days, he brought her wonderful drugs that drove her nearly mad with desire. Sometimes he would make love to her until she was finally satiated. Other times he would ignore her, laughing as she pleaded with him for relief. He painted her face and her nipples like a whore's, taking her as she wore a black garter belt, a whore's patterned stockings. But it was the drugs that were so wonderful, that took her to the heights of ecstasy; the ring, to which Victor tied the ribbons, or little golden chains with tiny bells. She felt that they were lost together in the wonder of their shared sensuality, their eroticism.

———

"You're the most beautiful girl in the world," Valerie cooed to the baby she held in her arms. Alexandra looked up at her with Victor's blue eyes. Her head was covered with soft dark hair. Her mouth was a pink rosebud.

"They are getting big," said Engvy, little Raymond suckling at her breast as she lay on a chaise nearby.

"Aren't they the most perfect, beautiful babies in the world?" Valerie said. "Don't you think they are, Engvy?"

"You are a good mother," Engvy smiled, shifting the baby to her other breast and wiping away a few drops of milk that dribbled onto her blouse. "It is almost time for me to leave. Another week, maybe, and then I go home to Sweden."

"Oh, I'll miss you, Engvy," said Valerie. "I've never been so happy as I have been these last few months. With Victor, and the babies. With you."

"It has been a good time for me, too," said Engvy, shifting the baby in her arms. "I have enjoyed knowing you, and having this rest." She sipped coffee that sat on a table next to the chaise. "But, it will be good to be back in school. It was so generous of Mr. Penn to give the bonus for the second baby. Twenty-five thousand dollars for the contract, and another ten thousand dollars for the bonus. Why, I am a rich woman, like you."

"We'll stay in touch, though, won't we, Engvy?" asked Valerie, stroking her daughter's fine hair as the baby drifted off to sleep wrapped in her pink blanket.

"It is in the contract that I just put this whole experience behind me," said Engvy thoughtfully. "It is just a job, and now it is finished."

"But, we have our friendship, Engvy," said Valerie. "That isn't part of the contract."

"Yes, Valerie," she replied. "Yes, we have our friendship."

They smiled at each other as the nurse appeared to take the babies inside for their afternoon nap.

It seemed so strange to be leaving, Valerie thought a week later, sitting beside Engvy in the backseat of the clinic's limousine as it sped toward the Geneva airport, where Engvy would take a commercial flight to Stockholm and Valerie would take the Penn International jet back to London, to her real life in the mansion in Regent's Park.

Valerie glanced at Engvy and thought how smart she looked, how different. Her hair was well cut, her makeup subtle, accentuating her pretty blue eyes, contouring her cheekbones. Her body was lithe and powerful again, and she wore a beautiful beige suit Valerie had given her, expensive beige leather shoes. On her lapel she wore the gold pin spattered with diamonds that Valerie had bought as a special present, a remembrance because she knew she would never see the other girl again. Just before they had left the chalet Engvy had told her that her name wasn't Engvy Erickson, and that she had been told never to give Valerie her real name because Valerie might try to find her later. Because Valerie was sentimental. It was all part of the contract, Engvy had pointed out with a sad smile. It had all made perfect sense before she and Valerie became friends.

"But I wanted you to know," said Engvy. "I didn't want you to think it was because I don't care for you, or value what we have been through together."

Standing in the doorway of the chalet for the last time, the girls had embraced. Like friends. Like sisters.

26

Milling photographers, reporters, and camera crews were waiting when Victor and Valerie, each of them carrying one of the babies, cleared customs at Heathrow Airport.

"Look over here, Mrs. Penn," called a reporter.

Valerie turned and smiled. Then she glanced at Victor, awkwardly cradling little Raymond, wrapped in a blanket. His grin for the cameras was boyish, proud.

"Oh, Victor," she said, when the two of them were settled in the backseat of the Rolls-Royce. "I'm so glad to be home."

He lifted one of her hands to his lips and kissed her open palm.

"I love you, my darling," he said.

She leaned to brush his cheek with her lips as the limousine swung onto the motorway leading to London. It was a perfect summer day, the sky a primary, seamless blue.

Gregson was there to welcome her home, to hope she was feeling quite well. To admire the babies as they all stood in the entry hall of the mansion. The chauffeurs were following Gregson's orders as they carried in suitcase after suitcase. The footmen were taking them upstairs to Valerie's suite, where her maid waited to begin unpacking them. Mrs. Wytton, the new English nanny, was clucking over the babies as one of them started to wail.

Little Raymond, thought Valerie. He was more bothered by confusion than Alexandra was. They were only fraternal twins, of course, and so they were quite different. Alexandra had her father's brown hair, his bright blue eyes that, even at only three months old, seemed so wise. Little Raymond's hair was a light brown, his eyes like her own, hazel that seemed green at times, flecked with yellow.

Valerie's secretary rushed in to greet her, to coo over the babies. She had a hundred messages, letters, cards. Presents for the babies filled an entire room.

Victor, his arm around Valerie's waist, led her into the drawing room where tea had been laid at a table next to a view of green lawns, formal flower beds. It was good to be home.

After a leisurely tea, Victor took her upstairs to the newly converted nursery wing. There were little bedrooms for Mrs. Wytton, her assistant, the maid who would help them with the details of caring for the babies. There was a darkroom where the photographer who would chronicle the routine of the babies could develop his prints when he came once a week. They all shared a little sitting room with a television set, a sofa, overstuffed chairs. There was a diminutive kitchen where they could heat water for tea when they didn't want to bother the downstairs staff.

Valerie gasped when she saw the nursery itself, the sunniest room in the mansion. Its walls were upholstered in pale yellow silk. There were filmy white curtains at the tall windows, toy chests on which sat teddy bears, dolls, every conceivable kind of toy. In the two bassinets, dripping with lace to the floor, little Raymond and Alexandra slept on their stomachs, each covered by a thin blanket, each little hand clenched in a fist. Mrs. Wytton, in her starched white uniform, her flat white shoes, the white stockings, beamed down at the babies as Valerie felt tears in her eyes. She leaned her head against Victor's shoulder, and he kissed the top of her golden hair.

"You must be exhausted, darling," he said sympathetically, holding her.

"I am," she said.

"Why don't you have a bath and a nap?" he suggested as they walked out of the nursery, closed the door behind them, and stood together in the wide hallway.

"Yes," said Valerie, feeling the weariness of the past year, of the impossible experiment that had somehow paid off. She thought of Engvy, her friend, whom she would never see again. "It's been a long year," she sighed. "A very long year."

His arm around her, her head on his shoulder, they walked slowly down the long hallway toward her suite. There were sprays of pale green cymbidia in her bedroom with its huge four-poster bed, the canopy and bedspread a flower-strewn chintz. Her clothes had all been put away in the huge mirrored dressing room. In the bathroom, Valerie saw her reflection in the mirrors, the hazel eyes dulled by fatigue, and the full, colorless lips where she had eaten off her pink lipstick hours before.

As she ran her steaming bath, she stepped out of her gray shoes, stripped off the jacket of her gray raw silk suit, the white silk shirt with the cowl neck. She unfastened her garter belt, peeled off the sheer stockings. Unscrewed the gold and pavé diamond earrings from her earlobes. On the back of each knee was a tiny scab where Victor injected her with the aphrodisiacs that drove her nearly out of her mind for him. Hidden in the folds of her genitalia was the narrow golden ring that matched the one she wore on the ring finger of her left hand.

Valerie lay in the steaming tub, running her hand over her high, firm breasts, the flat stomach, the narrow hips, her thighs conditioned to wrap around Victor's slim body.

He was her life, she thought. She would do anything to feel the way he made her feel. Anything.

Now they were home, together with their babies. A family at last.

Victor made gentle love to her that night, and she fell asleep wrapped in his arms, feeling the heat of his body against her own.

The next morning, Valerie, with her secretary, sorted through the flurry of invitations to be accepted or rejected. Many of her women acquaintances phoned to say how pleased they were that she had survived the ordeal of such a dangerous pregnancy, asking when they could stop by to see the marvelous infants. Roscoe and Caroline Danforth came for dinner, and Caroline laughed out loud when little Raymond closed one tiny hand around her bejeweled finger. She took Valerie in her arms and congratulated her that she had survived the births at all. Lady Anne arrived, marveling dutifully at the babies, whom she pronounced to be the most beautiful children she had ever seen in her life.

Their daily life resumed, and Valerie went off each morning to the conservatory.

In the evenings, there were dinner parties once more and, as the season began, the opera, the theater, concerts. Valerie's jewels were the talk of London, and Victor said he was trying to find someone to help her with her wardrobe, someone with the sublime, original taste that could take the level of her gowns to heights that would match the fabulous jewels he was always giving her.

The best time of the day for Valerie was at tea when Victor was home, and the babies were brought in by Mrs. Wytton for an hour. They would lie on a blanket on the floor, kicking and playing, as Victor and Valerie watched their every move, picked them up to coo at them, make faces. Valerie would look longingly after Mrs. Wytton when she collected them and took them back to their lacy white bassinets.

At first, Valerie had spent hours in the nursery, cooing over the babies, playing with them, unable to take her eyes off them. Sometimes in the middle of the night she felt such an overwhelming need to be reassured that they were there that she would creep out of bed, down the hall, and into the nursery, where she would stand over their bassinets, watching them as they slept.

Victor was very gentle when he told her that she was interfering with Mrs. Wytton's authority, that her behavior would only confuse little Raymond and Alexandra.

"But, I love them, Victor," pleaded Valerie. "I want to be with them all the time."

"Oh, my beautiful girl," he said, shaking his head. "I love them, too. I want to be with them all the time. But that just isn't the way babies are raised with people like us. I have my life. I have to go to the office. I have to attend to business. And you have your life. Your music, your practicing, supervising the house. Our social life."

Valerie conceded it was a very pleasant routine. If Victor was away on business, or too busy to get home, the twins would be brought to Valerie in her suite while tea was served to her. When Mrs. Wytton took them away, she would practice, or read, waiting always for Victor's telephone call from wherever he was. When Victor was home, the babies would be brought to them in the drawing room. And when the twins were taken away an hour later, she and Victor would go upstairs to her suite and make love. Then there would be time for a nap before they dressed to go out for the evening. Occasionally when they returned home after dining with friends, or from the theater, an opera, or a ball, Victor would tell her that he had found something new, something marvelous, to take them to even greater heights of ecstasy in each other.

Valerie would watch him as he prepared the hypodermic needle. When he was ready, she would obediently turn on her stomach, clutching the pillow as she felt the sharp sting in the back of her knee, the hot rush through her body, and she would be lost in a daze of lust. Sometimes she would sleep the next morning away, and when she awoke there would be the bitter taste in her mouth, the groggy feelings. She would stumble to the bathroom, unable even to remember what he had done to her. She didn't care. If it was what Victor wanted, she would do it. Anything.

And so it was very sweet.

Valerie watched Victor as he bounced little Raymond on his knee, her husband's face nearly as excited as the baby's. Valerie sipped her tea and reached over for a cucumber sandwich. The tea cakes, she saw, looked wonderful, all flaky pastry, custard, fresh fruit. On the floor, Alexandra turned over, her latest accomplishment.

An easel in front of them held the portrait Victor had commissioned of Valerie holding the twins. She studied it, noting the proud way she held her head, the cap of golden hair, the pale yellow hostess gown that Victor had picked out for her to wear. The babies, in her arms, were exquisite. Alexandra, with deep brown curls so like her father's, her dimples, the bright blue eyes. And little Raymond, with light brown curls, his green eyes flecked with gold. Valerie crossed her legs in their stockings, felt the satin ribbons looped through the golden ring caress her thighs. She looked at Victor reflectively and ran her tongue over her lips.

Victor was saying that he thought it might be rather fun if just the two of them slipped away for the weekend and went to the château in France, when Gregson appeared.

"Mr. Penn, you have a guest waiting in the entry hall. It's Mr. Raymond Penn."

Valerie felt the blood drain from her face. Victor was startled, she could see, and then amused.

"So, Raymond has finally come to see whether the latest additions to the family have all the necessary parts," he grinned. "Well, fine. Show him in. Bring another cup, and we'll even give him some tea."

In a moment, Raymond, tall and thin, wearing an exquisitely tailored gray suit, appeared in the doorway of the drawing room. He wore a gray silk tie, and his ascetic face, with his pale blue eyes and thin lips, was nearly as white as his shirt. He nodded at Valerie, his face expressionless.

"My dear chap," said Victor, rising to shake his brother's hand. "How good of you to stop by." He put an arm around Raymond's shoulders, drew him to Valerie, who sat rigidly in her chair. "Valerie, darling, isn't this jolly? Here's Raymond, stopping by at last to meet the twins."

"Raymond," she said.

He made a stiff little bow toward her.

Victor offered Raymond a chair, scooped up his namesake, thrust the baby into Raymond's arms.

"Isn't he something, old man?" said Victor as the baby looked up at Raymond, his eyes round with wonder. "And here's Alexandra. Isn't she a beauty?"

As Alexandra started to scream, Valerie jumped out of her chair and grabbed the baby from Raymond's arms. She sat down again, holding the baby tightly, cooing at her, trying to comfort her.

"I say, Victor," said Raymond. "Would you mind taking this one?"

Victor grinned, picked up the little boy, and pretended to toss him in the air. Little Raymond chortled with laughter, drool running down his dimpled chin.

"Well, what do you think, Raymond?" asked Victor, his eyes gleaming. "I knew you would be along to see the brats one of these days."

Carefully, he put the baby on the blanket on the floor, his eyes never leaving Raymond's face as his brother watched the little boy. Raymond caught his breath as the baby turned over, gurgling, trying to pull himself up on his hands and knees.

"Is he all right?" asked Raymond.

"You can see for yourself," said Victor carelessly. "He's perfect. So is the girl." He took Alexandra from Valerie's arms and put her on the blanket next to her twin. "Aren't they charming, Raymond?" he asked. "We're really a happy little family now that the babies have come."

Raymond sat fascinated, looking at the babies.

"I've just had this portrait done of Valerie with the children," said Victor. "What do you think of it, old man? I'm going to hang it over the mantelpiece in my bedroom so I can always see my beautiful family."

Raymond looked at the painting, glanced over at Valerie where she sat stiffly in her chair. His eyes were cold.

Valerie averted her eyes, flushing.

"It's a good likeness, don't you think?" Victor persisted.

"Yes, very good," said Raymond indifferently, looking again at the babies playing together on the floor.

Valerie counted the seconds, the minutes, praying that Raymond would stand up and leave. It wasn't until Mrs. Wytton appeared a half hour later to take the babies back to the nursery that Raymond finally rose. He made a little bow toward Valerie as Victor walked with him to the front door, where his car and chauffeur waited outside in the waning afternoon sunlight.

Victor's face was triumphant, his eyes glittering, when he came back into the drawing room. He leaned over Valerie to brush her lips with his own.

"I knew he would come around," he said.

"Why does he hate me so much, Victor?" she asked wearily, remembering the coldness in Raymond's eyes, his look of contempt mingled with something that was almost pity.

"He doesn't hate you, my beautiful girl. He envies our happiness. He was always envious of anything I had, even when we were children."

"He's so cold," she shuddered. "He scares me, Victor."

"Oh, my sweet girl," he said fondly, running his hand lightly over her breasts. "You're imagining things."

Valerie shook her head, remembering the way Raymond had looked at the twins as they played.

"Well, now that Raymond has made the first move, I think we should follow it up," said Victor, his voice brisk. "He cares about the babies. We know that, or he wouldn't have come. And, when he gets to know you, darling, he'll love you as much as I do. I just know it."

"Oh, Victor," said Valerie hesitantly, "do you really think so?"

"I'm sure of it," he said. "And I have a wonderful idea to make it come about. We'll take the babies and the nurse along with us to the château this weekend. And we'll ask Raymond to come, too. It's peaceful there, and there won't be anybody around to bother him."

Valerie felt a sinking in her stomach as she thought of spending a weekend in the same place as Raymond Penn, seeing the disdain on his face each time he looked at her.

"You can telephone and invite him in the morning," Victor continued. "Oh, darling. I'm so pleased that the ice is broken."

"Darling," said Valerie imploringly. "I couldn't call him. I just couldn't."

"But, my sweet girl," said Victor. "You're the lady of the house. Any invitation has to come from you."

Valerie slept fitfully through the night and awoke at dawn, dreading what she had to do. The morning passed and, finally, at eleven o'clock, she dialed Raymond's private number, which Victor had given her.

He answered on the second ring.

"Oh, Raymond," she said, "it's Valerie. It was so nice to see you last evening. Victor and I are going to take the twins and pop over to our place in the French countryside this weekend. We thought you might like to join us. It's very peaceful there. Victor thinks it's time we got to know each other."

Valerie heard a click and then the dial tone humming in her ear. She felt the tears as she slowly hung up the phone.

27

A year later the Penn International logo finally capped the dramatic pink marble and glass skyscraper housing the new corporate headquarters in New York. The apartment on Fifth Avenue was also ready for Victor and Valerie Penn, their children, and their staff.

Valerie stood in the drawing room seeing Central Park thirty stories below her. The trees were in bloom, the grass the pale green of spring. Taxis wound along the streets, a steady stream among the bicyclists, the horses and carriages. To the right was the Metropolitan Museum of Art.

The penthouse was in a perfect location. Mrs. Wytton and her assistant could take the twins for walks in Central Park, or watch them as they staggered over the grass, or sailed their boats in the pond, always accompanied by a bodyguard, of course. It was nice, too, to be so near the Metropolitan Museum and the Guggenheim, although the art on their own walls was probably as good, or even better. Valerie glanced at the Giotto that Victor had just bought for a record price hanging over the marble fireplace. It was magnificent, really. There was no question about it.

Like a blizzard of confetti, invitations to parties, and to balls benefiting one good cause or another arrived each day. Invitations to join the boards of Memorial Sloane-Kettering Hospital, the American Ballet Theater, the Metropolitan Opera Guild, and the New York Philharmonic. Victor joined the Metropolitan Club and the Union League Club. Valerie lunched with various women extolling the virtues of their causes at Lutece, Le Cirque, and the Four Seasons. She decided to concentrate her efforts on the Women's Committee of Memorial Sloane-Kettering, and on the New York Philharmonic. But mostly on Victor, of course, because it was around Victor that everything else revolved.

The streets of New York blazed with excitement and energy. Opening nights at the theater, the opera, the ballet, the symphony at Lincoln Center or Carnegie Hall were bigger than life, the women more extravagantly gowned, more lavishly bejeweled than in London; the men radiating power, immeasurable wealth. Next to New York, London seemed dowdy and provincial. Valerie felt dowdy and provincial, too, until Victor, on a quick business trip to France, met Mary di Stefano, a woman reputed to have the best taste in the world, and hired her to become Valerie's personal shopper.

Kyle Jones was on staff, too, as Valerie's music teacher. Soon after they moved to New York, Valerie had called the Juilliard School of Music to speak to her old, friendly competitor and offered him the job. Kyle, recovering from his second nervous breakdown, accepted. Now he lived in one of the apartments just below the two-story penthouse, to guide Valerie for an hour each afternoon with her studies.

Victor's private secretary, Brian Graham, always a trusted confidant, was made his executive assistant at a hefty raise. John O'Farrell, one of the young partners at the New York law firm handling Penn International's affairs, also became one of Victor's trusted confidants, flying with him to meetings all over the world. They frequently traveled to London to meet with Raymond Penn, the most trusted of all of Victor's confidants.

Even as they were settling into their new life in the hustle and bustle, the glamour and squalor of New York City, Victor's real estate agents in Beverly Hills were looking for a piece of property there for their permanent base. The looming skyscrapers flirting with the clouds, the vendors with their carts peddling hot dogs, soft drinks and pretzels, made him feel crowded, he told Valerie one night as they sat in the back of the limousine, stalled in crosstown traffic. His hand was under the skirt of her gown, stroking her thighs. When they were together, he never stopped touching her. Ever.

Victor wanted to be in America. Penn International had outgrown its London base and continued to grow with every branch that it opened, each company that it added to its list. Despite the attraction of the frenetic energy of New York City, what he really wanted were rolling lawns, a huge house set on those grounds, wide streets lined by rows of purple jacaranda trees, white magnolia trees, the purples and oranges of birds of paradise, the white and pinks and reds of impatiens and, most of all, greenhouses to grow cymbidium orchids, their feel to him like that of Valerie's own skin.

Victor wanted his own space. The jet was available to take them wherever he wanted to go, and the New York penthouse would be there if he had to stay for a couple of days.

Valerie's mouth went dry as she processed what Victor was saying. She felt giddy as she realized she was finally going home with the man who was the core of her life and with their beautiful children.

The hundred-acre estate that became their home was huge, even bigger than the Regent's Park mansion. Valerie and Victor puttered over the acres in an electric golf cart, accompanied by the architect who would oversee the remodeling. He sketched in plans for the swimming pool, the championship tennis courts, the two-story guesthouse with its five bedrooms and six baths that would be built to reflect the graceful lines of the mansion itself. Within three years, the Beverly Hills estate became the Penns' primary residence. Furnished and decorated to perfection, this was home to Valerie the moment she walked through the doors. It was the most beautiful house in the world.

The drawing room, with many of the pieces that had originally been in the mansion in Regent's Park, was magnificent. So was the dining room. The music room, with its red and yellow chintzes, the scores signed by Beethoven, Brahms, and Chopin, was her personal favorite, rivaled by her suite, with the Louis XVI pieces, mirrored walls, chairs upholstered in pink silk, the Bonnard hanging over the marble fireplace, and the nine-foot Steinway piano. Her bedroom was entirely in white and pale peach, with a little breakfast area overlooking the garden for the mornings after the nights Victor would spend with her, making cool, erotic love to Valerie as she lay still, silent, accepting.

Throughout the house were sprays of orchids from the greenhouse and cut flowers from the grounds. In the library were copies of the latest magazines, that morning's newspapers from around the world.

Under Gregson's guidance, the estate functioned at peak efficiency from the day after the Penns moved in. Twelve live-in help, among them a world-renowned chef, maintained the interior of the mansion. Full-time gardeners tended to the grounds. The security force, two men on each shift, monitored the grounds on banks of television screens in the guardhouse, or prowled the acres of the property with the Dobermans.

Delivery trucks came and went from the market, as well as from the dry cleaners and the laundry. The brown UPS trucks arrived daily with gowns, shoes, lingerie, and accessories that Mary di Stefano ordered from various designers and boutiques.

Early each morning, Valerie worked out with her personal trainer in the gym. Her hairdresser came, and then her manicurist and her secretary. When they finished with her, she practiced for hours every day at the Steinway in her suite. After lunch, usually with Kyle in the small dining room, the two moved into the music room for her lesson. Mary di Stefano usually arrived to meet with her at teatime, and then, if Victor was in town, he would be home by early evening.

That was the best time, of course. When Victor was home, when they didn't have a social engagement that evening, and when he wanted her. Valerie lay on her bed, propped up on one elbow, watching Victor as he slowly undressed, folding his coat, his trousers carefully over the back of a chair. His body, so familiar to her fingertips and mouth, was lean and muscular. Her eyes dropped to his flat stomach, his flaccid penis, his testicles. She shifted her buttocks on the bed, licked her lips, anticipating him.

He uncorked a bottle of champagne without a sound, poured it into two crystal flutes, came toward her. He smiled a boyish grin that always made her smile back at him. Always.

He handed her one of the glasses, touched it to his own in a toast, and sat next to her on the bed. His mouth on hers was wet, cold with the champagne. With closed eyes, she reveled in the smell of him, his evanescence.

She felt her pulse quicken as his mouth moved over her erect nipple, sucking. His long, slim fingers were splayed across her stomach, prodding, exploring.

"I can never get enough of you, my darling," he whispered as he stroked her thighs.

She was silent, still, luxuriating in his touch.

He kissed her mouth as her arms went around him, holding him as he explored her. He wanted her on her hands and knees, her legs wide apart, as he sat at the foot of the bed exploring her genitals with his fingers, his tongue. She was wet to his touch, and she could hear her heart beating in her ears. It was another hour, maybe more, before he pushed her flat against the bed and she felt the sting of a needle in the back of her knee.

Now, darling. Now.

She wanted to cry out for him to take her before she died for the wanting of him. He was telling her what to do with her legs, and she wound them around his waist as he guided his penis to the wet mouth of her vagina.

She gasped, as she always did when he entered her, and then they were together. They were one, Valerie thought. Truly one. Meant for each other from the beginning of time, two halves who had finally found each other to make a whole.

———

In the red Ferrari that Victor had given her for her birthday, Valerie moved with the traffic past the Beverly Hills Hotel, which sat, among the towering palm trees, manicured shrubs, and bright beds of flowers, like a big pink birthday cake.

A red light caught Valerie at the corner of Sunset Boulevard and Crescent Heights where, in those long-ago days, she had gotten off the bus, returning either from her lessons with Max Perlstein or from the evenings ushering at the Hollywood Bowl.

At the next corner, Valerie made a right onto the street where she had lived in the little apartment on the second floor with Vicki and Al and little Muffin. There was a parking place right in front and Valerie pulled into it. An enormous sadness welled up in her as she looked at the two-story building, with its fresh white paint, its neat lawn, the little hedge on either side of the walk.

It was all so long ago, she thought minutes later, as she turned the key in the ignition and the engine of the Ferrari roared to life.

Valerie drove with the heavy traffic north to the Hollywood Bowl. She made a left turn and moved slowly through the vast, empty parking lot. She parked, then hurried up the ramp to the Bowl itself, saw again the half shell, empty and still, in the bright, sunny day. She could almost hear the orchestra tuning up. Fifteen thousand empty seats tiered toward the top of the hill, which was fringed with shaggy trees. In the bright sky, the sun glistened on a silver jet that had just taken off from Burbank Airport.

Max Perlstein was glad to hear from Valerie when she called, and he invited her to come by for a drink with him and the girl he had been living with for a couple of years. He was doing great, just great, he said.

"I know," she laughed. "I read the papers, Max. I know about the two Academy Awards. I wrote to you, congratulating you."

"Well, kiddo," he said, "you're so high and mighty now that it's hard to tell."

"Oh, Max," she scoffed. "I'm not high and mighty. Nothing's changed."

Max's house was comforting and familiar. Max looked wonderful, too. His blond hair was shorter now, his tanned face a little more mature. Still he was the same old Max, in his jeans, his shirt with the sleeves rolled up to just below the elbow, the loafers worn without the socks. His girlfriend, Karen McGintly, was nice, too, and very attractive. She was writing a television pilot. The three spent an hour together over glasses of white wine, and when Valerie had gotten up to leave, there had been a flurry of kisses, and they had all said they must do it again very soon.

They wouldn't, of course, Valerie thought as she pulled out of the curving driveway. Max was so successful, and Karen was working, and Valerie knew they both thought she was just another rich matron who went to lunch with a lot of other rich women who talked about their clothes, and their trips, and the problems they were having with their servants. And if they thought anything else, she reminded herself as she turned onto Sunset Boulevard, they were giving her too much credit, because that was exactly what she did do. Exactly what she did talk about. Except for the problems with the servants, of course, because Gregson saw to all of that.

———

Valerie smiled in her sleep, turned. She reached out a hand for Victor, but the bed next to her was empty, the fragrance only her own perfume. Gradually, her thoughts arranged themselves in her mind. The crash of the Penn International jet. Charred bodies, four of them shot in the head, the fifth, Victor, dead of asphyxiation. Her husband, the center of her life, was dead. Raymond had said so.

Valerie bolted straight up in bed and covered her face with her hands. She shook with sobs as the whole ghastly mess came back to her, swept over her like the final curse of some diabolical natural force. Oh, Victor, she thought. My darling. My love.

28

As the headlines of all the morning tabloids screamed the latest details of the growing Penn International scandal, the funeral cortege, stretching on for several blocks, made its way behind the long black hearse carrying the mortal remains of Victor Penn. The coffin within was covered with a blanket of red rosebuds.

Inside the old stone church in the middle of London, the cloying scent of multitudes of flowers was almost nauseating. The vicar, in a black cassock with white and purple panels, was alternately unctuous and trembling at the wonder of conducting the service in front of a congregation of the great, the powerful, and the titled, all of whom had assembled to honor Victor's memory.

The grave, freshly dug, was discreetly covered with a carpet of artificial grass. Mary di Stefano stood with her head bowed, her hands clasping a worn Bible. Surreptitiously, she glanced over at Valerie in a simple black dress with a round collar and long sleeves, wearing a black hat with a veil. She was pale, even more than usual. The children stood on either side of her.

Little Raymond wore a gray suit, a white shirt, and a black tie. His head, with its mass of light brown curls, was bowed, his shoulders slumped. Alexandra, with her shoulder-length dark hair and bewildered blue eyes, the same color as her father's, clung to her mother's hand. The children were always so well mannered, so poised. Mary looked at their white faces and inferred their shock.

Raymond, in a black suit, a white shirt, and a black tie, stood ramrod straight next to Miss Furst, his assistant. John O'Farrell, Victor's attorney, was at Raymond's right. He would be, of course. Go where the money is, was John's motto.

Mary studied Valerie. For the past two days, Mary had listened to an eternity of Valerie's convoluted rationalizations. Victor was alive. Somewhere. And, as he was alive, he would send for her. She was his core as he was hers. Theirs was a perfect love.

All of which had its own logic, Mary thought. What

Valerie didn't seem to realize was that even if Victor were alive, Penn International was dead. Over. Ruined. With the death of the corporation went the houses, the tapestries and paintings, the furnishings, the *objets d'art*, the clothes and furs, the sweet little surprises like a diamond and sapphire necklace or the huge, perfect diamond ring. In fact, everything was gone, except for ten million dollars worth of trinkets in the safe-deposit box in a Beverly Hills bank where no federal agent, no bloodhound from the IRS, could possibly know about it.

She remembered John O'Farrell's words at tea yesterday. He had just flown in from Washington, D.C., where he had been negotiating on behalf of Penn International with the bank examiners, the IRS, and the Justice Department.

"The Federal Deposit Insurance Corporation is the agency," John began, pulling down his tie and unbuttoning the top button of his shirt. "They'll be moving into all of the branches of the bank in every city. They'll change the locks on the doors, dismantle the automatic teller machines. Count the cash in the vault, in the cash drawers. Of course, we won't know exactly where everything stands until after the audit. And, the way things are, that could take a couple of months."

"What happens then?" asked Kyle, leaning forward. He, like John, looked as if he hadn't slept in the past six months. There were dark rings under his eyes, and his face was drawn with fatigue.

"Well, we don't know," said John. "Maybe some other bank will take over if enough of the loans are good. maybe the FDIC will just shut it down."

"What about the businesses?" asked Kyle. "And all of the real estate?"

"Yeah, well, the problem with the businesses is the IRS," John said. "They'll be running things, doing the audits. Seeing where everything stands." He looked thoughtful as he added, "We could be looking at several years before everything is sorted out."

"What about the drug money, John?" asked Mary. "And the money from terrorist kidnappings? Have the banks been stripped?"

"I don't know," he said, shaking his head. "I'm not a banker. It'll come out in the audit."

"What happens in the meantime?" asked Mary, as she noticed Valerie looking down at her teacup. Trying to read the future in the leaves, maybe, although from what John was saying, perhaps it was better not to know.

"Well, all the assets of Penn International are being seized, at least temporarily," he said. "That means the estate in Beverly Hills, of course. Gregson and a small staff will be kept on. After all, the government wants to keep its property in good shape for the auction. And Daniel will be kept on to maintain the cars. Same reason."

"Oh, God," said Kyle, rolling his eyes.

"What I did get them to agree to was leasing the guesthouse to Valerie for a dollar a year for one year," said John. "So you'll all have a roof over your heads. And, of course, you'll all be able to take your personal effects from the mansion."

It hadn't been the most pleasant tea party she had ever attended, Mary thought, wondering if the vicar would ever finish his prayers. Neither did it help that every country in the world was cooperating with the

United States government in confiscating Penn International's assets until everything could be sorted out.

At least John had gotten the guesthouse for Valerie and the children. And it was already decided that Kyle would live there, too, until he could decide what he wanted to do. Mary would stay there for a while to get them organized. After all, it was the least she could do considering all the Penn money she had squirreled away.

Mary glanced again at Raymond, wondering once more at his extraordinary decision to have the funeral in so public a place. Raymond's face was stricken and he was actually clutching Miss Furst's arm. Oh my God, Mary thought, Raymond believed that Victor was indeed being buried.

Hoping that Valerie hadn't noticed, Mary glanced over to where the younger woman stood, holding tightly to the hand of each solemn child. Valerie's hazel eyes were panicky, her face white.

At last it was over.

Several people crowded around Valerie, offering condolences and bending to say a few words to little Raymond and Alexandra. As Mary strolled over to join the little group, she wondered if anyone else at the service had noted that Mr. Raymond Penn hadn't even so much as glanced in the direction of his sister-in-law.

29

Maybe it really was true about funerals and the rituals surrounding them, Valerie thought, her smile automatic and her handshake firm, as she sat in a Queen Anne wing chair in the drawing room of the Regent's Park mansion, accepting the condolences of those who had been invited back after the service.

Her dear Leon Stern was there, leaning over her. Taking her hand and kissing it. He looked older but as debonair as ever. "I am so sorry, my dear Valerie," he said, his eyes compassionate. "I am so very sorry."

"Thank you, Leon," she said. "I am so happy you could come." She shifted in the wing chair, letting the white ribbons threaded through the ring between her legs brush her thighs.

Mary sat with John O'Farrell by a window overlooking the grounds. They were deep in conversation, their heads together. Kyle, gesturing with his cigarette, was now chatting with Leon Stern. The few guests who were left were telling Alexandra and little Raymond how brave they were, how they must help their mother because they were all she had. The twins had a mid-afternoon flight back to Switzerland with their bodyguard. Financial empires could come tumbling down, fathers could be lost in plane crashes, but the school term still had to be completed.

Hours later, after the last guests had left, Valerie sank onto the huge four-poster bed upon which Victor had so patiently taught her the details of erotic love. All she wanted to do, as she unbuttoned the black wool dress, was lie down. Die. Make it all go away.

She took a long bath and crawled between the soft white sheets, nearly dead with fatigue. Thank God for the jewelry, safe in the bank in Beverly Hills. Ten million dollars, Mary had said. Why, that was a fortune. It would get them started again when Victor sent for her and the children.

As Valerie began drifting off to sleep, Victor's face danced in her mind. She heard the voice of the vicar. "Ashes to ashes, dust to dust." She saw once again Raymond Penn's set jaw, his expression, his hand as it clutched Miss Furst's arm for support.

Suddenly wide awake again, she bolted out of the bed and hurried down the stairs to the drawing room. Frantically, she tried to blot Raymond's stricken face from her mind. In the music room, she found a little peace as she played, until it was time for little Raymond and Alexandra to leave.

———

"Now, you be a good boy, darling," she said, bending to hug little Raymond as Daniel loaded their luggage into the boot of the Rolls-Royce limousine. "You'll take care of Alexandra, won't you?"

He clung to her, and she felt his tears on her cheek as Alexandra flung her arms around her as well. Valerie knelt, holding her children for a moment. Their bodyguard ushered them into the backseat of the car and ___ed the door. They were up on their knees, waving ___ ___om the back window, as the car moved away.

Valerie stood there until long after the car was out of sight.

Later, the limousine again rolled down the winding drive, with the verdant lawns on either side, the arching antique oaks. Reporters, television crews, motorcycles, vans, curiosity seekers all watched as Valerie Penn left the Regent's Park estate for the last time.

═══

The guesthouse had the usual configuration of rooms, including a maid's room downstairs and five bedrooms, each with its own bath and dressing room, upstairs. It was furnished with what Victor had tired of looking at in the big house, or what he hadn't decided he wanted to look at yet. It would certainly do for Valerie, Kyle, and the kids when they came, thought Mary di Stefano. Thank God, though, that she would soon be going home to her own apartment each night.

It was a glorious morning, Mary realized as she pulled into the parking lot behind the bank. This would be a little different from her usual visit to the safe-deposit box to pick out a necklace, a pair of earrings, a bracelet, perhaps, to accessorize a certain gown.

Inside, Mary looked into the face of a smiling, dusky-complexioned young woman. Strange, how she felt she was robbing the place as she told the young woman she needed to get into her safe-deposit box. Maybe it was because of the big canvas tote she was carrying, she decided, as she scrawled the box number on a form and signed her name with a flourish. The young woman raised her eyebrows as she read Mary's name.

"I'll get the key, Countess di Stefano," she said, releasing the low iron gate so Mary could enter the vault. The woman checked the number on the key.

"It's this one," Mary said, touching the box she had opened so often over the years. She inserted her own key into one of the two locks, and stood back as the young woman inserted a second key to release and open it. She pulled the box out of the wall, and, holding it in both arms, walked into the room next door and put it down.

"Will there be anything else, Countess?" the bank attendant asked shyly as she stood in the doorway.

"No, thank you," said Mary, and the door closed with a click. Settling into a chair, she wondered if perhaps they weren't being too hasty. Perhaps it would be more sensible to just leave the jewelry in the safe-deposit box and take out one item at a time as they needed the money. But Mary and Valerie had agreed that it might be wise to spirit away all the jewelry before the feds found out about it and attached it, as they were attaching everything else. They could always find some other place to put the jewelry, someplace where the feds would never look.

Mary pulled open the top of the safe-deposit box.

It was empty.

Slowly, Mary replaced the lid to the box. She pushed the buzzer under the table, and the dusky-skinned young woman reappeared.

"I'm finished," Mary told her. "Thank you for your help."

30

The electric golf carts used by the staff to negotiate the acres of the estate shuttled back and forth from the mansion to the guesthouse, carrying Valerie's clothes, Victor's clothes, a couple of Valerie's furs that hadn't yet been sent to storage for the summer, Victor's jewelry, all the watches and cuff links collected over the years.

Valerie's gowns, her dresses, the skirts, the sweaters, the peignoirs, the nightgowns quickly filled the walk-in closet in the master bedroom of the guesthouse and overflowed into the bedroom next door. Victor's hundreds of suits, dinner jackets, and topcoats hung on racks that nearly filled the room. Valerie spent hours each day sitting in the room near a window overlooking the guesthouse's swimming pool, the rolling acres of the estate. Sometimes, she walked among the racks, touching a jacket, a topcoat, imagining him in it. At night, she ceremoniously shaved her pubis, threaded ribbons through the golden ring between her legs, and crept into bed wearing one of his exquisite handmade shirts.

For the first few nights she had been back from London, she didn't dare to close her eyes. She knew what she would see would be Raymond's stricken face, his hand clutching Miss Furst's arm. She didn't want to see that, didn't want anything to contradict what she prayed would be the truth, which was that Victor was alive. She was nearly hallucinating with fatigue when Elliott had insisted she take a tranquilizer four times a day, at least for a few weeks.

Her mind seemed to be in neutral all the time. When Mary had come back from the bank and told her that all the jewelry was gone from the safe-deposit box, her only reaction had been to wonder how Raymond had managed to arrange that, too.

"Valerie," Mary had said, concern bright in her eyes. "This means you don't have any money. No real money at all."

"I guess so," Valerie had replied. "I'm going to have to think about what to do."

She was the only one who didn't have an option. She couldn't even kill herself because Victor would be sending for her soon. And because of the children, of course. Yes. The children. They were going to be home soon, and they would have to be taken care of, too.

What they were all waiting for, really, was for John O'Farrell to get back from London so he could tell them where everything stood.

———

"What did you say, John?" Valerie asked dreamily.

"I said Raymond has a proposition for you," he smiled. His coat was off, his tie was loose, and it was almost as if they were all old friends.

"Does Raymond think Victor is alive, John?" asked Valerie. "Did you ask him if he thinks Victor is alive?"

"No, I didn't ask him what he thought," said John, slumping into a chair and taking a long swallow of scotch and water. "Raymond's personality doesn't exactly invite questions."

"Because at the cemetery I got the feeling he may

think Victor is dead," said Valerie. "There was just a look on his face that made me think so. Of course, if that's what he thinks, he's wrong."

"Anyway, Raymond is willing to grant you an allowance of a hundred thousand dollars a year for life," continued John. "He thinks it would be best for the kids to continue their education in Switzerland. He would even be willing to permit the children to come to Beverly Hills during the summer holidays. He thought it would be fair if the two of you alternated between Christmas and spring break."

"I always wanted the children to live with us," said Valerie. "That was the one quarrel I always had with Victor. Of course, he was so traditional in his way. He wanted the children in the Swiss school, and I went along with him. I always went along with him. I thought it was the proper thing for a wife to do."

"The hundred thousand will continue to be yours even when you remarry."

"Well, I can hardly remarry," Valerie laughed lightly. "I'm already married."

"You're going to need money to live on, Valerie." John ran a hand through his hair. "There's the ten-million-dollar life insurance policy in your favor, but the insurance company will dispute that as long as the feds are nosing around. That could take years, as you know. The same goes for the missing jewelry. They are going to fight like hell to avoid paying that off." He sighed and took another gulp of his drink. "The hundred thousand that Raymond is offering is an alternative."

"Well, it isn't an alternative to me." There was a note of finality in Valerie's voice.

"Personally," said John, "I think the hundred thousand is only Raymond's opening offer. I think I could go back at him with a quarter million a year for life, and he would jump at it."

"I'm not selling my children to Raymond Penn for a quarter million dollars a year, or for any other amount." Valerie's hazel eyes were clear, her jaw determined.

"Hear, hear," said Mary, looking at the younger woman with new respect.

"What are you going to live on, Valerie?" John shook his head. "There will be plenty of money, but it's way, way down the line. How are you going to support yourself? How are you going to support the kids?"

"I don't know," she sighed, all the energy and resolve of the moment before ebbing away.

"We'll think about it tomorrow," said Kyle, his leg swinging quickly. "When we all get back to Tara."

"John, the wedding presents that Valerie and Victor got," Mary said suddenly. "They would be personal effects, wouldn't they?"

"Yeah, sure they would," he said.

"Well, I think that with my contacts, I could find buyers for them. It would give Valerie some cash flow for a while."

"Why not pack up the whole lot of them and send them off to Sotheby's?"

"Well, time, for one thing," said Mary. "It would take maybe a year to mount a sale that major. We can offer them little by little, buy some time."

"Yeah, well, running money is what we're talking about right now," he agreed. "I'll draw up the paperwork when I go into the office tomorrow. Any judge will go along with it. The poor widow. The orphans. It'll work."

"Our wedding presents," said Valerie, her voice quivering. "I can't sell our wedding presents. I can't."

"Look, Valerie," said Mary, "you don't have enough cash on hand to tip a parking lot attendant. You don't even have a checking account. We have to figure out a way to put the groceries on the table around here."

"Victor will never forgive me," Valerie said, shrinking into a corner of the sofa.

"He'll understand, Valerie," John said gently.

"John, you sound as if you think Victor is alive," said Mary.

"Yeah, I vote with the majority," John grinned. "I go along with the feds, the Justice Department, and the IRS. Victor Penn is alive, all right. I'd bet the farm on it."

I'll have to pull myself together, Valerie thought, emptying the bottles of pills into the toilet. No more pills. No more anything.

Wearing one of Victor's shirts, she walked among the racks of his clothing, feeling the softness of cashmere, of fine wool. What if he appeared tonight, she wondered, looking at the single bed pushed against one wall. He would think I'd lost my mind, sleeping in here among his clothes, as if a coat, a pair of trousers, were Victor himself. She opened the door to the bedroom and stood on the landing. The house was dark and silent, moonlight reflecting on the chandelier. Let him find me in the master bedroom where I belong, waiting for him when he comes.

But, what could she possibly do to earn money? The

only thing she could think of was to use her training as a pianist.

It was nearly dawn and Valerie was still turning over in her mind ways to get started again. It had been so long since she had had to think about anything except pleasing Victor. Victor had been her shield against the world, and they would be together again soon. She smiled at the thought of their perfect love.

Max Perlstein, with his Academy Awards and his Grammys, would know how she could get a concert career started. He was a huge success. She had read of his marriage to Karen and the birth of their daughter Rebecca in *Time,* and read of their divorce a few years later. She hadn't seen Max in years, but she knew he would help her. There was hope.

31

The double strand of pearls Valerie had taken to London for the funeral was composed of sixty-two Burmese cultured pearls, its clasp a five-carat emerald-cut diamond. Mary estimated it to be worth a half-million dollars, maybe more. When she walked out of the pawnshop on Melrose Avenue she had in her handbag a cashier's check for fifty thousand dollars, and a pawn ticket reading "Pawnbroker to the Stars."

Mary deposited the check in her bank account and headed north to the great estates above Sunset Boulevard and to the guesthouse on the most fabulous estate of them all.

"Fifty thousand dollars," said Mary, waving the pawn ticket at Valerie. "It's all safe and sound in my checking account."

"Fifty thousand dollars," said Valerie thoughtfully. "Is that a lot?"

"It depends how you look at it." Mary wondered for a moment if it was worth trying to help this spoiled child. Of course it was, she reminded herself. It was a beginning.

———

As appearances in their situation were everything, an assessment with which even John agreed, Valerie had spent two hundred thousand dollars of Kyle's money on a new, ice blue Ferrari convertible. Valerie and Kyle had also bought two Steinway pianos. It had taken four burly piano movers and a whole day to set them up in the library of the guesthouse.

The kitchen was always in a total shambles, with half-full containers of Chinese food, boxes of half-eaten pizzas, and the sink stacked with dirty dishes. The only things in the refrigerator were wedges of cheese, a jar of crunchy peanut butter, containers of potato salad or cole slaw, countless six-packs of diet Pepsi.

The rest of the house was even worse. There were newspapers and magazines everywhere, Kyle's overflowing ashtrays, empty glasses. On top of everything else, Valerie had the interior designers in, cheering up her own master suite for that magical moment when Victor would appear to resume his natural place as master of all he surveyed.

Every cent that Kyle had saved was being frittered away as if the world were going to end at midnight, and the fifty thousand dollars Mary had received for Valerie's pearls was a joke. Unless she could generate some income from the wedding presents, Mary thought, shaking her head, they would all be working at Saks before long. Even selling the wedding presents was only a stopgap measure.

When Valerie had grandly announced one morning that she and Kyle had some things that needed cleaning, Mary drew the line.

"Here," she said, handing Valerie the Yellow Pages. "We call this a telephone book. I'm sure you both remember how to spell *cleaners,* right? Well, look it up."

The two of them stood there, dumbfounded.

Mary simmered as she examined the lists she had made of her friends and acquaintances, everybody, in fact, who might be in the market for what she had to sell, and at the right price. She had already rehearsed her pitch, practicing in front of her bathroom mirror until she had it down pat. These were wondrous, rare items. The treasures of kings, princes, heads of state. The best of the best. From the collection of Valerie Penn.

It couldn't miss.

Valerie couldn't wait to speak to Max Perlstein after all these years. The sound of his voice gave Valerie a pleasant, little shock, but when she told him who it was, Max seemed almost embarrassed to hear from her.

"Gee, Valerie," he said, his voice flustered. "I was going to call. I was really sorry to hear about Victor, about everything coming down the way it has. But, I've been so busy with the show I'm putting together for Broadway. It's been a bitch, kiddo. It really has."

Valerie felt him wondering why she was calling after so many years.

"I've got to find something to do for a living, Max," she began tentatively. "I thought, maybe my music. It's the only thing I'm trained for. I thought you could help me get started again."

"So, it's as bad as it sounds, huh?" She heard the sympathy in his voice.

"Oh, there's money," she said vaguely. "A lot of money. But there are legal complications. You can imagine."

"Yeah, I can imagine. I've had some of my own. Not like the ones you're going through, of course, but there's been the divorce. Karen's career really took off and she wanted her space.

"Her attorney was the most materialistic bastard who ever came down the pike. So, there's been the property settlement, and alimony, and child support. Karen got custody, of course, but there was all the hassling about my visitation rights. I get my daughter every other weekend when I'm in town, and every Wednesday overnight." He paused.

"I know how busy you are, Max," Valerie said, "but I was wondering if you could find the time to see me for a half hour or so. Maybe, if you wouldn't mind, you could listen to me play."

"Yeah, sure, kiddo," he said after a beat. "Sure. Come on over."

Valerie, walking into the massive arched living room of Max's new Mediterranean house, noticed the pictures of Rebecca in silver frames. She was a pretty child with her father's blond hair and blue eyes.

Max approached Valerie tentatively, as if she were an invalid not yet starting to recover from some ghastly accident.

"You look terrific, Valerie," he said, putting his hands on her shoulders, brushing her cheek with a light kiss.

Valerie wanted to wrap herself in the warmth of his sympathy and beg him to hold her and cuddle her. "You look terrific, too." She smiled. It was true, she thought. His success had given him an almost compelling confidence.

Max's live-in housekeeper served them drinks in the living room, as the setting sun polished all of the silver picture frames into a sea of mirrors.

After a glass of wine, Valerie began to relax and feel comfortable again with Max. The telephone in the next room rang for the seventh time before the answering machine picked it up. Max didn't seem to care. He was smiling at her, enjoying her. Valerie smiled back, flushed, remembering the little crush she had had on Max as his ten-year-old student.

Finally, Valerie took her seat at the piano, feeling the same nausea she had always felt when the performance was important. Strange, performing for somebody again whose judgment she cared about, after all of those years of playing just for Kyle or Victor, when nothing was at stake.

She played a Beethoven concerto, hurrying through it because she had promised that she wouldn't take up Max's valuable time. She willed herself to slow down and to concentrate on Beethoven, on what he wanted to say.

To her ears, her playing sounded self-conscious and wooden. Finished, Valerie shifted on the piano bench and looked across the room to Max. In the other room, the telephone was answered again by the machine.

"I have good news and bad news," Max said after a couple of minutes.

Valerie waited, the blood rushing to her cheeks.

"The good news is that your technique is incredible," he said. "Pristine. Exquisite. Leon, Kyle. Working with Leon and Kyle sure paid off for you."

Valerie dropped her eyes.

"The bad news is that your concentration isn't so hot." His voice was thoughtful. "You've got a lot on your mind. It's probably all the shit that's been coming down."

"Do you think I have a chance, Max, after all these years?"

"Well, you know what it's like out there. There are always a lot of hot young kids coming up, and they're out for blood. Nothing's changed." He sipped his wine. "You're better than most of them, I'll give you that. Being a rich lady hasn't turned your talent to mush."

"Oh, thank you, Max," she said, tears of relief welling in her eyes. "Thank you." She buried her face in her hands, her whole body shaking. Max crossed the room to stand beside her, patted her shoulder.

"Well, that's the last time I give you a compliment, kiddo," he said at last. "But, I would give it a lot of thought before going ahead. People will see you as a curiosity, and they won't take you seriously. You know how grueling touring can be, and if it's decent money you're looking for, you're probably better off trying to win the lottery."

Valerie looked up at him, knowing everything he said was true.

"Think about it," he said again, and they said goodbye.

———

Mary had begun the initial calls to sell the wedding gifts. She was blitzed with questions about Victor Penn. Was he or wasn't he dead? Was it true that he had embezzled billions, had all those people murdered on the plane? She would begin her pitch about the marvelous Fabergé egg for sale, about the solid gold elephant with the diamond eyes and ruby collar, all from the collection of Valerie Penn. Just another trinket to be dusted, she would laugh.

Although there were no offers, there was interest. She could hear it in their voices.

"I think we're on to something," she told Valerie. "I think it's going to work."

32

Traffic on the freeway was light, but Valerie kept the Ferrari only a few miles over the speed limit. The twins were traveling from Geneva without their bodyguard for the first time.

Valerie swung off the freeway at the airport off ramp and approached the international terminal.

"You take a parking ticket," Mary had told her, "and you pay on the way out."

"Why don't you come with me?" Valerie had implored. "Show me how it's done. Just once. The next time I'll know."

Mary had just sighed irritably.

Every parking space on every level seemed to be taken as Valerie moved up another ramp, and another. Maybe she could just park in front of the terminal for a moment, and tell the guard she was fetching her children and would be right back. It was heartless of Mary to have made her go through this by herself.

A compact car backed out, and Valerie felt an odd thrill of accomplishment as she pulled the Ferrari into the empty space. Waiting for the light to change at the crosswalk among ten or twelve people, Valerie realized she was helpless, vulnerable, and alone. A teenage boy wearing a ponytail and an earring jostled her arm as the crowd pushed her along. Rock music from his huge radio battered her ears.

There must be at least three million people here, she thought, hurrying through the sliding doors into the international terminal. All of them were in jeans or shorts, wearing those hideous rubber sandals and tee shirts with sayings on them. The lines in front of the counters blended into each other. Overhead, voices generated by computers droned arrivals and departures. Why was this clean-cut, smiling young man offering her a flower? Not a reporter, she thought, feeling flustered. Oh, God. Please.

"No, no thank you," she murmured, brushing past him, searching the faces of the people emerging from the door marked Customs.

The twins were surprised to see her by herself, waiting to meet them. Oh, they are such beautiful children, Valerie thought, hurrying toward them, smiling. Alexandra's mop of brown curls was exactly the color of her father's, her blue eyes so like his. Her full mouth could have been Valerie's own. Little Raymond's hair was just a bit lighter, his eyes flecked with green like hers but shaped like Victor's. Oh, why aren't you here with me to meet our children, my darling? Valerie thought. Oh, Victor, I miss you so much I could die.

"Alexandra," she cried, stooping to gather them into her arms. "Raymond. How was your flight, my darlings?"

Then there were more hugs, kisses, their excited chatter as they told her how grown up they felt traveling by themselves, as they strolled together toward the exit.

Valerie was nearly beside herself with frustration by the time they finally got out of the parking structure. The smallest bill in her handbag was a fifty, and the fool in the parking booth took his time making change. Finally, she eased onto the freeway ramp, heading north on a beautiful summer morning under a hot sun in a perfect blue sky, pointed toward home with little Raymond and Alexandra, the two most beautiful children in the world. The trip had felt as though it had taken three days, and she couldn't wait to get her hands on a glass of wine. She didn't see why Mary couldn't have come with her just this once.

Valerie took the twins to the suite the interior designer had prepared for them. The sitting room was flanked by a bedroom, dressing room, and bathroom for each child. Alexandra's bedroom was all in dusty rose and a white the color of whipped cream. Raymond's room was in blues and beiges, just the color scheme for a little boy, the interior designer had assured her. Crates crammed with clothes, books, tennis rackets, fencing foils and masks, Raymond's soccer ball, Alexandra's saddle, and their chess set had started to arrive several days before the twins were due. Valerie had had to direct the maid as she unpacked each crate. Help was impossible these days, she thought to herself. Her own personal maid had never needed guidance. She had instinctively known just what to do, just where everything was to be placed. Everything had been so smooth, so orderly. Now there was only chaos. It was all so unfair.

Somehow everything had been put together before the children's arrival. Valerie saw their tentative looks, saw them catch each other's eyes.

"What's the matter, darlings?" asked Valerie.

In a moment, little Raymond answered in a high, uncertain voice.

"Mummy," he said, "are we very, very poor?"

Valerie felt a start of pleasure several weeks later when she answered the phone to Max's voice.

"Some friends of mine are having a barbecue on the Fourth of July," he said. "They have a house in Malibu Colony. I'm taking Rebecca, and I thought you and the kids might like to go, too."

"You mean you're asking me out?"

"Well, I guess you could put it that way."

"You're asking me for a date?"

"Oh, look, kiddo," said Max, annoyed. "I'm not asking you to run away with me to Sri Lanka and be mine forever. It's a big party, with a lot of kids, a few laughs.

I'm taking Rebecca, and I thought your kids might enjoy it, too. Don't make a big deal out of it, because it isn't."

"Let me check with the children, Max. I'll call you after lunch."

It *was* a big deal to her, Valerie realized as she replaced the receiver. She wondered what the twins would think about going somewhere with a man who wasn't their father. She really had to refuse. Not only wouldn't it look right, it made her feel guilty even thinking about it.

"Oh, fireworks," said little Raymond. "Like Paris on Bastille Day."

"Or Monte Carlo," said Alexandra. "Oh, Mummy, how super! Oh, can we go? Can we?"

"Say yes, Mummy," begged little Raymond. "Please!"

Mary was practically delirious with joy at the thought of having a day to herself.

"If you run out of gas and get stuck on Pacific Coast Highway," she said brightly when she was told about it, "don't call me. Promise you won't call me."

"Is Aunt Mary teasing, Mummy?" asked Alexandra, her blue eyes quizzical.

"Yes, darling," Valerie said with a tight smile. "Aunt Mary is teasing."

"I think I'll come, too," said Kyle. "At least there's the possibility of a decent meal, which is more than I can say for staying at home."

———

"I'm so excited, Mummy," said Alexandra, looking out the window.

"It should be fun, darling." Valerie felt a little excited herself.

She had spent hours deciding what to wear, what was elegant and yet casual enough for a day at the beach. She settled on a dress of coral cotton, with spaghetti straps and a skirt nearly to her ankles and coral earrings surrounded by tiny, perfect diamonds. Not real, of course, since very little of Valerie's jewelry was real these days. Her bare shoulders were covered by a fabulous cashmere shawl in the same delicate coral.

They were all ready and waiting long before twelve o'clock, even Kyle, in white gabardine twenties-style trousers, a blue and white striped, long-sleeved cotton sweater, and saddle shoes.

Max arrived with little Rebecca, her head full of blond curls, dimples darting in and out of her cheeks.

"What a beautiful baby," Valerie exclaimed.

"You look great, kiddo," said Max, looking her up and down.

"Not a baby," muttered Rebecca. "Big girl."

Kyle and the twins clambered into the back of the Chevrolet Blazer. Valerie and Max were in front, Rebecca between them.

It was a perfect day with bright sunlight, a clear blue sky, and just a hint of gentle breeze. There was almost no traffic, Valerie noticed, relieved, enjoying the sun on her bare shoulders. The twins, in back, craned their necks to look at the houses along Sunset Boulevard, at the lush planting, the bougainvillea in orange and deep pink climbing the walls surrounding each of the great estates. Cars filled with young people, pickups with surfboards, and vans blaring rock music jammed the road as they approached the beach.

"Is it soon, Daddy?" There was a tired whine in Rebecca's voice.

By the time they reached the Pacific Coast Highway, Valerie was perspiring in the blazing sun. The beach-bound traffic was backed up as far as she could see. An hour later, they finally pulled up to Malibu Colony. Perhaps a dozen cars, Porsches, Mercedes-Benzes, BMWs, a Cadillac Seville, Jaguars, and a Corvette were parked, bumper to bumper, in front of the house. Max squeezed the Chevrolet Blazer between a big Lincoln and a Lamborghini. As they walked the few feet to the gate, Alexandra, suddenly shy, clung to her mother's hand. Immediately inside was a tennis court where two middle-aged men, deeply tanned and in tennis whites, lobbed a ball across the net. A pair of lanky teenagers tossed a basketball through the hoop attached to the four-car garage.

Max, with Rebecca straddling his shoulders, waved idly to a couple a few steps ahead. The man was middle-aged, too, very tan, in pleated gray trousers, a matching gray silk shirt unbuttoned halfway down his chest matted with curly gray hair. The woman was in her early twenties, her hair peroxide-blond. She wore a strapless print dress stopping just above her knees, and strappy white sandals with three-inch heels. Valerie heard Max saying, "Say hello to Valerie, and this is Kyle."

Valerie didn't catch their names, but she nodded and smiled. The man rang the doorbell, setting off an assault of hysterical barking inside.

Valerie looked at Kyle, who rolled his eyes.

The day hadn't even started and she was already wishing she were back home.

33

A pair of red Irish setters set upon Raymond and Alexandra, almost knocking them down, frantically licking their faces.

"Knock it off," said Max firmly, and the dogs slunk away.

"Match point," called one of the men on the tennis court as their hostess, a short, smiling woman who looked familiar to Valerie, came forward to meet them.

"Say hello to Valerie," said Max, gently lowering his daughter to the floor. "This is Kyle." He gave the little girl a pat on her buttocks and she ran through the crowd of adults to the terrace, where several children were splashing in the swimming pool. On the beach a group of teenagers and some older men were playing touch football. The odor of hamburgers and hot dogs drifted into the crowded room, mingling with the fragrance of perfume and after-shave lotion.

"How do you do?" said Valerie.

"Oh, you're English. What fun that you're here to celebrate the Fourth of July with us."

She turned to chide a couple of ten-year-olds who were running through the house. "Stop that, you two," she ordered, and the boys slowed at once to a sedate walk. "Get yourself a drink," she said to all of them, "and the food is right over there, just through that door into the dining room."

There were platters of cheeses, cherry tomatoes,

pale green grapes, and long-stemmed strawberries laid out on the coffee table between two overstuffed sofas in front of a huge stone fireplace. A bartender poured drinks behind a bar in one corner of the room. Valerie felt the grit of sand under her shoes on the tiled floor. A Mexican maid in a white uniform offered her a platter filled with miniature quiches.

"No, thank you," she said.

"Out among the proletariat," murmured Kyle next to her, handing her a glass of white wine. "Can you see Victor in this crowd?" He took a gulp of his scotch and water. "How about Raymond? That would be even funnier."

Valerie glanced across the room at Max. He was standing with a group of his cronies, a big smile on his face. They were his kind of people, of course. This was his world. It was so different from the one in which she had always lived.

"Is it all right if we go in the pool, Mummy?" It was little Raymond in his swimming trunks, a towel over his narrow shoulders. Alexandra stood a step or two behind him. Her blue eyes, so like Victor's, expectant.

"Of course, darling," said Valerie, feeling miserable.

"You look familiar," a man was saying to her. "Are you an actress?"

"No, I'm not." She smiled, thinking that he looked familiar, too, although she hadn't recognized his name.

"I'm Valerie Penn," she said, and saw a look of horrified embarrassment cross his face.

"Well, it's nice to meet you," he said, trying to smile, backing away.

It got worse as the hours passed.

After a few drinks Max was talked into playing the score for his new musical. Success had certainly changed him, thought Valerie, watching him through narrowed eyes. Beside her, Kyle swung his leg in time to the music and dropped ashes onto his white gabardine trousers.

At dusk, the whole party moved out onto the tiled terrace, with its wicker furniture and huge terra cotta pots of petunias, pansies, and geraniums. Everybody drinking all afternoon had certainly contributed to the general hilarity, thought Valerie with disgust, shivering under her cashmere shawl. The laughter was raucous now, the conversation high-pitched, excited. Max had barely spoken to her all day, barely glanced at her.

Candles flickering in hurricane lamps lined the low brick wall leading to the sandy beach. Huge multicolored balls of light burst into the dark sky, dissipating in the chilling mist. Valerie huddled in her wicker chair, her legs underneath her, and wrapped the cashmere shawl tightly around her shoulders, remembering one wonderful night early in her marriage. She and Victor had been on their yacht, the largest yacht anchored that night in the Cannes harbor, the lights of the Carlton Hotel visible on the shore.

It had been summer, a perfect hot night, and fireworks had sprayed the black sky. Most of the crew was on shore for the festivities, and the steward who had stayed on board to serve them dinner had already gone below. The two of them had lain, wrapped in each other's arms, on one of the giant chaise longues used for sunning during the day. Valerie closed her eyes, remembering Victor's touch as he slowly undressed her. She almost felt his soft lips on hers, the tentativeness of his tongue, his hand pushing her legs apart, his fingers exploring the inner lips of her vagina. His mouth was sucking at her nipple, and she was tenderly running her hand through his thick, curly brown hair. She was holding his penis, guiding it toward the mouth of her vagina, which was flowing and ready for him.

"Are you okay?" asked a man's voice, breaking her reverie. She opened her eyes abruptly to see Max standing over her.

"I'm fine," she said coldly.

"Well, I think we better hit it if we're ever going to get home," he said. "Let's gather up the kids and go."

Driving home, Valerie stared straight ahead, wondering if the whole miserable day was ever going to end. Finally Max turned the Blazer into the driveway of the guesthouse. The twins were out of sorts when she woke them to tell them they were home. Kyle staggered past them up the stairs to his room. Rebecca was screaming.

"Well, good night, kiddo," said Max, giving her a little wave with one hand.

"Good night, Max," said Valerie, trying to smile. "I had a lovely time, and I'm certain the children enjoyed it, too."

"Yeah, it was fun," he said. "Great bunch of people, aren't they?"

"They were very nice," said Valerie, stifling a yawn. "It was sweet of you to ask us along."

"Well, I thought it would do you good to get out of the house." He grinned, taking a few steps back to the vehicle where Rebecca was leaning out of the window, still sobbing. "I've got to get my little princess to bed. I'll give you a call in a couple of days."

"Well, good night," said Valerie, with a dismissive wave. "Thanks again."

She closed the front door behind her, weak with relief to be home. Neither of the children looked very well, Valerie thought as she leaned over to put her arms around each of them and brush their cheeks with her lips.

Valerie thought she had been generous about the beach house in Malibu. She had complimented her hostess on its charm, and asked politely where they kept their residence in the city. It had turned out that it was their only home, but she couldn't possibly have known that. Nobody she had ever met owned only a beach house. She studied her reflection in the mirrored dressing room, and her exquisite skirt where someone's child had drooled on it.

She had barely gotten into bed and switched off the light when there was a timid tap on the door. Startled, she sat straight up, clutching the sheet to her breast.

"Yes?" she called, her voice trembling.

"Mummy, I don't feel very well," came Raymond's voice.

Valerie sprang out of bed and opened the door. She put her arms around the boy and felt his forehead, which was cool.

"Where does it hurt?" she asked, frightened, wondering what to do.

Wordlessly, he patted his stomach.

"We can go to the hospital," she said.

"Oh, no," he said, embarrassed. "It isn't that bad, Mummy. Really it isn't."

"Well, would you like to come to bed with me for a while?" she asked. "Perhaps you'll feel better with someone there."

"Oh, yes, Mummy," he said, smiling. "I'd like that very much."

A sick child. She had Max to thank for that, too. Valerie stroked Raymond's hair as he lay next to her in the king-sized bed. The little boy fell asleep almost at once. Valerie lay awake, listening to his steady breathing, wondering if he was all right. She put her hand on his forehead, and her breath quickened as she felt a film of perspiration. He was so beautiful, her little son. So intelligent, charming. She stroked his hair again, and a wave of tenderness swept over her, making her want to cry. Her son, and her beautiful daughter. She had her children at last.

———

Valerie had the coffee ready by the time Kyle, holding his head, warily navigated the winding stairway and made his way into the sunny breakfast room. He walked past Valerie into the kitchen where, in the refrigerator, he found some tomato juice. Valerie listened to the cupboard doors being opened and slammed shut, drawers being pulled open and then closed. Finally, Kyle reappeared, a Bloody Mary in his hand. His shoelaces were untied, a stubble of beard covered his chin, and his hair was a wild black halo standing out from his head.

"Oh, God," he said dramatically, sinking into one of the chairs. "Could somebody please turn off the sun?"

"It could be worse," said Valerie, sipping her coffee, which, she decided, tasted quite good. "We could still be in that ghastly house in Malibu."

"Spare me," he sighed. "I would rather have dinner with Raymond Penn than go through that again." He sipped his Bloody Mary, fumbled through his pockets for his lighter, and lit a cigarette. "Have you ever seen such awful people? If we had the money invested in plastic surgery by that crowd, we would be set for at least the rest of the century."

"Not only that," said Valerie, "but Raymond got sick, too. Poor little boy. All that awful food."

"What did you think was the worst part?" asked Kyle. "My vote goes for just being there at all."

"Mine goes to Max for playing the entire score of his musical, holding everybody captive to massage his ego."

"Oh, I don't know," said Kyle. "The score is great. When Max is picking up his Tony, we'll be able to say we heard it way back when."

"But don't you think it was rude of him to play all of it?" asked Valerie thoughtfully. "After all, it was a party. People must have been bored."

"But it was a show business party," Kyle pointed out. "I don't think anybody was bored." He brushed away the ashes that had just fallen on the front of his shirt. "Were you bored?"

"Well, no," she admitted.

"So what are you complaining about?" he asked.

"It just seemed like bad form," she said stiffly.

"You mean that Victor would never do it," said Kyle, taking another gulp of his Bloody Mary.

"That's right," she said.

"Well, he isn't Victor," said Kyle.

They had fun dishing the people, the middle-aged men with their starlet girlfriends, the couples, obviously married for many years, who even looked like each other. The women wearing huge diamonds in the middle of the day.

By early evening, Valerie was thinking that the day with Max hadn't been so bad after all. He hadn't been very attentive, of course, but he had a three-year-old to deal with. It wasn't until a couple of days later that Valerie realized she was jumping every time the phone rang or there was a knock on the door. She was surprised to realize she was hoping Max would be at the other end of the phone or standing there, his hands pushed into the pockets of his jeans.

34

The twins were frolicking in the swimming pool on a glorious early afternoon, as Mary carried a platter of pastrami sandwiches onto the terrace and set them on the umbrella-covered table. She had picked them up at a delicatessen in Beverly Hills that morning, after the long flight back from Paris the night before.

"So, anyway," she said to Valerie, who was a couple of steps behind her with a tray holding a pitcher of iced tea, glasses, soft drinks for the children, "there I was, sitting with the duchess in her *pied-à-terre* in the Sixteenth Arrondissement. She's about a hundred and twelve, you know, and it beats me why anybody that old still wants to buy things, but I told her about the Empire French Savonnerie carpet, and her face lit up. That one will come through, I think. Then she told me that if we knew of anybody who might be interested in her diamond tiara that belonged to the Empress Josephine, she would see that there was a commission in it for us."

"I get that, too," said Valerie between sips of her tea. "I'll call and say I have something I'm offering from my collection. Say, that alabaster dish inlaid with pearls. Whoever I'm talking to will say they don't want the dish, but that they have a museum quality Regency chair. If I can get it sold, there's a commission."

"What are you trying to say?"

"Well, it seems to me that there should be some way to bring all of these buyers and sellers together, don't you think? Maybe there's money to be made just by being brokers and taking the commissions. After all, we're going to run through the last of my things before very long."

"Maybe a catalog," suggested Mary. "We could put together a sample of the finest stock. We could use the things you have left to show people what we have in mind."

"We'll call it something like *The Best of the Best,*" said Valerie. "Or *One of a Kind.* We'll emphasize the rarity of the item, the exclusivity."

"They'll pay to be included," said Mary. "We'll take our percentage on everything that's sold."

"There are lists available for things like that, aren't there?" asked Valerie.

"Oh, I would think so," said Mary. "The fine auction houses, the art galleries, the magazines advertising the loveliest, most unique objects in the world."

Thus began *The Collection of Valerie Penn.*

Once Mary and Valerie had appointed Gregson the chief operations officer of *The Collection of Valerie Penn,* he helped them to set up a bookkeeping system and arrange the paperwork on the transactions. He was, after all, the most organized person in the world.

"What is your first name?" asked Mary.

"Paul," he said in his terribly proper English way. Mary remembered with a smile that he had actually blushed.

Daniel drove the children to and from school each day, leaving Valerie free to work with Mary and Paul Gregson on the details of their new company. Valerie had enrolled Alexandra at the Bryn Dale School for Girls in Holmby Hills, and little Raymond at the Yale School for Boys.

One day Valerie answered the phone. It was a little boy from the Yale School, asking for Penny.

"Penny?" she asked. "Do you mean Raymond Penn?"

"Yeah, Penny," the little boy said.

"Penny," she called through the open doors to the garden, where little Raymond was kicking around his soccer ball. "It's for you."

"Penny?" she said to him when he got off the phone.

"It's my nickname, Mummy," he said, a pleased smile on his face. "All the boys call me Penny."

Valerie happily realized she would never again have to call her son by his given name and be reminded of Raymond Penn.

Alexandra was making friends at her new school, too. Valerie would hear her giggling and laughing with some other little girl on the telephone. Sometimes they would have friends come to play in the early days of fall when the sun was still summer bright in the sky, and the flowers still a riot of color in the neatly manicured beds.

It was nearly nine o'clock one October evening as Mary left the estate for a little market in Beverly Hills before heading home.

She opened the glass door to the frozen food section and stood there, considering the macaroni and cheese, settling, finally, on the lasagna. It would take a couple of minutes in the microwave, and then she could go to bed.

"Oh, I'm sorry," she said, realizing the man next to her already had his hand on the package. The cuff of his coat was dark, perfectly tailored. There was the hint of a gold watch under his white shirt cuff.

"Mary," said a man's voice, surprised.

"Why, John," she said, smiling up into the handsome face of John O'Farrell. "What are you doing here? I thought you were in London."

"I just got in," he said.

"I'm just on my way home from the estate," said Mary.

"Well, listen," he said, glancing at the frozen dinner he held in his hand. "We can do better than this, can't we? Why don't we go somewhere and have some dinner?"

"That's the best idea I've heard all day." There was something so right about being with John O'Farrell, Mary thought, leaving her shopping cart in the middle of the aisle and walking out of the market with him.

"How about Le Restaurant?" he asked, starting his Porsche and throwing it into first gear.

"Fine." She nodded. "What a nice car."

"It's fun," he said. "A toy. I never would have

driven anything like this if I had stayed in New York. I guess I've become a California boy." He stopped for the red light on Santa Monica Boulevard, where a couple of teenagers were wheeling their bicycles across the street. "I like that little Mercedes-Benz you drive, too. It's one of my favorite models."

Mary could sense him appraising her, liking what he saw, as they drove along in the light traffic. It couldn't have been more than ten minutes before John was pulling up in front of the salmon-colored building on Melrose Place, with its discreet brass plate etched with the words *Le Restaurant,* and a parking attendant in a blue jacket and black trousers was helping Mary out of the Porsche.

"Good evening, Mr. O'Farrell," smiled the young maître d'hotel. "We're so happy to see you. It's been a long time, too long."

Mary noticed the scattered diners in the front dining room. "Would you prefer the garden room, Mr. O'Farrell? Or perhaps the small room, with four tables?"

"The small room will be fine, Robert." The maître d' slid the table away so that Mary could sit down on the banquette, with John next to her. She liked the way sitting next to John made her feel.

It was like being with an old friend, although better. When John made some point or other, he would put his hand on her arm for emphasis, and she liked that. By the time they were through with their first martini, she was touching him, too. "So, how are things going, John? How does everything look?"

"So far, so good. We're holding them off at the pass."

Mary told John how things were going for them,

about the great idea they'd had for the catalog offering exquisite, rare items for sale. About how it wasn't working. Hadn't worked, actually, since all that was left was Victor's jewelry, and all that was coming in was two thousand dollars a month sent by Raymond for the children.

"How about Max?" asked John.

"Oh, Valerie wouldn't take anything from Max," said Mary.

"I meant, is there anything going on between the two of them."

"I don't think so. Not yet, anyway."

"She's still waiting for Victor."

"Absolutely." Mary raised her glass in a toast. "To Victor Penn, wherever he may be."

"And what about you, Countess?" John touched his glass to hers. "I'm sure you're looking out for numero uno, or I don't know my girl."

"My girl." Mary felt a little tingle of pleasure at his words.

"I've put in every cent I had," said Mary. "I have enough money to pay the rent for the next couple of months, and that's it."

"You surprise me," he said, and Mary could almost feel his arm touching her own.

The waiter brought their appetizers. A salad of tiny shrimp, thin slices of avocado and papaya for Mary. A sweetbread salad for John.

"It was such a good idea," said Mary mournfully. "The best and the most beautiful things in the world, from the collection of Valerie Penn. If there was one thing Victor taught us, it was how to recognize the best."

"Yes, Victor certainly has impeccable taste," John agreed.

"Well, don't you think it's a good idea? The catalog?"

"Yes. Yes, I do. It's a brilliant idea."

"Well, what did we do wrong?"

"I think you need a business plan. That's what you're missing. With a long-range business plan, you can get venture capital. Somebody else's money."

"Oh, nobody is going to give us any money," sighed Mary. "We're just a couple of amateurs. Even when we go into a meeting at Sotheby's, or Christie's, we're treated like a couple of rich ladies playing around."

"But they would give it to me," John grinned.

"What do you mean?"

"The money. A venture capitalist would give the money to me."

"You mean you would be interested?" asked Mary, hardly able to believe what she was hearing, wondering if it were the martinis.

"Yes, I think so," said John. "I think it could work if you offer the service to people at no fee, and just take a commission when you sell something. That's how the real estate business works. Art auctions. Anything, really, where you're the middleman." He paused, tasted his salad.

"John, you don't realize how bad things are," Mary protested. "The phone is cut off. I was even going to charge the things I was picking up at the market."

"How much is the phone bill?" asked John.

"It's over four thousand dollars," said Mary sheepishly.

"Oh, that's nothing," said John, taking his checkbook out of his inside pocket. He wrote out a check and handed it to her.

"Oh, John," she said. "I can't take this."

"Fine," he said, "go without a phone."

Mary folded the check and put it in her handbag.

"Then, down the line, when we've got a track record," he continued, "that's when they'll pay to be in the catalog. It's all credibility, Countess. They'll be lining up."

He really could see the possibilities, Mary thought, sipping her drink. He was talking about renting office space in Westwood, or maybe Beverly Hills, for the address. Thinking out loud about structuring the business plan to be presented to the venture capitalists. All the time, his hand was on her arm, or her hand was on his arm. Mary felt his leg brush against hers for an instant under the table.

John was telling her why being a lawyer didn't satisfy him anymore. How law was always about somebody else and their problems, unless it was something like the United States Supreme Court, which was never going to happen for him now, considering the years he had spent with Penn International as his only client. Even when the Penn debacle was straightened out, if it ever was, the next client would probably be just as bad. He could quit. Walk away. Penn International would just drop another lawyer into his slot. Everybody was replaceable, after all.

Mary noticed that the other tables in the room were empty. Two waiters were chatting quietly. The maître d' stood in front of their table, smiling.

"Will there be anything else, Mr. O'Farrell?"

"Just the check," said John.

Standing in front of the restaurant, waiting for the parking lot attendant to bring the Porsche, John said he had something else he wanted to talk to her about.

"Yes," said Mary before he could say another word. "I want to go to bed with you."

"I'm pleased about that, Mary. Because going to bed with you is exactly what I'd wanted to talk about."

John's apartment was only a few blocks away from where Mary lived.

Some interior designer, maybe an old girlfriend, had done a terrific job, Mary saw. The living room had bleached wood floors, a couple of flagstone- and kidney-shaped tables, a curving banquette upholstered in white linen with pillows of all different sizes upholstered in the same fabric. There was a wall hanging by Claes Oldenburg, a box sculpture sitting on the coffee table, a seventeenth-century statue of some sort. There was a spiny cactus reaching nearly to the high ceiling in a corner of the room, one of its arms blooming with yellow flowers. A bedroom had been converted into a study, with book-lined walls, stacks of magazines, a big television set, and a wet bar with mirrored shelves filled with all sorts of glasses. The second bedroom was a conventional guest room with twin beds. The walls in the master bedroom had a heavy raked-paint finish, the king-sized bed covered by a tailored cotton spread.

Mary took off her suit jacket and hung it carefully over the back of a chair. John walked into the room, a glass of white wine in each hand.

"I need a shower," said Mary, taking the glass of wine from him.

"So do I." He leaned over to kiss her cheek. "You know, Countess, I may have forgotten how to do this. It's been a long time."

"They say it's like riding a bicycle. It comes back."

Mary watched John undress. She liked his broad

shoulders, and the curly black hair matting his chest. When he kissed her for the first time, his mouth tasted like the wine they were both drinking, and she liked that, too.

As he kissed her breasts, she ran her fingers through his thick, curly black hair, loving its texture. She thought of some of the others. Enrique di Stefano, and how she had thought she had died and gone to heaven when she managed to marry him. The odd tennis pro, the playboys, a movie star or two. Conquest sex, to see if she could. A couple of tycoons. A duke. A German count whose family owned vineyards that dated back nearly eight hundred years.

Then nobody. Not for a long, long time.

———

"Is that another one of your social skills, Countess?" John murmured a long time later, as Mary lay in his arms.

"What do you think?"

"Oh, absolutely," he said, stroking her hair. "Better than your tennis. Right up there with your chitchat at a dinner table. Better than that, even."

"You're not so bad yourself," she whispered in the dark, leaning over to kiss his shoulder, before drifting off into a dreamless sleep.

———

There was a pitcher of orange juice, eggs, bacon, and pork sausage, croissants for breakfast. Everything in the apartment was spotless, the furniture gleaming with polish, each leaf of every plant lovingly sprayed. A very good maid, John told her, as they sat in the enclosed patio high above the swimming pool and the gardens. He al-

ways called her when he was on his way back to Beverly
Hills so that she would stock the refrigerator with breakfast foods and see that there were fresh flowers in the
condominium. She had been with him ever since he had
moved to Beverly Hills from New York as an ancillary
worker to Victor Penn. An ancillary worker, but a highly
paid one. He had done just fine. He would bail out of
the firm a few months down the line, after structuring
the business plan for *The Collection of Valerie Penn*. He
would take with him everything he had acquired in his
pension fund and all the bonuses that had been piling up,
safe from the IRS.

Mary sat at the glass-topped table across from him,
wearing one of his robes. John had a lot of robes in his
closet, all of them, Mary guessed, gifts from women.
Robes were the sort of thing women always gave men
on their birthdays or at Christmas. She wondered who
had contributed the one she was wearing. It was maroon
silk, with a small fleur-de-lys pattern. In the best of taste.
Maybe the same one who had decorated the apartment.

"Would you like some more coffee?" he asked, his
hand on a handsome black thermos.

"You always talk about Victor in the present tense."
Mary handed him her cup.

"I guess I do," John said after a moment.

"Is it something you know for sure?" she asked cautiously.

He thought for a moment, glanced down at the
swimming pool where a workman was fishing out dead
leaves with a long-handled net.

"Well," he said, "I'm sure you can imagine what it
has been like over the last months. Meeting with investigators from different governments. Investigators on

every level. Criminal. Civil." He stopped again, searching for the right words. "They all talk about Victor as if he were alive."

"What about Raymond?" asked Mary.

"Raymond doesn't talk about Victor," he said. "Raymond doesn't have to talk about anything. There is no paper trail leading to Raymond. He can't be connected to Penn International."

"He really managed that," Mary said, admiration in her voice.

"He really did," agreed John. "Of course, he had some brilliant legal help from me."

"I'm sure he did," smiled Mary, raising her coffee cup to him. "What do you think, John?" she asked. "Do you think Victor is alive?"

"I don't know, Mary. I just don't know."

"Would you tell me if you did?"

"Yes, I would. For Valerie. So Valerie would know."

"Well, it's unlikely he's alive, or Valerie would have heard from him. Something, anyway."

"I've thought of that, too. I've thought of that many times."

Walking Mary back to her car, John put his arms around her and kissed her lightly on the mouth. She stood stiffly, wondering what he would say. About another meeting. About when they should all get together to talk about business. About the two of them. About how sensual, how passionate it had been for him when they had made love, the way it had been for her. About how he would be moving in with her that night. Or, why didn't she move in with him? About how they would be together forever. But she didn't want that. She didn't know what she wanted, but she knew it wasn't that.

"Well, thanks for dinner," Mary said, smiling up at him. "I'm really glad you decided not to go home last night and just scramble some eggs."

"So am I," he said.

"I'll have good news when I see Valerie. Thanks for the check."

"Oh, sure."

"That wasn't just conversation, was it?" added Mary. "About the business, I mean."

"Do you mean was it just a ploy to get you into bed?" He grinned. "You really don't have a whole lot of trust in men, Countess."

"I've never had any reason."

He kissed her again and hurried toward his car, turning once to wave good-bye to her.

35

Valerie didn't even realize she was regarding Max as a potential lover until she looked into the mirror after her bath one evening, and saw that she was unconsciously letting her pubic hair grow back. To see the fine golden hairs covering her mound of Venus after so many years made her feel as if she were already being unfaithful to Victor, even though Max had never so much as kissed her. The only times he had even touched her was when he would give her a friendly hug. Sometimes, he tousled her hair, too, the same way he tousled Rebecca's. With affection, or appreciation. Because she had made him laugh.

Other than that, nothing.

Valerie didn't even know if Max was interested in her, or if he was ready to be interested in anybody. His relationship with Karen was still very much on his mind. It seemed to him, as he went over and over it with Valerie, that he had given everything to the relationship he had to give.

With all of the pressure Valerie felt from the investigators, it was always such a relief when the phone would ring and it would be Max with tickets to the latest Disney screening, suggesting that they take the children and go out for a hamburger afterwards. Before too long, Max was calling to suggest that just the two of them have dinner, or that she accompany him to some black-tie benefit where he was to be one of the celebrity guests.

It felt good to spend an hour in her bath, to take the time to do her makeup, to pick an exquisite gown, and to have Mary coordinate her jewelry and furs. For a few minutes, anyway, it was just like old times.

She liked to be with Max. There was a comforting familiarity about him, and they had so much to talk about. Karen, of course. Victor. The children. His work, and her financial problems.

Valerie knew that Max saw other women. She saw photographs of him with them in the newspapers, and read their names linked together in the society columns. When he called her from New York and asked her to come to the opening of his musical, *A Tale of Two Cities,* she told him she would love to, but that she, Mary, Paul Gregson, and John O'Farrell had business commitments and she couldn't take the time. She sent flowers instead, a lavish spray of green cymbidium orchids.

It wasn't until the venture capital had been committed and they had settled into their beautiful office in a graceful old building in Beverly Hills that Valerie finally had a moment to think about anything besides work. What she found she was thinking about was Max Perlstein, partly because he was there, and partly because she felt so good when she was with him.

They were so different, Max and Victor.

Victor, so elegant, so incomparable. When they were together, his total concentration had been on her and the time they were sharing. There was a luminous quality about him, something quicksilver that she could never quite grasp. And of course, the lovemaking. She remembered the way she would lie awake and long for him, waiting for him to come to her and bring her alive.

So, if Max wasn't ready for a relationship, neither was she. She would wait for Victor. He was her love, her core, and the only man who had ever been in her life.

———

Oriental carpets partially covering a hardwood floor, fine English antiques, a Gainsborough painting accented the office of *The Collection of Valerie Penn*. Mary was on the telephone when Valerie entered the room.

Mary looked fabulous. Valerie watched her across her Sheraton desk, gesticulating with one hand, murmuring words of agreement with whoever was on the other end of the line. Her gray-streaked blond hair was cut just below the jawbone, and she wore a beige cashmere sweater with the sleeves pushed up, a charcoal gray silk blouse underneath. On the sweater was the gold and diamond brooch that John O'Farrell had given her a couple of months earlier.

"Max has invited the children and me to Sun Valley for the Christmas holidays," said Valerie as Mary put down the phone. "He has some friends who have a big house there. They've offered to let him use it."

"It sounds great," said Mary. "And the kids will have a ball, won't they? They really must miss being able to ski all the time."

"It's his turn to have Rebecca," said Valerie. "She was with her mother on Thanksgiving."

"Oh, no wonder you're hesitating," said Mary with a laugh. "I don't know that I would look forward to spending seven or eight days with Rebecca. Or seven or eight minutes, for that matter."

"Well, there's Kyle," said Valerie. "We always spend the holidays together."

"Oh, don't worry about Kyle," said Mary. "He'll be delighted. He has a hot invitation for Christmas, and he really wants to do it. He asked me if I thought it would be all right with you."

"Of course it's all right." Valerie felt a sting of disappointment that Kyle would prefer to spend his Christmas somewhere else.

"John and I are spending the holidays at his condominium in Aspen," Mary continued. "So, there we'll all be, out on the slopes, breaking various bones in our bodies and praying for the moment when après-ski is announced."

"That sounds wonderful, Mary. How is everything going?"

"Oh, it's slow, but sure. I've found the most exquisite light yellow diamond that's about to go to auction in San Francisco. It weighs nearly thirty-eight carats, and it's worth a million dollars, minimum. I think we can get it for the catalog next month. It will be quite a coup."

"I meant between you and John."

"Oh, we're just fine. We have a giggle."

"Do you love him?"

"We don't think in those terms, sweetie. We have a marvelous time together. We laugh a lot. Best of all, we're a team. We care about the business and about getting the job done."

"Do you think I should go?" asked Valerie.

"You mean to Sun Valley with Max? Why not? He's the oldest friend you have. And it'll be wonderful for the kids."

"You know," began Valerie, feeling the blood rush to her cheeks, "he's a man, and I'm a woman and, well, you know."

"But there isn't anything like that between the two of you," Mary prompted.

"Well, no." Valerie felt foolish.

"Well, what else would you do?" asked Mary. "Stay here and feel sorry for yourself?"

Valerie waited until she and the children had finished dinner that night to mention Max's invitation. They were delighted, running up the winding staircase to their suite to sort out their ski clothes and equipment.

Nothing fit.

Valerie had hundreds of outfits for lounging around in front of the fireplace after a day of skiing, but nothing to wear on the slopes. Victor hadn't permitted her to learn to ski because she might break an arm, a wrist, and he wouldn't allow her to take that chance.

The next morning the three of them visited the most

exclusive ski shop on Rodeo Drive in Beverly Hills and charged thousands and thousands of dollars' worth of ski clothes, boots, and accessories. Afterwards, Valerie took the children to lunch at an upscale coffee shop and watched them gobble hamburgers and French fries drenched with catsup, sucking their chocolate malts to the noisy end.

That night, Valerie thumbed through the Yellow Pages under "Physicians" until she found a women's clinic about thirty minutes south of downtown Los Angeles. Three days later, she lay with her legs apart, her feet in stirrups, as a gynecologist, without comment, snipped apart the narrow ring that for so many years had intersected the inner lip of her vagina.

"Do you want it?" the gynecologist asked Valerie.

"Oh, yes." She sat up on the table feeling oddly naked between her legs. She turned the ring over and over in her hands before returning to the tiny cubicle to dress. She paid in cash before driving home.

———

The twin-engine Beechcraft taxied to the airport building. A few people in bright-colored ski jackets and boots stood outside, waiting for friends to debark. The door popped open and Valerie followed Max, who held Rebecca in his arms, as they carefully picked their way down the aluminum stairs.

New snow glittering in the sunlight blanketed the landscape, the roofs of the chalets, and the Sawtooth Mountains on the horizon. The icy mountain air was like pinpricks on Valerie's face as she saw all of their luggage being loaded into a rented four-wheel-drive vehicle. The twins scrambled into the backseat, laughing and interrupting each other as they chattered away. Rebecca was quiet, looking out at the silent, white landscape, her big blue eyes wide with wonder.

The house was beautiful, a huge A-frame, with a three-story glass wall facing the mountains. In the living area, a roaring fire blazed and crackled in a huge stone fireplace. On the walls were bookshelves jammed with books, and paintings of American Indians. Indian artifacts were displayed in a hanging glass case. There was a Remington sculpture of a cowboy on a horse on the coffee table. The furniture was large and overstuffed. A huge fur rug lay on the floor in front of the fireplace. The housekeeper, a pretty dark-haired college student in jeans and a plaid shirt, showed them to their quarters. The twins were taken to the children's dormitory, a huge room with eight single beds and two adjoining bathrooms. Rebecca was to stay in a large bedroom with the housekeeper. Max had the master bedroom, with a broad view of the mountains. There was a huge bed with a massive oak frame, a fur rug, and more bookcases stuffed with books. The adjoining bathroom was cunningly done in turn-of-the-century western.

"Cute, huh?" grinned Max.

"Cute," she agreed, taking in the four-legged bathtub, the flocked wallpaper, the old-fashioned washbasin with its wooden cabinets. The lush towels hung on brass hooks molded like lariats, and the light shades were Tiffany glass. Looking closely, Valerie saw that they were signed Louis Comfort Tiffany, at that.

Her own room had a double bed with a down comforter, an oak bureau into which she unpacked her bulky sweaters, her shirts, and the lacy panties she had taken to wearing. The large mirror reflected endless miles of glistening snow outside, the mountains in the background. Valerie remembered the winter she had spent in the château at the clinic in Switzerland when Engvy was pregnant with the twins, their long walks with the snow crunching under their boots, and Victor arriving every other weekend to sweep her into his arms. The tears were hot in her eyes as she thought of Engvy, a doctor by now, married, probably with children of her own.

There was a knock on the door, and the twins burst in, laughing and bidding her au revoir before they clattered down the stairway, off to the slopes for the day.

It had been a good idea to come, Valerie decided, as she and Max jolted along in the four-wheel-drive, slowing for the skiers who sauntered across the street. They stopped at a market as well stocked as any on the west side of Los Angeles, filling two shopping carts with a goose and all the trimmings, plus eggs and sausages and bacon, freshly baked bread, and flaky sweet rolls with raspberry, lemon, and strawberry fillings for breakfast Christmas morning.

They picked out a tree, a ten-foot fir. They stopped at an old-fashioned dime store and bought silver, blue, red, green, and yellow ornaments, boxes of tinsel, and for the top of the tree, an angel with golden hair who, Valerie agreed, looked just like Rebecca.

Max set the tree up in front of the huge expanse of glass facing the snow-covered landscape. They trimmed the tree together with Rebecca, and the multicolored lights reflected in the window in the gathering dusk. The twins, rosy cheeked and exhausted, finally limped back in time for dinner, arguing heatedly about which of them had been the more daring during their day of downhill racing.

A freshly-laid fire roared in the fireplace, candles burned in their holders on the dining room table, and they all applauded as the housekeeper carried in the goose, browned to perfection, stuffed with a dressing of apples and prunes. There were tiny roasted potatoes sprinkled with fresh parsley, slivers of string beans. Vivaldi's *Four Seasons* played on the stereo. Valerie sat at Max's right and watched him expertly carve the bird and heap each plate. After dinner, Valerie sat at the piano, and they crowded around, singing, "Oh, Little Town of Bethlehem," "Silent Night, Holy Night," "Ave Maria."

It was nearly eleven o'clock before the housekeeper took Rebecca up to bed and the twins shuffled after each other up the stairs, gripping the handrail with happy fatigue.

Valerie sat on the rug in front of the fireplace, her arms clasped around her knees, staring into the flames. Max knelt beside her, a bottle of champagne in one hand, two glasses in the other.

"How about a glass of champagne, kiddo?" His voice was gentle, edged with weariness.

"Oh, Max," she said, looking up at him. "You're so kind to me. You're such a decent person, such a nice man."

"You're going to make me blush." He grinned, handing her the glasses, and twisted the cork. There was a pop, and foam flowing, and Valerie caught the spill with her glass.

"You've been such a friend," she continued as he sat beside her, raised his glass to touch hers.

"Well, I try to be. That's what it's all about, isn't it?"

"I don't know. I never thought about it one way or

another. There was always my music, my career. That didn't leave time for anything else, really."

"You coulda been a contendah, kiddo." He laughed.

"Oh, I don't think so. As soon as Victor came along, nothing mattered but him. I gave it up like a shot. You knew I was going to do it. You warned me on our wedding day."

"Well, it happens." Max gave her a hug. "That kind of money is pretty seductive. And managing that kind of lifestyle, well, even on my level, it eats up a lot of time. On Victor's level, there probably wasn't time for much else."

"Victor always wanted me to be there for him." She leaned against Max's shoulder. "He wanted me to be waiting, to drop everything to go someplace with him if he wanted, to be there when he got home."

"Yeah, well, a lot of guys are like that."

"There hasn't been anybody in my life besides Victor. He was the only one, ever. I never even kissed anybody else but Victor. Oh, there was a boy I liked when I was at the conservatory. We did a little wrestling in the backseat of his father's car. But it was nothing." She paused for a moment, and gave a little laugh.

"I should hope not," said Max with mock horror. "God, I don't even want to think about some punk trying to kiss Rebecca."

"Max," she said, "would you kiss me?"

He pushed her away and looked at her.

"Valerie, are you sure that's what you want?"

"Please, Max, just a kiss. I'm not asking you to run away with me to Sri Lanka."

He laughed, and took her into his arms. His lips on

hers were soft and gentle. Valerie put her arms around his waist and clung to him, feeling guilty but remembering how good it felt to kiss a man. How different it was from kissing Victor. Victor's kiss was erotic, a teasing first taste of all that was to come. With Max, a kiss was somehow more earthy. Valerie felt her breath coming faster as the two of them lay, their arms entwined, on the fur rug, their mouths locked. Valerie felt the heat of the flames on her feet and legs. She opened her mouth and embraced his neck.

Max kissed her hard, rubbed his cheek against hers. He hadn't shaved since early morning, and the faint stubble of his beard felt rough against her face.

"It's getting late," he said shakily, sitting up. "We had better call it a night, kiddo. Those little monsters will be up before dawn to get their haul."

Valerie lay on the rug, looking at him silhouetted against the fire, his elbow on one knee, and felt an almost overwhelming compulsion to throw herself into his arms, to beg him to hold her, and comfort her.

"Max," she said tentatively, "will you hold me? I mean, would you mind?"

"Sure, sweetheart," he said, reaching down and pulling her up into his arms. He petted her blond hair as if she were a tired child. "You've really had it, Valerie," he said, his voice so sympathetic that it almost brought tears to her eyes. "I understand, kiddo. It's been tough."

"Would you hold me all night, Max?" she asked, her voice pleading. "Would you hold me while I sleep?"

"Oh, Valerie. Of course I will, sweetheart." He kissed her awkwardly on the forehead. "Of course I will."

Valerie went to her room, bathed, and put on a nightgown and robe. Max was already in his pajamas and in bed when she tapped on the door.

He held out his arms to her. Slipping off her robe, she crawled into bed beside him, felt his arms wrapping around her waist. She fell instantly into a dreamless sleep, until she awoke with a start to the first rays of dawn bathing the room in pale gray. Turning on her elbow, she saw Max's back as he lay asleep. His head was buried in a pile of three down pillows, his breathing steady, slow. Valerie reached over and grazed his shoulder with her fingertips. She crept out of bed and, grabbing her robe, silently left the room.

Turning back the satin-covered down comforter on her own bed and pulling the sheets up to her throat, she couldn't remember when she had felt more refreshed.

How sweet Max had been to understand, she thought as her eyes closed. How good it had felt to go to bed in a man's arms, to feel protected again, shielded from the world.

36

Valerie was already stirring in her sleep, the smell of freshly brewed coffee drifting into the room, when the twins flung open the bedroom door and bounded onto her bed. Sleepily, she hugged them, felt their kisses on her cheeks, and told them she would be down in a minute. It was only after they had slammed the bedroom door shut that it all came back to her. That she had asked Max if she could sleep with him, had fallen asleep in his arms and awakened to find him next to her in bed.

She shook her head, wondering how she could have done such a thing, as she quickly showered, dressed, and hurried downstairs. Max was waiting at the foot of the stairs, a Polaroid camera in his hands.

"Smile," he commanded, and there was a flash of light.

"Merry Christmas," she said, averting her eyes, then walked with him into the living room where the twins and Rebecca were poised at their packages as if waiting for the sound of the starter's gun. Rebecca wore a little red Santa Claus suit and a Santa Claus hat with a bell. She smiled at Valerie, showing dimples. Valerie felt her eyes misting with tenderness as the camera flashed again. Outside the three-story window, fresh snow sparkled in the sunlight. A fire blazed in the fireplace. Valerie leaned over and hugged the little girl. The housekeeper came in with a tray loaded with cups, a thermos of coffee, muffins, sweet rolls, toast, a pitcher of freshly-squeezed orange juice, glasses.

It was fun, Valerie thought, to watch the children tear open their packages, toss the red, silver, and green paper into the fireplace to watch it flare for an instant before they opened the next gift. Alexandra was screaming with laughter, holding up the jeans Max had gotten her, the sweatshirt that read, "Los Angeles Philharmonic Support Team." Penny, very serious, was showing Rebecca how to talk to a teddy bear that repeated everything she said. Rebecca was gazing up at Penny, her blue eyes wide with love, her Cupid's-bow mouth ringed with jam from a half-eaten sweet roll discarded among all the wrappings, the ribbons. When she told her teddy bear that she loved him, it was with Penny's soft English accent. Valerie wiped away a tear as she watched the children playing, heard their shrieks of laughter; she was comparing this morning with the formality of the Christmas mornings she and Victor had shared, when Alexandra and Penny would open a gift, politely thank their parents, and neatly refold the wrapping paper to be whisked away by Gregson.

Buying anything for Victor had been among the most anxiety-producing events of the years she had spent with him. Months before a special occasion, Valerie would wake in the morning with her stomach churning, because what did one buy the man who, quite literally, had everything?

For Max, Valerie had found a letter written by Arnold Schoenberg to Thomas Mann. Schoenberg, famous for his atonal compositions, had very much influenced Max's own work. She watched the real pleasure on Max's face as he lifted the framed letter out of its wrappings, saw his expression of surprise and delight.

She caught her breath when she opened Max's present to her. It was a copy of the album she and Maria Obolensko had recorded all those years ago in London, mounted and framed the way his own gold records were.

"Where did you ever find it?" she asked him later, as they puttered along in the four-wheel-drive vehicle past the miles and miles of A-frame condominiums, each roof a white quilt of snow, on their way to the ski lift that would carry Alexandra and Penny to the top of the most expert run. She and Max would play in the snow with Rebecca who, still in her Santa Claus suit, was waving and smiling to the skiers trudging past them.

"Do you really like it?" he asked, turning to face her, studying her expression.

"I love it, Max." She saw from the way his shoulders relaxed that he knew she meant it.

"You're not exactly the easiest person to shop for, kiddo," he laughed, spotting a parking space.

"Neither are you." She smiled, realizing how good it made her feel to give somebody she cared about something that really pleased him. She did care about Max, she realized, feeling a wave of guilt over what she had done the night before, wondering how she could have done such a thing when she was Victor's wife. Mrs. Victor Penn.

It was dark at five o'clock. They were all tired from their day in the snow, the cutting wind that stung their cheeks, a bad fall by Penny, and Rebecca was long past her nap. Everybody devoured the Christmas dinner of golden brown turkey, sage and mushroom stuffing, mounds of mashed potatoes dripping with gravy, cranberry sauce, yams whipped with brown sugar, butter, and marshmallow, biscuits with butter and honey, tiny green peas, and creamed onions. Mince and traditional pumpkin pie followed dinner.

After the children went off to bed, Valerie lay, overwhelmed by fatigue and food, wrapped in a blanket on the sofa in front of the fireplace. Max, in jeans and a bulky sweater, sat on the fur rug studying the flames. He poured another glass of white wine for himself and turned to Valerie to see if she wanted more.

Valerie shook her head, content, thinking about what a wonderful day it had been. The best Christmas ever, she thought guiltily, with all of the children playing in the snow, the wonderful dinner, and Max, with his Polaroid, snapping pictures of every move they made. How different from the photographer who had all but lived with her and Victor when the twins were small, chronicling their days, developing his film in a darkroom constructed for him in the residence, a security measure so that no pictures of little Alexandra and Raymond Penn would end up on the third page of one of the London or New York tabloids.

Asking Max if she could sleep with him last night, well, that had been a weakness of the moment, a result of the strain she had been under. All those awful hours being questioned by the investigators from the Justice Department, the FDIC, the IRS. The money worries that never seemed to end. She didn't even want to think about the icy expression that would be on Paul Gregson's face when he saw the bills from the ski shop where she had outfitted Alexandra, Penny, and herself for the trip, and the bills from the stores where she had bought Christmas presents for Rebecca, Max, Mary, Kyle, and Daniel.

No, she didn't feel guilty any longer that she had spent the night in Max Perlstein's bed. They hadn't done anything, after all. He hadn't even kissed her. So, there wasn't a thing to feel guilty about.

Max stood, stretched, covered a yawn.

"Little boy, you've had a busy day," he said. "I think I'm going to go up."

"Mmmm," murmured Valerie, her eyes half closed, pulling the blanket up around her throat, luxuriating in the heat from the fireplace. She felt peaceful for the first time in so long, all troubles at bay, at least for the moment.

Max was standing there, looking down at her, one

thumb in the pocket of his jeans. Wordlessly, he reached out his hand.

"Do you think we should?" she asked tentatively.

"Same deal, kiddo," he said quietly.

She let him pull her up onto her feet. Leaving her hand obediently in his, she followed him up the stairs to the master bedroom and into his bed, where she slept like a child, safe in his arms.

———

Max made New Year's reservations for the two of them at the Sun Valley Lodge, the lodge in the old movies Valerie ran across when she flipped through the channels of the television set in the middle of the night, unable to sleep with worry.

Crimson ski pants, Valerie decided, and an exactly matching crimson cashmere sweater with long sleeves and a scoop neck. A simple pavé diamond and ruby necklace, diamond and ruby earrings. She twisted her wedding band as she decided on the full-length Russian sable, a gift from Victor two years earlier. Valerie cradled the coat in her arms, snuggled it against her face, and hurried downstairs to the living room where Max was sprawled on the sofa, watching television with Alexandra and Penny, who were already in their pajamas.

Both of the twins protested vigorously at being left behind like a couple of babies. There was Rebecca, of course, but she really was a baby, already in bed, fast asleep. They wanted to come along, too. Valerie kissed both of them good night, hugged them, wished them a Happy New Year, wondering if, perhaps, it hadn't been better when they were more docile, those perfect little children of not long ago. Finally, she and Max were out of the house, the cold air slapping their faces, and Max helped her into the passenger side of the four-wheel-drive vehicle. Somewhere in the night there was the tinny toot of horns, a cry of "Happy New Year."

The lobby of the Sun Valley Lodge was jammed with revelers. Valerie flinched as somebody threw a handful of confetti at them. Several of the people who had glanced in their direction when they came in recognized Max. She clasped his arm as they walked toward the hostess, a blond girl in ski clothes who looked as if she had graduated from high school the year before. She knew who Max Perlstein was, though, Valerie thought proudly. The girl led them through the crowded dining room, where everybody was tooting horns and calling New Year's greetings, to a booth with dark red leather seats, the table draped with a white tablecloth. A candle flickered in a miniature hurricane lamp. "We'll have a bottle of champagne," said Max to the waitress, another teenager in a jaunty skirt and white blouse. "The best you have."

Max ordered bottle after bottle of champagne. The eight-piece orchestra played standards from the thirties and forties. Somebody must have told the leader that Max Perlstein was there, because the band swung into a medley from the score that had won him an Academy Award the year before. Nearing midnight, they danced together to something slow Valerie didn't recognize, her head nestled in Max's neck, both of his arms around her waist.

At twelve o'clock, the band began "Auld Lang Syne," horns croaked, and guests threw streamers and confetti as they wished each other Happy New Year. Max leaned down to kiss Valerie on the mouth, his arms tightening around her. His lips were soft, and when Valerie opened her mouth to his, he tasted of champagne and longing.

"What do you think, kiddo?" The two of them clung together, rocking to the music, as the crowd milled and jostled around them.

"I think I'm very happy," she whispered into his ear, still feeling the shock of his lips on hers.

"You want to go?" His mouth was against her ear.

"All right."

"You're sure?" he insisted.

"I'm sure."

They didn't speak on the way home. The huge A-frame was in darkness, and the pale moon gleamed on the three-story window, and on the snow leading up to the front door. Clinging to his hand, Valerie followed him up the dark stairway and into the master bedroom. Valerie sat at the foot of the bed, her fur coat open. Max leaned down and kissed her mouth again. Then he stood up, stripped off his bulky sweater, and tossed it over the back of the chair.

"You're sure you're sure?" he asked softly.

She sat silently, her eyes closed, her hands clasped together on her crossed legs.

"I don't want you to do this because it's New Year's Eve, or because of the champagne. I don't want you to do this because you're lonely, or just because of anything."

She shook her head.

"And, no promises, Valerie," he continued. "I can't promise you anything."

"I know." Her voice was small.

"Look, there's the door," he said, gesturing toward

it. "Why don't you go to bed, and we'll talk about this again in broad daylight. When we haven't had three bottles of champagne between us."

Valerie slid off the bed. The fur coat dropped to the floor. Slowly, she wriggled out of the cashmere sweater and the ski pants and stood in front of him in her lacy white panties. She put her arms around his neck and leaned up to kiss his dry lips. He kissed her hard, forcing open her lips with his thrusting tongue. He held her shoulders and looked at her in the moonlight reflected from the snow outside.

"You're beautiful, sweetheart." His voice was husky, trembling, as he unbuttoned his wool shirt, threw it over the chair, and stepped out of his boots, his jeans. "Get into bed. I'll be right there."

Valerie sat up against the pillows as she watched him stepping out of his underwear. She saw his pale, flat buttocks, the long back, his sloping shoulders. She turned her eyes away as he moved toward the bed, felt his weight on the other side.

There had been an innocence about the nights they had spent together thus far, the terms defined. It was friendship, solace, not just for her but for him. Two old friends who shared a love of sorts. With a few words, the rules had changed. She looked over at Max, who was propped on one elbow. His blond curls were outlined by the moonlight, his face in the shadows solemn.

Tentatively, she reached over and touched his shoulder, and felt him recoil. She heard him take a deep breath as he took her in his arms and kissed her lips. She felt a small shock at his hand on her hip, peeling off the lacy white panties, leaving her exposed, vulnerable. His hand was between her legs, exploring, as he touched the lips of her vagina. She was dry, unyielding, her body protesting the stranger. Still, her nipple was erect under his mouth, and her legs parted as he stroked her.

"I don't think so, sweetheart," he said thoughtfully, pulling away.

"Help me, Max," she pleaded.

She pushed back the covers, and her hand found his flaccid penis. She held it, stroked it, felt it harden, as she kissed him, seeing Victor's face in her mind, feeling Victor's penis in her hand. Victor. Her love. Her core.

"You're right," she said, turning her back to him, wondering how she could ever have thought of doing such a thing. It must have been the champagne, the tension, the crazy loneliness.

Max wound his arms around her, and she felt the heat of his chest against her back, his penis relax again against her buttocks.

"Let's sleep, sweetheart." His voice was gentle as he kissed the back of her neck. "Happy New Year."

"Happy New Year, Max," she whispered, her face buried in her pillow.

In a moment, she heard his steady breathing. She wanted to dart out of his bed and rush down the hall to her own bedroom. She wanted to bathe, wash away his touch, the mouth on hers that hadn't been Victor's, on her breast, the hand exploring between her legs. Odd that she had never realized her body was a temple to the love she and Victor shared. Of course, it was too late now. No way to turn back the clock.

Max stirred in his sleep, and Valerie felt a familiar rush of tenderness for him. He felt good next to her. He groaned in his sleep when she reached under the covers to touch his penis. It was soft, of course, and so there wasn't any way to tell much about it. But it seemed to be large, like Victor's, the foreskin at its head circumcised. It hardened to her touch. Funny how powerful it made her feel to play with Max while he slept. She never would have dared to do such a thing with Victor.

Well, Max probably thought he was having a dream, a nice dream, Valerie told herself as she reached idly between her legs, rubbed her clitoris, stroked the inside of the lips around the entrance to her vagina, felt the wetness, her desire rising. Her fingers couldn't even find the place where the ring had pierced her. It was as if it had never been there. Valerie leaned down, took Max's penis in her mouth, ran her tongue over its head, sucked it, and felt it swell.

She leaned over and kissed Max on the mouth, running her tongue over his lips. She was already guiding his penis into her when Max opened his eyes and pulled her down on top of him, sucking her mouth as she sat astride him.

It hadn't been that good, Valerie thought later, lying beside him. It had been too much of a surprise. Both had been clumsy, like athletes trying to figure out each other's game. It had been too fast. What had been good was the next time, at dawn, when Max had awakened her with his hands between her legs, his penis hard as a rock against her buttocks.

They were figuring it out.

Later, when they were back in Beverly Hills, Valerie asked him if there had been others since he and Karen had separated.

"Only bimbos, sweetheart."

"Bimbos?"

"Yeah, you know. All of those little chicks who run

around, the ones who will drop their pants for anyone who has an assistant director credit on a television show that manages to make a cable channel some morning around three o'clock.''

"Well, with your celebrity, you must really have to fight them off.'' She tried to smile, to keep her voice light, unconcerned.

"Yeah, I'm a hot ticket,'' he said thoughtfully. "You know, I just can't understand them. I mean, what could it possibly do for them?''

"I'm sure I don't know,'' she said with a tight smile, her hand trembling as she picked up her wineglass. "Now, tell me,'' she said, changing the subject, "what does Rebecca's therapist say about her progress?''

That was what it was, much of their relationship. About the children, his domestic life and hers. Their work lives. The sex, of course. Hot and lusty, but their secret. They never shared a bed when the children were around. Max had promised her nothing. He was making no commitment. There was no reason to confuse the children.

Still, it was the no promises, the no commitments, that drove her nearly insane with jealousy. She knew that all of those girls were waiting, ready to jump on him, and there was nothing he had ever said or implied that would give him one guilty stab if he said yes to every one of them.

37

"Good evening, Mrs. Penn." The uniformed chauffeur was waiting for Valerie outside the American Airlines terminal at Kansas City International Airport.

"Good evening." She smiled as he helped her into the backseat of the shining black Cadillac limousine. When she traveled on business, which she seemed to do almost incessantly these days, Valerie carried a single suitcase. This time, though, she was continuing on to New York the next afternoon to meet Max for the Tony Awards, and the ball afterwards at the New York Hilton. Max's musical, *A Tale of Two Cities,* had turned out to be as fabulous as everyone had said it was going to be. All of the reviews were raves, and it was sold out for months. Critics and the Las Vegas money were betting it would be a sweep. Valerie watched the chauffeur through the window as he loaded her six suitcases into the trunk of the car. She leaned back, clutched the collar of her pale mink coat, and sighed. It had been a long day.

Valerie hurried through the crowded lobby of the Westin Crown Center to the reception desk, where the bellhop stood waiting. There was only one message at the desk, from her secretary confirming her appointment the next morning with Mr. Henry Mueller of ConAir, Inc., at ten o'clock. There was nothing from Max. She felt a sting of disappointment and wondered what he was doing that kept him too busy to call. Wondered with whom he was doing it.

Valerie registered, smiled at the clerk as she said good night, and followed the bellhop to the elevator. She would order a pot of tea from room service, and then call the children to say good night. She saw so little of them these days.

Both of them had been having problems.

There had been a meeting requested by the headmistress of Alexandra's school. "She's a lovely child," the headmistress said. "She's very intelligent, excellent at her studies. She's on the tennis team and the swimming team."

"Then what's the matter?" asked Valerie.

"She's very shy," the headmistress said. "She doesn't relate to the other children as well as we would hope."

"That's why I decided that she should come here," Valerie said. "She and her twin brother are so close that they seem to need only each other."

"There was her father's tragic death," said the headmistress.

"Yes, there was," Valerie agreed, lowering her eyes.

"Well, perhaps when the tragedy recedes in Alexandra's memory . . . " said the headmistress, letting the rest of her thought drift away.

"Perhaps," said Valerie.

Alexandra's nightmares, which had begun recently, seemed to be getting worse. In them, Victor would come and sit beside her on her bed and tell her he would be sending for them soon. Alexandra would rush into Valerie's room in the middle of the night, sobbing hysterically, and Valerie would hold her daughter, soothe her, telling her that everything was going to be all right, until, finally, the little girl would fall asleep in the king-sized bed.

The report from Penny's school was much the same. He was shy and remote, didn't relate to the other boys.

"But they must like him," said Valerie. "They've given him a nickname. They telephone him. They come over to play. He goes to their houses."

"He's too well behaved," the headmaster commented, "and he won't take any initiative."

Too well behaved. Valerie couldn't believe the headmaster's words.

"Well, discipline is viewed differently where he attended school in Switzerland, and he'll adjust, don't you think?" asked Valerie. "There have been so many major changes in his life."

"Of course," the headmaster had said, his voice comforting. "I'm very sorry about your recent loss, Mrs. Penn. It's a terrible tragedy."

"Thank you," said Valerie, as she had so many times, looking across the desk at him, meeting his eyes. He didn't think Victor was dead, either.

Penny didn't have nightmares. It would be during the day, or at night when Valerie was tucking him in, that he would suddenly ask her if Daddy was really dead and, if he wasn't dead, which was what all the other boys at school said, where was he? Why didn't he come home?

Valerie wanted to suggest that he ask his uncle Raymond when he phoned, which he did frequently. Instead, she tousled Penny's hair. "I don't know, darling. I just don't know."

The children were in limbo. And so was she.

Valerie would be sitting in some first-class lounge, waiting for a flight. She would catch a glimpse of the back of some man's head that was so like Victor's, even to the way his brown hair curled at the nape of his neck. Valerie would feel the blood rush from her face and her breath coming faster. The man would turn. Of course it wasn't Victor.

Max wasn't in his room at the Plaza when she called, still wasn't in when she tried an hour later. It was nearly two o'clock in the morning. She lay awake for hours, picturing him with someone else in his arms, kissing her, making love to her. Lay awake, vowing not to meet him in New York. Vowing never to see him again. If he wanted somebody else, that was fine.

Exactly at ten o'clock the next morning, Mr. Mueller's personal assistant ushered Valerie into the chief executive officer's large corner office. The huge windows looked out onto a golf course and a tranquil blue lake. On one wall were photographs of some of the private jets ConAir, Inc., had sold over the years to multimillionaires and major corporations the world over.

Henry Mueller rose from behind his glass and chrome desk and extended his hand. "Good morning, Mrs. Penn."

"How do you do?" she smiled, shaking his hand.

She saw that Mr. Mueller was in his middle fifties. He was dressed in a beautifully tailored gray suit and a maroon tie with a subtle white stripe. Gold cuff links caught the sunlight streaming through the windows.

"We were delighted when you telephoned, Mr. Mueller," she said.

"Well, I've been following *The Collection of Valerie Penn* with a great deal of interest." He smiled. "I liked that article I read about you last month. Very, very interesting. I thought we might fit right in."

"Thank you," she replied. "I hope we'll be working together soon."

"I understand from my wife and her friends that to have a copy of your catalog on the coffee table gives almost as much status as owning any of the things in it."

Valerie smiled, waiting for him to continue.

Henry Mueller leaned forward. "Now, Mrs. Penn, the DC-10 we want to feature in the catalog as soon as possible is currently the property of an Arab sheikh. As you can imagine, discretion is most important."

"Our operation is totally discreet," said Valerie, with a quick smile. She paused, watching his knowing nod. At this level all their clients had the same concerns. "Every item we offer has a special computerized code. If an individual on our mailing list is interested in an item in our catalog, the customer uses the code to access our electronic mailbox. The seller is then accessed through his computer system."

"That's fine," he said heartily. "Well, I suppose your people will be in touch with us to make the necessary arrangements."

"We certainly will," said Valerie with a smile as she rose. "It's been nice to meet you, Mr. Mueller."

"And it's been nice to meet you, Mrs. Penn," he said, taking her hand. "May I add that I was very sorry about your husband's death."

"Thank you," she said. Henry Mueller walked her to the door and opened it.

"How did it go?" asked Mary when Valerie called the Beverly Hills office from the airport VIP lounge.

"Max didn't call," said Valerie. "When I tried him at the Plaza, he wasn't there. He wasn't in this morning, either."

There was a moment of silence at the other end of the phone. "I meant the meeting with Mueller at Con-Air." Mary's voice was cold.

"Oh, it was fine," said Valerie, sensing Mary's annoyance. God, I'm like every other woman, she thought as she hurried to board her flight. I was a credible business presence in the meeting with Henry Mueller. But it isn't business that's on my mind. It's Max.

Oh, God, she prayed as the smiling stewardess led her to her seat in the first row of first class, please let me not ask him where he was. Please.

38

The entrance to the Plaza, old, imperial, with its ornately carved columns on either side of its massive doors, was familiar to Valerie as the chauffeur drove up. She glanced impatiently at her watch, and saw that it was nearly five o'clock. Max would be pacing the room, waiting for her, as anxious to see her as she was to see him. And, whatever happened, she wouldn't ask him where he had been the night before or that morning when she had called him from Kansas City and listened to the telephone ring until she couldn't stand it anymore.

Valerie knew that she was more beautiful than she ever had been in her entire life. She saw it in the glances of the men, the other women, as the doorman helped her out of the backseat of the limousine.

Walking up the stairs to the entrance of the Plaza,

she caught a glimpse of her reflection in the glass doors. She had always been tall, with that wonderful posture that Lady Anne Hallowell had beaten into her when she was a girl, and she was as slender as she had been as an eighteen-year-old bride. Her face was more defined now, the high cheekbones, the straight nose, the full, sensuous mouth. The big eyes, either hazel or green, depending, framed by the long, curly lashes. She had let her hair grow, too, and in the glass doors she saw the pale nimbus of it, a lion's mane surrounding her face, the matching pale mink coat, the long legs in sheer stockings, the narrow ankles, the long, slender feet in high-heeled shoes. I must admit I'm really a triumph, Valerie thought to herself as she strode into the lobby of the hotel, felt her feet sink into the thick carpet.

So, why did she almost burst into tears when the clerk at the reception desk said that Mr. Perlstein wasn't in the room?

"I'm sorry, Mrs. Penn," he said, as the bellhop stood beside the baggage trolley waiting expectantly. "There doesn't seem to be a message for you."

Valerie fumbled in her handbag, found a ten-dollar bill, and handed it to the bellhop.

"Would you please take those up to Mr. Perlstein's room?" she asked, giving him one of her best smiles. And, turning to the clerk behind the desk, she said, "When Mr. Perlstein comes in, will you tell him I'm in the Palm Court, having a cup of tea?"

"Certainly, Mrs. Penn," he said smoothly. "I'll be happy to tell him."

Why am I afraid to go up to the room, order tea, have a hot bath? Valerie wondered as the maître d'hotel led her to a little table for two not far from the orchestra.

Around her, well-dressed women sat in twos or threes, shopping bags imprinted with the logos of Bloomingdale's, Henri Bendel, Saks Fifth Avenue at their well shod feet. There were several well dressed couples, a smattering of men together. A couple of men alone.

Well, she didn't know why, but, on the other hand, she did.

Some bimbo would still be there, lying among the tangled sheets, savoring the conquest she had made the night before. Max Perlstein, supposed to take it all the next night at the Tony Awards. She looked impatiently at her watch, thinking she could go home. Come to think of it, she would go home. She was looking around for the waiter, when she saw Max striding across the room, looking rumpled and very tired, a big smile on his face.

"Well, hello, kiddo," he said, leaning over to kiss her lightly on the mouth before he sank into the chair next to hers. "You're looking like about thirty million big ones on the hoof. How was good old K.C.?" He paused for a moment, looking around for the waiter. "I've missed you," he said, looking back at her. "God, you look great."

Around the room, people were glancing their way and then putting their heads together, nodding. Yes, it was Max Perlstein. From the pictures in the newspapers, the magazines. The television talk shows. The orchestra leader raised his baton. Eight pieces started to play the overture from *A Tale of Two Cities*. A middle-aged woman in furs proffered a piece of paper, asked Max for his autograph. He was flushed with pleasure as he signed it and handed it back to her.

"I'll have a glass of white wine," he said to the

waiter hovering above them. "Do you want anything else, sweetheart?"

"No, thank you," she said coldly.

"I can't believe how screwed up things are," he said, leaning back in his chair, his hands in his pockets. "We're fifteen minutes over. The network is screaming bloody murder. The girl who's supposed to sing the number from *Let's Do Lunch* has laryngitis. It's chaos, total chaos."

"I tried to call you last night," she said, hoping her words were like a blade of ice penetrating his heart.

He took a long sip of the glass of wine the waiter put before him, and then set it down.

"I didn't get back here until nearly four o'clock in the morning," he said, smiling, as he covered her hand with his. "Those bastards at the League of New York Theaters and the American Theater Wing say no freebies, none at all. Do you know what that means at two hundred and fifty bucks a pop, and we've got fifty performers in the cast?" He paused and looked at her expectantly.

She sat silently, wanting to pull her hand away.

"Well, that's over twelve grand for tickets," he went on. "Try selling that to the money people. No way."

"What did you do?" she asked, leaning toward him, thinking how tired he looked with those awful dark circles under his blue eyes. But he was exhilarated, too. Valerie could feel the electricity emanating from him, the sheer, unadulterated joy of loving what he was doing. A couple of well dressed men walking by stopped to pat him on the back, to wish him luck the next night. Max smiled his thanks, his eyes filled with pleasure. He looked about twenty, Valerie decided, wanting to put her arms around him. Proud that she was sitting there with him.

"What could I do?" he asked, turning back to her. "I bought tickets for everybody. No way was I going to have any of the performers not be there. They did it, after all."

Valerie stared at him, fascinated.

"And, do you know what time I was out of here this morning?" he asked. "Six o'clock. I might as well be sleeping over at the theater. Save the hotel bill." After taking another sip of wine, he added, "But I couldn't have done that, could I? After all, I had to have somewhere to sleep with my gorgeous woman, didn't I? I couldn't very well fuck Valerie Penn in the back row of the Hellinger Theater."

He was looking at her, his eyes mischievous, his expression mock-serious.

"But, all I've been doing is talking about myself," he said solemnly. "Tell me about you. What do you think of me?"

The old actor's joke, Valerie thought, laughing as she leaned over to kiss Max on the cheek. God, he was a darling.

He glanced at his watch, the Rolex she had given him, with all the dials and hands that did everything.

"You know, we've got to be at the Meyerhoffs by eight o'clock. That's the latest," he said. "I don't know about you, but I'm bushed. Could you use a nap?"

"Yes, darling," she said. "I've bought a new dress for tonight."

"That's great, sweetheart," he said, scrawling his signature on the check lying on the table in front of them, adding a tip. "You'll knock them dead." He helped her out of her chair, took her elbow, waved to some people at the tables around them who broke into a smattering of applause. "I don't know how I got this lucky." He smiled, shaking his head. "All of this for *Two Cities* and the most beautiful woman in the world, too." He hugged her to him as the elevator in front of them opened its doors. "I must be doing something right," he almost whispered.

The room on the tenth floor was large, with a double bed, nightstands on either side of it, and a low table at its foot on which one of Max's suitcases was sitting. There was a sofa flanked by two chairs. A week's worth of the *New York Times, Variety,* and the trades from Hollywood were neatly stacked on the coffee table in front of the sofa, a lavish arrangement of tiger lilies, baby orchids, and ferns sat on the bureau. Valerie saw her reflection in the mirror hanging over it an instant before Max closed the door, pulled her into his arms, and kissed her hard on the mouth.

"If you're wondering who sent you the flowers," he murmured, nuzzling her neck, "I did."

He moved away from her, taking off his blue blazer, pulling his tie loose, unbuttoning a couple of buttons on his shirt and pulling it over his head. He stretched, yawned, and flopped onto the bed.

"You know, I'm seriously thinking about fucking you," he said. "What are your views on that?"

"Ummm, it sounds good to me," said Valerie, glancing toward the wall where her suitcases were stacked. "But I've got to unpack."

"Later," he said huskily, and she went into his arms, smelled the dried perspiration under the after-shave lotion, felt him almost quivering with fatigue as he pulled her onto the bed, fumbling with the buttons on the coat of her beige suit jacket, the zipper on her skirt.

When she was lying nude on top of the bed, he rose, undid his belt, stepped out of his trousers. They dropped to the floor, and he kicked off the loafers he wore without socks. Then he was back on the bed, holding her with one arm as he struggled out of his undershorts with the other.

He loomed above her, looking down into her face, before he leaned down and kissed her on the mouth, cupped one of her breasts in each of his hands, leaned down and kissed one nipple and then the other. Valerie stirred beneath him as her arms went around his neck.

She was ready for him, gave a gasp of pleasure as she wound her legs around his waist, pulled him down, found his mouth with her own. They moved together, finding their familiar rhythm. Valerie felt her breath coming faster as Max buried his face in her neck. Stopped. She felt the heavy breathing of his chest as it crushed against her breasts. Heard a gentle snore. She lay with his sleeping body on top of hers, his penis growing soft inside her body.

It had taken a while before they were good together, before they had learned each other's rhythms. In those first days, Valerie reacted the way Victor had taught her, lying there waiting for Max's touch, initiating nothing and holding back any reaction she had when they were making love.

"I'm not pleasing you," Max would say, disappointed.

"Oh, but you are," she would protest.

"I couldn't be," he said. "You never respond, you never move."

"But, Victor . . . " she began. "Well, I just want you to be pleased, darling."

"I don't care what Victor wanted," he said brusquely. "What will please me is being able to please you."

And, slowly, she had come to trust him physically, to move in rhythm with his body, to cry out when she felt the hot rush of orgasm.

She hugged him tightly to her, kissed the golden curls on his head, before she inched her way from under him and got out of bed to unpack the dazzling gowns she would wear during the two-day celebration of the Tony Awards.

───

In a figure-caressing beaded gown the color of her pale golden mane, a copy of a magnificent canary diamond necklace at her throat, matching earrings, Valerie stepped out of the bathroom into the hotel room where Max was just fastening the last of his onyx studs, and stood there until he became aware of her presence.

He stopped, looked at her appreciatively, and gave a long whistle.

"Is it all right?" She smiled, knowing that she had never looked better in her life.

"You're absolutely gorgeous, baby," he said, coming over to kiss her neck, to breathe her perfume. His eyes were glistening with pride as he held her away from him, examining her closely. "I love you, Valerie," he said.

"I love you, Max," she said, feeling the shock of his words. Of her own.

"We ought to do something about it, kiddo, what do you think?"

She pulled away from him, took a couple of steps into the middle of the room.

"I don't know if I'm free, Max."

"Valerie," he said softly. "Look how long it's been, and there's been nothing from Victor. There's a plot in a cemetery in London with his name on the headstone."

"Oh, Max," she sighed, sinking into one of the chairs beside the coffee table. "I just don't know."

"We're so right for each other, baby," he said, kneeling in front of her, taking one of her hands. "We have a great time together, don't we?"

"Oh, yes, Max. We do. We always do."

"And we're practically family," he reminded her. "We go way back. No surprises."

"I know," she said slowly. "There isn't anybody who knows me as well as you do."

"I still remember that scared little kid who came to audition for me." He smiled. "God, you were scared."

"I *was* scared." She laughed. "And I didn't play that well. But you took me on anyway."

"Oh, you were good," he protested. "Don't ever think you weren't. But, I probably felt something that I didn't realize. I probably felt that somewhere down the line we were fated for each other."

"Oh, you're being silly," she said as he took her hand to his mouth, kissed her palm.

"I always kept in touch, though, didn't I?" he said. "The Christmas presents all the time you were living with Lady Anne, the letters, the clippings I always used to send you."

"You were my lifeline," she said reflectively.

"There wasn't anybody else, not after my parents disappeared."

"And don't forget," he said, rising to his feet, smiling as he saw her pensive face, "I danced at your wedding. That's got to count for quite a bit."

"Yes, I suppose it does," she said, taking a deep breath, banishing the thought of Al and Vicki, banishing the thought of Victor.

"We'd better get out of here," he said, pulling her out of the chair. "Let's go see how our chances really look. Everybody will be at the Meyerhoffs. They always are. And those are the pros, the toughest audience in New York."

By the time Max and Valerie stepped off the elevator leading directly into the marble foyer of the Meyerhoffs' thirty-room penthouse apartment, it was already jammed with New York society, people with famous names and celebrated faces from all walks of the city's creative life. As they pushed their way through the crowd, the waves of expensive perfume mingling with the cigarette smoke, the excited conversations, the occasional screech of laughter, Bobby Short at the piano caught sight of them and switched from the tune he was playing to one of the three hit songs from *A Tale of Two Cities*.

Max was pulled away from her, engulfed by all his well-wishers offering congratulations, assuring him that the next night at the Tony Awards his show would take them all. That it would be a repeat of *A Chorus Line*. A repeat of *West Side Story*.

For the Tony Awards the next night, Valerie wore skin-tight black satin with a low décolletage, slit up the sides nearly to the knee. Her jewels were a blaze of dia-

monds around her neck, one important diamond bracelet, a ten-carat pear-shaped diamond ring on her right
hand. Her wrap was a black mink scarf that she could
wrap around herself three times. Scattered applause
greeted them as they made their way down the aisle,
found their seats in the rows where the *Two Cities* company was sitting.

And it was a sweep. Every time a presenter would
open an envelope the winner was *A Tale of Two Cities*.

In the backseat of the limousine carrying them to
the awards gala Max kept saying over and over that he
couldn't believe that *Two Cities* had taken it all, kissing
Valerie, hugging her, and telling her how much he loved
her.

The chauffeur opened the door and Valerie stepped
out, her furs wrapped around her shoulders, to a murmur
of appreciation from the throng. When Max stepped out
after her, the crowd broke out in applause, cheers, and
even a couple of the paparazzi stopped snapping their pictures for a moment to come up, shake his hand, pat his
shoulder, and tell him that they had known it all the time.
Valerie's eyes were wide with excitement as she watched
the crowd around him, saw the graceful way he was handling all of it with his usual, self-deprecating, charming
little shrug, as if to say, "Oh, anybody could have done
it. It just happens to be my turn, my fifteen minutes in
the spotlight."

He's really an angel, Valerie thought as she took the
hand he stretched out to her.

———

The forty-piece orchestra on the stage of the grand
ballroom was already playing the score from *A Tale of*

Two Cities when they strode through the doors. The glamorous crowd all stood and applauded, and it was ten minutes before Valerie and Max made their way through all the well-wishers to one of the *Two Cities* tables.

It was all so exciting that afterwards Valerie never could sort out the details of what had happened, of who had said what, who had been the most perceptive about Max's genius. The only thing she did remember was that at the very end, when the master of ceremonies asked Max to come up, cries of "Bravo" and "Author" brought Max to the stage. He had grabbed Valerie's hand and dragged her up the stairs with him, hugged her tightly with one arm as he took the microphone with the other.

"Thank you all," he began. "The Tonys belong to the cast, all the brilliant people behind the scenes, my investors, all you wonder women with your theater parties. And, as the frosting on the cake on this, the happiest, most wonderful night of my life, ladies and gentlemen, my friends, my peers, I have asked this beautiful woman, Valerie Penn, to marry me."

For an instant, Valerie stiffened with shock. When she looked up at Max, her eyes were wet, her face burning.

———

It was nearly three o'clock before Max was closing the door to their room behind them.

"You're quiet," he said, untying his bow tie and opening the top button of his shirt. "It was exciting, wasn't it? God, I can hardly believe it."

Valerie sat down on the sofa, her furs still wrapped around her shoulders. "Max," she said.

"What, sweetheart?" he asked, taking off his dinner

jacket, reaching behind his back to unfasten his black satin cummerbund.

"Do you really want to marry me?" she asked.

"Hey, what is this?" he said, grinning at her. "Do you want me to ask you on bended knee? Should I make an appointment with your father to ask for your hand?"

He walked over to her, tousled her hair, and leaned down to kiss her lips.

"Tell me, baby," he said, lowering himself onto the sofa next to her and putting his arm around her shoulders. "What's the matter?"

Valerie told him the rest of it, the part of the story he didn't know. About Cini Schuyler, the girl who was just out to have a little fun. About her unknown father, who was probably a member of the mob. That was what Vicki had told her, and, as Max knew, Vicki had always been a pretty good judge when it came to what was happening.

"Yeah, well, families," said Max at last, leaning back against the sofa. "They can be a bitch."

Valerie huddled silently, the black fur caressing her pale skin.

"Let me tell you a little something about my family," he said with a weary grin. "You know, when I was little, about the age Rebecca is, or maybe even a year younger, it was at the end of the Second World War. And do you know what it was like in our house?" He paused, and she saw the set of his jaw, saw the pain in his face as the memories pushed into his consciousness, found their way into words.

"All my mother did, may she rest in peace," he continued, "was pace the floor wringing her hands, or whisper on the phone to my aunts. You know my late father?

That big, successful philanthropist, that pillar of the community?

"Well, back then he was on his way to getting rich. The way he was doing it was by selling tires on the black market. And right about then, it looked as if he was going to be prosecuted. That was what my mother was so worried about, because he would have found himself in the slammer."

"What happened then?" asked Valerie.

"Oh, the war ended," he said. "He wasn't prosecuted. One tire store became a chain. Then it went to mufflers, batteries, the works." He leaned forward, drumming on the coffee table with the tips of his fingers. "Then he went public, and then he sold out for millions."

"It didn't have anything to do with you," she said.

"And your family doesn't have anything to do with you," he said. "That's my point."

"I guess not," she said doubtfully.

"You're a wonderful woman, Valerie," he said, patting her shoulder. "You have a lot of strength. Look at how you've come through this mess Victor left you with. And, you're raising a couple of great kids."

"Ask me again," she said.

"Ask you what?" he asked.

"Oh, you know," she said, turning her head.

"Will you marry me?" he asked, his eyes shining.

"Yes," she said, leaning over and kissing him.

"Well, I'm glad to hear it," he said, "because I'm really tired, and I want to go to bed."

"What a good idea," she said.

"And, if you're a very good girl, I'll let you come to bed with me," he said.

"And, if you're a good boy, I may take you up on your offer," she answered, relieved that she had told him the truth, and more relieved that he didn't seem to care.

———

When the waiter from room service came with breakfast the next morning, he brought all the morning papers. Valerie looked at the picture in the middle of the front page of the *New York Times,* which was directly over a two-column story headlined, *"A Tale of Two Cities* Sweeps Tony Awards." In the picture, Max was standing, an exultant look on his face, holding the Tony Award up in the air with his right hand. His left arm was around Valerie, hugging her to him. She looked at the picture of herself, at the tall, slender body in the skin-tight black satin dress, the jewelry sparkling, her mane of blond hair, at the adoring expression as she gazed up at Max.

The expression was the same as it had always been in pictures of herself looking up into the face of Victor Penn.

39

Valerie's office in the graceful old building in Beverly Hills that housed *The Collection of Valerie Penn* had French doors that led into the interior courtyard with its terra-cotta tiles, trees, shrubs, and neat flower beds. The walls of the office were a faint pink with a slight texture, the upholstered pieces covered in a flowered silk. The chimneypiece was a pale pink marble. There was a lot of pink, navy blue, and gray in the oriental rug, the gray picking up the granite veined with the pink of her desk, the round table surrounded by four Chippendale chairs for casual meetings.

The office is really glorious, Valerie thought as she sat at her desk a week after she had returned home with Max, a pile of letters in front of her to be signed. "I'll miss it," she sighed, smoothing her linen dress, which was almost the same color as her mane of pale hair. She stood up and strolled over to the doors leading into the garden. But I'll phase myself out over a year, then Mary and John can carry on, she thought.

She and Max hadn't decided where they were going to be married, but they were all going to live in Max's house in Holmby Hills. They were already planning to convert one whole wing on the second floor into space for the children, with a central living area, and bedrooms for Penny, Alexandra, and Rebecca.

The children had been delighted when she and Max had told them they were going to get married.

"Oh, Mummy, Mummy," Alexandra and Penny bubbled, throwing their arms around her in the living room of the guesthouse. "Oh, that's so wonderful."

Valerie kissed their cheeks as they wiggled in her arms. Then they rushed across the room to where Max sat, hugging and kissing him, too, as he beamed, looking embarrassed.

"We'll be a family," said Alexandra, as little Rebecca clambered onto her father's lap.

"Will you be my mommy now?" asked Rebecca.

"Karen is your real mommy, darling," said Valerie, her arm around Penny's slim shoulders. "I don't think she would like it if you called some other lady your mommy. So you just keep calling me Valerie."

"A little sister," said Alexandra, her face flushed with excitement, her blue eyes bright.

"It's smashing," Penny had pronounced. "Oh, I must say, I know we'll all be so happy."

Isn't it ironic that it's turning out to be Max and me, Valerie thought, walking back to her desk. Why, that was my secret fantasy from the time I was a little girl. "God, I love him," she whispered with contentment as she sat down to sign the first letter.

Max had dug in his heels when she had told him that Kyle had to come along, too.

"He's a grown man," Max had protested.

"He isn't," Valerie had said.

Kyle had been her teacher, and he had been with her all the way when Victor disappeared. He needed to be where he would feel safe, where he could decide what he wanted to do with his life.

And now she would have time again to devote to the Young Musicians Foundation, the Los Angeles Philharmonic Orchestra.

Yes, everything is going to be just fine. She smiled, remembering their conversation that morning about her engagement ring.

"You have such beautiful jewelry," Max said. "What kind of an engagement ring can I give you that would be half as good as what you already have?"

"It's all fake." She laughed. "Copies of what I had."

"That makes it easier," he said, putting his arm around her, cupping her breast in one hand. Kissing her hard on the mouth. Today Max was in Malibu, working with the producer on the details of the new film he was scoring.

The intercom on her desk buzzed, interrupting her thoughts.

"Yes, Kim," she said.

"Valerie, it's Jess Murphy from Penny's school on one."

"Hello, Mr. Murphy," she said, trying to put a smile in her voice.

"Well, hello, Mrs. Penn," said a hearty voice on the other end of the line. "Welcome back to Los Angeles. I saw you on television the other night at the Tony Awards."

"Well, thank you," she said.

"And, congratulations on your engagement," he added. "My very, very best wishes."

"Thank you," she repeated, wondering when he was going to get to the point, whatever it might be.

"Tell me, Mrs. Penn," he said, and Valerie felt her stomach clench with fear as she heard the difference in the shading in his voice, its tentativeness, "was there some appointment Penny had today that he didn't tell us about?"

"What do you mean?" she asked, her hand at her throat, her heart fluttering faster and faster.

"Well, was he going to the doctor, or to the dentist?" he asked. "The boys are supposed to check with the administration office if they intend to leave the campus before the end of the school day."

"You mean he's not there?" said Valerie, trying to keep the sound of panic from her voice.

"Well, he was in his history class earlier. But after the eleven o'clock break, he didn't turn up at his English

Lit class." There was a pause, a faint feel of disapproval, when the voice continued. "You know, Mrs. Penn, some of the boys can be very thoughtless about not letting us know when they have to be elsewhere."

Had the housekeeper, Kyle, or Penny himself said anything about a doctor's appointment, the dentist? Valerie ran over the twins' calendar of commitments in her mind. There was nothing. Nothing at all.

"He didn't have any appointments today, Mr. Murphy," she said, her voice trembling.

"Well, sometimes the boys go for a little walk down to the fast-food place at the corner," the voice said. "We try to stop them from doing it, but they do it anyway." He paused for an instant, then added, "Maybe that's what happened."

But his voice said that wasn't what had happened, Valerie thought, her mind racing wildly.

"What should I do, Mr. Murphy?" she asked in a little girl voice she hadn't heard from herself in a long time.

"I think you'd probably better get over here as soon as you can," he said kindly. "I'm going to call the police."

"I'm leaving now," she said, and hung up the telephone.

She picked up the intercom to the receptionist.

"Kim, Penny has disappeared from his school," she said, finding it hard to catch her breath.

"Oh, no . . ."

"They're calling the police. I've got to get over there."

"Oh, God," said Kim. "I'm sorry. I'll try to reach John and Mary."

"Thank you," she said and hit one of the outside lines to call Max.

"I'll meet you at the school, sweetheart," he said instantly. "It's at the foot of Ventura Boulevard and Benedict Canyon, right?"

"That's right," she said, gulping for air.

"Okay," he said. "I'm getting in the car, Valerie. I love you." Then he added, "Is there anybody there who can drive you?"

"No, no," she protested. "I don't need anybody to drive me. I'll see you there."

She almost went mad, keeping the powerful Ferrari in first gear as she made her way through the crowded business section of Beverly Hills, but at Sunset she put her foot down on the gas pedal and, in a record fourteen minutes, turned into the parking lot of the Yale School for Boys. Three black-and-white police cars were already parked near the administration office. Valerie hurried into the low brick building where she found Jess Murphy, several blue-uniformed policemen, and a detective questioning a couple of boys from Penny's history class. Both of them looked terrified, their eyes round, their faces dead white.

"I'm Valerie Penn," she said, walking up to the plainclothes officer, putting out her hand. "I'm Penny's mother."

"Lieutenant Carter," he said, reaching out a hand to shake hers. "I'll be with you in just a minute."

Everything had been the same as it always was, each of the boys maintained. Penny hadn't said anything about leaving to meet anyone. Neither of them had seen him at the eleven o'clock break. More boys were brought in, questioned, their eyes wide with fright, or excitement, as one after another all said the same thing. They hadn't seen any strange vehicles, or any strange people. Just the other boys, the masters, the maintenance men, the gardeners.

Somehow, Alexandra appeared, hurrying over to her mother, arms outstretched. Her eyes and nose were red from crying, her cheeks streaked with tears. How would they have known where Alexandra went to school? Valerie wondered as she held her daughter in her arms, stroked her dark hair, kissed the top of her head. Any of the other boys would have known, she decided. All anybody had to do was ask.

Then, Mary and John were hurrying into the room. Paul Gregson was there, too, and Daniel. Mary saw Valerie, eyes darting about the room, searching.

"What is it, sweetie?" Mary asked, holding her hand so tightly that Valerie could feel Mary's nails digging into her palm.

"Max was in a meeting in Malibu," she said. "I called him just before I left the office. He said he was leaving immediately to meet me here."

Valerie watched Mary's face, saw her calculating how long it would take Max to get from Malibu to the school. The corners of her mouth were white, and her eyes, when she looked at Valerie, were wide with alarm.

"John," she called to John O'Farrell across the room, where he was in conversation with the school's headmaster. "Max was supposed to be meeting Valerie here. He was leaving Malibu at the same time that Valerie left the office in Beverly Hills."

John nodded thoughtfully, ran one hand over his chin, and sighed.

"Is there a radio anywhere?" he asked the headmaster.

"No, no," Valerie cried. "Don't turn it on. I don't want you to turn it on."

40

Kyle, at his Steinway in the library, his third scotch and water of the day in front of him, was thinking that he sounded pretty good, that maybe he should get his act together and take it on the road, when the housekeeper came into the room and told him that there was something about Max Perlstein on the radio.

"*¿Dónde está?*" he asked obliquely.

"Come," she said impatiently.

Probably some movie deal, Kyle thought, picking up his drink as he followed her down the hall and into the kitchen, where the radio was playing mariachi music. He turned to look at the housekeeper, who gestured toward the radio, meaning, he realized, that he should flip the dial and see what he could find. It didn't take long. It was there, leading the first news broadcast he found.

"Max Perlstein, winner of two Academy Awards, several Grammy Awards, and, only recently, eleven Tony Awards for his first Broadway musical, *A Tale of Two Cities,* was killed earlier this afternoon when his car went out of control on a sharp curve on Sunset Boulevard. The car burst into flames after pinwheeling down a cliff. Witnesses said that Perlstein had been driving at dangerously high speeds."

"*Es muerte,*" said the housekeeper.

"*Muerte,*" said Kyle. The ice cubes in his glass jumped in his trembling hand.

"According to Mr. Perlstein's spokesman, Perlstein had been on his way to meet his fiancée, Valerie Penn, the widow of the late international financier Victor Penn, as Mrs. Penn's son, Raymond, had disappeared this morning. So far there has been no trace of the boy. Funeral arrangements for Max Perlstein are pending."

Kyle walked slowly back to the library, sloshed some more scotch into his glass, and lit a cigarette. Hitting the remote control on the television set, he saw the police barricades a few miles west on Sunset Boulevard, a shot from a helicopter of the black Maserati Max had loved so much, its mangled remains being lifted by a giant crane.

What the hell is going on? he asked himself, running a shaking hand through his hair. He looked at the car, thought about Penny disappearing from school.

———

It was a couple of hours and many drinks later before Kyle thought he had it figured out.

It was Raymond.

He had found out about Valerie's engagement to Max. Through Miss Furst, probably, who would have brought the papers, that picture of Max and Valerie at the Tony Awards and the news of their engagement splashed all over the front pages even in London. Raymond decided there was no way his brother's widow was going to marry anybody else, much less a composer of popular music. So, good-bye, Max Perlstein.

Penny was part of the same thinking. The kid was Raymond Penn, the heir to the name of Penn. That implied a lot, none of which included just being another nice kid in an expensive Los Angeles suburb. Raymond had said right from the beginning he wanted Penny to continue his education in Switzerland. He wanted to share Penny's time with Valerie on school holidays. He wanted to keep his hand in, keep the old influence going. Kidnapping Penny was the inevitable next step.

Kyle shook his head, staggered at how naive he and Valerie had been to think they could just pick up the pieces of their lives and get on with things after Victor disappeared. Find success. Find happiness. Find love—at least for Valerie. The key was Raymond, and the point was family honor.

We could all be killed, Kyle thought. He took the bottle of scotch with him as he staggered up the stairs to his room and fell on the bed.

———

There were all kinds of cars in the driveway outside, Kyle saw a few hours later when he looked blearily out his window. Valerie's Ferrari. Mary's old Mercedes-Benz. John O'Farrell's Porsche 928. A beige Buick that looked like a rental car. A couple of nondescript gray or beige numbers. A couple of black-and-whites.

He threw some water on his face and poured himself another drink.

Kyle weaved a bit in the doorway of the drawing room. Mary was there, looking haggard in a pair of jeans, tennis shoes, and an old sweater. John O'Farrell. Another blond guy about John's age, in a suit that looked as if he had been sleeping in it. A few other guys who looked like cops, or the FBI, or something. Probably the FBI, Kyle thought. When a kid was kidnapped, it was always the FBI. He stood there, grinning helplessly, wondering where Valerie was.

"Is there any news?" he asked.

"There's no sign of Penny," said John. "The police didn't turn up anything in the house-to-house search. The helicopters are still searching the whole area."

"What about the other kids?" Kyle asked. "Did any of them see anything?"

"One of them thought he saw Penny talking to someone, a Latin male in his late twenties," said John. "The other boy with him said that it was an old guy in his sixties."

"What do you think?" asked Kyle, turning to one of the detectives.

"We don't know yet," he said. "Logically, it would seem that the boy's disappearance must be connected in some way with the brake cable on Mr. Perlstein's automobile being cut. What the connection is, if there is one, we don't know."

So, the brake cable was cut, Kyle thought. Well, he would have bet the farm on that one. "When's the funeral?"

"Tomorrow morning at Forest Lawn," said Mary.

"The old black-suit trick again," Kyle croaked. "In this little social group, it's best to have it ever at the ready."

"It's at eleven o'clock," said John. "Family members only. We're not invited. Max's ex-wife was on the phone to Valerie, screaming that she had killed Rebecca's father." His mouth was tight with anger. "Cute, huh?"

"Where is Valerie?" asked Kyle conversationally. "She's usually around when we have these little gatherings. Or, has she gotten bored with the whole drill? Another engagement, perhaps."

"She's upstairs," said Mary. "With the nurse."

"Not feeling so hotsy totsy, huh?" asked Kyle, lurching over to the cart with the bottles, glasses, ice bucket, and mix on it, and pouring himself another tumblerful of scotch.

"Oh, she's okay, considering," said Mary. "It's Alexandra."

"Well," said Kyle, his drink running down his chin, "I think I'll just lurch up the stairs and say hello."

A nurse in white was just coming out of the door to the children's suite.

"Valerie," called Kyle, looking around the sitting room with its television set, tennis rackets in a corner, chessboard on a table where there was a game in progress. "Valerie, where are you?"

Valerie stood in the doorway to Alexandra's bedroom, a finger at her lips. Her face was ravaged. She put her arms around him.

"Oh, Valerie," he sobbed. "Oh, Valerie. I'm so sorry."

She walked with him to the sofa, held him in her arms as he sobbed, gulping for air.

"We were wrong, weren't we?" she said at last. Her voice was very low, reflective.

"Oh, Valerie, we were so wrong. So wrong."

"I still can't believe I was so stupid I didn't realize what he would do when he saw that picture. I've gone over and over it in my mind and, Kyle, I never gave it a thought. It was as if I had forgotten he existed."

"Who are we talking about here?" he asked hesitantly.

She stood up, pulled him to his feet, and he stumbled after her into Alexandra's bedroom. The girl lay still as death, her dark curls tumbling over the lacy white pillow. Her face was white, her blue eyes open, staring at the ceiling, seeing nothing. An I.V. dripped fluid into her small arm.

"Do you think we're talking about her father?" Valerie snarled. "Do you think her own father would do this to her? Do you think Victor doesn't know what Penny means to her?"

She turned away from the bed, her whole body shaking. "Raymond Penn," she said through clenched teeth. "I'll kill him if it's the last thing I ever do."

———

It was through a haze of shock later that Valerie realized John was introducing her to Sid James, a lawyer friend of his who was also a private investigator.

"Penny's uncle, Raymond Penn, is responsible for all of this," she said, then stopped for a minute, took a couple of sips from the glass of water in her hand, her eyes filling with tears. "I know he has Penny. He wouldn't let his namesake be raised by another man. That's how distorted he is." She paused again, fighting for control. "But, Max . . . Max was innocent."

"These incidents could be independent of each other," speculated Sid James, making notes on a little pad.

"Mr. James," she said coldly, "these two incidents

are related. Penny is with his uncle, either in London or wherever he has taken him. All you have to do to get Penny back is to contact his uncle."

"It isn't that easy," Sid James said, making more notes. "He may not cooperate. At the moment, there isn't any evidence linking him to your son's disappearance, and, Mrs. Penn, you're accusing him of murder. That's a serious charge, considering there is no evidence."

"I know I'm right," Valeric insisted. "He killed my husband, his own brother. I'm sure of that now. I would have heard from Victor before this if he weren't dead."

She bowed her head, sobbed into her soaking handkerchief, her shoulders shuddering with grief and rage.

"Maybe you should take a tranquilizer, Mrs. Penn," suggested Sid James, closing the notebook.

"Come on, sweetie." Mary put her arm around her friend's waist. "Come on. Let's go upstairs and see if you can get a little rest."

———

Two days after Penny's disappearance, Alexandra's doctor admitted her into the Children's Psychiatric Unit at UCLA.

Valerie sat beside her bed in the large, pretty room and held her daughter's limp hand. "Alexandra, my exquisite daughter," she whispered, looking at the child's empty face. Little Alexandra, keening for her lost twin when she made any sound at all.

"Oh, my darling, what do you have left? Your father died in disgrace. I tried to do my best, but it took me ten years. All you have is Penny. And now he's gone. No wonder it's all coming apart for you."

She looked at her daughter's body, still except for the barely discernible rise and fall of the blanket on her chest, saw the staring eyes, the I.V. needle taped into a vein in her arm. She put her head on Alexandra's hair, so soft, so fine, so like her father's, and she wept until there were no more tears.

———

A week later, Alexandra was sitting up in the hospital bed, able to watch television for a few minutes before her concentration waned. She was eating a bit, too. The staff was encouraged, Valerie was told by a nurse one afternoon.

"You're looking much better, darling," Valerie said brightly as she walked into Alexandra's room. There was a tinge of color in her daughter's cheeks, even though the expression in her eyes was still flat. "How do you feel?"

"Oh, much better, Mummy," she said quickly, dropping her eyes with embarrassment. "I'm sorry I was so much trouble. I do hope you'll forgive me, Mummy."

"Oh, darling." Valerie sighed, sitting down and taking the little girl's hand. She brought it to her mouth and kissed it.

"I can't think what the other girls at school must be saying," Alexandra said, her eyes far away. "They probably all think I'm such a baby."

"I'm sure they don't think anything of the kind, darling," Valerie said, waves of love for her daughter sweeping over her.

"I'm so sorry about Uncle Max," she said, her voice indifferent. "He did drive too fast, though, Mummy. I was scared sometimes. I really was."

"Yes, he did drive too fast," agreed Valerie, the tears ready to come, the way they always were when she thought of Max.

"Now Rebecca doesn't have a daddy either," she reflected. "Just like Penny and me." She turned her eyes toward her mother, in contact for an instant. "Isn't that too bad, Mummy?"

"Yes, darling, yes, it's terrible."

"Mummy," the little girl began, and stopped.

"What is it, Alexandra?" prompted Valerie, her look encouraging.

"It doesn't matter."

"Darling, what were you going to say?"

"Well, I was just thinking." The little girl hesitated.

"What were you thinking about, baby?" said Valerie, wanting for a moment to shake her.

"Well, I was just thinking about Uncle Raymond," she said at last, one finger twirling a dark curl.

"What about him?" asked Valerie.

"Well, I was just wondering why he didn't take me, too," she said apologetically. "I mean, if he took Penny, why didn't he take me?"

Valerie's muscles tensed. She started to speak, then stopped.

"Do you know something?" said the little girl, her eyes wide. "I wish he had, Mummy. I mean, I would miss you terribly. And Uncle Kyle, and everybody else, and my friends at school. But I wish he would have taken me, Mummy. I really do."

"Oh, darling, don't say that," cried Valerie. "The authorities are working on it. That nice friend of John O'Farrell's, Sid James, is a very smart detective. He's working on it, too. Penny will be home soon."

"Do you really believe that, Mummy?"

"I certainly do," Valerie said, her voice firm.

"We'll help each other, darling," she added, wishing she could think of something more positive to say. Knowing there wasn't anything.

———

Valerie had to hand it to Sid James. Through his London office, he persuaded Scotland Yard to call in Raymond Penn to assist them in their inquiries. A friendly judge even issued a search warrant, but no trace of Penny was found in the Belgravia mansion.

Valerie tried, too. She dialed the number she had for Raymond, but never got an answer. She wrote letter after letter, describing Alexandra's perilous emotional state, imploring Raymond to contact her about Penny.

41

Valerie adjusted her coral and pavé diamond earrings and smoothed the soft coral wool of her skirt. She stood in front of her suite's mirrored walls in the Beverly Hills mansion she had recently purchased. The face that looked back at her was now among the most familiar in America, pushed to a level of national recognition by a hurricane of television appearances, magazine covers, and stories in the national and international press. She paused for a minute, studying her reflection, then grabbed her Russian lynx coat and hurried downstairs to the waiting car.

As the chauffeur buzzed open the tall wrought-iron gates, Valerie opened her Filofax to check her New York schedule. She stared at the date on the page. It was a year to the day since Penny's kidnapping and Max's murder.

God, has it been that long already? She shook her head. Requests for interviews had come pouring in after her son's disappearance and Max's death. Valerie had protested against exploiting the memory of Max, and Penny's kidnapping, but Mary and John had advised her to do the Barbara Walters special, the story in *Time.* The new public relations person had polished Valerie's television skills and had sleekened her appearance.

With her increased visibility, *The Collection of Valerie Penn* began to soar. They had outgrown their offices and were in the process of moving to three floors in a new building in central Beverly Hills. When the time had come for all of the Penn International assets to be auctioned off, John, Mary, Paul Gregson, and Valerie took the presentation they had spent months preparing to the decision makers at the FDIC and the IRS. They had gotten exclusive listings on every item on the basis of Paul Gregson's plan to feed only five percent a year into the market to avoid flooding it.

Everything they had set out to do with the business had been accomplished. They were the biggest of the big time in their field, and, individually, very, very rich.

And, like it or not, it was all because of Victor Penn.

———

Valerie had telephoned Mrs. Wytton, the nanny who had taken care of the twins until they had gone off to school in Switzerland, asking her to come to Beverly Hills and be a companion to Alexandra until she was herself again. Alexandra was doing fairly well now. She went to school and saw her friends. She played tennis, swam, and her fencing was so good that her coach was even talking about the Olympics. Valerie realized that Alexandra was keeping herself so busy with physical activity that she never had time to think about the loss of Penny. Or her father.

In her own way, Valerie had done exactly the same thing. When Penny had disappeared, when Max was murdered, she had poured her energy into the business. Penny was constantly in her thoughts, and only the conviction that he was safe, with Raymond, kept her sane.

She was numb.

"Good morning, Mrs. Penn. I hope you have a pleasant flight," smiled a stewardess as Valerie strode aboard the plane. A second stewardess took her fur coat as Valerie found her seat on the aisle. Nodded her thanks as a stewardess handed her a copy of *The Wall Street Journal*.

"Valerie," said a man's voice with a bit of a southern drawl, delighted recognition.

She looked up at the man who stood in the aisle of the plane, at the lean, elegant figure, the shock of white hair incongruous with the youthful face, the innocent blue eyes, the cleft chin.

"Why, Harry Cunningham," she said. "I didn't know you were in Los Angeles."

"You didn't?" he said, looking amused, as he stepped past her, settled into the window seat next to her. "Well, I guess I better fire my press agent."

Valerie tried to remember where she had first met

Harry Cunningham. Perhaps in some greenroom back-stage before a television show, where Harry Cunningham was about to have his ego massaged as he parried with the host or hostess, maintaining, as always, that he would never allow any president to appoint him secretary of state. Valerie seemed to recall that he gave everything he earned to charity and lived off the income from his trust funds. It was the grandfather who had made all the money, wildcatting for oil in Louisiana. The father had thought it was crooked, or something, and had become a preacher.

Harry Cunningham, writer, lecturer, one of the intellectual movers and shakers. His icily reasoned diatribes were published in the *Atlantic, Forbes, Manhattan, inc.,* his syndicated column, and in his books. An attractive person, Valerie thought, more at home with the great, the rich, the celebrated than they were with each other.

Now where had she met him? Definitely East Coast. That was Harry Cunningham's native habitat, at least when he was in the United States.

"Bring me a shot of cognac, would you, please?" he asked the stewardess. "A three-star Hennessey will be fine."

Cognac with his coffee at nine o'clock in the morning, Valerie thought, remembering more about Harry Cunningham. A bit of a drunk. A barroom brawler who occasionally took a punch at a photographer.

She opened her copy of *The Wall Street Journal*, still unable to recall where they had met for the first time.

Over his second cognac, Harry Cunningham decided he wanted to talk.

"You must spend a lot of time flying between Los

Angeles and New York," he said, falling into his familiar interviewing style. "What takes you east this time?"

"I'm appearing on the *Today* show in the morning." Valerie smiled as she realized she had also immediately fallen into her interviewee mode, her gaze fixed on Harry's face.

"Now, what's the strategy there?" he asked. "Is it because the corporation is after new markets? Has something spectacular come your way that you want to boast about?"

"It's really just general maintenance at this point," she replied. "Since the government picked us to handle the disposal of the Penn International assets, we're rather in the position of, say, the Getty Museum. They have such a huge endowment, fifty-four million dollars a year, that, if they were greedy, they could outbid any other museum or private collector in the world. They could end up with, literally, everything. That isn't the way they do it, though." She paused, the way she usually did when she was delivering this particular speech. "We feel the same responsibility. We have so many items in our inventory that, if it were all to be offered for sale at the same time, the market would be ruined for decades."

"So, your television appearances, your lectures, are a matter of corporate goodwill," he suggested.

"That's right," she said. "I'm the image, a sort of walking, talking trademark."

"How do you like that role?" he asked lazily, enjoying the game he knew they both were playing.

"It's a dirty job, but somebody has to do it." She laughed.

"No, seriously," he protested, with a little wave of his hand. "I really want to know."

He's good, Valerie thought, looking into his blue eyes, so clear despite the two cognacs. He really did make her feel as if he wanted to know, the mark of the great interviewer.

"Well, it was hard to get used to," she admitted. "I did my first interview when I was fourteen years old. I was a pianist then, something of a child prodigy. I won a competition, and that attracted some attention from the press."

"Yes, I do remember reading that," he said.

"I dissociate myself from what I'm doing," she said. "It's the only way I can bring myself to do it."

"What does that leave for you?" he asked.

Valerie glanced at the front of the cabin, where the stewardess was locking the movie screen into place. She turned to Harry Cunningham, and smiled before she turned away.

"Nothing," she said at last.

"What are you going to do about it?" he asked.

"I'm not going to do anything about it," she said. "I'm just going to go on. I've worked very hard for what I've achieved, and I'm proud of that. Being the image for the corporation may not give me any satisfaction, but it's part of what I do. I'll make my appearances. I'll hope that my daughter finally faces her father's death and her brother's disappearance, instead of just pretending they never existed." She paused for a moment, wondering what there was about Harry Cunningham that had brought all of this out.

"I'm sorry," he said, and she knew he was sorry, sorry for her, sorry for what had to be done to survive.

"Your father didn't sell out, though," she said, calling on details of his life that she had read about or heard him refer to on television.

"He was a brilliant preacher," said Harry in a thoughtful voice. "He believed in everything good for mankind, and that was how he lived his life. Rigidly, according to the Good Book."

"He must have been a wonderful example for you," she said. "I envy you."

"Don't," he said shortly. "Everything he ever did was a reaction to his own father, the crook. He took the course he did because my grandfather overwhelmed him. Because he knew he would never be half the man my grandfather was."

"You don't talk about this on television." She smiled.

"It was really awful, as a matter of fact," he said brightly. "Church every night. Three times on Sundays. No radio, no television, no movies. He was so afraid that if he deviated at all from the most fundamentalist point of view, his world would all shatter into a million pieces."

"And yet, he let you go," she prompted.

"Yes, the best schools. Choate, and then Princeton. His son had to be an educated man." He smiled again. "I didn't see my first movie until I got to Choate. *The Bridge on the River Kwai,* with Alec Guinness and William Holden. I was so excited I knew I'd never forget it as long as I lived."

"You know," she said several hours later, after lunch had been served, "I've been trying to remember where we met, and I just can't."

"So have I," he said with a sheepish smile. "I was just starting to think that maybe we hadn't met, that maybe it was just secondhand, through television and magazines."

"This really is funny," she said, her eyes glittering, alive with pleasure. "What a commentary on the times."

"Well, I ran through every place it could have been," he said. "New York. Washington. Los Angeles. Places in Europe. Then I even thought it might have been at Raymond's, but, of course, it couldn't have been. Raymond and I are always the only ones there."

"Raymond?" Valerie felt her ears start to pop as the plane began its descent.

"Raymond Penn," he said.

"You know Raymond?" she asked, incredulous. "You know Raymond Penn? You've been in his house?"

"Well, yes," he said, surprised. "I've known him for a long time. Ten years or so."

"Do you mind if I ask you how you know him?" She tried to make it sound like the most natural question in the world.

"Oh, it was over some article of mine in *Harper's*," he laughed. "He wrote me an anti-fan letter, disagreeing with every one of my conclusions. I can't even remember what the article was about. Roland Barthes and semiotics. Something like that."

"And you wrote back."

"Yes, I wrote back. In fact, he was right and I was wrong. Then I was in London on some seminar, and he read about it in the *London Times*. He called me at my hotel and asked me to come and have supper with him at his house." The city was visible in the gray dusk below them. Overhead, the No Smoking sign blinked on.

"He's a recluse, and he doesn't go out," Harry added. "Of course, you know that."

"Yes, I know that," she said, trying to absorb that he and Raymond knew each other, and that Harry had actually been in the house in Belgravia. She saw Penny's face in her mind. "I need to talk to Raymond. Do you think you could arrange it, Harry?"

"Why do you need me?" he asked, surprised again. "You mean he won't talk to you?"

"He never thought I was good enough for Victor," she said in a voice ugly to her own ears. "I have to reach him, Harry. He has my son. I know he does."

"Oh, Valerie," he sighed. "My God. I'm sorry I've upset you."

"Harry, I have to talk to Raymond," she pleaded. "I've telephoned. I've written him dozens of letters. I've sent him telegrams. I just don't know what else I can do."

"Listen, Valerie," he said. "My car is waiting at the airport. Why don't I drive you into town and we can talk about it on the way? Even have dinner tonight, if you're free."

"Oh, my car is waiting, too," she said distractedly.

"Well, are you free for dinner?" he pressed.

She nodded, feeling hope for the first time in months.

The plane touched the runway, the jet engines roared, and passengers began to gather their belongings as the plane bumped along on the way to the terminal.

He was only a few inches taller than she was, Valerie noticed as they strode along together to the baggage area, where their chauffeurs were already waiting at the carousel. There was something compact and feisty about him, a belligerence repellent at the same time that it was attractive.

They shook hands at the curb outside the terminal,

as the chauffeurs loaded their luggage into their limousines, and agreed that he was to pick her up at the Pierre at eight o'clock.

The maître d'hôtel at the Four Seasons couldn't do enough for them. He led Valerie and Harry Cunningham to a banquette in the Pool Room and moved the table so the two of them could sit down.

"Could you bring us a bottle of Roederer Cristal?" Harry asked. The maître d' smiled and said he would attend to it at once.

Valerie looked around the pretty room with the large, shallow pool in the center, the celebrities occasionally dabbling a surreptitious hand in the water, the huge arrays of flowers, the vast expanse of windows.

"You're sure you wouldn't rather be in the bar," said Harry.

"No, I love it here," she said. "I always have."

"Yes," he said. "It's a nice room. And, if they don't make it as a restaurant, they can always turn it into a bank."

He really is amusing, Valerie thought later, a little giddy from the champagne. He's not at all the sarcastic intellectual he seems on television.

"What do you think of Raymond's house?" he asked as he toasted her at dinner, their champagne glasses ringing.

"I've never been in it," she admitted. "I've always had visions of cobwebs and dust. Miss Haversham's bedroom. That sort of thing."

"Oh, it isn't like that at all," said Harry.

"Well, what's it like?" she asked.

"There are a lot of books."

"And a torture chamber."

"No torture chamber," he said, smiling wryly. "If there is a torture chamber, it isn't part of the grand tour."

"That's odd," she said thoughtfully. "I was so sure Raymond would have a torture chamber. Somehow, it suits him."

"Maybe it's in the basement," said Harry.

"Well, they always are, aren't they?" she pointed out. "Where does he keep the dolls?"

"What dolls?"

"I've always heard he has a collection of dolls."

"Books," he reminded her. "Lots of books."

"Right," she said. "Books. Harry, about Penny. Can you help me? I know Raymond has my son, or at least knows where he is . . . " Valerie pleaded, tears welling in her eyes. "Every clue has led nowhere. The police have put the case aside, but I'm his mother. I know he's alive, and Raymond has the answers. You're the first hope I've had in a year. Harry . . . can you?"

Harry squeezed her hand and brushed a tear from her cheek. "I'll call him first thing in the morning, Valerie. I'll see what I can do."

———
———

It had been a long time since she had laughed so much with anybody, a long, long time since she had had so much fun, Valerie thought. She was back in her suite, returning Mary's call. There was the tail end of laughter in Mary's voice when she answered the phone.

"I was just wondering if you planned to drop into the New York office," Mary said.

"Oh, yes," said Valerie. "Right after the show in the morning."

"Good," said Mary. "They're anxious to put on a presentation for you, show you what they're doing." John's voice came from somewhere in the background, shouting hello. "How's it going?"

"Oh, fine," said Valerie. "Harry Cunningham was sitting next to me on the plane. He took me to dinner at the Four Seasons."

"The barroom brawler," laughed Mary. "Did he punch you out?"

"He's really awfully nice, Mary. All southern charm, and a real gentleman."

"Oh, sure, Valerie," said Mary patiently. "His second wife had him arrested for assault and battery. You do remember that, don't you?"

"Oh, he explained all of that. She's Italian, very hot-tempered. Really, he's very sweet. He's going to be at the Sloane-Kettering benefit tomorrow night, too."

"Well, I'm sure you will give him the pleasure of a dance," said Mary dryly.

"And, Mary, you're not going to believe this," she continued, "but he knows Raymond."

"Our Raymond?" Valerie could hear the interest in Mary's voice.

"Yes, he goes there for dinner when he's in London. He and Raymond have long, philosophical conversations."

"That's interesting. This could be the first break about Penny, couldn't it?"

"That's what I thought, too," said Valerie. "Oh, Mary . . ."

"We'll have to go slowly, sweetie. Don't do anything about it until you get home, all right? Maybe John should call Sid James and tell him about it. God, a personal contact to Raymond Penn. It could be a real break."

"Harry promised that he would come up with some sort of a plan. I'm sure he will, Mary."

"Well, it sounds as if you had a wonderful time," said Mary after a moment.

"Oh, I did," enthused Valerie. "I can't remember when I've had so much fun."

42

Valerie was already out of the shower and putting on her makeup in the bathroom of her suite in the Pierre when the phone rang with her wake-up call. She had slept fitfully, if at all, all her thoughts of Penny. Could Harry Cunningham somehow convince Raymond to let him come home? How? She had tried to envision scenarios all night, and she hadn't come up with a thing.

The *Today* show interview was a breeze. Riding on her elation about Penny, she was even better than she usually was.

Once out of the television studio, Valerie stopped at the Fifth Avenue offices of *The Collection of Valerie Penn* to meet with the small but dedicated staff. A group of winners, she thought, pleased with their enthusiasm.

By the time she was back in the limousine, it was mid-morning, the traffic bumper to bumper, the sidewalks swarming with pedestrians. Arriving at the hotel, she realized she could lie down and close her eyes for half an hour before getting ready for her luncheon with an important art dealer.

Valerie glanced at her box behind the reception desk, saw that there were no messages, and checked her watch. The office in Beverly Hills wouldn't even be open for another hour. A man's voice said, "Mrs. Penn?"

Valerie turned to see a young man in top hat, white tie, and tails, holding a red, heart-shaped candy box. She took a step away from him as he started to sing "Girl of My Dreams." Some of the other people in the lobby smiled, and others stopped for a moment to listen. He grinned as he finished the song, handed her the heart-shaped box, and danced away.

———

She put the box down on a table in her suite and looked at it with wary distaste, then went into the bedroom to hang up her sable coat, ease off the high-heeled lizard pumps. Finally she untied the silver ribbons, lifted off the top, and saw a small, white envelope sitting on a chocolate bed. She read it aloud. "Girl of my dreams, I've finally found you. I'll see you tonight. Save the first dance for me, the last dance for me, and all the others, too. Harry." Valerie's eyes welled with tears. The meeting with Harry Cunningham wasn't supposed to be about the two of them. It was supposed to be about Penny.

She sat down, her brow furrowed, and stared at the wall without seeing it. She remembered how much fun she and Harry had had the evening before when it hadn't been about Penny, but about him and her. There was something there beyond his acquaintance with Raymond. There was a spark.

But it had to be stopped before it started, she decided, reaching into her handbag for her Filofax. She called TWA reservations, changed her flight, and canceled her appointments for the rest of the day. Even though Raymond had Penny, there was still Victor's honor, family honor, to be upheld. The fact that Raymond considered Harry Cunningham a worthy intellectual adversary wasn't enough to keep him alive.

An hour later, she sat in the back of the limousine, deep in thought, as the chauffeur maneuvered through traffic to JFK for her flight back to Los Angeles.

———

The organ-grinder came first, right out of Central Casting, with a big, black mustache, a gold earring, a red bandanna, and a tiny monkey who enchanted the office staff while the man ground out "Girl of My Dreams."

The music box was on the third day. It was antique filigreed silver, with a red silk interior cushioning a glowing tear-shaped crystal.

A singing dog was next.

On the fifth day came a chorus line of five girls and five boys, all strutting and kicking in unison as they sang "Girl of My Dreams."

A pizza was next. The delivery man bustled into Valerie's office, his head down, giving the impression of a large nose and big glasses with dark rims. He waited while she opened the flat white box. Inside was a deluxe-sized pizza, the words "Girl of My Dreams" spelled out in flat anchovies.

She looked up at Harry Cunningham, just as he was removing his Groucho Marx nose and glasses.

"You can't say that I'm not persistent," he said.

"I really liked the singing dog."

"Yes," he agreed. "I thought that was a nice touch."

"I don't want to do this, Harry."

"Well, why don't we give it a try and see how it works out?"

———

Harry was staying, as usual, in a pink bungalow at the Beverly Hills Hotel. Valerie sat in a nondescript beige station wagon, usually used by the housekeeper to run errands, in a parking place twenty steps away. In the glow from the streetlight overhead, she looked in the rearview mirror and saw that her lipstick was fine. She wished that she had never agreed to have dinner with him.

Harry had suggested that they dine at Chasen's, but Valerie insisted that whatever they did together had to be discreet. Even as she had dressed in the pale gray cashmere top, the gray wool trousers that were an exact match, she had fought with herself to keep from canceling.

Harry opened the bungalow door at her tentative tap, a wide smile on his face. He was wearing a striped shirt, a pair of pleated trousers, and narrow Italian shoes.

"Where are the acrobats?" she asked, feeling his eyes taking her in.

"No acrobats," he smiled. "But caviar and champagne. Vodka."

"I'll take the champagne," she said, looking around the cozy room with its chintz-covered sofa and matching curtains, the stacks of *New York Times* that reminded her, with a sudden stab, of Max.

"I'll take the vodka," he said.

"I thought you would," she said, sitting primly on the sofa, crossing her long legs as he popped the champagne and poured a glass for her. He toasted her with a half-filled glass of vodka and ice before replenishing it.

They made stilted small talk about presidents and secretaries of state, about the trip Harry was to make to Europe the next week for high-level meetings with dignitaries in the governments of England and France, and the economic summit he would be attending in Brussels. They discussed the yacht that had belonged to Aristotle Onassis, perfectly restored, that had come the way of *The Collection of Valerie Penn* and had been sold even before the contracts giving them the exclusive listing had been signed.

Harry ordered dinner from room service, Maine lobster for him, grilled salmon for her, and a couple of bottles of pouilly-fuissé. At the tap on the door, Valerie went into the next room, where she stayed until she heard the front door close.

They started to relax a little with the rest of the champagne. After dinner Valerie kicked off her sandals and curled her legs under her, as Harry leaned down and kissed her on the mouth.

"I'll call and have all this debris cleared away," he murmured against her lips.

"Oh, just put it outside. Everybody does."

"You sound experienced, madam," he grinned. "Do you spend a lot of time in this bungalow with strange men?"

"Whenever I drive down this street I always see tables sitting outside the doors, waiting to be taken away."

"Well, I'm glad about that," he said. "I wouldn't want to think of you in this bungalow with any strange man—except this one."

Holding her hand, Harry led her into the bedroom and took her into his arms. She had to make an effort not to pull away. She could feel his penis hard against her body through the fabric of his trousers.

"God, I want you," he whispered, clinging to her, as she stood stiffly in his arms. "Tell me you want me, Valerie. Tell me."

"Oh, Harry." She pulled away. "Maybe we better not. I don't know how I feel about this."

He leaned against the doorjamb, crossed his arms in front of him, and looked at her for a minute. Two minutes.

"Tell me what you thought about when you were dressing to come here," he said at last, his southern drawl more pronounced than it usually was.

"What I was thinking about was that I should call and cancel."

"But you didn't," he pointed out.

"No, I didn't."

"So, you knew you were having dinner with a man who is very attracted to you," he continued. "You must have known that. It took me a lot of time to teach that dog how to sing 'Girl of My Dreams.' " He grinned, a wonderful, infectious grin.

"Did it?"

"Oh, yes. He couldn't get the chords at all. He wanted to drop the whole thing and go with something

classical. *Pagliacci,* he suggested. More his style. Well, I
wouldn't hear of it.''

"Oh, Harry. It was wonderful of you to stand up
to him like that.''

"I suggested we have dinner at Chasen's,
L'Ermitage, Spago,'' he continued. "You didn't want to
do that. No, you wanted to have dinner here. Just the
two of us, a couple of bottles of champagne, and a bedroom right through the door.'' He stopped. "Valerie,
what was I supposed to think?''

"I know.''

"Well, what do you want to do? You can leave. Or,
you can stay.''

"I'll stay,'' she said, her voice meek.

"Fine. Now, let's go to bed, because what I want
to do more than anything in the world is make mad, vio-
lent love to you.''

There was a quality about Harry Cunningham, a
self-confidence, almost an arrogance, that had made
Valerie think he would be a wonderful lover. She took
off the cashmere top, stepped out of the trousers, and
waited for him to come to her. He kissed her, unsnapped
her gray satin brassiere, and removed it carefully. As they
stood, he cupped her breasts with his hands and leaned
down to kiss one pale, pink nipple, then the other.

"Beautiful,'' he said huskily. "More beautiful than
I had imagined.''

As she stood there, he sank to his knees in front of
her and reverently peeled off the brief bikini panties. "A
natural blond,'' he said, looking up at her. "I would have
bet on it.''

She stood transfixed. He seemed to be all penis, his
narrow shoulders, hairless chest, slender legs and arms

barely able to support his erection. He took her hand and led her to the bed, pulled back the covers, and watched her lie down and wait for him. He slid onto the bed next to her and was tentative as he took her in his arms and kissed her again on the mouth. His hands were practiced as he caressed her breasts, his mouth eagerly sucking on her erect nipples. Valerie looked down at his shock of white curly hair and felt herself responding to the fingers sensuously stroking her clitoris. His caresses enflamed her senses, awakened desire so long denied.

She lay drenched with sweat, with longing, her legs spread to receive him, before he mounted her. He paused, his hands entwined in her hair, his penis caressing her wet vagina.

"Tell me you want me, Valerie," he whispered urgently, his lips hardly touching her. "Tell me."

"I want you, Harry," she moaned. "Oh, please, please. Yes, I want you."

He thrust into her, and she felt her own heat, her first shuddering orgasm as he moved faster, his cries announcing his own orgasm, the spurt of his semen.

He held her afterwards, running his fingers through her tangled hair, traced her profile, outlined her breasts, her body.

She heard his breathing, slow and steady, as he slept, and wondered how she could have gone so long without this.

Silently, Valerie stole into the bathroom and hurried into her clothes. When she left the bungalow, she pulled the door quietly closed behind her until she heard the click of the lock.

———

Harry was on the phone at eight o'clock the next morning, his voice purring with contentment.

"Did I dream all that?" he asked. "Were you really here?"

"Oh, yes," she whispered into the receiver. "I can still feel you, Harry. It's so nice."

"Why did you leave?" he asked. "I wanted to wake up with you, darling. I reached out for you, and you weren't there."

"I had to get home, Harry. There's Alexandra, the staff. I thought you would know that."

"Well, I forgive you," he said lazily. "What about tonight?"

"Same time, same place?"

"I can't wait."

She felt herself wanting him again. Right then. Right there.

———

He was wearing an exquisite dark suit, a striped tie, and he still smelled of soap from his shower when he opened the door to Valerie at nearly eight o'clock that night. She stood, clutching the collar of her full-length lynx coat, tendrils of her long golden hair caught by the gentle breeze.

"Hello, you glorious creature," he said, kissing her on the lips and leading her into the living room. "We've got dinner reservations in a half hour. That'll give me just enough time for a nip at the vodka bottle, and we'll be off."

"I've got a better idea," she said softly, moving away from him.

"Oh, what's that?" he asked.

Slowly she turned, her coat whispering to the floor. She stood nude except for her high-heeled sandals, her body, perfumed and oiled, gleaming in the soft light.

She heard him suck in his breath.

"I've been thinking about you all day, Harry."

"Oh, God, darling," he said, stepping toward her. "I've been thinking about you all day, too. About touching you. About making love with you. About how much better it would be the next time. And the time after that."

He was already taking off his jacket, stripping off his tie, as he followed her into the bedroom, his eyes never leaving the long glorious legs, the swell of her buttocks.

The four remaining nights that Harry was in Beverly Hills, Valerie appeared close to eight o'clock, tapping on the door. Under her lynx coat she would be wearing a nightgown, ivory, with spaghetti straps and lace inserts, or black satin. Lilac. On his last night, she was nude again.

"You know," he said later, as they lay in each other's arms in sheets wet and tangled from lovemaking, "I've never had anything like this, not since I was a very young man."

"What's that, darling?" she murmured contentedly, kissing his neck, tasting the salty dried perspiration with the tip of her tongue.

"Well, always in the past," he said, "whether it was with my wives, or the women I was involved with, I always had the feeling that they were with me because of who I was, the public figure. But with you, I don't feel that way. You don't care about any of that. It's as if you care just about me, being here, alone. That's never happened to me before."

"Oh, darling," she said, kissing his jaw. "I feel the same way. We're our own secret, here in our own little place."

"I think there's a song to cover this." He laughed, tightening his hold on her.

"When we find out what it is," she said, feeling his penis hardening under her touch, "we must teach it to the singing dog."

"Some other time, my darling."

43

Harry called her every day from Europe and, once his plane had landed in New York City, he begged her to come the next day to see him, or the next. Anything.

"This weekend," Valerie said into the receiver. "Alexandra is going to be spending it with a girlfriend. I was worried about her going, but her therapist says it's a good idea. That it will build her confidence."

"Oh, darling," he said, "that's wonderful. There's a gala benefit at the Waldorf-Astoria on Saturday night. Bring your prettiest dress. I can't wait to show off my beautiful girl."

"No, let it just be us," she protested. "I'll come, Harry, but only if we stay in your apartment. I just want to see you, darling. I can see those people anytime."

"Oh, sweetheart," he sighed. "You're so wonderful. I've never known anything like this."

Valerie told only Kyle about her trip to New York. She flew coach, paying cash for her ticket and using her maiden name. She wore the simplest cloth coat she had, no jewelry, a scarf over her pale hair, and dark glasses. Arriving in New York, she signaled for a taxi and gave the driver the address of Harry's Olympic Tower apartment.

Harry was waiting for her at the door, had barely closed it behind her before he was holding her in his arms and kissing her. He tore off her coat and fumbled with the buttons on her beige silk blouse. They made fierce, fast love on the oriental carpet in the entryway. Harry was sobbing, his eyes tightly closed, as he spurted into her. He lay across her, panting, their clothes a jumble around them on the floor.

"Welcome to New York," he finally managed to say, kissing her closed eyelids, her smiling lips, inhaling the faint perfume that lingered in her tangled hair.

———

She didn't awaken until nearly noon in his king-sized bed. At its foot were a pair of Louis XV benches. On the tables on either side, a pair of carved-wood griffins had been converted into lamps.

Harry stood in the open doorway leading into the bedroom wearing a blue silk dressing gown. He was holding a silver tray with a silver coffeepot, and a crystal pitcher filled with orange juice that glittered in the bright sunlight streaming through the curtains. Valerie smiled at him and flung one arm across his pillows. "Good morning, darling."

"You know," said Harry finally, looking across the room at her, "I think the most beautiful thing I've ever seen is you, lying there in my bed, and knowing in my heart that you're all mine, and that you always will be."

She didn't get to see the rest of the apartment until he had taken her again. When she was glowing from her shower, wrapped in one of his robes, they went through to the grand drawing room on the first floor. The room was breathtaking, with crystal chandeliers and formal sofas, a copy of a Louis XVI chimney piece that *The Collection of Valerie Penn* had bought from a French count. The dining room was charming, with walls and curtains in a subtly patterned linen, the furniture in the manner of Louis XV, with oversized armchairs and a large parquetry-topped table seating eight. The huge study, also on the first floor, was jammed with books, stacks of papers, and manuscripts. A word processor sat on a table that ran along an entire wall. The kitchen was all stainless steel, equipped with a hotel-sized stove and more cooking equipment than Valerie had ever seen. Next to the kitchen was the suite in which the housekeeper lived during the week.

Along the wall, beside the winding staircase, were several superb Impressionist paintings. Besides the master bedroom, with its black marble bathroom and Harry's walk-in closet in which there must have been two hundred suits, as many pairs of shoes, and shirt and sweater drawers, there were two more bedrooms, one obviously used as a guest room, the other as a backup library, every inch of it jammed with books and file cabinets.

Holding hands, they strolled back to the master bedroom. They looked out the window at the skyscrapers, towering apartment buildings, and condominiums of New York. Far below, the people of the city swarmed, the size of ants. The traffic on the street was a colorful, slowly moving snake.

"It still takes my breath away when I look out this window," said Harry, "even after all the years I've lived here."

"It's the most perfect apartment in the world." Valerie nestled against him as his arm encircled her waist. "Oh, Harry, who would want to be anywhere else?"

He leaned down and kissed her, and she saw that he was getting hard again.

———

There was a minor skirmish on Sunday afternoon when he wanted to send her to the airport in his Rolls-Royce. "Harry, no. I'm tired of all that."

"How can you be tired of all of that?"

"Try to understand, darling." She stood in the doorway, holding her single piece of luggage, leaning up to kiss him good-bye.

"I'll come down in the elevator with you. Walk you to the front door like a well-brought-up southern boy."

"No."

The short weekend had been so much fun, she thought in the elevator, tying her scarf over her pale hair, slipping on the dark glasses. Dinner the night before had been "Lutece-to-Go," picked up by the chauffeur. Brunch that morning had been "Tavern-on-the-Green-to-Go," a mouthful, Harry had laughed, which was what one could also say about their brunch.

They played games, conjuring up fantasy dinner parties where the guests would be people, living or dead, they wanted to meet. Alexander the Great. Greta Garbo. Sigmund Freud. George Bernard Shaw. Or, dinner parties where everybody had the same last name. Sherlock, Larry, Oliver Wendell, and John Holmes. Michael, Andrew, and Jesse Jackson. Ulysses S. and Cary Grant. They watched television, giggling and touching, and holding hands. They read each other passages from their favorite books.

Most of the time, they made love. Endless, tireless love.

Our little den of iniquity, Harry called the apartment. "I'm going to call my decorator tomorrow," he said, "and get us a mirror for the ceiling over the bed. I don't know why I didn't think of it before."

"Oh, Harry," she chided, smiling.

She was always smiling.

He was starting to press her, though. He wanted to see her house, and meet Alexandra and Kyle. She made vague excuses. He didn't like it, but he accepted it.

"You know," he had said, "if this is a game you're playing to intrigue me, you're really succeeding."

"It's not a game," she had answered.

———

He sent her stuffed dogs, one with a music box inside that played "Girl of My Dreams." Porcelain dogs from Austria, when he was there for meetings. A fluffy dog wearing a polka-dot dress, a topaz and diamond necklace wound several times around its neck. Postcards from Hong Kong and Singapore and Washington, D.C., where he was spending more and more time.

The private line on her bedroom phone was ringing as she hurried along the upstairs corridor, dragging her sable scarf on the carpet as she rushed to answer it.

"Hello, girl of my dreams." Harry was calling from the spartan bedroom of the *pied-à-terre* he kept in Washington, D.C.

"Oh, Harry." She smiled. "I'm so glad it's you, darling."

"I've been calling you every ten minutes for the last two hours," he said mildly, but she could hear a slight slur in his voice.

"Oh, I went to a benefit," she said. "It was all very last minute. Some friends had a table, and a couple they had invited dropped out. They called."

"How was it?" he asked. "Did you have fun?"

"It was quite grand," she said. "It was for Saint John's Hospital, at the Beverly Wilshire Hotel. The ballroom looked marvelous, with all these tall orchids and burning candles as centerpieces. Barbra Streisand sang, and you know what it takes to get her to do anything. The chair said they raised over three hundred thousand dollars, so it was wonderful."

"You should have called me," he said slowly. "I would have flown out and escorted you, darling."

"Oh, Harry, there just wasn't time. I didn't even know about it until five o'clock."

"Who did you go with?"

"Well, I didn't go with anybody," she said, hearing the defensive note in her voice. "They had somebody pick me up, of course."

"Who was it?" he demanded.

"Nobody. Somebody's son. An attorney."

"Are you going to see him again?"

"Harry, why are you doing this to me? Why would I see him again?"

"I guess I'm just a little jealous," he said, the smile back in his voice. "I guess I would like to walk into a ballroom with you on my arm, Valerie. I think about that once in a while."

"Oh, darling, I wish you were with me. Right now. I'm so happy that we're together."

"I don't know that I would call this together," he said, his voice thoughtful.

He didn't tell her he loved her as they said good night.

Maybe he's going to stop seeing me, Valerie thought as she lay awake in bed, her mind whirring as the hours passed. It's natural for Harry to want to go out to dinner, to walk into a party with me on his arm. But I can't take the chance that something might happen to him because of me.

She was relieved when Harry didn't call the next day, or the next. It's best for him, if not for me, she mused. But I wish I didn't miss him so much.

"I'm in London," he said when he called a few days later. "I've just left Raymond Penn."

Her hand clenched the receiver.

"Valerie, I'm convinced he had something to do with Penny's disappearance," he said. "He was just a little too casual when I brought it up. But I got the feeling the boy is fine."

"Did he say that?" Her voice was faint.

"It was something I sensed. You know, listening beyond words."

"Did you tell him about us?"

"I didn't do it like that. It was just part of the chitchat, sort of, 'Wasn't that terrible about your nephew, and what do you think happened?' That sort of thing."

"You didn't mention me at all?"

"Not a word."

"Thank God," she whispered.

"Darling, I've been invited to the Red Cross Ball in Monaco. What do you think? Does it sound like fun to you? Would you like to come here, and we can fly over together?"

Valerie had attended the Red Cross Ball several times on Victor's arm, exquisite, bejeweled, the reflection then of his wealth and power.

"I can't, Harry. We're in the midst of important meetings."

"Okay," said Harry, his voice edged with disappointment. "I'll call you when I get back to New York tomorrow night."

Harry had started to tease her when he would find her name linked with some available man around town, or a picture of her with somebody in the society section of one of the ten or twelve newspapers he read each morning as he flipped the television set among the three network news shows.

"You know, I'm starting to feel just like some backstreet hooker." The purr in his voice was tinged with querulousness. "You go out with all these guys, but I'm the only one you go to bed with. Is that it? Or are you fucking them, too?"

"I'll see you at the apartment tomorrow night. You know that, darling. Please don't do this to me."

"I don't know what I'm doing to you. I don't see why a simple statement of the facts is doing something to you. Oh, darling." He sighed. "I love you."

Valerie's last appointment the next day was nearly an hour late, and she fought the traffic on the way to the airport. She spent nearly a half hour circling through the levels of the parking structure before she found a space for her nondescript car. The plane was an hour late taking off, and ran into heavy weather halfway through the trip. She shuffled through the terminal, lugging her single suitcase, feeling as though she had been traveling for a month.

Outside the terminal, the gutters were flooded, and the rain beat a steady tattoo on the asphalt of the street. It was another fifteen minutes before she got a taxi, and, when they got to the bridge, traffic in all eight lanes was backed up as far as she could see. Eventually, the skyline of New York City, the occasional twinkling light, became visible through the heavy mist and rain.

"You know, I've been trying to think where I've seen you before," said the driver of the cab, a heavyset man chewing on the stub of a dead cigar. "And it finally came to me. You're Valerie Penn, ain't you?"

"No, I'm not. Other people have said that, though."

"It's a compliment, lady," the driver assured her. "She's a great-looking broad, I'll tell you that."

"Well, thanks," said Valerie.

Finally, they pulled up at the Olympic Tower. She pushed the fare and a big tip into the driver's waiting hand. Harry will probably be worried, she thought, rushing to the elevator bank in the soaring indoor atrium, grateful that there was an elevator waiting. As the doors slid shut, she ripped off her scarf and tried to push her damp hair into some kind of order. She had just enough time to apply a little lipstick before the doors opened onto Harry's floor.

It took only a minute to let herself into his apartment and close the door behind her. Harry loomed in front of her, his face mottled with rage. She cringed at the fury in his eyes, the snarl on his lips as his hand lashed out and slapped her across the face.

"What did you do, cunt?" he demanded, hitting her again. "Stop somewhere for a quickie on the way? Some stud you picked up on the plane, maybe? One of those nelly boys you go dancing with back in Beverly Hills?"

"Harry," she gasped, touching the corner of her mouth where it was already beginning to swell, feeling a trickle of blood. "What . . ." She staggered back against the table in the entryway, grabbed it for support, suddenly found herself lying on the carpet at his feet in puddles of water, strewn flowers, shards of china.

"Oh God, my head," she thought, as she felt the searing pain. Dazed, she looked up into Harry's stricken face.

"Oh, my God," he moaned. "What have I done?"

It was the last thing she heard before she lost consciousness.

———

It was still raining steadily, and the light in the master bedroom was as gray and clouded as Valerie's mind. Her whole body ached, and she knew her mouth and eye were swollen. She buried her head in the pillow, trying to remember what had happened, what had brought it on.

She felt Harry standing over her, and then his hand, tentative on her hair.

"Darling," he said. "How do you feel?" It was his

soft, southern voice again, so rational now, full of unspoken apologies.

"I've made coffee," he pleaded. "Here, darling. Drink some coffee. You'll feel a lot better."

He was gently moving her aside, sitting beside her on the bed. Leaning over to kiss her hair, her ear.

"I never want to see you again, Harry," she whispered, struggling to sit up.

"I'll make it up to you," he implored. "I promise you it will never happen again."

She turned away as he leaned over, trying to kiss her on her mouth.

"It's just that I love you so much, Valerie." He began to sob. "I can't stand the thought of you being with anyone else. It was getting so late. I'd had all that cognac, and all of these wild thoughts started to push against each other in my mind. I kept remembering those pictures of you with other men. I kept seeing you in bed with them, doing what we do together."

She felt his body shake the bed with his sobs.

"You've got to tell me why you won't be seen with me, Valerie," pleaded Harry, taking huge gulps of air as tears coursed down his cheeks. "It's driving me fucking out of my mind. Tell me, darling. I'm begging you."

"It's Raymond," she blurted. "I'm afraid Raymond will kill you the way he killed Max."

His body stiffened with shock.

"Why would Raymond kill me?" he asked at last.

"Because of me. Because I have to be faithful to Victor."

"But Victor's dead. Even the government finally decided that."

"I know. But Raymond doesn't care. He'll kill you

if he finds out about us. And maybe this time, he'll kill me."

He looked at her with wide, clear eyes. Then he threw back his head and started to whoop with uncontrollable, happy laughter.

"He killed Max," she insisted. "He'll kill you."

"You mean that all of this has been about Raymond? You mean it isn't because you've really been involved with somebody else?"

She nodded, running the tip of her tongue over her swollen mouth.

"Oh, darling." He scooped her up in his arms, hurting her as he kissed her hard on the mouth. "This is wonderful, wonderful. I'm so happy. I'm so relieved. I was so sure it was somebody else. I just couldn't figure out what else it could be."

"You don't understand Raymond," she said grimly.

He kissed her as she lay inertly in his arms. "Raymond isn't going to kill me," he said.

"How do you know that?"

"Well, if he does, he's going to have to stand in line. A long, long line."

"What do you mean?"

"Do you know how many death threats I get?" he said, smiling. "Three, four a week. Sometimes I get even more."

"But they're cranks," she murmured. "They don't mean it."

"Oh, they mean it, all right," he said, holding her against him. "That's why I have a chauffeur who's a bodyguard. If nobody else has ever managed to get a shot at me, I don't think we have to worry about old Raymond."

"I worry about Raymond." She sighed. "I worry about him all the time. I worry about what he's doing with my son."

"We'll get your son back, too," he whispered against her hair.

44

"I can take a taxi," Valerie offered as they stood on the sidewalk outside the front entrance to the Olympic Tower. Harry's chauffeur waited at the curb beside the open back door of the Rolls-Royce.

"That's over," he said, putting his arms around her and kissing her hard. "I love you, darling." He held her away from him by her shoulders and looked into her eyes.

She looked at him, trying to put a word to the expression she saw there. Shame. Regret.

Valerie was home in Beverly Hills by four o'clock. The sky was a pale blue, and a mild sun shone on the manicured lawns. In the distance, she heard the splash of the waterfall in her fern garden.

Valerie walked slowly down the massive hall, wincing with pain at every step.

She heard her footsteps echoing as she looked into room after empty room. No voices were coming from the terrace, or the swimming pool outside. She remembered it was Sunday. The housekeeper, maids, and cook were off.

Opening the door of the library, Valerie saw Kyle and Alexandra at the backgammon table, their heads bent over their game. The afternoon sunlight filtered through the curtains. Kyle's hair was a wild, black mass, his face unshaven. His feet were bare, and a cigarette dangled from one of his musician's hands. Alexandra, her brown curls bobbing forward as she leaned over the table, was in blue jeans, a big sweater, and pink socks.

Simultaneously, they looked toward the doorway. Their faces went white.

"Oh, Mummy," Alexandra cried out, jumping up from the table.

"So, he finally beat the shit out of you," muttered Kyle, looking down at the board again, finishing his move.

"It was nothing that exciting," said Valerie, trying to keep from wincing as she lowered herself onto the sofa. "Just my taxi sliding into another car in the rain. I hit the partition. That's all."

"Oh, Mummy," Alexandra repeated, her blue eyes wide with shock. "You could have been killed."

"It was nothing, darling," said Valerie, watching her daughter begin to process the possibility of more loss. Total loss this time. "Look at me," she commanded. "It's just a few bruises, Alexandra. I'm fine."

"Yes, Mummy," she said, getting her control again. The polite, perfect little girl, her eyes with the same far-away look they'd had in the first months after Penny's disappearance.

Valerie looked helplessly at Kyle as the two of them watched the robot return. Kyle mouthed the words, "Should I call her therapist?"

Valerie shook her head, and started to talk about the

accident and how trivial it really was. About the rain and the two fire trucks trying to get through, and how much worse the traffic was these days than when they had lived in New York. She talked about how smooth the flight had been coming home, and the light traffic on the freeway. Anything that came into her mind, as Alexandra stared into space.

"You know what I could use, though," said Valerie in a hearty voice. "I would just love a nice cup of tea."

"Shall I get it for you, Mummy?" asked Alexandra.

"Would you mind, darling?" asked Valerie, wondering if the little girl was really all right now, trying to keep the mood light as if nothing had happened.

"Oh, no, Mummy," said Alexandra, moving toward the door, her body relaxed now. "Would you like tea, Uncle Kyle?" she asked from the doorway.

"I'm ready for a drink," he said gruffly.

"I'll just be a minute," said Alexandra, with another quick smile at her mother. "Oh, Mummy, you gave me a scare. I'm so happy that you're all right."

"What brought it on?" Kyle asked, after Alexandra had been gone for a minute or two. "Did you disagree with his opinion of the Common Market?"

"What do you mean?"

"Why did he beat you?" Kyle slouched over to the drink caddy, where he splashed scotch into a glass.

"It was the taxi, Kyle," she said wearily. "Harry was wonderful. He took care of me all weekend."

"Sure, Florence Nightingale with a dynamite right hand," he scoffed. "You know, sometimes I think women all have a screw loose. You meet a guy, he has a reputation for punching people out, and you say, 'Oh, no. He would never do that to me.' " He lit another cigarette, and took a big gulp of his drink. "And then, surprise, surprise. He punches you out, just the way he's punched out everybody else."

"It wasn't that way," she insisted. "I swear it wasn't."

"You know, we've been friends for a long time, Valerie. I didn't think we lied to each other."

"We don't."

═══

"I'm so glad you're all right, Mummy," said Alexandra as they kissed good night later. "A taxi skidding in the rain, well, that isn't anything. Not really."

"I'm fine, darling." She willed an enthusiastic note into her voice and gave her daughter a hug.

In her own suite, Valerie finally felt the tension seep out of her and the fatigue envelop her like a shroud. Hobbling across the sitting room, she unbuttoned her lime green silk shirt and unfastened with trembling fingers the hooks on her matching skirt. As she peeled off the sheer panty hose in her huge, mirrored dressing room, she caught a glimpse of herself in the sea of mirrors. Her smooth white breasts and pale pink nipples were incongruous against the smudged gray bruises running down one side of her rib cage. A purple bruise covering one hip was spreading over her rounded buttocks. She took a deep breath, feeling a stab of pain, as she limped over to the mirrored wall and leaned forward to examine her face. One eye was half closed, its lid swollen and purple, already tinged with bilious green. Her mouth was split. She flinched with pain when she touched her cheek with tentative fingers.

Gratefully, she lowered herself into her steaming

bath, felt the soothing hot water blanket her aching body, and she tried to make sense of what had happened over the past two days. Tried to understand, finally, why she had stayed after what had happened.

Cautiously, she dried her aching body with the fluffy white towel, flinching when it touched the ugly purple bruise on her hip. Kyle was right, she thought, pulling a flannel nightgown over her head. She knew Harry's reputation for violence, and she had gone ahead with the relationship. Because he loved her.

She dragged herself across the room, feeling worse by the second. She turned down the cream-colored satin quilt on her four-poster bed and tried to find a position where she didn't hurt quite so much.

The shrill ring of her telephone sliced through the stillness.

"Are you all right, darling?" Harry asked, his voice a honeyed, southern purr. "How was your flight home?"

"It was fine," said Valerie, her hand trembling. "We were right on time."

"I've been trying to call you. I was worried about you."

"I was downstairs, watching an old movie on television with Alexandra and Kyle."

"Well, I was worried, darling. I love you, you know. I can almost feel you, still in my arms."

"Yes, Harry," said Valerie dully.

"Valerie, you've got to forgive me," he pleaded. "You've got to understand that I was crazy with jealousy. Now that I know what it was, that you were only thinking about me, it'll never happen again. You're the best thing that's ever happened in my life. I don't want to lose you. I'll do anything not to lose you."

"I forgive you, Harry," she said.

"Now, tell me you love me, darling," he purred. "I'm not going to let you off the phone until you tell me you love me."

"I love you," she said at last.

"I love you, too," he said. "I'll make it up to you, darling. I promise you that."

"All right," she said.

"I love you," he said again, and there was a click.

She lay awake, staring at the vague forms of the furniture in the bedroom, trying not to move. She thought about Harry and how she felt about him now, and what she was going to do. She had thought she cared deeply about him until two days ago. Where could those feelings have gone? She was still awake at three o'clock in the morning when there was a faint tap on the door. It was Alexandra, looking like a little ghost in her white nightgown, padding across the floor.

"I just wanted to be sure you were all right," she said hesitantly from the foot of the bed.

"You should be asleep, darling." Valerie put out her arms to her daughter.

"Are you all right, Mummy?" she asked, coming into her mother's arms.

"I'm fine, sweetheart." She held the little girl, kissing the top of her head. "Would you like to sleep with me? Would that make you go to sleep, do you think?"

"Oh, yes, Mummy." Alexandra crawled over her and slipped under the covers.

Valerie held the child in her arms, rocking her as she had never been allowed to do when Alexandra was a baby. Finally, she heard her soft, steady breathing and fell asleep, too, her pale head against her daughter's dark curls.

———

Alexandra was already gone when the tiny alarm clock next to Valerie's bed tinkled seven o'clock. Looking in the mirror after she had put on her makeup, Valerie saw that she looked better than she had the day before, although her mouth was still puffy, and so was her cheek. Her eye was nearly open, and with makeup, it didn't even look like a black eye.

———

"What happened to you?" asked Mary, from the doorway of Valerie's office. Her eyes were wide with concern.

"It was pouring in New York," Valerie murmured lamely. "There was a big tie-up on the bridge going into the city. Everybody was sliding into everybody. It was in the taxi. The partition."

"Harry must have just about fainted when you walked in," said Mary, looking at her curiously.

"He was wonderful." Valerie ran her hand over her swollen cheek. "He took care of me all weekend."

"Well, that's awful, sweetie." Mary's voice was sympathetic. "Is anything broken? Have you seen a doctor?"

"It's just my face, Mary. Nothing's broken."

"Just your face," Mary snorted. "Our international beauty, our image, and it's just your face." She looked at Valerie closely. "We'll have to put off that cover shoot for *Business Week.*"

"Oh, God, that's right," said Valerie. "I'll see that

somebody lets them know. And I'll see you in the meeting in two minutes."

"I'll have your coffee poured, sweetie," Mary smiled as she left the office.

45

Every morning before she dressed, Valerie would examine her bruises, watching them slowly fade. Every night, when she was reading in bed, her stomach would lurch at the ring of the phone. She knew it would be Harry, telling her he loved her. He was off in Sweden, Italy, and then to Japan for meetings.

"I'm going to be there Friday, darling," he said. "Same time, same place. All right? I can't wait to see you, Valerie."

"I can't wait to see you, Harry," she said, feeling sick at her words, a fine film of perspiration covering her forehead.

"We'll have fun, darling. It'll be like it was in the beginning."

"All right, Harry," she whispered. "Same time. Same place."

Valerie bathed for an hour, powdered and perfumed her body. She applied just a touch of makeup and brushed out her pale golden hair until it was like a cloud around her face. Harry opened the door of his Beverly Hills Hotel bungalow to her knock promptly at eight. Champagne was cooling in an ice bucket. She sat primly on the sofa, clutching her coat around her as he uncorked the bottle. She watched his hands as he touched his own glass to hers and toasted her. The girl of his dreams.

"Why don't you take off your coat and stay awhile?" She heard the awkwardness in his voice, the embarrassment at seeing her for the first time since he had slapped her.

Slowly pulling back the fur, she watched the expression on his face as he saw the pale breasts, the naked line of her body, the black lace garter belt holding up sheer black stockings, the golden pubic hair between her legs. Just as it was in the beginning.

Except it wasn't.

He stood, put out his hand to pull her up, and led her into the bedroom.

He took off his tie, unbuttoned his shirt, slipped out of his trousers, his undershorts.

She dropped the coat to the floor and stood patiently as he unhooked the black garter belt, peeled off her stockings. Led her to the bed.

"I appreciate this, darling," he murmured, his mouth against her ear. "I love it that you're trying to make it easy for me. I love you."

She pulled his head down, found his mouth with hers, and licked his lips until he kissed her, caressing the inside of her mouth with his tongue. Trying to decide how she felt, she decided that she didn't feel much of anything. He kissed her breasts, ran his hands along her body, bent to thrust his tongue into her navel as his fingers explored the folds of her genitals as they had so many times before. As he kissed her mouth again, lovingly, tenderly, she found herself thinking about her appointments the following week.

"Let's go get some dinner," he said gruffly, sitting up. "I've made a reservation in the dining room." He looked at his watch on the nightstand. "We can still make it."

"But I can't," she gasped.

"Why not? Do you expect Raymond to turn up with an Uzi and blow me away?"

"I don't have any clothes."

"You have your coat." He grinned. "Nobody will know."

After wine with dinner, Valerie was feeling almost glad that she was there. He had his arm around her waist as they returned to the bungalow and was nuzzling her neck as he somehow managed to get the door unlocked.

They managed to make love, and they showered together later, soaping each other.

"I wish you didn't have to go," he crooned, touching her chin with his fingers as they stood at the door of the bungalow.

"I have to get home." She kissed him on the cheek.

"What about tomorrow?" He caressed her shoulder under her coat. "I'll tell you what. I'll make a dinner reservation for eight o'clock somewhere. Jimmy's, maybe. Or Le Chardonnay. I'll come by for you around seven. Have a glass of wine. See the house. Meet Alexandra and Kyle."

"I don't know, Harry."

"I'll see you at seven," he said. "Now, you drive carefully, you hear? I don't want anything happening to my girl."

"I'll talk to you tomorrow," she said.

"I love you," he called after her, as she hurried to

her housekeeper's nondescript car jammed between a limousine and a red Jaguar.

———

"It's not much, but you call it home?" said Harry the next night after she had shown him the house. The two of them were sitting with a glass of wine in the library. "How many rooms are there in this place?"

"Thirty," said Valerie.

"Not counting bathrooms," said Harry.

"No, you never count bathrooms," said Valerie. She noticed Alexandra peeping in the doorway.

"My goodness, Valerie, is this your daughter?"

He was on his feet at once, leading her into the room. "Why have you been keeping this little beauty such a deep, dark secret?" Alexandra blushed deeply. Her eyes were shining as Valerie introduced them.

"Yes, Harry, this is Alexandra. Alexandra, may I present Mr. Cunningham."

Later, at Jimmy's, Harry leaned toward Valerie. "You know, Alexandra is lovely. Graceful, too. Like a dancer. She's really a knockout. She'll sure have all those old boys jumping through hoops when her time comes."

Harry was admiring, and Alexandra was infatuated.

Instead of taking a noon flight the next day, Harry turned up in a taxi just after lunch. He borrowed a tennis racket and volleyed with Alexandra. An hour later both of them returned, perspiring and laughing, to the terrace next to the swimming pool where Valerie sat under a striped umbrella, reading a sheaf of sales reports. The day drifted away, and Harry started to look at his watch, waiting for the limousine that would take him to the airport for his ten P.M. flight back to New York.

"Will you come to the airport with me?" They sat at the table in the small dining room, drinking a last cup of coffee. Alexandra, her eyes wide with excitement, stared at her new idol as if she had never seen anybody quite so wonderful in her life.

"Can I come, too?" she asked, bouncing in her chair, wiggling like a puppy.

"It will be past your bedtime," said Valerie automatically. "There's school tomorrow."

"So, you will come," Harry said to Valerie, his tone satisfied.

"Oh, I want to come, too," Alexandra begged.

"Next time, pumpkin," Harry promised her with a big smile.

Self-conscious, Valerie and Harry sat next to each other in the backseat of the limousine as the chauffeur headed toward the airport.

"I've been carrying this around with me all weekend," Harry broke the silence as he reached into the pocket of his coat and pulled out a jeweler's box. He pressed it into Valerie's hand. "I didn't know if you would want to accept this from me." He was silent for a moment. "I still don't know," he added abruptly.

"It's for your right hand. Nothing serious, darling. It's just my way of saying I'm sorry. That's all."

Perhaps it's just a trinket, Valerie thought. The weekend with Harry had been good. It was nice to have a man in her life. A man in Alexandra's life.

"You didn't have it wrapped," she said, turning it over in her hand.

"They would have charged extra." He grinned.

She snapped it open and caught her breath as she saw the ring nestled in the black velvet. It was a marquise diamond, around eight carats, she estimated with her practiced eye, flanked by two tapering baguettes. It was clearly such an important stone that part of her wondered why she didn't know about it, and why, if it were available, it had never been a possibility for the collection. At a minimum, it was worth half a million dollars.

"Of course, you're a hard lady to give a piece of jewelry," he said, and she could hear the smile in his voice. "You probably know exactly what it weighs, where it came from. I was really taking a chance."

"No, I don't know where it comes from."

"It was my grandmother's," he said quietly.

"Your old granddaddy sure must have been rich."

"He sure was." Harry smiled.

"I can't accept it, Harry," Valerie said, snapping the box shut. "I'm just not willing to make the commitment to you, to us, that accepting it would mean."

"It doesn't mean anything," he protested, and she could hear the edge of anger in his voice. "I'll tell you what, darling. You just take it on trial, like that rug you have in your house that you're thinking about buying. How about that?"

"I can't."

"Then, I'm going to just roll down this window and throw it into the street," he said casually.

He would, she thought. He really would, to make his point.

The limousine came to a stop in front of the American Airlines terminal. Harry gave Valerie a quick kiss on the cheek and sprinted out of the car. He grabbed his suitcase from the chauffeur's hand, turned as he reached the door to the terminal, and gave her a wave.

Well, I won't wear it, Valerie decided. I'll just keep

it a couple of days, and then send it back with a note. Then she remembered Alexandra's expression as she looked adoringly at Harry Cunningham across the dining room table. She remembered how much fun the weekend had been, that silliness at dinner at the Beverly Hills Hotel with her wearing only the fur coat. The lovemaking later, and the next night, too, when she had given herself up to him, to her pleasure.

———

"Who's this Ralph Sprague?" he asked mildly in one of his nightly calls a week later.

"Ralph?" she said. "Oh, he's a local philanthropist. Very active, with United Way mostly, and the Music Center." She leaned back against her pillows. It had been a long day at the office, then dinner with friends. "In fact, we're on the same committee. It's a support group for the Philharmonic."

"Yes, so I read in the paper this morning. 'Valerie Penn and Ralph Sprague, huddling in a quiet booth at lunch at the Bistro Garden.' Did you see it, darling?"

"Harry, Ralph Sprague is nearly ninety years old. He uses a walker to get around. A nurse goes everywhere with him. He's a very brave man. Anybody else would just sit in his house and wait to die."

"Darling, I just don't want to read about you and other men anymore," he said evenly. "I don't care if he's being lowered into his grave."

"That's not reasonable, Harry." Valerie felt the knot in her stomach, the tightness of her jaw.

"Do it for me, darling," he purred. A direct order. She almost felt the sting again of his hand across her face.

Her body tensed.

"Did Alexandra tell you I phoned her this afternoon?" Harry chuckled. "We must have talked for fifteen minutes. We're good buddies, Alexandra and myself. Real good buddies."

"She told me." Valerie heard the tremble in her voice.

"Well, she was happy I called, wasn't she?"

"Yes, she was happy," said Valerie.

Harry Cunningham treated Alexandra as if she were a princess. He admired her, told her how pretty she was, and predicted that soon every boy who saw her would be falling at her feet. Harry sent her matchbooks for her collection from the summit meeting in Iceland, printed with the date, place, and the occasion. Matchbooks from a meeting at the Kremlin, unprinted, with the date, place and occasion noted on the inside cover in Harry's careful handwriting.

Alexandra's blue eyes would light up whenever she came home from school to find an envelope from Harry among the rest of the mail. Inevitably, it would be covered with colorful stamps from whatever country Harry was visiting.

Alexandra would toss the matchbooks in the brimming basket in the sitting room of her suite, and take the stamps to school to show to her girlfriends. Valerie would often find her daughter at her dressing table, experimenting with lipstick and a little eye shadow, sweeping her mass of shiny brown curls on top of her head, emulating the models she saw in magazines. She noticed Alexandra posing haughtily in front of her full-length mirror.

Harry Cunningham was the first to make Alexandra feel like an attractive female. In return, she thought he was the most handsome, brilliant, charming man who had ever lived. She was madly, wildly infatuated with him, which was just what Harry had in mind. Valerie watched Alexandra, saw her shining eyes glued to the television set whenever Harry was on, saw her squinting as she read his articles from one magazine or another, saw her reading his books, a dictionary at her side.

———

"Darling, I've got just the occasion for our public debut." It was Harry's usual nightly call, this time from his *pied-à-terre* on Dupont Circle in Washington, D.C. "There's a big benefit next weekend, one of those three-day numbers, for Ford's Theater—you know, where Lincoln was shot. Everybody is coming in from all over. The private jet set. There'll be a reception at the White House, standing in line to get our picture taken with the president and his wife. Parties from morning to night."

"What day?" she asked dully.

"Well, if you fly Friday morning, it will be perfect. You'll get in around six. We'll have time for a little rest, maybe even a cuddle, and then the White House. That's the first night."

"We're making our final selections for the next catalog on Friday, Harry. And all through the weekend. You know that. It's always the same. Every month."

"Oh, darling." His voice was imploring. "It's such a perfect time. I'll be so disappointed if you don't come."

"But Harry . . . the catalog."

"I'll tell you what," he said brightly. "I'll make a few telephone calls. See who's coming from Los Angeles in a private jet. I'll arrange for them to bring you along. Would you like that, darling?"

"I can't come, Harry. I have to work."

"They can do it without you, Valerie."

"Oh, all right," she said, resigned. "But don't bother about calling to try to get me a lift. I'll take a commercial flight. It doesn't matter."

"Oh, darling. I'm so happy you'll come. Your first time with me in my town."

"Yes, Harry."

"And darling, you'll bring your prettiest dresses? And your furs? You'll do me proud?"

"Yes, darling."

"And bring along that little old friendship ring I gave you, too. It's not doing anybody any good sitting in a drawer."

"All right."

"I love you, darling," he whispered, his mouth close to the receiver. "Thank you. Thank you for being you."

She hung up the receiver and rushed for the bathroom, getting there just in time to heave up her light supper. She sat on the marble bathroom floor, her head against the toilet, gasping for air, hating the sour taste in her mouth. Even her body was protesting. Her stomach was bloated, her breasts fuller, the nipples enlarged, sensitive even to the touch of a silk shirt covering them.

Valerie told Mary she was going to the three days of parties in Washington, D.C.

"Some people have all the luck. Maybe if I got another boyfriend," Mary joked. "Somebody who doesn't want to stay at home all the time."

"I'll trade you," Valerie laughed.

"You keep away from John," said Mary, smiling. "What are you going to wear?"

"Well, I hadn't really thought about it," said Valerie.

Valerie and Mary went through the possibilities, covering every moment of each day. Furs, jewelry, shoes, handbags were strewn all over Valerie's suite.

"Twenty-six suitcases?" Harry asked with alarm when he picked her up at the airport with the rented limousine. "Twenty-six suitcases for three days? What happened to the girl I used to know, the one who would turn up in New York for a weekend with one itty-bitty suitcase?"

"You told me you wanted to be proud of me," she said, waving her right hand, the ring glittering in the waning afternoon sunlight.

"Oh, my love," he said, grabbing her and kissing her hard on the mouth. "Oh, thank you, darling. Thank you."

"It's adorable." said Valerie, looking around the entry hall to Harry's Dupont Circle apartment.

"It's small," he said, blushing.

"It's perfect."

"I love you. Are you happy you came, darling?"

"Yes. Yes, I really am."

For once, the selections for the next catalog would

be made without her. Nobody would know the difference. And it was good to get away to just have fun, for once, with no business appointments. She smiled at Harry, a radiant smile, feeling better than she had in weeks.

He stepped toward her, took her in his arms, and kissed her lips. She felt herself respond to him in a way she hadn't for a long time.

"Do we have time?" she whispered into his ear, holding him around his waist as she stood wrapped in his arms.

"We'll make time," he said hoarsely, and she could feel him hard against her.

Then they were lying together, nude, on the narrow bed. Her breath was coming faster and faster as she wound her legs around his waist, urging him to enter her, feeling him push into her as he brought her to orgasm almost at once. It took longer for him, and she came again before she felt his movements grow faster, and heard his anguished moans as if he were in pain. He fell across her, and she ran her fingers over his back, wet with perspiration.

"It hasn't been like that with us for a while," he murmured, a hand under each of her buttocks.

She was silent, kissing his gray hair. She sighed, wanting him again.

"Come on, you vixen." He laughed, pulling her up. "Let's go show these folks a pretty lady."

For the reception at the White House, she and Mary had picked out something conservative to wear, a white, crepe cocktail suit, floor-length and slit up the sides past the knee. A chunky turquoise necklace, earrings to match, and, of course, Harry's ring. Her blond hair, brushed out, was long and flowing.

Harry, in tuxedo and black tie, stood in the tiny entryway. He gave a whistle of appreciation as she struck a pose at the top of the stairs, one hand above her head.

At the White House, Valerie fought to keep back the tears of pride and patriotism as the Marine band, in their dress uniforms, played at the head of the huge, winding staircase she ascended on Harry's arm. With a cluster of other guests, they were given a tour of the Red Room, the Blue Room, and several wings of the White House mansion. Later, they sauntered into the East Wing for cocktails, and received a smile and a few murmured words from the first lady, in her signature red, and a firm handshake from the president. Harry nodded several times as the president spoke close to his ear.

Every four seconds, it seemed, Harry was introducing her to somebody else, smiling proudly, showing her off. Valerie smiled, too, exchanged pleasantries, agreed that the food was superb, that the first lady was getting prettier by the year.

"You know what I was thinking, darling," murmured Harry that night, crawling into bed beside her and pulling her close to him. "I looked at all those attractive women there tonight, listened to their pretty little laughs, their charming chitchat. Then I looked at you. The most attractive woman of them all, the prettiest laugh, the most charming conversationalist in the room. And so smart, so successful, too."

He kissed her hair, held her more tightly against him.

"I couldn't believe my luck," he continued. "That I would be the one who got to take you home. To my bed. That I would be the one who would be able to kiss you and touch you."

"Oh, darling," she whispered. "I'm so happy I came."

"Maybe I should have passed on those last two cognacs," Harry chuckled ruefully.

"Why don't we see what we can do about that?" Valerie found his flaccid penis with her hand. She leaned down to take its head in her mouth, as his fingers explored her genitalia and pushed apart the lips, preparing her for him.

Valerie woke in the same position, with Harry's fingers caressing her vagina, massaging her clitoris with a finger wet with his own saliva. She lay silently, her eyes closed, her breath coming faster, as she felt him spread her inner lips, the head of his hard penis searching, helped by his guiding hand as he pushed into her. It was over in a few minutes, and she heard his shuddering sigh as he pulled out of her and rolled over on his back.

She propped herself up on an elbow and looked at him, feeling his semen and her fluid, sticky between her legs.

"Hangover hots." He grinned, pulling her face down to kiss her mouth. "Did you mind?"

"I don't mind anything you do." She smiled. "God, it's never been this good between us, has it, Harry?"

"Maybe it's something about being at the seat of power."

"Maybe it's just being away from all the responsibility."

"Now, don't you go all serious on me," he warned. "This weekend is about having a good time."

They just made it to the brunch with Harry's friends

at the Jockey Club. They found each other's eyes over mounds of fluffy scrambled eggs, kippers, bacon, sausage, blueberry muffins, and long-stemmed strawberries that were to be dipped in powdered sugar. Two hours later, the limousine took them to an exquisite town house in Georgetown, where they caught the tail end of another brunch, and had a few glasses of champagne as they mingled with the thirty guests, all excited about the black-tie benefit that night at Ford's Theater. The entertainment would be taped for viewing on network television a few months down the line.

"How about a little nap?" Harry said, twirling the tip of an imaginary villain's mustache once they were back in the bedroom of his *pied-à-terre.*

She turned to see him looking at her with a love, an adoration, she had never seen in a man's face before. Not even Victor's.

"Why, Harry," she said, taken aback.

"What's the matter, Valerie?" He grinned. "Didn't you think I meant it?"

"Well, yes," she said.

"Then, don't be surprised," he said, moving toward her where she stood in front of the open closet. He took one of her breasts in his hand, and bent to suck the nipple. "You know, this is how I like you best. Just before your period, when your breasts are swollen, and you have a little tummy on you." He patted her stomach, took her other breast in his hands, leaned over and kissed her mouth.

"It's all your Italian wives," she teased, laughing.

"Now, how about that nap," he said, leading her to the bed. "After all, madam, I'm a busy man."

Hours later, Harry dressed, watching her as she applied her makeup in the tiny bathroom mirror.

"You go downstairs," she suggested, still wrapped in her terrycloth robe. "Have a glass of wine, or something. Put out the cat."

"We don't have a cat," he protested, laughing.

"Well, go downstairs anyway."

"But I want to watch you dress."

"And I want you to be surprised."

Valerie wound her hair into a chignon, wet her finger and fashioned curls in front of each ear, a suggestion of bangs. She pulled on sheer black panty hose and stepped into black satin pumps with pointed toes and three-inch heels, which would bring her to exactly Harry's height.

Then the dress, the hit of the Paris collections. A black top with long sleeves and a deep décolletage, the skirt hitting midthigh, a pouf covered by a swath of shocking pink satin, and a huge bow in back. Impossible to sit down in, of course, impossible to find a wrap for, but with the impact of a blast from an elephant gun. Valerie fastened the graduated collar, set with seventy-two emerald-cut diamonds, around her neck, secured a round diamond earring in each earlobe, and slipped Harry's exquisite marquise diamond ring on the ring finger of her right hand.

She crept soundlessly down the staircase and stood in the doorway to the tiny drawing room. Harry was watching the traffic lumber by in the late afternoon sunlight.

"Harry," she said softly.

Startled, he turned.

He didn't have to say anything.

———

The president and the first lady were already seated in the first row of Ford's Theater, and Valerie saw, with a thrill of satisfaction, that both of them turned to watch her at Harry's side as they found their seats. She found a position that was fairly comfortable and crossed her long legs, unavoidably showing a flash of thigh.

"You're the most gorgeous woman in the world," Harry murmured in her ear, his arm draped carelessly over the back of her seat. "Every man in this theater wants you."

"As long as you want me, darling."

"Oh, darling, I love you," he said under his breath.

She put a finger to her lips, kissed it, and touched his mouth as the lights dimmed, the orchestra began its overture, and the curtains parted.

———

The Corcoran Gallery was white marble, with a dramatic staircase leading to a second level, more marble, more galleries, and then a private reception room behind high mahogany doors. Valerie and Harry joined the reception line, shaking hands with cabinet members, several senators, three members of the Supreme Court, the president again, and the first lady, who complimented Valerie on her dress.

Downstairs, Harry introduced her to more senators, congressmen, and media figures whose names and faces she knew almost as well as her own, as they wended their way through a crowd that must have numbered eight hundred, perhaps more, to a table for two under a fabulous Jackson Pollock painting. Valerie managed to take a sip of wine before they were surrounded by friends of Harry's who pulled up chairs to join them.

"Would you like to dance?" asked a voice in her ear. He was a good-looking young congressman, with a famous family name, she seemed to recall from Harry's hurried introduction a few moments earlier. Presidential material someday, Harry had murmured. She tapped Harry's arm. "Do you mind, darling?"

"Oh, God no, darling," he said, giving her a quick grin before turning back to his conversation with several dignified men whose names she couldn't recall. Serious matters, she thought, taking the hand the congressman reached out to her, smiling as he led her to the dance floor. He took her in his arms, crooning the words when the orchestra played an old standard. Valerie caught Harry's eye, saw his big smile, and waved to him.

———

Harry was quiet going home in the limousine, reflecting, no doubt, on the discussions in which he had been involved throughout the evening. Enough, she thought, to give him fuel for a few magazine articles, or some new insights for use at his next round of economic seminars.

"Oh, darling, I had such a wonderful time," she said, throwing her arms around him as soon as they were home, the door closed behind them.

"I saw that," he muttered, pushing her arms away.

"Harry . . . what?"

"Dancing all night with that asshole. Glued to him. Rubbing up against him." He glared at her, contempt veiling his eyes—or was it cognac? "And that dress, as if you were about to start dancing the cancan."

"Harry." She touched his arm.

"Get your hands off me, you slut." He raised his hand as he turned.

Valerie screamed at the sharp sting of the slap against her cheek. She stared at him. His look was as horrified as her own.

"Oh, God, darling," he gasped. "I'm sorry."

She stood there for an instant before bolting past him up the stairs to the bedroom. She scooped up her daytime handbag and her stack of credit cards. He was standing at the doorway when she rushed down the stairs.

"Don't go," he begged. "Please, darling. I didn't mean it."

"Get out of my way." She fought to open the door as he tried to push her back. "Let me go."

"Oh, I get it," he sneered, standing aside. "You're going to meet him, aren't you? You little slut. Haven't I fucked you enough to keep you satisfied? What are you? Some kind of nymphomaniac? Is that it?"

She ran past him out of the house and along the deserted street, his words echoing in her ears, until she found a taxi. She crawled, panting, into the backseat.

"Where to, lady?" asked the cabdriver, a jowly man in a baseball cap, huddled in a big sheepskin coat against the late-evening chill.

"The airport," she panted. "The one in Baltimore."

"National's a lot closer. Twenty minutes instead of an hour, and they've got the same planes."

"Please, just take me to Baltimore, all right?"

"Oh, I get it." He squinted at her in the rearview

mirror. "A fight with the boyfriend, and you figure he'll be right after you."

"Something like that," she said, her cheek starting to throb from Harry's slap.

"You're Valerie Penn, aren't you?"

"Yes," she replied, stroking her cheek, remembering the fury in Harry's face.

"You want a little piece of advice, Valerie?" The driver met her eyes in the mirror.

"What?" she asked, getting annoyed.

"If I was you, I'd take off those rocks you're wearing and put them in your purse. Somebody could live like a king forever on what you've got on."

"They're all fakes," she said, which they weren't.

"Well, not everybody would know that," the driver said. Valerie took off the necklace, her earrings, the ring. "Say, you must be awful cold without a coat. Here's something you can put over your shoulders."

"Why, that's so nice of you," she said as he handed her a baseball jacket so old it read "Brooklyn Dodgers."

"I'm a nice guy," he said proudly. "And, I've got a thermos of hot coffee, too. Care for a cup?"

Valerie let the tears come, hot, furious tears for the end of her and Harry, once and for all.

"There, there," the driver said as she sobbed into one of the tissues from the box he handed her. "No guy is worth it, Valerie. They're a dime a dozen. With your looks and your money, you can have anybody."

47

By the time Valerie's twenty-six suitcases arrived at the mansion in Beverly Hills two days later, her private telephone numbers were already changed.

"If he calls through the switchboard, I don't want to talk to him," she told the receptionist at her office. "If there are letters, telegrams, packages, don't even tell me about them. Just send them back. And send this back to him, too." She reached into her handbag and handed her the ring.

He got her, of course, through Alexandra, calling her on the regular number at home, asking her, very casually, to put her mother on the phone.

"This is despicable, Harry. Using a child this way."

"I had to talk to you, darling." His voice trembled. "I'm sorry, really sorry."

"You're sorry every time."

"Darling, I'm doing something about it." The words came quickly, spilling over each other. "I've stopped drinking. It's always been the cognac, the booze. That's been the problem. Well, I'm not doing that anymore. I haven't had a drink since you walked out of the house. I'll never drink again. I'm getting help, darling. I'm going to see someone. A psychiatrist."

"Oh, God," she said, running a hand through her hair.

"Don't say anything now," he begged. "Let me prove it to you. Please."

"What does the psychiatrist say?" she asked finally.

"Give me a month. Try to trust me, darling. Please. I can't stand the thought of losing you, Valerie. I love you."

And she wanted to trust him.

But she knew that it would take more than a psychiatrist to help Harry Cunningham. He would have to want to change, for himself, and it seemed to Valerie that he was much too pleased with himself for that to ever happen.

The jury was out on her and Harry.

"Is there any tenderness here?" Dr. Feldman palpated Valerie's lower abdomen as she lay on the examining table.

"No, that's fine."

"How about here?" He prodded a little higher, around her appendix.

"That's fine, too."

His fingers danced over her neck, under her arms, searched for the unusual in her breasts.

"Well, you seem to be all right." He turned to his nurse. "The tech got a blood sample, didn't she? And urine?"

"Yes."

"Get dressed, Valerie. I'll see you in my office when you're ready."

Five minutes later she sat down in front of his large desk as Elliott dropped into his chair and fumbled for a pen.

"Well, you're fine. Nothing out of the ordinary. Everything is just the way it should be."

Valerie started to breathe again, relieved.

"And the nausea, the knots in your stomach, that's been, what, a couple of weeks now?" He scrawled something on the pad. "Have you been under any particular stress?"

"You know there's always stress. I just wanted to be sure that's all it is, Elliott. Stress I can handle."

"Maybe it was just a little too much weekend in Washington." He grinned. "I saw the pictures in the papers. Harry Cunningham . . . is that new?"

"I don't even know if I want it anymore," she sighed. "That's the stress, Elliott."

He jotted down her answers about her diet, her exercise regime.

"I'll give you a call when the test results come back," he said at last. "Maybe you have a little iron deficiency. You ought to have your gynecologist take a look at you, too. It might be some female thing."

"What do you think?" asked Valerie, removing her heels from the stirrups and swinging into a sitting position on the edge of her gynecologist's examining table.

"Well, I'll have to see the test results, but I would say that you're pregnant, Valerie. Three weeks, give or take a day or two."

Pregnant. The word hung in the air.

"I can't be," she blurted.

"A lot of my patients say that."

"You'll see."

"Well, the lab results will be back the day after tomorrow," said the doctor. "I'll call you the moment they arrive."

"You have copies of the lab tests Elliott made," said Valerie. "They don't show anything."

"That was last week." The doctor opened the door to the examining room. "That was too early."

Valerie stood nude that night in front of a wall of mirrors in her dressing room. She smiled bitterly as she ran her hands over her body. Her breasts were swollen and sensitive, the nipples enlarged, a shade darker than their usual pale pink. Her stomach was slightly bloated, though her hips were as narrow as they had been on her wedding night.

"The results are positive. There isn't any doubt at all," the doctor said two days later, her voice kind, maternal.

"I'd better come in and talk to you," Valerie said.

The scans of her Fallopian tubes showed that she was fine. The endocrinologist's workup revealed no hormonal imbalance. Valerie Penn was a normal, healthy young woman.

Her gynecologist hadn't even changed expression as Valerie told her she had been part of Gordon Lerner's earliest programs, that the twins had been fertilized in vitro, then nurtured to term by a surrogate mother.

"And none of it was necessary," Valerie concluded.

"No, it wasn't."

"Then, what was it all about?"

"I don't know," said the gynecologist.

———

She knew she had to call Harry. What would she say? She didn't want to marry him. If she had Harry's baby, they would be in a tug-of-war for the rest of their lives. She ran her hands over her breasts and her stomach again, remembering how she had always wanted this.

She decided she wouldn't call. Not now, not with things the way they were.

"You and Harry," said Mary, raising her eyebrows. "Young lovers in trouble. What does he think about it?"

"He doesn't know. I tried to tell him, Mary. I had my hand on the phone a dozen times. I just couldn't do it."

"I'll come over to the hospital around seven," promised Mary. "At least I can keep you company for a couple of hours. What about Alexandra?"

"I told her it was a female thing, and I'll just be in the hospital overnight," said Valerie. "You're a darling, Mary."

"So are you, sweetie." Mary gave her an awkward hug. "I'm sorry you have to go through this. You know that."

Valerie was admitted to UCLA's medical center, examined and prepped for surgery the next morning.

A couple of minutes after seven, Mary pushed open the door with her shoulder, staggering under a mammoth horseshoe of flowers. Kyle stopped by a few minutes later, and they stayed until a nurse arrived. Valerie washed down a sleeping pill with a sip of water and lay her head down. The fragrance of the flowers hung cloyingly in the room.

Alone at last, she thought bleakly.

48

Valerie turned it over in her mind in a million different ways. The *in vitro* fertilization had been staged.

How easily she had assigned the blame for Penny's disappearance, Max's murder, the crash of the jet and of Penn International itself to Raymond. It hadn't even crossed her mind that it might have been Victor.

The *in vitro* fertilization had nothing to do with Raymond. No, that was Victor. Her husband, Victor Penn. Why?

A pregnancy wouldn't have done. There could be no protruding stomach, no breasts drooping with milk, no hips widening for the rite of birth, she realized. Not for Victor's toy. Or maybe that wasn't it at all.

Valerie was still awake, sitting up in the narrow bed, when the black night dissipated into a smoky gray dawn. The door of her room was pushed open, and she saw a nurse, silhouetted for a moment in the doorway. Valerie blinked as the lights in the room came on.

"This is a tranquilizer, Mrs. Penn." The nurse put a tray on the table next to Valerie's bed. She picked up the syringe. "I'm sure the doctor told you. It'll take effect in about fifteen minutes. Then we'll be back to take you to surgery."

It was as easy as her gynecologist had said it would be, Valerie thought, fighting her way out of the anesthesia several hours later. She felt a little tender, and she felt the sanitary napkin between her legs, but that was about all. She ate ravenously when lunch arrived and, when Daniel appeared in the doorway to take her overnight bag, she was dressed, made up, and feeling almost herself.

Harry's telephone numbers in New York and Washington were ribbons of responsibility undulating through her mind. She tore off her clothes and hurried to the bathroom, where she stood under a scalding shower for a long time, washing away the memory of the hospital, the surgery, washing away the guilt.

As she soaped her bare pubic area, shaved for the surgery, she put her hand against the marble shower wall and steadied herself. Her thoughts were fragmented, cocooned in cotton. Her trembling hands could barely turn the faucets off before she sank to the floor of the shower.

It was several minutes before she felt her strength returning.

She hobbled into bed, and was asleep almost before her head hit the pillow. She awoke at dusk, and the face of Victor Penn was etched in her mind as if in stone.

She stood at her window, looking out at the acres of garden enveloped in the gray evening light.

She gazed out of the window, barely able to discern the shapes of the trees, the bushes, the flower beds in the encroaching dark. No, it wasn't Raymond who had taken Penny.

It was his father who had taken him.

Victor Penn.

And what else had Victor done?

Suddenly, nothing seemed too farfetched, too monstrous. She realized that the buzz she heard was her telephone intercom, that it had been buzzing for a long time.

49

"It's Alexandra, Mrs. Penn," said Mrs. Wytton in an anxious voice when Valerie finally picked up the receiver. "She's in the library, watching the news on television. There's something on it about Mr. Cunningham."

"I'll be right down." Valerie jammed the phone down and pulled on a robe as she rushed down the stairs.

"Alexandra," she cried, rushing across the library, grabbing her daughter, rocking with her as the little girl moaned. On the television screen, Valerie saw a network correspondent standing in front of a restaurant. On the awning over its mahogany doors was its name, Larousse.

Washington, D.C., thought Valerie. Harry had told her about Larousse. Great Frog food, he had said.

"Alexandra," whispered Valerie into her daughter's ear. "Guess what. I've got wonderful news for you, really wonderful. It's about Penny, darling," she said. "Don't you want to hear about Penny?"

Alexandra's moans subsided gradually. Valerie could feel her response as she held the slender body in her arms. The little girl hugged herself tightly.

Valerie's eyes met those of Mrs. Wytton, who stood in the doorway. Kyle appeared behind her, along with Mary di Stefano, white as a sheet, and John O'Farrell, pale under his perennial tan.

Alexandra turned beseeching blue eyes toward her mother's face. Her nose was red, running, her cheeks wet with spent tears.

"Mummy," she said softly, "Mr. Cunningham is dead. He was shot by some terrorists who were trying to assassinate the vice president. The vice president and Mr. Cunningham were having lunch in that restaurant. Larousse. Isn't it funny to name a restaurant for an encyclopedia, Mummy?" Valerie felt a shudder, which she realized was her own.

"And, do you know what the newscaster said? He said that these were real terrorists. They all had machine guns."

"Yes, darling," said Valerie numbly.

"What is it about Penny, Mummy?"

"He's alive, Alexandra," whispered Valerie.

"Oh, I know that. He's with Uncle Raymond."

"No, he isn't, darling. He's not with Uncle Raymond. He's with Daddy. He's with your daddy."

Valerie saw Mary open her mouth as if she were about to speak, saw Kyle's questioning, raised eyebrows. John started to shake his head, and then he stopped.

"Oh, Mummy. He isn't."

"Yes, he is, darling. I've never been so sure of anything in my life."

———

Alexandra was curled up on the sofa, finally asleep.

Valerie sat with her feet up on the coffee table, as her gynecologist had instructed. She watched the news reports as Alexandra, in her sleep, let out a soft moan. Valerie listened to her daughter's breathing return to normal, and began to tell Mary, John, and Kyle what she had figured out about Victor.

Much of it was new to all of them.

The *in vitro* fertilization Victor had staged.

The fact that her real mother was a woman named Cini Schuyler, and her real father was not known.

Since Victor had staged the *in vitro* fertilization, it made sense that he had staged the crash, too. He was alive, somewhere, and he had Penny.

"Okay," said Kyle, the ashes from his cigarette dropping onto his shirt. "Granted that all of it is true. But knowing all of this and fifty cents will get you to Westwood on the bus. I mean, so what?"

"So Penny is what," Valerie said. "If I can find Victor, I know I can find Penny."

"How are you going to find Victor?" Kyle took a slug of his drink. "God knows, the government tried to find Victor. And not just one government, mind you. Lots of governments. The insurance companies tried to find Victor. Probably even some angry depositors tried to find Victor. Nobody seems to have managed it yet." He paused to refill his glass. "Clever chap, that Victor Penn. I always gave him that."

"I don't know." Valerie stroked Alexandra's shoulder as the child stirred in her sleep.

"We'll come up with something, sweetie." Mary patted Valerie's arm.

At the door, Mary hugged her tightly.

"We're so sorry about Harry," she said.

Valerie just shook her head.

———

Valerie knew she never would have seen Harry again. No, when she decided to have the abortion she had closed the book on them. Her eyes were red and swollen when she picked up the *Los Angeles Times* the next morning and saw the headline about the attempt on the vice president's life.

An assassination attempt, she thought scornfully. It wasn't an assassination, and it wasn't an attempt. No mistake had been made at all. The intended victim was Harry Cunningham, and his murder had been successfully executed by men hired by Victor Penn. Just like the murder of Max Perlstein and the passengers on the Penn International jet.

It was all so terrible. So unfair. So like Victor, she realized, as the words formed in her mind. Terrible. Unfair.

Yes, that was Victor.

Who else? she wondered, pouring herself another cup of coffee. Al and Vicki Hemion? Probably. Cini Schuyler? She didn't have a doubt in the world about that one. Engvy Erickson, so she wouldn't say anything? Even Victor wouldn't do that. Or would he?

She didn't know anymore.

The offices of Sid James occupied the entire thirty-seventh floor of the General Motors Building in New York City. The elevator opened directly onto the graceful reception area, with English antique furniture, well-tended plants, and a discreet sign etched in brass, reading, *Sid James*. A receptionist led Valerie down the long hall toward a huge corner office.

Valerie thanked the receptionist with a smile. When the door closed, she walked over to the shelves of law books, bound in red leather, lining a wall. She examined a shelf of tennis trophies awarded to Siddon Corbett James III, at Phillips Exeter Academy. There were framed pictures of rows of smiling boys in tennis whites, holding rackets. She searched those sixteen-year-old faces and found Sid in the middle of the front row, his blond hair shorter and his frame twenty pounds lighter.

There were other pictures, too. His father, dead for years, whom she recognized from photographs in business magazines. His mother, the dowager, in lace and pearls, holding a Yorkshire terrier on her lap. His sisters and his brother, who now ran the family business.

When Sid came in a couple of minutes later, Valerie was standing at the window watching Central Park shimmer in the sunlight.

"Nice day," commented Sid.

"Beautiful," said Valerie, walking slowly across the room. Sid's secretary came in a moment later with a carafe of coffee and croissants, and Valerie began to talk.

Finally Sid closed the yellow legal pad and rifled through the pages of notes.

"A lot of this is rote," he said. "I think where we start is with Cynthia Schuyler. According to your foster parents, she was from somewhere in the east. She would have been about, what, twenty, twenty-one when you were born?" He made another note on the pad. "Something like that, anyway. So, we can start checking county courthouses, birth certificates for those years, give or take a couple."

"I'm a rich woman, Sid," said Valerie, watching him. "I can pay you anything you want. Is this really something you want to bother with? Or do you think it would be better if I went to somebody, well, smaller?"

"Anything for John O'Farrell." He grinned. "We

didn't do that blood brothers stuff at Harvard Law, of course. But still, we always come through for our friends."

"No, really . . ." she said, her words trailing off.

"Oh, look, Valerie," he said leaning back, crossing his legs, "all I've ever tried to do is go my own way. Have a little fun, a few laughs. That's why I wouldn't major in business at Harvard, the way my father wanted me to. He threatened to disinherit me, too. And my poor kid brother, Roddy, got stuck with running the department stores." The legal pad was on the coffee table now, and Sid slouched in the chair, his hands behind his head, enjoying himself. "So I thought, Why not law? Clarence Darrow, and all those hot lawyers I'd read about. The ones who got plays written about them. That was all right for a while, and then I went out for a Rhodes scholarship. I had a terrific time in England for the year I was there, and I picked up a doctor of jurisprudence, too."

"Yes, living in England was fun," said Valerie. "I'm surprised we didn't meet at some house party somewhere."

"We wouldn't have been going to the same house parties." He laughed. "Not with you married to Victor Penn."

"Maybe not."

"Then it was time to start practicing, to put all of this education I had acquired into action. Time to make my mark." He stretched out his legs. "So I got a job at the biggest and best law firm in New York. I lasted six months. I've never been so bored."

"Why not the tennis?" asked Valerie, gesturing to all the trophies and pictures.

"You mean turn pro? Just be a jock? No, not intellectually challenging enough. So I decided to become a

private detective. Sam Spade, maybe. Or Philip Mar-
lowe. It sounded exciting. Lots of action, adventure." He
smiled again, looking at her. "So I became a detective.
And what did it turn out to be? Industrial espionage.
Computer components. The automobile industry. That
sort of thing."

"So it didn't work out to be as exciting as you
thought it would be," said Valerie.

"Well, there were some basic problems," he said,
his expression serious. "I couldn't stand straight bour-
bon, for one thing. And I never could get the hang of
drinking in the morning."

"That's too bad."

"And, another thing. I never could find a secretary
named Effie."

"That's even worse."

"But there was a bright side." He pulled himself up
in the chair and leaned forward with his elbows on his
knees.

"What's that?"

"I knew my father wouldn't disinherit me," he concluded. "And he didn't."

He was nice, she thought, trying to put her at her
ease like this.

"So we'll start with Cynthia Schuyler," he said.
"And I'll do some thinking over the next couple of days.
Come up with some sort of a plan from there."

"I was planning to fly back to Los Angeles on the
two o'clock flight," Valerie said.

"Well, that's fine. I'll go over this with a couple of
my people. As soon as I have something tentative in
mind, I'll give you a call."

"Thank you." She rose and extended her hand.

"Oh, incidentally," he said as they stood at the door

to his office, "I was sorry to hear about Harry Cunningham. He was a smart guy. I met him a couple of times. But he was a feisty son of a bitch."

"Thank you," she said. "But it wasn't going to come to anything."

"We'll talk in a couple of days," said Sid, dismissing her with a smile and a wave.

Valerie strolled quickly down the long corridor. In moments she was heading toward the airport for her flight back to Los Angeles, where she would never again answer the telephone to Harry Cunningham's purring southern voice telling her he loved her.

Valerie was staring pensively out of her office window several days later when her secretary buzzed. "Valerie, your manicurist is waiting in the reception area, and Sid James is calling on line four."

"Are you going to be around this weekend?" he asked. "I thought I would fly out, sit down with you. And John, if he's available."

"I can put you up in the house," she offered. "There's a guest wing."

"No, no," he said. "I'd rather be on my own. That's my style."

"Whatever you want."

"We've put ads in the personals column in the *Los Angeles Times*," said Sid. "We've also put ads in the *Hollywood Reporter* and *Variety*, asking people who might have known Cynthia Schuyler to contact us at a box number out there. We're offering a reward."

"You must let me know how much all of this is costing," said Valerie.

"Oh, don't worry about that." Sid laughed. "You'll

be getting my hotel bill, too. And my rental car. The works. This is a business arrangement, Valerie. I'm sure you know about business arrangements."

"Oh, yes," she said, nodding at her manicurist, who stood in the open doorway to her office. "Business arrangements are something I know about."

She put the telephone down, feeling better than she had in a long while. Finally, they were moving forward.

51

"That was a great dinner," commented Sid, leaning back on the sofa. He had his legs crossed on the coffee table in front of him, a snifter of brandy in one hand.

"I taught the cook everything she knows," said Valerie, relaxing in a big armchair, her arms crossed on her lap in front of her.

"She's lying," said Kyle, standing at the drink caddy, pouring himself another scotch. "Valerie didn't even know how to use the telephone to have pizza delivered. Didn't even know what pizza was, in fact. I tell you, Sid, it wasn't easy."

"Well, neither did you," said Valerie, noticing that the ashes from his cigarette were about to fall on the Aubusson carpet. Again.

"But I'm a genius," Kyle reminded her patiently, returning to the seating area. "I'm not supposed to know things like that."

"God, remember all those little dinners at the big

house?" Mary was nostalgic. "Oh, that chef. He was the genius."

"Now you're hurting my feelings," said Kyle.

"We've sure gotten some interesting answers to those ads we put in the *Reporter* and *Variety* about Valerie's mother." Sid took a sip of brandy.

"I don't want to hear anything dirty," said Kyle, sitting down, lighting another cigarette. "I'm easily shocked."

"Alexandra is in bed, isn't she?" Sid looked over at Valerie. Smiling.

"Oh, not yet," said Valerie. "But she's upstairs in her suite."

"She's a pretty girl," said Sid. "The boys will be falling at her feet in a few years."

"Yes, that seems to be the consensus of opinion," said Valerie wryly.

"Maybe I should play something," mused Kyle. "A little after dinner music. No charge, of course."

"Cini was really something," said Sid. "Of course, none of these people is really putting anything in a first letter. Not without knowing what kind of money we're offering for information. And they don't want to jeopardize themselves. We could be the police, or something."

Valerie felt a little queasy.

"One of them did say, though, that she was one of the three most expensive women in town," said Sid. "She got a thousand dollars a night, and that was more than thirty years ago. Big money back then."

"Big money right now," said John O'Farrell, glancing at Valerie, who was looking down at her hands.

"Well, I'm glad we're dealing with the best of the best," said Kyle. "Wouldn't it have been awful if she were just a run-of-the-mill person? One of the top two hundred, say?''

"I've set up some meetings tomorrow with these people," Sid continued. "Let's see if they're for real, or just bullshitting."

Sid reached down for his briefcase and drew out a chart, which he spread on the coffee table. Printed out were electronically prepared boxes, each with a name in it.

Valerie read the chart several times over. Victor Penn. She would see him in hell, she thought.

The plan detailed by the computer printout was simplicity itself, already under way, in fact, from the moment Sid's people in New York had started to call up birth certificates all over the East Coast to locate Cynthia Schuyler's parents. Her own grandparents, Valerie realized, shaking her head as Sid pointed to the appropriate boxes. And if not the grandparents, their brothers, sisters, cousins. Someone to give them a start.

My relatives, Valerie thought as Sid went on. My aunts and uncles. My children's roots. Silently, she cursed Victor, hating him with a fury that brought tears to her eyes for denying her her family.

Through the relatives, Sid said, they would find Cynthia Schuyler. Through Cynthia Schuyler, they would find Al and Vicki Hemion, they would find out why they had left Los Angeles without a trace. How much they had been paid, and, more important, by whom.

"Of course, I'm assuming that some of these people are alive," he continued, his voice thoughtful.

"What if no one is alive?" Valerie asked. "What if you come up with conclusive evidence that all three of them are dead?''

"Then we press on. With money and time, you can find out anything. Everybody who has ever touched your life as it related to Victor Penn will be questioned. In Europe we'll contact everyone we know about, especially Lady Anne Hallowell. She's, perhaps, the most important link in the chain. And Miss Furst, of course. Raymond Penn's secretary.

"Does anybody know her first name?" asked Sid, looking around the circle of their faces, his pen poised over a box with her name in it.

"I know I've got it in an old address box somewhere," said Valerie. "Margaret, I think."

"Okay," said Sid. "I'll get it from you when I call you tomorrow, late afternoon. After I've seen some of these flakes."

And Raymond Penn, of course. Somebody had to talk to him. Because, if anybody in the world knew where Victor was, it was Raymond Penn.

Sid was folding up the computer printout, snapping open his briefcase, placing it carefully on top of a stack of manila file folders.

"Do you think you'll have time for a couple of sets of tennis?" asked John, rising. "We've got championship courts at the house, Sid. I'd like you to try them out."

"I wish I could, John," he said as they all moved toward the entryway. "But I'm just not going to have time."

———

"Three out of the four showed," Sid told her when he telephoned the next afternoon around five o'clock. Miraculously, Valerie had actually managed to doze for thirty minutes or so. "I'm sloshing around in coffee," he added. "It sure isn't easy being a private dick."

"Who were they?"

"The one I met at the diner was a woman, early sixties, I would say. Marci Nelson," Sid began. "She's a masseuse, and she used to go over to Cini's apartment on Doheny when she was living there to give her a massage about three times a week. She said the apartment was gorgeous. Lots of nice furniture, paintings, crystal, the works. Cini told her that some john was paying for it. Apparently, her specialty, from what this woman says, was sadomasochism, and Cini didn't particularly care whether she was serving or receiving, as we say in tennis. She laughed when she talked about one john, an important official in the state government, who she whipped so hard she put him in the hospital. He loved it, though. As soon as he was on his feet, he was back on the phone, begging her to see him again."

Valerie was silent.

"Do you really want to hear all this?" asked Sid, his tone solicitous. "There isn't any reason, you know. I'm seeing all three of them again over the course of Monday and Tuesday. Taking sworn affidavits with a court reporter. Just to have it all on the record."

"Go on," said Valerie, and she took a deep breath.

"This woman would set up her abortions," he said. "Cini didn't pay much attention to birth control. She would have one, oh, every couple of months. This woman would take her, wait for her, drive her home. Take care of her for a couple of days. Then a couple of weeks later, when she was all right again, she was back at it. She had a lot of nice jewelry. Things that johns would give her. And beautiful clothes, this woman said. She had a red Thunderbird, that little two-seater that used to be so popular. Some john had given her that, too. And they all took her to the best places. All of them wanted to have her on their arm when they were in public. This was in the last days of Ciro's, the Mocambo, Romanoff's.''

"Who else did you see?" asked Valerie.

"A bartender who used to work at one of the hotels in Beverly Hills. He set up tricks for her."

"Who was the other one?"

"This was a guy she made a couple of movies for. That was in the days when you sold movies like that out of the trunk of a car. He tried to convince her to make more. He told her he would make her a star, the biggest in the business. She laughed at him. Said she'd only done the movies as a lark. To be able to watch herself on the screen doing all of that.''

"Oh."

"The fourth one, the woman who didn't show up, said in her letter that she used to be the landlady at the apartment building where Cini lived. Not the apartment on Doheny Drive. Another one, a little earlier. She had her answering machine on when I reached the number, no return address on her letter."

Valerie sighed.

"This woman, Marci Nelson, knew Vicki. She used to go to that beauty salon where Vicki worked on the Sunset Strip to have her hair done. She and Vicki knew each other by sight, but that was all. And Cini's pimp, the bartender, knew Al from around. They'd worked a couple of places together when Al was a little down on his luck, tending bar."

"Well, it's a start," she said, feeling numb.

"I'll keep trying the number for the woman who said she was Cini's landlady. And then, as I told you, there are the sworn affidavits first thing next week."

"Well, thank you, Sid. I'm very grateful."

"And, Valerie," he said, his voice softer. "There isn't one of them who thinks Cini Schuyler is still alive. They all said the same thing. The way Cini was going, the only thing she could have had in mind was committing suicide. Nobody could have kept on living the life she was living and survived. Nobody."

Several days later, Sid caught Valerie in Atlanta where she had given a speech on style for corporate women at the annual convention of the National Secretaries' Association.

She sat at the desk in her hotel room, making notes on a little pad, as she listened to Sid, who was giving her the first reports from his people in London.

"So, it was Victor, personally, who called the conservatory about the scholarship," she said slowly. "And it was Victor, personally, who told them that I was its recipient, and that I would be staying with Lady Anne for that year." She paused, looking over her notes. "I don't see anything here about Lady Anne."

"She wasn't in," reported Sid. "She hasn't called back yet. My man may have to take a run down to Cap Ferrat if he isn't able to reach her in a few days. But you'll be happy to know we traced Julian Unwin. He says he's always felt badly about cutting you off when you were both teenagers, but Lady Anne's chauffeur had taken him aside and pointed out that it might be better for his career if he didn't have to try to play the violin with ten broken fingers."

Oh, she had been so hurt. She had felt so used all of those years ago. It hadn't been that at all. Suddenly, she felt light as air about her first love.

"He has a couple of children now, a boy of ten and a girl who has just turned five. A nice wife who writes film criticism. And he only performs enough to impress the parents of his students at Eton. At any rate," he finished, "he sends you his very best regards. He also said he would love to hear from you. He'll come up to London when you're there, and take you out for a nice dinner, if you have a free evening."

He paused to peruse his notes. "Nothing on the chauffeur. Nothing on that personal assistant of Victor's, Brian Graham. Nothing yet on Claude Vilgran, either.

"But I've been thinking about your mother." Even the notion of Cini filled Valerie with vague feelings of dread. "We've been drawing blanks with the Schuylers we've talked with all over the East Coast. I've been wondering if perhaps Cini's last name really wasn't Schuyler, that she didn't come from a good family in the east. If, maybe, that was just part of the story. I think I'll run a check on her in California. It can't hurt, at any rate."

Valerie felt Sid's attention wander. She heard a woman's voice in the background saying, "Hello, darling. Am I early?"

"Hold on a minute, will you, Valerie?" When Sid returned, he was a bit breathless, with a smile in his voice. "I'll call you as soon as I have anything."

"All right," she said. "And thanks, Sid."

Back home a few days later, she carefully opened a large package from Sid James. On top of the stack of material was a handwritten note from Sid saying he would call her when he had more information for her.

Next was a three-page computer printout of figures, and the first itemized bill. The total on the bottom was large enough to make Valerie wince.

Under the bill were transcripts of all the interviews. Word for word. She glanced over the stack, picked out a phrase here and there.

"Mrs. Penn's gynecologist will be happy to release her medical records upon receipt of a notarized request from Mrs. Penn herself."

"Julian Unwin is a man in his mid-thirties, slightly balding, who works as a . . ."

"Leon Stern is a man in old age, wearing a well-cut pin-striped suit with a carnation in its buttonhole . . ."

Valerie laid her head on the stack of transcripts and cried.

Sid James was on her private line a couple of nights later, startling her, as she lay propped up against a few pillows, reading *The Wall Street Journal.*

"I hope this isn't too late for you," he said.

"It's only ten o'clock here," she reminded him.

"Yeah, well, I just got in. But it's the first chance I've had to call you."

She felt her body tense under the covers.

"We've come up with something out there," he said. "Female infant named Cynthia Schuyler, born about the right time in Los Angeles. Good Samaritan Hospital. Father, Ralph Schuyler. The mother, Natalie Johnson Schuyler."

"Oh, God," she whispered.

"The operative here who came up with it ran a

check through the Department of Motor Vehicles in Sacramento," he continued. "They've got a new Cadillac El Dorado registered to a Ralph Schuyler. The address is in Palm Desert."

Ralph and Natalie Schuyler, thought Valerie. Maybe they were her grandparents. She mouthed the names silently.

"I had a telegram sent," he said. "You know, one of those lawyer things, hinting at the possibility that they were beneficiaries of some estate. Asking them to call collect as soon as possible. That should bring a call tomorrow."

"Oh, Sid." She heard the strain in her voice.

"Now, don't cry," he said. There was something sweet in his tone. "I've got more. My operative in London had a meeting with one of Lady Anne's acquaintances, Sir Harold Carrington."

"Sir Harold," murmured Valerie. He had been a frequent guest at Lady Anne's dinner parties, she remembered.

"The most interesting piece of information concerns the house on Green Street."

"What about it?"

"She didn't have a house on Green Street," said Sid. "It was Sir Harold's understanding that Lady Anne had been living out of the country because she was nearly destitute. When he heard that she was taking the house on Green Street, the Daimler, the chauffeur, and you, he'd gone back to his own sources to find out what was up."

"What did they say?" she asked.

"They didn't know anything, either. Everyone figured that some trust fund had matured, and they let it go at that. She was always very well liked in London. Everybody was happy for her, happy to have her back on the scene."

"Has anybody been able to get in touch with her?"

"Not yet. But I just wanted to bring you up to date, Valerie. I'll let you know when I hear from Ralph Schuyler. Who knows? This could be the break we've been waiting for."

"Thanks, Sid."

"Did you have a chance to take a look at my bill?"

"Yes, I did. I passed it along to my accountant."

"Now you know what I meant when I said this is a business arrangement." He laughed. "Good night, Valerie."

53

"Well, at least they saw me," Sid told her a week later, calling from Palm Springs. "But all they did was stonewall. Yes, their daughter's name was Cynthia Schuyler. Yes, they had lived in Los Angeles where Mr. Schuyler had a store in Beverly Hills, on Rodeo Drive. The store was the Ascot Riding Shop. They sold riding togs, saddles, boots, that sort of thing. They said they hadn't heard from their daughter in more than thirty years. They think she's dead."

"Maybe they do," said Valerie.

"Yeah, maybe they do."

"Are you coming to Los Angeles? It's only a twenty-minute flight. We could have dinner."

"I've got to get back to New York." His voice was distracted. "They're calling my flight now. I'll be in touch."

Replacing the receiver, Valerie slowly realized that even if Cini were dead, Natalie and Ralph Schuyler were, indeed, her grandparents.

Sid had found her grandparents. A piece of her past.

———

At seven o'clock the next morning she was on the phone to Sid.

"Do you think my grandparents would want to see me?"

"Well, I don't know."

"I've been thinking about it. I want to see them, Sid. I really do."

"Well, they don't know about you, Valerie. I hinted around at the possibility that Cini might have had a child. They just looked blank."

"I need to see them, Sid," she said quietly.

"You could write them a letter, I guess." His voice was thoughtful. "We can come up with something plausible, if you give me a minute."

"I thought I would just run down there."

"What are you going to say?"

"I don't know right now. I'll think of something. They're old, after all. I want to be careful, cushion it. I'll think of something."

Valerie sat, stalled in traffic in her black Ferrari Testarossa, just after nine o'clock in the morning. The sky was clear above the skyline of Los Angeles, though the air was dense with gasoline fumes. Vehicles were backed up as far as she could see. Maybe she should have had Daniel bring her in the Rolls, she thought. At least she could have caught up with some paperwork from the office or reread the transcripts that Sid had sent her. She had already studied them for hours.

Valerie felt as if she would recognize Cini's masseuse if she saw her on the street. From the words on the page, Valerie could sense her admiration for Cini, even envy. Cini could wrap any man around her little finger, take a john for everything she could get.

She noted the indignant tone in Daniel's interview. Well, yes, he had been British Special Services before Mr. Penn had hired him many years ago. Of course he was one of his bodyguards. But he had been as staggered as anybody when the Penn International jet crashed, and Mr. Penn with it. When the government allowed him to continue with the Penn estate to maintain the automobiles, he had stayed because he felt a responsibility to the memory of Mr. Penn, and to poor Mrs. Penn in her desperate situation. How happy he was now that everything had been put right again by Mrs. Penn's own efforts. Truly a remarkable lady, and he was proud to be in her employ.

Paul Gregson's words had been much the same. The sense that it wasn't seemly for Mrs. Penn to be in such straits, and so he had offered to help. It was the only decent thing to do, under the circumstances. As for his own success as chief operations officer of *The Collection of Valerie Penn,* it was a turn of events beyond his wildest dreams.

The interview with John O'Farrell. With Mary. With Kyle, who'd said he could count on one hand the times he had been alone with Victor Penn, and, at that, they had been at opposite ends of a sixty-foot corridor.

The traffic started to move, and within fifteen minutes the towers of downtown Los Angeles had receded in the rearview mirror.

Valerie remembered the interview Sid's operative had conducted with Julian Unwin. Every sentence reflected his pride in his talented children. Tears had welled in her eyes when she read Julian's words about her. He had really liked her. He had thought she was the most beautiful girl he had ever seen. Like a fawn.

The latest transcripts had arrived just the day before. Included were the medical records she had requested from her first gynecologist, the one she had visited when she hadn't conceived after a year of marriage to Victor.

"Valerie Hemion Penn is a healthy nineteen-year-old girl, her organs normal in every way. There is no reason she can't become pregnant and carry a successful pregnancy to term." Added in pen, evidently an afterthought, the gynecologist suggested that perhaps the problem might lie with Mr. Penn. "Mr. Penn might consider having a sperm count. If it is low, I would be happy to recommend a course of action."

She read the transcript over and over again, remembering the agonized look on Victor's face when he told her the gynecologist's tests had revealed blocked Fallopian tubes and a hormonal imbalance. She could never get pregnant. Never.

———

Valerie's plan to make contact with her grandparents without unduly shocking them was, she thought, inspired. She had telephoned the sales director at their condominium complex the day before and told him she was interested in a condominium for John O'Farrell's parents. After viewing the available units, she would ask to see the restaurant at the golf club on the property at just about one o'clock. She would pray to God that Ralph and Natalie Schuyler would be having lunch there, and ask the saleswoman to point them out. She'd talk to them somehow, without scaring them to death.

"It won't work," Sid had said decisively. "Besides, it won't accomplish a thing. Cini is one dead broad, if you want to know what I think. You're just being sentimental."

"Sid, it's what I want to do. They're my family."

"Well, whatever happens," he said, "it's a nice drive."

And it was a nice drive, Valerie thought, moving at a speed so slow that the Ferrari was on the verge of stopping altogether. The massive oleander bushes lining either side of the freeway were already in bloom, their flowers white and deep pink amid spiky, dark green leaves. She lowered the windows, hoping for a powerful, sweet fragrance, and got instead a quilt of desert heat.

54

After what seemed like an endless hour touring the Charleston View Community, the saleswoman led Valerie to a booth at the golf club for lunch.

Valerie had dressed simply in a white sharkskin suit with a pleated skirt, a scoop-necked black shell under the jacket, black-and-white patent leather pumps, and onyx and diamond jewelry. Nothing flashy. Just a simple day-time outfit, enough to make Ralph and Natalie Schuyler turn to each other and say, "Isn't that Valerie Penn?" "Didn't we see her on television not long ago?"

Now she felt overdressed as she looked around. The saleswoman was waving greetings to men in bright golfing clothes, their hairlines receding, their freckled scalps peeling. Women in pastels, their perfectly coiffed hair either pale blond or white, exchanged a pleasantry or two as they passed the table.

And finally, the Schuylers. Ralph, a tall man, tan and gray-haired, in a bright rose shirt and white trousers. And Natalie with a hint of a tummy in her golfing skirt and hair so blond that it was nearly white. A tan face, hazel eyes with flecks of yellow, and a wonderful, warm smile as she leaned forward. "How nice it is to meet you, Mrs. Penn. We've seen you so often on television, we recognized you right away."

"Ralph, Natalie, there's plenty of room at our table. Why don't you join us for lunch? Mrs. Penn is looking for a condominium for your good friends Mr. and Mrs. O'Farrell."

Valerie studied the Schuylers, searching for something familiar in the bone structures or the laugh wrinkles.

"Now, what's this about Mrs. Penn knowing friends of ours?" asked Ralph, after ordering a diet Pepsi with ice.

"Well, her business associate is John O'Farrell," said the saleswoman. "Mrs. Penn tells me you met his parents on a Caribbean cruise, and told them what a wonderful place the Charleston View Community is."

Ralph and Natalie's eyes met.

"What have you seen, Mrs. Penn?" Ralph's expression was quizzical as he turned to Valerie.

"I've shown her a two-bedroom penthouse with a

really spectacular view," said the saleswoman, "and we've toured the grounds."

"It's a lovely place," Valerie said.

"As long as you're here, Mrs. Schuyler and I would like you to take a look at our place. See what we've done with it. It'll kind of show you what the O'Farrells can do. How are the O'Farrells, anyway?" Ralph's eyes were speculative and cold. "Don O'Farrell, wasn't it? And his wife, Louise?"

"John O'Farrell, Sr.," replied Valerie in a small voice. "And his wife, Anita."

"Oh, yes," said Ralph Schuyler, giving an almost imperceptible shake of his head. "John O'Farrell, Sr., and his wife, Anita. How could I have forgotten?"

———

They were outside, in the midday desert heat. "Mrs. Penn, come along now and take a look at our condominium before you do anything else," insisted Ralph. Natalie shot him a curious glance.

"Thank you, Mr. Schuyler." She smiled openly at the tall, gray-haired man. "I would love to."

Ralph Schuyler helped her into the backseat of his golf cart. "I'll have Mrs. Penn back at your office in no time at all." He waved at the fluttering saleswoman.

Everything in the Schuylers' apartment was in shades of beige, ivory, or pale brown. Behind her, she heard the click of the door as Ralph closed it decisively.

Valerie knew her face was very pale as she turned to face him.

"While we're on the subject of our dear friends, the O'Farrells," said her grandfather, "I think we have another acquaintance in common, Mrs. Penn. A lawyer from New York."

He moved into the living room, motioning for Valerie to follow, and gestured to the sofa where she was to sit. She crossed her ankles primly, one hand over the other in her lap. Natalie lowered herself cautiously into a lounge chair across from her.

"Sid James," said her grandfather.

Valerie moistened her bottom lip with her tongue, trying to organize what she had to say.

"He turned up a few days ago," her grandfather continued. "As it turned out, we weren't the beneficiaries of some estate. No, it was about our daughter, Cynthia. He wanted to know where she was. And now you turn up with this cock-and-bull story about these O'Farrell people on a Caribbean cruise, or some other nonsense. Mrs. Penn, I would feel justified in calling the authorities over this harassment."

"Cini was my mother," stuttered Valerie, feeling the blood rush to her face.

It was a few moments before Natalie took a breath. "Who wants an iced tea? Father, how about you? Mrs. Penn?"

———

"Every time we saw you on television," her grandmother smiled, Valerie's birth certificate on the table in front of her, "I said to Ralph, 'That girl is the image of our Cini. The very image.' "

"Please call me Valerie . . ."

"You call me Natalie, my dear." She leaned over and patted Valerie's arm. Three feet of blue leather-covered photograph albums were stacked on the coffee table.

"Well, it was rough on girls back in those days." Her grandfather sat with his legs crossed, the expression on his face open now, unguarded. "Not like these days. You couldn't just walk in and get an abortion. No, it was a big thing. The disgrace. The quacks. You could die in some back alley somewhere. I wish we could have helped her. But I never realized . . ."

"So, she didn't tell you about the pregnancy," prompted Valerie.

"Not a word," said Ralph. "She turned up one night. This was when we still had the big house in Cheviot Hills. The one where Cini grew up." He took a sip from a can of diet Pepsi. "She said she was really in trouble, that she had crossed some man who was big with the mob in Vegas. She had to get out of town because he said he was going to kill her. She was scared to death."

"I had my hand on the phone to call the police," interjected Valerie's grandmother, remembering. "I really did. I said to her, 'Cini, that's what the police are for. When decent people have problems, they call the police.' But Cini said not to call them. That we'd only make it worse."

"She said she was leaving town," said Ralph. The look on his face made Valerie realize he was seeing Cini's face on that long-ago night. His terrified daughter. "She asked for money, of course. Which I gave her."

"She was a good girl, a good daughter," her grandmother insisted. "She was home every night by twelve o'clock. If she was out of town, she called every single day."

"Anyway," said her grandfather, "that night when she came to say she had to leave town, she gave me the keys to this little Thunderbird one of her boyfriends had given her. She told me to sell it and hold on to the money and she would be in touch."

"You mean, Cini always lived at home?" asked Valerie, thinking about the Doheny Drive apartment.

"Oh, yes." Her grandmother's eyebrows arched in surprise. "After all, dear, she was only twenty years old."

"Did she call?" Valerie asked. "Did she tell you where to send the money?"

"She certainly did," Ralph replied. "She called from Portland, Oregon. She must have been waiting out the last couple of months before you were born." He looked away, his mouth set, thinking about his beautiful daughter, alone in Portland to bear her illegitimate child. Valerie knew Ralph was wishing he could go back and do things differently, that he could have been there at her side, protecting her.

"She was so frightened," added Natalie. "She kept saying over and over again that we were never, ever to tell anybody where she was. If we did, she would be killed."

"Did anybody ever ask?"

"Oh, yes," said Ralph. "Men would come into the shop. They would be waiting for us, sitting in big cars, when we got home from work. We'd get telegrams, letters, like the ones your friend Sid James sent. We just didn't say anything. Not then. Not now."

"It must have been terrible for you," murmured Valerie. "Terrible."

"Terrible for you, dear," said Natalie, patting her arm again. "All those years of not knowing your mother. Now, tell me," she said, the smile on her face reminiscent of Valerie's own, "why are you looking for her now? Why not years ago?"

"Victor told me he had looked for her and couldn't find her," she whispered. "Naturally, I believed him."

"Why would he lie to you?" asked Ralph.

"I just don't know."

"When did you find out?" Her grandfather's brow furrowed.

"Not long ago. That's when I went to Sid James. To find my mother. To find Cini."

"You poor little thing," said her grandmother, dabbing the corner of her eye with a tissue.

"Sid realized after speaking with you that she was dead and that this was useless." She looked at her grandfather, seeing her cheekbones in his, and at her grandmother, recognizing the green-flecked hazel eyes, like Cini's. Like her own. Like Penny's. "But I hope you don't mind," she continued, pleading now, tears welling in her eyes. "I hope it doesn't upset your lives to know you have a granddaughter. And great-grandchildren. Alexandra. My son, Penny."

She was sobbing into the tissue her grandmother had handed her. Above her, she felt her grandfather hovering, his hand on her shoulder, awkwardly patting her with concern.

"Maybe you should lie down for a few minutes, dear," said her grandmother.

"No, no," protested Valerie. "I'm fine. Just fine." She patted her cheeks dry and took a deep breath. "Actually, this is such good news, I'm having a hard time realizing it's true."

She told them about Al and Vicki Hemion, who had raised her and how she had believed they were her own parents until she went to England. How they had disappeared, too. Paid off, perhaps, to get out of her life.

"So you thought that if you could find Cini," her grandfather began, "she might be able to tell you where these people, the Hemions, are, and that would lead to your husband?"

"To Penny," she whispered. "To my son. I had always thought Penny was with his uncle, until I found out that Victor had lied to me. I'm following every lead to try to find my son."

"And even though Mr. James feels that Cini is dead, and that a visit to meet us would tell you nothing, you came anyway?" he asked.

She nodded.

"Why is that, Valerie?"

"Because you're my grandparents."

"Well, that's a very good point," Ralph said. "Yes, I can certainly see that." The room became quiet.

"You're wrong about one thing, though," Natalie broke the silence. "Cini isn't dead."

"What?"

"Your mother isn't dead," her grandmother repeated. "She's fine."

"We could telephone her right now," Ralph added. "Tell her you're here."

"No," Valerie gasped. "Not yet."

Relaxed now, Natalie talked about Cini, a wealthy, very social widow living like a queen in Dallas. "Leave it to Cini," Ralph added, shaking his head with pride. "The whole bottom dropped out of the oil business and it didn't even affect her. Her people saw the whole thing coming. She sold out in time, and she's richer than ever."

"Did they ever have children?" asked Valerie, imagining half brothers, half sisters. A family.

"No," said Natalie. "She tried, too. She would have loved to have given Bubba, her husband, a son or a daughter." Her eyes flickered over Valerie. "Here you were all this time, right in Los Angeles, just a few miles from our house in Cheviot Hills, and none of us knowing about the other." She lowered her head over the scrapbooks and flipped a couple of pages. "Look at Cini in this one."

Valerie saw Cini's beautiful face, her voluptuous body in pose after pose. Cini, a lovely child, with pale blond braids. Cini, about four, kneeling with her arms around a cocker spaniel. Cini, darling, exquisite, with that crazy look in her eyes.

There were no pictures after the ones taken at the Hollywood nightclubs and on the beaches.

"We've never had a picture of her or even a letter," said Ralph. "We haven't even seen her in all these years. There are just the telephone calls once in a while. And if we want to reach her, we have a number. An answering service, which always reaches her a few minutes after we call."

"So she's still frightened," Valerie said softly. "After all these years, she's still frightened."

"Yes, we've thought about that," admitted her grandfather. "We've wondered about the terrible thing that must have happened to keep her so afraid."

Later, Natalie put a platter of different cheeses, crackers, and duck pâté on the coffee table, and Ralph opened a bottle of white wine. All Natalie wanted to do was talk about Cini. About what a beautiful child she had been, and bright as a whip. But she had been a wild one. She would cut classes. She wouldn't do her homework. So Ralph and Natalie had sent her off to a private school for girls only, and very disciplined. That had seemed to work, at least until she graduated.

Her grandmother remembered those long-ago days when they would have to wait to hear from Cini in Portland, Oregon, with no way to contact her. Once the money from the sale of the Thunderbird had been wired to her there hadn't been a call for months. Finally, she called collect, using a phony name. She was in Dallas, working as a secretary in one of the big oil companies.

"That was my doing, of course," said Natalie proudly. "I always told her, 'Cini, keep up your secretarial skills, and you'll always be able to take care of yourself.' "

"She'd met Bubba," added Ralph, "the head of the oil company, and they were going to get married. She wanted us to know that Bubba loved her, and that he would take care of her."

"So, after that," said Natalie, picking up the thread of the story, "it was all about the home Bubba had bought for her. The round-the-world cruises. The parties they went to. The clothes she bought. Then a couple of years ago, the sad news that Bubba had died. Cancer, it was. Of course, he had been years older than Cini. Thirty, maybe forty years older."

"They must have had a wonderful life," said Valerie thoughtfully.

"I think so." Natalie sighed. "She just called us, in fact. Not more than three weeks ago." She ran her hand over her husband's shoulder. "She sounded just fine. Didn't you think so, Father?"

"I sure did."

Glancing at her watch, Valerie saw that it was after nine P.M. She leapt to her feet. "I really must leave. It's a long drive back to Beverly Hills."

"Valerie, dear, let us give you our telephone number." Her grandfather scribbled a number onto a piece of paper. "Here's the number of Cini's answering service in Dallas. All you have to do is use our name, and she'll call you back within an hour at most. Would you like us to call her first, tell her to expect your call?"

"No," said Valerie. "Thank you, but I'd like to approach her on my own."

Her Ferrari Testarossa, gleaming in the moonlight, was the only car left in the parking lot. "Drive carefully, dear," said Natalie. Valerie smiled. It seemed to her that was something grandmothers were supposed to say.

Then she was backing out of the parking lot, waving to them as they stood, her grandfather's arm around her grandmother's shoulders.

She drove through Palm Desert to the highway, in love with the black sky, the moon silhouetting the cactus, the tumbleweeds, and the desert. In love with the thought of her grandparents, their arms around each other as they waved good-bye to her. Wondering what it meant that Cini was alive.

55

"You're kidding me," said Valerie into the receiver. "Sid, Conni Considy is one of our best customers. Every time a really fine ruby comes our way, we call Mrs. Considy first. She has one of the finest collections of rubies in the world."

"Have you ever met her?"

"Well, no." Valerie played scenes in her mind of the many parties, benefit balls, luncheons, and brunches she had attended in Dallas for one reason or another. "I don't think so."

"Have you ever seen her picture?"

"I must have. Some magazine, or the Dallas papers. Women like that always have their pictures in the newspapers or in *Town & Country*. Tell me. What does she look like?"

"I don't know. I haven't been able to find a picture of her. I had one of the researchers check the Dallas papers, the society magazines, everything. There just aren't any pictures of Conni Considy. Or Cini Schuyler."

"She's still scared," murmured Valerie. "After all of this time, her own parents don't even know what name she's living under. And there isn't a picture of her to be had."

Valerie slowly replaced the receiver. Conni Considy, the widow of one of the richest oil barons in Texas, Brother Considy. Brother. Bubba. She jumped as her telephone intercom buzzed.

"Hi, sweetie," said Mary from her office down the hall. "John is meeting with the company lawyers tonight at six. Nothing important. Just a catch-up sort of thing. Now, you and I can either join them, or we can go out and have dinner together, just the two of us. I can't remember the last time we did that."

"Sid just called me, Mary. It's Conni Considy. Conni Considy is Cini Schuyler. My mother."

"You mean Conni Considy our collector?"

"Yes. Sid doesn't think she'll see me."

"Well, in her position I can see why. Let's talk about it at dinner. How about L'Orangerie at eight o'clock? My secretary will make a reservation."

———

She was already at a banquette set for two in the pretty, high-ceilinged room, sipping a martini over the rocks, when Valerie slid in next to her, brushing her cheek with a kiss. "I ordered a bottle of your favorite wine, sweetie." Mary smiled as the wine steward filled Valerie's glass. "This is almost a celebration." She touched her glass to Valerie's.

"Getting Conni Considy to sit down and talk with you can't be any harder than starting *The Collection of Valerie Penn*."

"But how am I going to get to her, Mary? Should I just go ahead and call her?"

Mary tapped a finger to her lips. "No, it can't be a telephone call. You're going to have to be standing in front of her. That's the only way you're ever going to get her to talk to you. You can't give her even the slightest hint beforehand."

As the maître d'hôtel approached their table to take their order, Valerie said slowly, "I think I have an idea."

———

Valerie waited until eight o'clock in the morning to telephone Sid. She gave him the name of Myrna Francis, married to Bucky Francis. She had run into the two of them recently at the airport in Dallas.

"She's very, very social. If you could have a researcher check her charities against Conni Considy's charities, we might find a couple that match."

"And then what?"

"I'll have Myrna arrange the meeting with my mother."

"Okay. I'll start the computers working."

Both Myrna Francis and Conni Considy were on the boards of the Greater Dallas Diabetes Association and the Southwestern Chapter of the Retinitis Pigmentosa Foundation. They knew each other.

Myrna Francis was thrilled to hear that Valerie

would be in Dallas for two days, that she had both evenings free, and that she was interested in seeing Myrna and her husband.

"Well, my dear Valerie," cooed Myrna Francis, "you just consider both your evenings taken. What would you like to do? I have it. How about a little dinner party right here at home? We have the best chef in Dallas. A true genius. He trained in one of those three-star restaurants in the south of France."

"That sounds like bliss, Myrna," said Valerie.

"Now, I thought we could have ten," said Myrna. "Or we could have twelve. We'll want to have a handsome, eligible man for you, Valerie. Someone amusing, of course. And Bucky and I make four." She paused for a moment. "Is there anybody you know here in Dallas you'd like me to invite?"

"We have a very good client who lives there. I would love to meet her, of course. I wonder if you might know her."

"Well, who's that?"

"Her name is Conni Considy."

"Conni!" screeched Myrna. "Why, Conni is one of my very best friends. We've known each other forever. Of course I'll invite Conni. She'll love it. She'll just love meeting a big celebrity like you."

"Oh, that's wonderful, Myrna." Valerie hadn't meant anything quite so much in a long, long time. "I can't wait to see you. Give my love to Bucky."

———

Cocktails at seven, dinner at eight, Myrna Francis had said. Valerie glanced anxiously at her watch. It was only ten minutes to seven. "Could you drive around for about fifteen minutes, please?" she said to the chauffeur.

"I'd like to be back here at exactly five minutes after seven." She glanced over at the handsome building with its graceful, tree-lined entry, a doorman opening the back door to a Lincoln limousine. The late afternoon sun glittered on the top stories of the building next to it.

"Certainly, Mrs. Penn," he said, catching her eye in the rearview mirror.

A quarter of an hour later the car glided to a stop in front of the Francises' condominium. The doorman opened the back door to the limousine and leaned forward to help Valerie out of the car. He held open the towering glass door and gestured toward the bank of elevators in the mirrored wall.

Waiting for the elevator, Valerie studied her reflection. The cloud of blond hair, the hazel eyes that looked green, reflecting the emeralds and diamonds around her neck, all set off perfectly by her ivory cocktail suit. The expression on her face for one unguarded instant was that of an abandoned child.

The doors to the elevator opened into the foyer of the Francises' apartment. "Valerie, you look just gorgeous," cried Myrna, both of her hands grasping Valerie's. "You remember my husband, Bucky, of course. And this is Chet Williamson, our interior designer."

"You've certainly done a wonderful job with all of this fabulous space, Chet," said Valerie graciously as she walked with him toward the windows to look down at the trees, the plantings, the swell of Turtle Creek below. Valerie glanced toward the foyer, where the elevator doors were sliding open again. Myrna's hands stretched out to take those of the woman who stood there, put an arm around her, and led her in Valerie's direction.

Valerie felt a lurch of recognition that nearly brought her to her knees.

Cini.

Her hair was a rich auburn, her nose in profile exactly like Valerie's own. She was glorious, wearing a dove gray crepe dress with long sleeves, her creamy breasts swelling to fill the décolleté neckline. Around her neck blazed a choker of perfect rubies. Another ruby, more than twenty carats and surrounded by diamonds, shimmered on her right hand.

Myrna introduced them, and Valerie felt her mother's hand in her own. The shock of that flesh against her own. She looked into eyes that were more golden than her own, but flecked with green.

"It's so very nice to meet you, Mrs. Considy."

"Oh, call me Conni. Everybody calls me Conni."

"And you must call me Valerie."

"It's such a pretty name. You know, I always said to myself that if I ever had a little girl, I would name her Valerie."

"Thank you." Valerie swallowed hard, taking a glass of champagne being offered by one of the staff. The interior designer was saying something about the light on the trees below. Valerie was nodding, watching her mother, who was smiling up at a handsome, white-haired man. Valerie knew the type of woman her mother was very well. She had met her over and over. In drawing rooms, in dining rooms, in ballrooms, for as long as she could remember. That sleek surface, smoothed and honed by the care that only money could buy. Empty. Self-absorbed. Thinking about the next jewel. The next trip. The next gown.

At the dinner table, Valerie sat at Bucky's right, and Conni on his left. Valerie's escort, a recently divorced investment counselor, was talking about Dallas, about how bad times were. She tasted nothing, trying not to

be too obvious as she watched her mother flirt casually
with their host.

Coffee, brandy, and dessert were served by Myrna's
staff in the drawing room, as the lights of Dallas twinkled
in the distance. By eleven o'clock, guests were beginning
to glance at their watches. Myrna led them couple by couple to the elevator, chirping good-byes.

Conni stood in front of Valerie. "It's been so lovely
to meet you at long last, Valerie, after all the marvelous
jewels your collection has found for me." Valerie took
her mother's hand again and looked into those eyes that
were so like her own, the curve of cheekbones and lips
so similar.

"I was hoping you might be able to find a couple
of minutes to see me tomorrow," said Valerie.

"Oh, you have a lovely surprise for me," said Conni,
glee in her voice. "Something wonderful has come on
the market?"

"Would it be convenient?" pressed Valerie, wondering what she would do if Conni said that it wouldn't.

"Of course, my dear," Conni replied in a hearty
voice. Valerie could almost see the mind working, wondering which magnificent ruby was available from which
collection, and how dearly she was going to have to pay
to add it to her own.

"Come at four. We'll have tea."

———
———

Cini's mansion, behind tall wrought-iron gates, was
only a few minutes from Valerie's hotel. A pair of pea-
cocks strutted on the rolling green lawn as the limousine
pulled up to the entrance. Inside, the marble floors, upholstered walls, and twenty-foot ceilings left an impression of unrelieved white. Sunlight beamed through a

wall of glass in the morning room, where Conni motioned Valerie into a chair.

"Isn't this nice that we have a chance to really sit down together?" Conni asked. Valerie looked at Conni carefully in the bright sunlight. She noted Cini's perfect skin, perfect earlobes with ruby earrings, a flawless neck, creamy breasts in a pale green hostess gown. "As you can imagine, I was awake all night, trying to guess which stone had come into the collection." She ran the tip of her tongue over her bottom lip. "Wasn't that a nice party last night?" she continued. "Their chef, well, he is an artist. There's no question. And the condominium is lovely, don't you think?"

"Lovely," agreed Valerie.

"Of course, I would never want to live in a condominium. A bit stultifying. No, I like to be able to roam around. Take a step on my own grounds."

Valerie sat silently, watching Cini's mouth wind around the words, until finally the older woman stopped.

"Are you all right?" she asked.

"You don't know who I am," said Valerie, searching her face.

"I beg your pardon, my dear?" said Conni, a bit taken aback.

"I'm your daughter."

Conni's face went dead white with shock.

"I'm your daughter . . ."

"I'm afraid you must be mistaken, Mrs. Penn." Conni's tone was like ice.

Valerie snapped open her handbag, took out the folded photostat of her birth certificate, and let it flutter onto Conni's lap.

"I've hired detectives," Valerie whispered, her eyes locked with Cini's. "They ran advertisements in the

trades, in the *Times.* They found people who knew you
when you lived in Hollywood. They've taken sworn affidavits.''

"I don't know what you're talking about, Mrs.
Penn," Conni said, the eyes beginning to glitter. With
fear, Valerie realized, because if Valerie had found her,
others could as well.

"The detectives checked birth records all over the
east. They found a Cynthia Schuyler who was just about
the right age." She glanced up to see the horror, the dis-
may, etched on Conni's face. "Of course, it wasn't you.
Then they decided to try California. They found you
through your parents, Ralph and Natalie."

There was a soft noise from the direction of the
doorway and the maid appeared, smiling, pushing a tea
caddy with a silver tea service.

"Leave it there," Conni snapped. "Get out."

The maid's eyes widened in shock as she hurried out
of the room.

"They wouldn't tell the detective anything," Valerie continued, her eyes beseeching. "They said they
hadn't heard from you in thirty years, maybe more. So
I went to see them. I showed them my birth certificate.
They said that whenever they had seen me on television,
they were always struck by how much I looked like you.
Just the same as when you were my age."

"Yes, I had always thought that, too," murmured
Conni, looking off at the garden, perhaps, or at nothing.
"But, I didn't think anything of it. Just one of those coin-
cidences."

"They believed me," said Valerie. "They didn't
know what to think about it. About me, that is. Because
they didn't know about the pregnancy. But they gave me

your number at the answering service, and they promised not to call you. It would be my surprise."

Cini was pensive, listening.

"And what a surprise," Valerie said slowly, "to find out who you were. Conni Considy, one of our major clients."

"What is it you want from me?" Conni asked.

That was a good question, Valerie thought. It was the one question she really couldn't answer. I want you to be my mother. I want you to love me. I want to start all over again.

"I want the truth," Valerie said at last.

"This is pathetic," Conni sneered.

"Where are Al and Vicki Hemion?"

"How would I know that?" Conni asked incredulously. "I haven't been in touch with Al and Vicki Hemion in twenty-five years."

"They disappeared years ago," said Valerie, tears filling her eyes. "You left me with them. You never even bothered to see what had become of me."

"You certainly aren't implying that you have any argument with me about that!" Conni looked at her as if she had taken leave of her senses. "I figured you'd probably try to become an actress, like Vicki, if you were pretty enough. Then you'd get married." She leaned forward, looking hard into Valerie's face. "Look at you. You're one of the most beautiful women in the world."

"I want you to tell me who my father is." Valerie's voice was small. "You were so terrified you left town. You're still terrified. Your own parents don't even know the name you're using."

"You're going to have to forgive me, Mrs. Penn," Conni said coldly, glancing at the diamond watch on her wrist. "I have an engagement, and I have to start getting ready."

"I'll go." Valerie rose wearily to her feet. "Please, Mrs. Considy. I need to know who my father is. Just tell me that, and I promise I'll never bother you again."

Conni looked into Valerie's face with disinterest.

"I'm afraid I can't do that, Mrs. Penn. You see, I don't know." She glanced at her watch again. "And now you really must forgive me. I'm sure you can find your way out."

56

Valerie was seething with hurt and anger by the time she returned home to Beverly Hills and called Sid in New York. It was all she could do to tell him what had happened.

"My own mother, Sid," she stammered. "She dismissed me as if I were nothing."

"Maybe I should give it a try," said Sid, his voice thoughtful. "It sounds to me as if Conni might respond to the coaxing of a big, handsome man. Especially one with a stack of sworn affidavits that the Dallas newspapers might like to see about one of their leading society figures."

"I won't stoop to that level," she said, her voice cold.

"It's all we've got, Valerie. It's our only leverage to find out what she knows."

"But she's frightened, Sid. That must be the reason she was so cutting."

"I'll let her know I'll be discreet," he promised her.

Sid called a few nights later, just as she was sliding into bed.

"I've just left Cini. She let me take her to dinner, even after I told her I was working for you."

"What did she say?" Valerie's hand trembled on the receiver.

"Not a lot. She stuck to the story that she doesn't know who your father is. She said she left town and went to Portland to have her baby because of the disgrace in those days."

"That's not what Vicki told me."

"She said Vicki was wrong."

"I guess she would."

"She's something," Sid noted, admiration in his voice. "I called a friend of mine from college and asked him to leave my name at the Petroleum Club. I had just about tasted my first drink when she walked through the door, blazing with rubies and diamonds. All that red hair. She was on me the minute she saw me."

"She's attractive, isn't she?"

"She's beautiful," Sid agreed. "Anyway, I pulled out all the stops. I told her I would see that the editors of all the Dallas newspapers got copies of our sworn affidavits."

"What did she say?"

"She laughed. She told me to go for it."

"God, she's tough."

"She asked me to go to bed with her," he added.

"And did you?"

"I declined, with thanks. I told her I didn't do things

like that while I was working. Then she asked me if I was your lover."

"What did you tell her?"

"Well, I wasn't going to lie, Valerie. Anyway, we had a couple of drinks, a nice dinner. She was very good at brushing her leg against mine under the table. I even thought she was going to grope me for a minute there. It got me all excited, in fact."

"Sid." There was a hint of disapproval in her voice. "We're still nowhere."

"She did tell me one thing, Valerie. When they were all kids in Hollywood, having a good time, Al always said if he ever got a stake, he wanted to move to Australia. He liked the idea of a new country. When I get back to New York tomorrow, I'll have somebody send a telex to Sydney to start checking it out."

"Did she say anything about me?" she asked wistfully.

"Just that you didn't know when to let well enough alone," he said gently. "Maybe she's right, Valerie."

Valerie was resolute. "No, Sid. I'll never rest until I find my son, and the truth about my past. I'm sorry, but there's nothing Cini Schuyler can do to stop me."

———

A couple of days later, Sid was on the telephone again.

"We've gotten a letter from the attorney for the doctor who performed the *in vitro* fertilization. He says that all of Dr. Gordon Lerner's records are sealed to protect the integrity of his research, and to insure the privacy of the couples who participated in his early experimental programs. We can try to get them unsealed. But, if we have to take the bastard to court, it could take a couple of years. That's the problem.''

"There were others at the surgery,'' she reminded him. "There was Gordon Lerner's assistant. There was a nurse. There was an anesthesiologist.''

"That's right. I'll call London and have somebody take a run down there. Maybe a little bribe might get us a look at the records.''

———

When Sid called again, it was to tell her that he had finally gotten through to Lady Anne Hallowell at her villa in Cap Ferrat.

"She said she'll talk, but only to you, Valerie.''

More lies, Valerie thought bitterly. Like everything else about my life.

"I'm planning to be in London for the tennis matches at Wimbledon in a couple of weeks,'' Sid was saying. "I think I should be with you when you speak with Lady Anne. I can run over a little earlier, if you want me there. I'll be an objective listener.''

"Yes, I think it would be better if you're there,'' she said slowly, wishing it weren't so.

———

It was odd to think that Lady Anne had been in her life for nearly twenty years, Valerie thought. Lady Anne had raised her, really, no matter what her reasons would turn out to be. Valerie sat in the bay window of her suite, looking out at the stony beaches of Nice and the blue Mediterranean just across the Promenade des Anglais. The room service waiter tapped on the door and wheeled in a breakfast cart with a pitcher of orange juice, flaky warm croissants, freshly made strawberry jam, and a pot of coffee. Valerie felt her stomach tighten at the thought of their meeting, only a few hours away now. Their only contact over the last few years had been through small presents on birthdays and Christmas, and notes of sympathy and distress when Penny disappeared and Max was murdered.

Valerie was already sitting in the lobby of the Hotel Negresco, glancing over the front page of the *International Herald-Tribune*, when Sid dropped onto the sofa next to her. He wore a white polo shirt and chinos and carried a blue blazer over his arm, his blond hair freshly blown dry.

"The car's here. You ready?"

Valerie sighed and folded the newspaper in her lap.

"Ignorance isn't bliss," he reminded her. "Let's go."

Sid had rented a Mercedes-Benz convertible for the beautiful drive along the French Riviera. The early summer sun caressed their faces and shoulders, and glittered on the soft swells of the Mediterranean. The traffic moved steadily along the Lower Corniche, past vacationers picking their way down to the rocky beaches, splashing in the surf, sitting on folding beach chairs under brightly colored umbrellas.

By the time Sid made his turn onto the narrow, tree-shaded lane leading to Lady Anne's villa, Valerie's mouth was dry. They stood together at the low-arched front door, hearing the call of the bell from somewhere inside. The door opened, and a maid led Valerie and Sid through rooms with low ceilings, comfortable furniture upholstered in bright fabrics, occasional fine antiques, and bowls of flowers everywhere.

Lady Anne stood on the terrace with her back to them, her arms crossed in front of her, facing out to the shining blue sea. She turned as she heard their footsteps on the tile and walked gravely toward them, leaning to press her cheek against Valerie's.

"This is Sid James, Lady Anne." She was surprised at the tremor in her voice, at Lady Anne's nearly white hair and the network of wrinkles around the corners of her eyes and mouth.

Lady Anne held out her hand to Sid, smiled graciously, and motioned them to a table set up for luncheon. The maid poured each of them a glass of white wine and returned with salads of crab, shrimp, lobster, an urn of butter, a freshly baked baguette.

Sid set his tape recorder in the middle of the table and adjusted the microphone.

"All right, Lady Anne," he said.

"Well," she began, drawing a deep breath, "I had been living in modest circumstances in a little villa not far from where we are now when I received a note from Claude Vilgran. We'd met socially several times. He wrote that you were coming to London to study at the London Conservatory of Music. He described you as a 'talented young relative of the Penn family.' As the Penns felt a certain amount of responsibility to you, it was decided that you should spend the year in an environment appropriate to the family's station. I, with my impeccable social credentials, he wrote, would provide that background; the Penns would be delighted to pay me for my services. A house in Mayfair would be leased and properly furnished. There would be a proper staff, and a chauffeur-driven limousine would be at our disposal. And all of the other amenities. Whatever, he said, I felt would be necessary.

"And he also promised me a bonus of two hundred thousand pounds. Not a fortune, of course, but it would certainly add to my financial security in the future. And so I agreed.

"It was so tempting," she said, looking at Valerie with pleading eyes. "The thought of being in London again for a year, of being able to entertain my friends in a lovely home. To have a car again, and a driver. To be able to live the way I did while I was growing up, the way I lived with my late husband before estate duties took nearly everything.

"Penn International owned the house on Green Street. I hired the inside staff, but Claude Vilgran insisted on providing us with Bernard, the chauffeur.

"Then, only a few days before you were scheduled to arrive in London, Monsieur Vilgran informed me that you were not a member of the Penn family, but only a student to whom Penn International had awarded a scholarship. Then Monsieur Vilgran told me to introduce you as my own niece. I was baffled.

"Things had seemed to go along smoothly enough. You were so charming, my dear, and I did enjoy seeing to your tutors and guiding your development. It was almost like being a mother, in fact. We were having a wonderful time for a while, Valerie.

"Then your parents disappeared, and the whole situation began to seem very peculiar. I didn't know what to think or whom to believe. Either the Hemions had been paid to get out of your life, or they had been killed. And," she added, "neither alternative would have surprised me. By then, it was too late for me to back out. All I could do was wait to see what happened next, try to maintain appearances by going about our usual routine, and hope for the best. And then, you got involved with that boy at the conservatory." She smiled at Valerie, reaching over to pat her knee.

"Julian Unwin," said Valerie.

"Bernard called Monsieur Vilgran at once. I tried to reason with him." Lady Anne shook her head. "I told him you were a young girl, and it was only natural for you to want to have friends. But he said you weren't to see the boy. He said he didn't care what I told you, but it was to be finished right then.

"I remember calling you into my suite and telling you that you must devote all of your free time to catching up socially. So that you would be prepared to deal with the level of people you would meet as your career developed. It was all I could think to say," Lady Anne sighed. "Then you saw that boy again. Several times."

"And you found out," said Valerie.

"That was the end of any pretense. Monsieur Vilgran said I wasn't to let you out of my sight unless Bernard was physically guarding you. He instructed me to have a gynecologist examine you to be sure your hymen was intact. I was in fear of my life," whispered Lady Anne, looking at Valerie, her eyes wet behind her bifocals. "I was so upset for you, my dear. You were the innocent one."

"Oh, Lady Anne. I felt guilty because you were stuck with me. I had nowhere to go," said Valerie. "I felt so bad because you were supporting me. There didn't seem to be any end in sight."

"Instead, you were supporting me." Lady Anne's voice was hoarse. "And, no, there didn't seem to be any end in sight. There were your competitions, of course. My dear Valerie, you were so talented. The concerts you gave. Then you performed at the Albert Hall. And Victor came backstage afterwards to your dressing room. I had made plans, of course, for a supper to celebrate your success and your seventeenth birthday. But Victor wanted to be alone with you. When he came over to ask me if it would be all right, I said to myself, 'Is this it? Is this what all of this has been about?' "

"He didn't bring me home until morning," Valerie remembered.

"Well, I had been up all night, literally walking the floor," recalled Lady Anne. "I couldn't decide what was going on. I thought, perhaps, it was just as it seemed. You were making a reputation, and he was just being polite. Even when he sent you that Degas sculpture, I didn't know for sure. He was known for his extravagance." She paused, thoughtful.

"When he called to tell me he was picking you up at the conservatory and taking you to the country for lunch, that Bernard didn't have to bother to fetch you, well, that's when I realized what was happening. My function had been to train you to be a proper wife for Victor Penn."

"Did you ever confront him with it?" asked Sid.

"Oh, no," said Lady Anne hastily. "It was unspoken. Everything was very proper between Victor and myself. I knew that my job was just about finished at that point. When he took you to Paris," she said to Valerie, "I almost held my breath until Victor formally asked me for your hand."

"Were you relieved?" Valerie asked sadly.

"Oh, yes. All that was left to do was the wedding. That took a lot of planning, of course. Weddings like yours always do. Every day when I woke up, I said to myself, 'This is one day closer to the end of it. This is one day closer to my freedom from the Penns.'

"All this time, I kept asking myself, 'Why this child?' You were lovely, of course, and growing more beautiful every day. And so talented. But there had to be more to it. There were other beautiful and talented young girls. Wellborn, young women whose families would have killed to land a man like Victor Penn. The question 'Why Valerie Hemion?' kept going round and round in my mind.''

"And I wasn't even Valerie Hemion," said Valerie slowly. "My real mother, Lady Anne, was a woman named Cini Schuyler, a friend of Vicki's. Sid found her in Dallas. I met her for the first time last week."

"Ah, that's the missing link. Now everything fits into place, Valerie. The Penns must have known your mother. Don't you remember the first night we ever went to Victor's mansion?"

"Oh, yes."

"Well, I've never seen a look on the face of a human being like the one on Raymond Penn's when he first met you. I'll never forget it. It was as if he were looking at a ghost. He must have realized the moment he saw you that you were Cini's daughter."

Valerie was still.

Was that all Raymond had realized? Perhaps he realized he was meeting his own daughter. Or Victor's. She looked at Sid, saw his awareness of those possibilities flash across his face.

"I'd begun to think . . ." Valerie's voice trailed off.

Lady Anne shuddered, her face in her hands.

"Oh, my dear. I've always cared for you, Valerie. You have been like my own daughter. Can you ever forgive me?"

———
———

It was dusk by the time they saw the rooftops of the city of Nice undulate over the softly swelling hills. Valerie had been silent since they had pulled away from Lady Anne's door.

"Valerie." Sid's arm was around her shoulder. "Are you all right? You look as if you could use a little dinner. What do you feel like?"

"Nothing," she said quietly.

Sid was looking at her, his eyes intent.

"We'll go out," he was saying. "We'll have a wonderful dinner somewhere, a couple of bottles of wine. I know just the place. It's about an hour's drive from here, up in the mountains, at Saint-Paul de Vence. You go upstairs and dress. It'll be fun."

"I'm sorry, Sid. I just don't know how I feel right now. I need to be alone. To think."

"We'll think together," he said, concern in his voice. "We've been a good team so far, Valerie. Let's not stop now."

———

Soaking in her bath, Valerie closed her eyes, her mind a jumble of questions. Cini Schuyler. Raymond. Victor. But how did it all fit together? Claude Vilgran would know, of course. He had set all of this in motion. But, how was she ever going to find him? And, even if she did, why would he tell her anything?

As she stepped into the lobby and saw Sid standing near the doorway, she had to agree that it had been a good idea to go out. He smiled as he noticed her walking toward him. "You look fabulous," he said, leaning to kiss her cheek.

"Thank you, Sid." Valerie wanted to reach up and push the blond curl on his forehead back into place.

It was nearly an hour before they approached the little village high above Nice and pulled up to the Restaurant Colombe d'Or. Sid took her elbow as the maître d'hôtel led them to a table by the window. He smiled broadly as he helped her into her chair and gestured toward the view of the whole valley, sparkling down below.

Sid conferred with the maître d'hôtel about the wine, tasted it when it was presented, and nodded his approval. "To the future, and the eventual answers to all your questions, Valerie."

"Sid," said Valerie, finally, "it's Claude Vilgran. He knows everything: why Cini has been running scared, why Al and Vicki disappeared, and where Victor is keeping Penny. Oh, Sid." Valerie sighed. "I can't get this afternoon out of my mind. We've come a step closer, but I feel as lost as ever. And everything seems to point to Claude Vilgran. Do you—"

"Valerie," Sid interrupted, his hands closing over hers, his eyes willing hers to look at him. "We're going to get to the end of all this together. London will give us some more answers. You've been so brave, come so far. For tonight, give yourself a gift. Relax. Try to push it all out of your mind. I know how hard it is, but try. Okay?" He smiled, squeezing her hands.

"Sid," she said thoughtfully, "you know I came to Europe only to see Lady Anne. I should get on a plane tomorrow morning and go home."

"No, you shouldn't."

"Why not?"

"Because I don't want you to, Valerie. Because I want you to come to Wimbledon with me. We'll have a good time."

"Why?" she asked, frowning.

"I like having you around."

"So what's changed?"

"Well, when I first met you, I thought you were just another spoiled bitch like so many of the women I grew up with." He searched for words. "But when I said we're a pretty good team, I meant it. That's new, to feel as if somebody is on the same team with me. I like it."

"I thought your style was free and easy. No commitments."

"Yeah, well, maybe I was just waiting for the right person to come along," he said, grinning.

"I'm not interested, Sid."

"Are you kidding?" He laughed. "Of course you're interested. You've been wanting to touch me all evening. I can feel you fighting to keep your hands off me."

"Mr. James, you're the most arrogant man I've ever met."

"But it is true, isn't it? That you want to touch me?"

Valerie shrugged, nodded.

"Well, if you lean forward and I lean forward," he said, "we can just kiss."

"Here? In front of all these people?"

"Oh, Valerie, come on," he chided. "This is France, the country of lovers."

They kissed, a light kiss, leaning over the table as the waiter stood patiently, waiting to serve their escargots in garlic butter.

"Very nice," said Sid approvingly, popping an escargot into his mouth.

"Yes," she agreed. "I thought so, too."

It was nearly one o'clock before they were back in Nice. As the doors of the old-fashioned lift stopped at her floor, Valerie hesitated for a moment. Sid stepped out of the elevator with her, their footsteps soundless on the carpet, as Valerie found the key to her room. She paused in front of her door. Looking up into Sid James's face, she saw the mischief mixed with desire in his blue eyes. She wanted again to reach up and push back that one blond strand that kept sliding down over his forehead.

"What do you think?" he said huskily, putting a hand on either side of her waist.

"It was a wonderful evening," she whispered.

"I thought so, too." He brushed the top of her head with his lips. "I have another good idea. Why don't I come in with you, and we'll make love for a few hours. See how we get along in bed."

"I'm not interested, Sid. I told you."

"But you do want to touch me. You did say that."

"Well, yes. But that's only a physical attraction."

"It's amazing. Your whole family says that to me. That's just what your mother said."

"Did she?"

"Word for word. Just think of how sweet it will be, Valerie. Here's your chance to find out what your mother couldn't have."

"That would be cheap of me, Sid. Going to bed with you just to get back at Cini in some way."

"Well, if I don't care," he said cheerfully, taking the key from her hand, and unlocking the door, "why should you?"

It felt wonderful to be in the double bed with him, to be in his arms while he kissed her cheeks, her eyelids, her mouth. The clear, warm air from the open windows made the curtains flutter, caressed their bodies as they lay wrapped in each other's arms.

Valerie's lips moved over those broad shoulders. Her tongue traced that hawklike nose, touched the center of his lower lip as she felt the wetness between her legs. The wetness she hadn't felt in so long.

"Sid," she whispered, pulling away. "I can't."

But, Sid's fingers were pushing her legs apart, were fondling her genitalia, feeling the wetness there, and he was saying, "Don't worry, darling. I'll take care of you."

And, later, when they were both through, and she was lying, panting, in his arms, her eyes closed, he held her tightly. "Stay here, darling," he whispered. "Fall asleep in my arms."

Valerie drifted off to sleep in his arms, feeling safe and protected. Just before the soft tendrils of unconsciousness wiped her mind clean, the image of Cini passed through her thoughts. Cini, who had borne her and given her away, and who, if it had been her choice, would have seen to it that Valerie had never walked the earth.

Cini, who had made a pass at Sid James, and been refused.

She moved in Sid's arms, found his forehead, wet with perspiration, and kissed it.

Too bad for Cini, she thought, a smile on her lips.

57

London, below, was shrouded in mist and fog as the plane descended into Heathrow. The limousine waiting for Valerie and Sid took them to the Connaught Hotel, where Sid's secretary had reserved a suite.

"Great news," said Sid as he returned to the suite that evening. He kissed her hard, squeezing her until she was laughing and pulling away to catch her breath. "The guy we're using in Australia thinks he has a lead on the Hemions. He had checked everywhere." He stripped off his Burberry raincoat and loosened his tie.

"I know." Valerie nodded, sinking onto the bed.

"First he found nothing," he said, pulling off the jacket to his suit. "Then he started to think about that little dog you mentioned. Muffin, the poodle. Well, Australia is like England. An animal entering the country has to spend six months in quarantine. So he checked with animal control in Sydney. Nothing. Animal control in Melbourne. Nothing. Animal control in Perth. There she was.

"An apricot poodle named Muffin, in quarantine at just that time. We should be hearing more in a couple of days."

"That sounds wonderful," said Valerie as her thoughts careened off each other. So Al and Vicki might be alive. She felt a stab of pain as the old feelings of abandonment washed over her.

Sid leaned over, ruffled her pale hair, kissed her forehead. "Gee, you're nice to come home to," he said, wonder in his voice. "I could really get used to this, buttercup."

Buttercup. Buttercup, he'd said, because her blond hair and fair skin reminded him of fields in the country, of picnics under sunny skies, with everything all green and yellow. Valerie cradled his head, listening to the snap and pop of the fire in the hearth. She kissed his hair.

"You're getting carried away," she murmured.

"I like getting carried away." His voice was content as they lay comfortably together. "I never get to get carried away. It's always on guard. Watch what I say. Watch what I do. Be responsible, of course, and leave no false illusions. No promises, implied or otherwise."

"But this is different, isn't it?"

"Of course," he said, winding his arms around her. "You care only about my body. You told me so."

———

She had just come in the next afternoon when Sid telephoned her from the countryside near Gordon Lerner's clinic. He had decided to see for himself what he could find out. "I drove carefully," he said. "I'm staying at a place called the Twelve Bells."

"Did you find anybody?" she asked anxiously.

"Yes, the head of records at the clinic. How's that? I'm taking her to dinner tonight. As far as she knows, I'm a medical writer for a journal in Pennsylvania. Doing a behind-the-scenes look at *in vitro* fertilization."

"Good luck, Sid. I hope it goes well." Valerie knew that if anybody could find the information they needed, it would be Sid, with his charm. Even she was succumbing to it, in spite of herself.

After midnight, Valerie was still turning fitfully in the double bed, unable to sleep, missing Sid next to her. Outside a sudden flurry of rain pounded against the windows. Through the open bedroom door she heard a sound. Valerie lay still, her heart beating, as she heard a key turning in the lock, the sound of the door opening and then closing. Almost silently.

Somebody from Victor, she thought. He must be aware by now that she had hired a detective. He must know that she was trying to find him and Penny. Was it

Victor himself, that dark, looming figure next to the bed? she thought wildly, her eyes tightly closed, the taste of fear bitter in her mouth.

"Valerie," a voice whispered. "Valerie."

It was a man's voice. There was a hand on her hair, fingers caressing her.

Then she was in Sid's arms as he sank onto the bed and held her against his damp raincoat, kissing her forehead, her mouth.

"I couldn't sleep without you," he murmured against her hair. "I kept looking for you in that bed, and you weren't there."

"I looked for you, too," she whispered, her mouth against his cheek.

He sighed as he stood up, undressed, and came into their bed, taking her into his arms as hers went around his neck. She looked up into his face, into blue eyes earnest and sincere.

"I hope this isn't getting to be one of those nasty habits, like heroin or something," he said as he leaned down and kissed her mouth. She felt the awakening of desire and an almost silly happiness that he had gotten in the car and driven back through the rain and sleet to make love to her and sleep in her arms.

Later, she thought. There would be time later to hear what Sid had uncovered about the Lerner operation, to debate their next move.

"Simple, old-fashioned lust is my style for a rainy night," he said, moving down the bed, outlining each of her breasts with his tongue. He traced her navel and her hipbones before pushing her legs apart and burying his head in her pale pubic hair. His tongue caressed her inner lips, played on her clitoris, as she moved down, too, found his hard penis with her mouth, closed her lips over its head, and began to suck rhythmically. Her vagina was flowing an hour later when he finally entered her, letting her guide his penis into the welcoming mouth between her legs, and pushed into her hard. She felt his chest, the blond hair covering it matted with perspiration, against her breasts. His mouth sucking her lips, his tongue licking her teeth, as they moved together to orgasm.

"I'll miss this," she said later, after they had showered and he had carried her back to bed, tucking her in as if she were a child. Kissing her mouth, her forehead, her earlobes, before he wrapped himself around her to sleep.

"You don't have to," he said, nuzzling her neck.

It seemed to Valerie that she had hardly closed her eyes before the alarm clock was ringing. In less than another ten minutes, the waiter was pushing in the breakfast table, leaning over to light the fireplace.

Valerie was already sipping her coffee in front of the roaring fire when Sid came into the room, all showered, dressed, and smiling.

"Gordon Lerner has quite an operation going at the clinic, according to the woman I took to dinner last night." He sat across from her and poured himself a cup of coffee. "You and Victor weren't the only ones using his services way back then. So did American millionaires and their wives. A head of a European state. A tin billionaire from South America."

"But they all had fertility problems," said Valerie. "Real ones."

"Not at all," he corrected her. "They had no problems at all. In some cases, the egg was actually fertilized in the wife's body by the husband in the traditional way, and then it was removed from the wall of the uterus and implanted in the surrogate mother to be carried to term. In other cases, it was the way you and Victor did it. *In vitro* fertilization in the lab, and then implantation in the surrogate mother."

"Why?"

"Because the woman didn't want her body disfigured by a pregnancy. Or because the husband didn't want it."

"I don't understand."

"The prerogatives of the immensely rich. Why should a rich woman go through a pregnancy, ruining her figure and depriving her husband of her sexual services, if there's a poor woman who can be hired to go through it for her?"

"Was there a file on me?"

"No. That letter from Gordon Lerner's attorney was right on the money. All of his files have been taken away somewhere, sealed, to preserve the privacy of his patients. You can see why. It would be a bombshell if it came out he was providing this service to people whose needs could be considered, shall we say, frivolous. That wouldn't be so hot for his 'savior-of-the-human-race' image."

"So, Victor was just doing what a lot of other rich men were doing. He just didn't bother to tell me."

"It looks like it." Sid leaned over and pulled Valerie up. "Come on, buttercup. Walk me to the door of our humble home. I've got to get back out to the countryside."

"You scared me last night," she admitted as he secured his arm around her waist. "I heard the door open, and I thought I would die."

"I should have called," he said apologetically.

"Did you bring your gun?" she asked, keeping her voice light.

"To England? Not a chance. They would have me in nick as soon as I stepped off the plane."

"But you're a private investigator," she persisted. "You have the right."

"Not here," he said, kissing her. "I wouldn't take the chance."

"Are you going to be back tonight?"

"Of course. Now that you're getting used to me, I have to keep the momentum going, don't I? What are you going to do today?"

"I'm going to call Maria Obolensko, and try to see her if she's in town."

"I'll call you around teatime." His arms tightened around her and his mouth found her lips. "You're a great fuck, do you know that?" His voice was soft, playful.

"So are you." She kissed him again.

She caught Maria at home.

"What do you want?" Maria demanded, her voice cold.

"I would like to see you."

"About what?"

"About the past. About the time when we were friends."

"Before you dropped me as if I were dirt," Maria flared. "Come at five o'clock this afternoon, if you must."

———

The sky was sullen and the rain, just starting again, was beginning to spatter the windows of the limousine as it drew up in front of Maria Obolensko's Eaton Square town house. Valerie moistened her lips, a little nervous to see Maria again, as she stood on the stoop, rang the bell, and heard inside the hysterical yapping of small dogs. That was new, thought Valerie, remembering Maria's Dobermans. The door opened to three tiny Yorkshire terriers, pink bows in their topknots, hurtling out. She knelt to pet them and felt the flurry of little wet tongues on her fingers and hands.

The girl who answered the door could have been a model for Degas, with her pale blond hair pulled into a ballerina's bun on top of her head, her wide, light blue eyes, high cheekbones, and full mouth. She had a dancer's body, slender as an adolescent boy's, with barely formed breasts and no hips. Long legs in tight, washed-out jeans, tennis shoes.

"I'm Ariel," she said as she scooped up one of the little dogs and stepped aside for Valerie to enter the house.

"I'm Valerie Penn," she said, thinking how familiar the girl looked, how she herself had looked very much the same when she had been that age. The girl helped her out of her raincoat and ran her long fingers over the sable lining.

"Maria will be down in a minute," she said in a sweet, shy voice. "Tea will be served in the drawing room."

"Thank you," said Valerie as the girl smiled and moved gracefully, soundlessly, to the foot of the stairs and glided up, the dogs leaping and bounding around her feet.

Valerie strolled into the drawing room and saw that everything was chintzes now, fine antiques. The El Greco was gone, replaced by a Cezanne landscape. There were several other paintings as well, in gilt frames. A Manet. A Signac.

Maria's arrival was heralded by the yapping of the

Yorkies. She posed dramatically at the entrance to the room until Valerie turned from the chimneypiece and smiled at her.

Maria wore cream-colored lounging pajamas and high-heeled pumps in the same color. Her black hair was sleek against her head, coiled at the nape of her neck. Gold and pavé diamonds glittered in her earlobes. Her high cheekbones were even more elegantly etched by the years. Her mouth, as usual, was a slash of scarlet. Her black eyes gleamed malevolently.

She indifferently brushed Valerie's cheek with her own, as Ariel, looking self-conscious, peeped into the room from the doorway.

"You met Ariel?" She gestured toward the girl.

"Yes."

"I found her in New York last year. She is one of my greatest fans. She is a dancer."

"I could tell."

"All of this is for her." Maria gestured around the room. "All of this chintz, and these old pieces of furniture. Ariel likes to have things cozy. And I like it, too. It is a nice change. For the moment, anyway."

"How is the duke of Weyburn?" Valerie asked carefully.

"Impossible. A pig," her hostess muttered, the expression on her face darkening. "He lives in France now, and Acapulco, also. He is always on the phone, begging to see me. I don't go, of course."

"My firm sold his estate here in England."

"Yes, he told me that." Maria patted the sofa next to her, making a place for Ariel to sit beside her.

"Have you seen the villa in Acapulco?" asked Valerie, sipping her tea. "We found that one for him, too."

"So, you got two commissions." Maria laughed, one

hand resting on the girl's thigh. "You finally got some sense. Of course, you had help. That Mary di Stefano. The fake countess. I would see her around at house parties in the old days. All of her hostesses with their jewels locked up so she wouldn't steal them. Or their husbands."

"That wasn't how Victor saw it," she replied, cautioning herself to resist Maria's baiting. "When Victor hired her, he said everybody on the Riviera thought she was the most wonderful person in the world. Her hostesses all said they simply couldn't do without her."

"Well." Maria shrugged, picking up a tea cake and popping it in her mouth while the little dogs wiggled at her feet, begging for a taste. "You're here to ask me about Victor, no?"

"Yes, Maria. That's exactly why I'm here."

It had been Claude Vilgran, an old friend whom Maria knew from house parties in France, Italy, and England, who had introduced Maria to Victor Penn in the days when she was still in need of a patron to subsidize her career, and to pay for the beautiful surroundings she felt to be her right as a supreme artist.

"Of course, Victor was very impressed with me." Maria ran her hand over Ariel's thigh. "He knew I was a genius, and so he wanted to be with me. I decided to try it out with him." She sighed, sipped her tea. "But, it didn't work between us."

"Why not?"

"I laughed at him." Her black eyes flickered with the memory. "I thought he was such a silly child, with what he wanted."

"In bed, you mean."

"Oh, yes. In bed. Of course, in bed."

"What did he want?"

"You told me he shaved you," said Maria abruptly, sitting up straight. "It was right after he had married you. I remember when you said that, one of those days when you were raving over Victor, your darling. I almost threw up, if you want to know the truth, Valerie. He wanted to shave me, too. Not just my bush, but my head, too. He wanted to have a hairless little creature to do things to. To tie up. To drug. 'Oh, it won't hurt you, my exquisite girl,' he told me. 'It will be wonderful. You'll love it.' Can you imagine?"

"My exquisite girl." Valerie clenched her teeth and felt her fury at Victor well up again.

"I asked him what he would pay me and he named a very large amount," continued Maria. "And so we had a weekend together at his castle in the country to see how we would get along."

"How was it?" asked Valerie, curious now.

"A fiasco," Maria chortled. "He took one look at my black bush, and he shriveled up, like a little worm." She laid her head back against the sofa, laughing to herself, remembering. "So we decided to call it off. He gave me a magnificent diamond and ruby necklace, and earrings to go with it. You understand, he was very anxious that I not say to anybody that he was a failure." A smug smile played on her lips for a moment. "And after that, whenever I wanted anything, I would just call him up, so sweet, and say, 'Oh, Victor, I need a new dress. I need a car.' And he would send over a check at once. Because, you understand, he didn't want me to tell on him."

"I understand," said Valerie.

"And then Claude found me the duke of Weyburn."

"Where did I come in?"

"Oh, that's right. You." Valerie realized Maria had actually forgotten why she was there. "Well, I always knew that Victor would have to marry somebody very, very young. So he could train her, you know. To satisfy all of his little whims. Somebody who would know nothing about what a sensual life should be. You understand?"

"Yes," said Valerie.

"And then, Claude came to me one day. He said he had met the most adorable child, so charming and sweet. A niece of Lady Anne Hallowell's. He said that he thought you would do for Victor Penn, if he could only get Victor interested in you. So I came in to help with your career. To make you famous enough so that Victor should notice you. Claude gave me such beautiful things for the help I gave you," Maria recalled.

"But what was Claude's relationship to Victor?" Understanding was beginning to dawn in the corners of Valerie's mind.

"Why, he worked for him. For Raymond, too. He would go around the world finding things for Victor to buy. And he would do anything in the world that Raymond wanted done. It had always been that way, ever since the three of them came to England together."

"From where?" asked Valerie, her heart pounding.

"Oh, I don't know that. That was Claude's secret. He never would tell me, no matter how clever I was when I asked him."

"Did you have an affair with Claude?"

"Oh, no, not an affair." Maria wagged a finger at her. "A dalliance now and then together, when we were very bored. But not an affair."

"Do you think he would see me?" blurted Valerie.

"Claude?" Maria was thoughtful. "Well, you know,

he might. He is not at all well, and he is very bored. It might amuse him to see you."

"Where is he?"

"I can't tell you that, Valerie. I will first have to ask him if he wants to see you. And then, if he does, I will tell you."

"Oh, Maria," she pleaded. "I really need to see him. If our friendship meant anything to you, try to make him see me."

"All right, Valerie." Maria sighed imperiously. "I will call him tonight. And I will call you later at the Connaught."

"Thank you, Maria."

"But, there is something that I would like you to tell me in return. When Victor died, why didn't you just find another rich man? You could have gone on with your music. You could have had a wonderful life on your own in the arts. After all, business is so vulgar."

"I loved Victor," Valerie murmured. "I couldn't think about another man."

Maria's expression was a combination of superiority, contempt, and wonder that anybody could have been so naive.

═══

The two women and the yipping dogs scampering around their feet walked with Valerie to the front door.

Valerie shook hands with Ariel, who stood encircled by Maria's arm. Valerie leaned forward to brush Maria's cheek with her own.

"You're looking older, you know," Maria remarked.

"We all are, Maria," she replied, and there was a

smile on her face as she hurried through the mist to the waiting limousine, then turned to wave good-bye to the woman who had been, in her own convoluted way, her friend.

58

Valerie walked into the small, elegant lobby of the Connaught Hotel and saw that it was crowded with men and women who all looked vaguely familiar. The television talk-show host and his pretty new wife. Movie stars and movie moguls. One of the best-known entertainment attorneys in Beverly Hills. All there for Wimbledon, she realized. Valerie shook her head, trying to clear the thoughts that had been swirling around since she had left Maria's.

In the little suite, she leaned over and put a match to the wood that had been laid for a fire. In the bedroom, she hung her raincoat on a hanger on the back of the bathroom door so that it could dry. Turned over and over again in her mind the conversation with Maria.

Yes, Claude Vilgran was the key. She hoped it would amuse him to see her. He had to see her. Because it seemed that she had been wrong about everything, and Claude Vilgran was the only one who could straighten it out.

She jumped when the telephone's two short rings creased through the silence in the little drawing room.

"Are you all right, buttercup?" asked Sid on the

other end of the line, his voice concerned. "You sound a little odd."

"Oh, Sid," she said, wanting to cry at the welcome sound of his voice, "I saw Maria this afternoon. It isn't Victor. It's Claude Vilgran. He was responsible for starting it. All of it."

"It's interesting you should say that. I called to let you know I'm on my way back. I've got news, too. Nice timing, huh? It will give us just enough time to compare notes, fuck each other into insensibility, and get in the mood for Wimbledon."

"It's raining," she reminded him.

"I can fuck while it's raining."

"Sid . . ."

"It will stop," he assured her. "The sun may not always shine on the British Empire these days, but it always shines on Wimbledon."

———

Light streamed through the curtains as Valerie awakened in Sid's arms the next morning. The rain had stopped, a full day before Wimbledon was to open.

Slipping into her velvet robe, she stole into the drawing room to call room service and light the fireplace.

"Where are you?" called a querulous voice from the next room. "I'm lonely and you don't even care."

Sid was propped up on a couple of pillows, his hands behind his head, his blond hair a tousled mass, his blue eyes bright. He caught his breath at the sight of Valerie as she stepped into the bedroom.

"God, you're beautiful, Valerie," he said in a soft voice. "I can't believe my luck that you've let me into your life."

"You're not bad yourself, Siddon Corbett James

III." She laughed as she slipped out of her robe. As she walked toward him, she could see his eyes travel slowly down her body, then meet and hold hers. There was a tap at the door in the other room, and Valerie pulled her robe back on and opened the door to the waiter.

Valerie took Sid's coffee into the bedroom and slipped, nude, under the sheets as the telephone rang twice.

"Sid James," he said into the receiver, then nodded at what he was hearing. He looked interested, excited.

"The guy in Australia found the Hemions," he said when he had hung up. "He interviewed them. His tapes have been transcribed, and they're coming into the London office on the fax machine right now. Pages and pages, they say. They'll be sending them over by messenger as soon as they're all in."

Al and Vicki. Alive.

Valerie lay back against her pillows, shaking her head, unable to believe it.

———

Al and Vicki lived in an expensive suburb of Sydney in a ranch-style house with a large front lawn and a swimming pool in back. Vicki served Sid's operative cocktails and little crackers shaped like fish in the den, which was nicely furnished with modern sofas and chairs, a glass coffee table, and a built-in bar. Along one wall were framed photographs of a woman who Sid's operative assumed was Vicki in her starlet days. The other occupant of the house was a black toy poodle, also named Muffin.

Al had opened a restaurant in Sydney that had caught on called Rick's Place. It served American beer, hot dogs, and hamburgers. A pianist played American pop tunes in the bar, and, in the dining room, old American movies were shown. Within a couple of years, he had opened several other restaurants throughout Australia, which were also successful.

At the time in question, Al had been approached by a man who informed them that his principal, who wanted to be nameless, was prepared to pay the Hemions two hundred thousand dollars to get out of Valerie's life. The conditions were that they were to emigrate to Australia or New Zealand, whichever they chose, and that they were never to contact Valerie again.

Valerie skimmed the transcript.

Vicki Hemion: We were dead broke. We thought it was Valerie's dad who had found her and wanted to take care of her.

Al Hemion: We just took the money and ran.

Vicki Hemion: We couldn't turn that man down. There was something really scary about him, even though he was a perfect gentleman. We both had the feeling that if we didn't do what he wanted, things would really get bad for us.

Al Hemion: What she's trying to say is that we both thought that sucker would have us killed.

Vicki Hemion: So it all worked out. We're talking to you now because so many years have passed. It couldn't matter anymore, and we want to put Valerie's mind at ease about us. You could have knocked me over with a feather when I read that she had married Victor Penn. I turned to Al and said, "So, that was what it was all about."

Al Hemion: It was all I could do to stop this sentimental broad from sending a wedding present.

Vicki Hemion: When the babies were born, I felt as if they were my very own grandchildren. I wanted to jump on a plane and go see my little Valerie. Hold those dear, little babies.

Al Hemion: I wouldn't let her. Besides, by that time Valerie had gotten pretty grand. I couldn't see Victor Penn being too happy to see Vicki if she had come knocking on the door.

Vicki Hemion: My heart practically broke for Valerie when Victor Penn was killed on that plane. When it turned out that he had been a thief, and the whole company fell apart, I cried for Valerie, I really did.

And when her little boy was kidnapped and her fiancé . . . well, I didn't sleep for weeks.

Al Hemion: But she's done great. That company of hers is fantastic. We even know people who have managed to get a copy of that catalog they put out. She's turned out so beautiful. Every time I see her picture in the papers, I can hardly believe that it's our own little Valerie. She was always such a tiny little thing. So shy.

Vicki Hemion: Except for her music. We were always so proud of her music. Why, I stopped working so I could take her around. Al and I were at every concert. She was a wonderful pianist.

Al Hemion: Yeah, she was great. Really great.

Vicki Hemion: Give her our love, will you? Will you tell her we would love to hear from her sometime? That we hope she will find it in her heart to forgive us?

(Operative thanked subjects for their time and hospitality, and left his card in case they had anything to add to what they had told him.)

The last page of the fax report was a reproduction of a photograph of Al and Vicki Hemion. They looked older, Valerie saw, and both had put on some weight. They were standing in front of the ranch house. Al had his arm around Vicki's waist, both were smiling, and in Vicki's arms was a small black poodle.

Valerie felt Sid's eyes on her as she turned the last page.

"Are you all right, buttercup?"

"Oh, Sid," she murmured, wiping away tears, and laughing at the same time.

59

Valerie huddled in her raincoat and watched Wimbledon's top seed drill an ace. His opponent stood there shaking his head.

A light rain began to fall, and umbrellas all over the stands started to pop open.

"They're going to call it," said Sid, disgusted. "We're just going to have to go back to the hotel and spend the rest of the day making love."

"But first I need to stop by a few jewelry shops," said Valerie to Sid. He held the umbrella over their two blond heads with his arm around her shoulder.

"You need a fix?" he grinned.

"I've finally figured out why Maria hasn't called us about setting up a meeting with Claude Vilgran."

———

In an antique jewelry store off Portobello Road, she found a bangle bracelet made of twin intertwined snakes, their bodies formed of gold scalework and accented with opaque white enamel. The heads, which met, were decorated with two pear-shaped pearls, cabochon ruby eyes, and pavé-set diamonds.

Sid gave a low whistle when he saw the price. Twelve thousand American dollars, exactly twice what Valerie had intended to spend. "If I keep on hanging around with you," he said, "I'm going to have to get a second job."

"I know Maria." Valerie wrote out a check and a gift card and handed them both to the salesperson, along with Maria's address in Eaton Square.

———

By the time they returned to the hotel that afternoon, there was a message from Maria Obolensko asking Valerie Penn to telephone back as soon as possible. Valerie's heart raced as she lifted the receiver.

"He's going to see me tomorrow," she said a few minutes later, after she had said good-bye to Maria.

"I'm coming along," said Sid. "Where is he?"

"He's living in a village, Saint Helion's Bumstead. It isn't too far away from Cambridge."

"Great," smiled Sid. "I'll show you my college. The old alma mater, and all of that."

———

The twenty-one colleges of Cambridge University were spread all over the city of a hundred thousand people, located on the banks of the River Cam. Birds chirped in the ancient trees that bent over the river with the weight of the days of rain.

They had a late lunch in a pub in the center of Cambridge. Afterwards, they wandered through the main line of colleges. Magdalene. Saint John's. Trinity, where Sid had studied during the year he had been on his Rhodes scholarship. At Clare College they stood on the stone bridge, with its thick stone balls on its parapets, looking down at the gray river, Sid's arms wrapped tightly around Valerie, his cheek resting on her hair. "I love you, Valerie."

"I think I love you, too, darling," she said hesitantly.

"We'll get it right, Valerie," he said, pulling her closer.

They were in Saint Helion's Bumstead by mid afternoon. The chauffeur pulled up in front of a tobacco shop where several men in overcoats were looking at the newspaper headlines on the racks outside. Lowering the electric window, he asked one of them where he could find the residence of Mr. Claude Vilgran.

"It's to your left, at the top of the hill. You can't miss it," the man assured the chauffeur. "We thought you'd be for Monsieur Vilgran. He gets all the limousines that come to Saint Helion's Bumstead."

60

The old vicarage where Claude Vilgran lived was charming, with a sloping roof and pretty windows. It was set twenty feet back from the country road. In the front garden were a pair of graceful oak trees, and flower beds bloomed on either side of the steps leading to the front door. Sid's knock was answered by a dark woman in a uniform.

"Valerie Penn and Sid James," he said. "We have an appointment with Monsieur Vilgran."

"Come in," she said, standing aside. "He expects you."

The woman led them into a little sitting room looking onto the back garden.

It was among the loveliest rooms Valerie had ever seen, filled with antique pieces by artisans whose work even she didn't know. The chimneypiece, where a fire burned, was wood, ornately carved with fruit and leaves. "Exquisite," she murmured, shaking her head. The carpet, navy blues and reds, a hint of yellow, was a silk warp Tabriz, a masterpiece worthy of any museum. There were several eighteenth-century landscapes hanging in gilt frames on the walls. Unfamiliar, but breathtaking.

"Welcome to my home," said that familiar voice, oily, ingratiating, but subdued. Valerie turned from the painting she had been examining to see Claude Vilgran in an aluminum wheelchair being pushed into the room by a manservant. A plaid blanket covered his legs. His hair was thinner, and his face was the color of old wax.

"Claude," she said as she moved toward him, extending her hand. His grasp was surprisingly firm as she introduced Sid.

"Oh, yes, Mr. James. Department stores, isn't it, and a little gumshoeing on the side? Do sit down," he said, pushing himself next to an enchanting nineteenth-century table as the housekeeper returned with silver trays, a tea service, and a bottle of sherry. She served the three of them silently and vanished, closing the double doors to the room behind her.

"Your home is beautiful, Claude," said Valerie. "Exquisite. And your things. Even I don't know what some of them are, or where they came from."

"Well, that would be reasonable, wouldn't it?" said Claude. "After all, finding beautiful things is the way I've always made my living. Obviously, with my own home, I would have the best for myself."

"Touché."

"You know, the truth is, this is the first home I've ever had," he said, looking around, the ghost of a smile playing at the corners of his mouth. "I've always lived in hotels or stayed with friends. I was quite the social butterfly until my little accident."

He paused, looking at the two of them, a hint of amusement in his eyes. "Oh, you're both too polite to ask. Of course. Well, it was a small stroke, in fact. Too much good living. Too many bottles of champagne. Just one oyster too many, perhaps."

"I'm sorry," Valerie murmured.

"It isn't that bad. On my good days, I can even walk. On the others, well, there is a bit of weakness in my right leg. And sometimes, I have trouble holding things with my right hand. Otherwise, I am relatively unimpaired, except, of course, for the natural ravages of age."

"Where would you like to start, Monsieur Vilgran?" asked Sid, testing the tape recorder. "How do you fit into all of this? What about Victor Penn? Raymond Penn? And Valerie. How does she come into it?"

"You mean this isn't just a visit to an old friend?" he asked, his tone ironic, as he looked over at Valerie on the sofa, her fists clenched in her lap.

"Claude, I'll pay you anything you want," said Valerie. "Anything."

"Well, I have been thinking about that since Maria told me you wanted to come to see me. Two million dollars is my figure." He looked over at her, his eyes taunting her.

Two million dollars, thought Valerie, quickly calculating her assets in her mind.

"Fine."

"If I had known you were going to do so well, and that you are so generous, I might have been on your side, my dear."

"I didn't know there were sides."

"Yes. That was always the problem with the game. That you didn't know there were sides."

His hand trembled slightly as he picked up his glass, took a sip of the sherry, and turned to Sid. "Don't think I'm going to talk into that thing, Mr. James." He waved his glass at the tape recorder. "No, you can put it away or I say nothing."

"Victor and Raymond Penn are the sons of a prominent German businessman, baron von Pentheim, who fled with his wife and his two children to Argentina shortly before the end of World War II. They were escaping prosecution for using slave labor in his munitions factories. Using the millions he smuggled out of Germany as a base, the old baron quickly added to his fortune with cattle ranches, mining, logging, and then financial institutions in his new homeland. My own father was a French collaborator who had also fled to Argentina. He worked for the baron, managing his estate. I was a brother to Raymond and Victor, in all but blood. We were classically educated by private tutors, and when they were sent by their father to England to make their mark in the larger world, I went with them. I could be trusted, of course, to do anything either of them wanted to be done.

"The times we had." Claude smiled. "We were everywhere. Based in London, of course, because that was what the old baron wanted. But Paris, too. Rome. New York. Acapulco. All along the Riviera. And Los Angeles. Oh, the boys loved Los Angeles. The movie stars, the polo matches in Santa Barbara. All of those adorable little girls trying to break into films. They would do anything if they thought the man was important enough."

"Cini Schuyler," said Valerie slowly.

"Yes, Cini. I was the one who found Cini. I'll never forget it. It was at the Coconut Grove in the Ambassador Hotel, down on Wilshire Boulevard, which was still so popular in those days. Everybody used to appear there. Lena Horne. Frank Sinatra.

"I was there with friends, sitting at a table in front.

At the next table, in a group of eight or ten, I saw an absolutely beautiful creature. All of that blond hair, and those hazel eyes with something yellow in them. Amazing cheekbones, and a full mouth. Aah, that mouth." He glanced at Valerie. "She was far more voluptuous than you are, my dear. She was wearing something low-cut, with a little sprinkling of rhinestones around the neckline covering those wonderful, creamy breasts. She stood to dance with her escort, and her waist was so tiny. Those hips. The legs. She smiled at me when she walked by our table, and she had a mad glitter in her eyes. I remember thinking, Oh, she would certainly do for the boys. They will just love her.

"At some point I went over, gave her my card and asked her to call me. I saw her run her dear little tongue over her lips, thinking about it. I didn't know what she was at that point, of course. She said to me, 'I'm expensive.' And I said to her that that was even better, that she was a professional."

"So, she called," said Valerie.

"Of course she called." Claude smiled.

"Which one of them was it?" asked Valerie, trying to keep her voice steady as her heart pounded madly.

"Oh, it was Raymond," said Claude. "Victor would have taken her in a minute, but Raymond liked her. And so Victor deferred to his older brother. It had to be somebody special to interest Raymond, even then."

Raymond Penn. My father.

"Mr. James," said Claude, "here, give Valerie a bit more of this sherry."

"Are you all right, darling?" Sid's voice showed astonishment and concern.

"Go on, Claude." Valerie took a huge breath.

"You see, when we were all growing up, since Raymond was the elder son, the old baron placed all of his hopes in him. The baron was, shall we say, rather intemperate when it came to disciplining Raymond. As luck would have it, Raymond came to like being punished. To him, it was a sign of love. He sought women who would give him that. Cini, of course, was more than happy to oblige. She adored it."

"Did he tell you about it?" asked Valerie, barely comprehending Claude's words.

"Oh, yes. We used to talk about things back then. It was whips and chains, and all of that." He grimaced. "With your mother as the beautiful, glorious dominatrix. Cini Schuyler, of course, realized she was on to a good thing. She became pregnant and tried to blackmail him." He paused to sip the sherry. "And I set out to kill her on Raymond's instructions. She slipped away," he admitted, "but I never stopped trying to find her. It didn't occur to me that she would actually have the child." He paused and looked at Valerie. "And how is your dear mother, Valerie? Did you have better luck in finding her than I did?"

"No."

"Well, actually, with the life she was leading, I'd be astonished if she were still alive. I recall that she was experimenting with drugs. And all those men and women. When she didn't turn up after a couple of years, I just assumed she had done what she seemed to have in mind all along, which was to commit suicide."

"Trying to blackmail Raymond certainly showed that," noted Sid.

"It certainly did," agreed Claude. "Did you find her parents?" he asked, turning to Valerie. "Such a nice couple. Such an unlikely pair to have produced the glorious Cini."

"She's dead. They told me so."

"At any rate," Claude continued, "I had other work to do, mostly for Victor. Raymond was always quite austere, but Victor loved things. He was his mother's favorite, which is so often the case with a younger son, and the baroness loved things, too. She loathed being locked away in Argentina with no society, nobody to entertain, nobody to see her clothes, her jewels. But she was a good German wife to the end, and she did what her husband desired. She left Victor her taste for paintings, furniture, lavish homes, and all of the treasures the world has to offer. And that became my job. Traveling the world to find those things for Victor. It was a good life, I must say. Staying in the best hotels, meeting the most amusing people." He met Valerie's eyes. "You know, when I saw you at the Hollywood Bowl, I was astonished. Here was a little usherette who was a dead ringer for Cini Schuyler, and just about the right age to be the child she had carried by Raymond.

"Over the next few days, I arranged an accidental meeting with one of the secretaries in the administration office of the Hollywood Bowl. I took her to lunch, flattered her a bit, and I found out your name and address. There was nothing to it. One of my men entered your apartment, found your birth certificate, and photographed it. Of course, you didn't know."

"You didn't tell Raymond you had found me," said Valerie. "You didn't tell anybody."

"Oh, yes," he corrected her, the hint of a smile in his eyes. "I did tell somebody. I told Victor."

"What did Victor have to do with it?" asked Valerie, puzzled. Sid squeezed her hand, then put an arm protectively around her shoulders.

"Raymond was austere, and Victor was lavish. I

knew if I had told Raymond about you, he might have said, 'Kill her,' and that would have been that. But you were a Penn. Or rather, a von Pentheim.

"Victor was enchanted when I told him I had found you," Claude continued, his eyes gleaming. "With all of his love and respect for Raymond, he was also terribly competitive. 'Oh, let's bring her to England,' he said."

"What did he have in mind?" asked Sid.

"Very little, actually." Claude smiled. "He thought it would infuriate Raymond. It would be an amusing new game. So we came up with the music scholarship, and everything else."

"You monster," Valerie gasped at the insolent look on Claude's face.

"Now, now, my dear . . ."

"And what about the Hemions?"

"The most direct solution would have been to just have them killed."

Killed. Valerie remembered the murdered passengers of the Penn International jet. Max Perlstein. Harry Cunningham.

"Killed? Is it that easy, Claude?" Valerie couldn't control the trembling in her voice.

"But we decided against that. If they had been murdered, you see, the authorities would have made you, as next of kin, return to Los Angeles while their investigation was going on. Since you had no relatives, you would have been made a ward of the court and placed in a foster home. That wouldn't do. Not at all."

"So they had to disappear," said Sid.

"Yes." He nodded. "Victor was so thrilled I had pulled everything off that he gave me a painting. Van Gogh's *Hyacinths*."

"You must have gotten a fortune for it when you sold it," Sid observed.

"Oh, I didn't sell it," said Claude, faintly surprised. "I wouldn't sell a present from Victor. It's hanging in the dining room. You'll see it when we go in for dinner. You will stay for dinner, won't you?" he asked anxiously, looking first at Valerie, then at Sid. "It's for the staff, really. They were so excited at the thought of guests. It's so difficult to get people to come all this way. Everybody is so involved."

His expression was solemn as he stared into the embers in the fireplace.

"Yes, only Raymond comes." He sighed. "And Raymond has always been so austere. He really doesn't care for good food. He'll have a glass of wine, of course. But he has other concerns. Things of the mind, I believe. The life of a recluse is just right for him. I never imagined my life would turn out to be as reclusive as his."

61

Despite its vaulted ceiling, the dining room was small. The chandelier above the Chippendale table was gilt, Italian, with six burning tapers. The bare wood floor gleamed, reflecting the candlelight; the walls, painted in a nondescript off-white, picked up the white of the hyacinths in the van Gogh painting hanging across from Claude at the head of the table. A fire burned brightly in a fireplace with a simple marble chimneypiece.

"That's the problem with having such an important painting," Claude mused as the cook ladled steaming green pea soup from a tureen into bowls. "You can't do a thing with the rest of the room. Everything has to be simple, simple, simple. Such a bore.

"Isn't the soup marvelous?" asked Claude, meeting Valerie's eyes. "They've been planning the menu since yesterday. They decided it would all be local fare. From the village."

In spite of herself, Valerie agreed it was the best soup she had ever tasted.

"They've brought your chauffeur into the kitchen," added Claude. "So don't worry about that. He's getting his dinner, too. I told them only one glass of wine for him, since he'll have to drive all the way back to London tonight."

"Thank you," said Valerie.

"How does London look to you these days?" asked Claude, using his left hand to spoon the soup.

"Lots of building. Excavations everywhere."

"Yes." He nodded. "A pity."

"It's just like New York, or Los Angeles," said Sid, wiping the corner of his mouth with his linen napkin. "All major cities seem to go the same way."

"Yes, they do," agreed Claude, looking at Sid.

"You had Valerie in London, and the Hemions out of her life," Sid reminded Claude. "What happened next?"

"Oh, yes. As I said, Victor was so excited about the whole situation. The house in Green Street was all set up, with Lady Anne there to attend to the child, and Bernard to keep me current with everything that happened." He glanced at Valerie as she steeled herself for what might come next. "He couldn't wait to see you."

"It was three years."

"Oh, no, not at all. He saw you at the opera, in Lady Anne's box at Covent Garden, shortly after you arrived in England. He looked at you through his opera glasses several times."

"And?"

"Well, no offense, my dear," said Claude, touching Valerie's arm. "But he was very disappointed."

"Oh, really?" She felt the set of her jaw.

" 'But she's just a baby,' was what he said to me. 'She's a provincial child.' I remember saying to him, 'But Victor. Those wonderful bones. That mouth. The eyes. Those strange hazel eyes with the yellow flecks, and those long, long lashes. Think of the potential.' "

"And what did Victor say?" she asked, feeling the rage well up within her.

"He said to do what I wanted, that he didn't care. I decided to bide my time, keep to my plan, and eventually get his interest. So I paired you with Maria Obolensko."

"So you brought him people as well as things," said Valerie slowly.

"Like a pimp," said Sid.

"You don't offend me, Mr. James," Claude said, smiling slightly as he met Sid's eyes. "It was my role in life to provide Victor with what he wanted, just as it was my father's role in life to do the same for the old baron."

"And you provided for Raymond, too?" asked Valerie.

"He wanted less. He is a celibate. He always was, except for that brief time just after we left Argentina. He has been ever since."

"That isn't what people say," Valerie reminded him. "The little boys, the torture chamber . . ."

"Oh, my dear . . . all nonsense," he said shortly as his manservant appeared with a huge silver platter and began to carve a saddle of lamb.

"I kept telling Victor how well you were developing," he continued, after the manservant had returned to the kitchen, leaving them alone. "I kept saying that Lady Anne was molding you into a truly superb young woman. That you were more charming than any other girl in England, and your beauty was astonishing. He was still uninterested. Until, that is, Maria saw to it that your talent was recognized by the critics. When you were talked about by the people Victor saw socially, the people who matter here, he finally decided he would meet you, to see what sort of a young woman you had turned out to be."

"I gather he liked what he saw," Sid muttered.

"He was utterly charmed. My plan had worked. But I've always known what Victor wanted. Often, before he knew it himself."

"Did Raymond know about me?"

"Well, that was very wicked of Victor and myself." Claude smiled at his own cleverness. "We didn't tell Raymond. He didn't know you existed those first three years. There wasn't any reason, you see. Raymond knew about all of the major expenses of the corporation, but the expenses of Lady Anne and the Green Street house were so minor he never would have been bothered with such petty amounts. So the first time Raymond learned about you was after the fact, after Victor had already begun seeing you."

"Exactly when did he find out about me? Do you remember?"

"Certainly. Victor and I planned it very carefully. It was the first evening he had you and Lady Anne to dinner and bridge at the Regent's Park mansion. Raymond was there, as I am sure you recall. When you walked in, and Raymond saw this *jeune fille* with the face of Cini Schuyler, he knew at once who you were. He was beside himself with anger and humiliation. We kept telling him we had thought he would be amused."

"Was he amused?" asked Sid laconically.

"Not at all. When Victor decided to marry Valerie, Raymond declared their relationship over. They were no longer brothers."

"He didn't stick to it."

"Oh, no. Of course not. The old baron wouldn't hear of it. Victor and I had counted on the old man interceding, and he did."

"So we were married," Valerie prompted.

"A beautiful wedding, didn't you think?" asked Claude, his eyes misting. "Quite the most beautiful wedding I have ever seen. So extravagant.

"He was so pleased with you, my dear. Your beautiful body, your exquisite face. He used to tell me how lovely you were, how soft your skin was to his touch. He said your genitalia were the most perfectly formed he had ever seen. And he was quite a connoisseur, as you can imagine." He turned to Sid. "Do you agree, Mr. James, that Valerie has perfectly formed genitalia?"

"I have never thought of it quite that way, Monsieur Vilgran," Sid said pleasantly, as Valerie looked at her plate, her cheeks hot.

"Then the old baron started to clamor for a grandchild," reminisced Claude. "A boy."

"I wanted a child, too," said Valerie. "I wanted to give Victor a son. Desperately."

"Well, that didn't really matter," Claude pointed out. "But as the old baron wanted an heir, something had to be worked out. It sent Victor into a terrible tizzy. He knew he would be repelled by your body forever if you went through a pregnancy. He talked to me about it. 'Claude,' he said, so upset, 'I would never be able to touch my little girl again. To see those lovely small breasts engorged like some farmyard animal's. To see her flat stomach bulge. I couldn't take it.' You see, Victor didn't intend to share your body with anyone, not even his own child. So here was his quandary. He wasn't nearly satiated with his physical pleasure in you, and he wouldn't jeopardize it. At the same time, he had to satisfy his father with a grandson."

"And so, Gordon Lerner's *in vitro* fertilization," said Sid.

"Finally, Victor had a chance to please his father," said Claude. "To present him with something Raymond never had. A grandson."

"We never used contraception," remembered Valerie. "Victor wouldn't hear of it."

"My dear, it was almost impossible for you to become pregnant by Victor," said Claude mildly. "His sperm count was too low."

All those years I was convinced it was my fault, Valerie thought bitterly.

"Did you find Engvy Erickson?"

"No, that was Gordon Lerner."

"I loved her. She gave us our children." Valerie looked out the window, tears welling in her eyes.

"Victor knew you cared for her. So, it was really such a pity about the accident." The manservant began to remove their plates while the cook prepared dressing for their salads.

"What accident?" asked Sid.

"The automobile accident. It was on the highway

near the airport when she returned to Sweden, driving into Stockholm with the young man who had come to pick her up. Both were killed instantly."

Valerie closed her eyes and felt the blood drain from her face.

"She wouldn't have said anything," she whispered a moment later.

"Well, we didn't know that, did we?" Claude smiled.

It was Sid, after dinner, who wheeled Claude back into the drawing room for dessert, coffee, and brandy. A fire burned brightly in the fireplace. The curtains had been drawn and candles in silver candelabras flickered on several of the charming occasional tables. Next to the fireplace, the coffee was waiting for them in a magnificent Georgian silver coffeepot. Dessert was a tarte tatin, made with apples from their own trees, Claude pointed out, as Sid placed him next to the tea table. On the table in front of the sofa sat an array of cognacs, brandies, and sweet liqueurs set on a silver tray along with crystal balloon snifters and small crystal glasses. The manservant bustled among them, serving the tarte tatin, the coffee, a cognac for Sid, and a glass of port for Claude.

"It was a sublime dinner," said Valerie to the manservant. "Please tell your wife."

"Yes," added Sid. "Give her my compliments, too. It was marvelous."

"Oh, thank you, madam, sir," he said, beaming. "She'll be very pleased that you both liked it."

"It is possible to live as a civilized person, even in a remote village like this one," Claude observed, a look of pride on his face, as he turned to his servant. "Thank you, Louis. That will be all for tonight. And, thank Francoise." He kissed the tips of the fingers on his left hand.

"It was superb." Claude smiled at Valerie. "Do you think you're getting your money's worth, my dear?"

"God, what a question—"

Valerie interrupted Sid by placing a hand on his arm. "Yes, Claude," she said.

"Good." He leaned back in his wheelchair and looked around his drawing room, seeming to savor every detail.

"But there's more," said Sid, sipping his cognac.

"Oh, yes," agreed Claude. "There's more."

"What about the crash of Penn International?" asked Sid.

"Oh, that. Well, it was the old baron who thought of using the banks to launder ransom money collected by terrorists in kidnappings. There was a lot of that going on in South America back then. And as the practice spread to Europe and the rest of the world, he included those countries as well." He paused, sipping his port. "He was a financial genius. Quite ahead of his time. When drugs became popular, and with Colombia so near, well, it was obvious to include drug money."

"Were you involved in all of that?" asked Sid.

"Yes."

"But that wasn't enough," prompted Sid.

"No, all of it was to finance a more ambitious plan

when Raymond and Victor were sent to London. They had to be substantial, make the Penn presence felt. Of course, it soon became obvious that Victor would play the public role for the corporation, and Raymond would function behind the scenes as Victor's adviser."

"Did John O'Farrell know what was going on?" asked Sid, slowly. Valerie watched his face, saw him realize, realized herself, that John must have been involved.

"Certainly. How can anything be going on without the lawyer knowing about it?"

"But he left," Sid pointed out.

"Yes, he left." Claude nodded. "Something happened to John O'Farrell after awhile. He seemed to lose his taste for the larger game, as we saw it." He looked at Valerie, licked his lips, and shook his head. "He was quite outrageous. He was the only one who knew where Raymond was culpable in the Penn International situation, the only one who could link him to it and bring him down, as it were. With what John knew, Raymond could have been prosecuted and sentenced to a long term in jail."

"I'm surprised Raymond didn't just have him killed," Sid observed dryly.

"Oh, it's not that easy with a lawyer." Claude laughed. "John had all sorts of evidence squirreled away somewhere that would have had Raymond up on charges if anything happened to him. Raymond knew that.

"First of all, John came to Raymond and negotiated trust funds for the children's education and their support money. Then, using the same leverage, John extracted from Raymond the seed money to start up *The Collection of Valerie Penn*."

"I always thought John had put up his *own* money," Valerie murmured.

"He's a lawyer, my dear," Claude pointed out. "It is anathema to a lawyer to use his own money for anything. Surely, now that you are a businesswoman, you have noticed that. You have done marvelously well, my dear." He made a mocking bow toward her. "Despite ourselves, we have all been very impressed with what you have accomplished."

"What do you mean, 'we all'?"

"Well, Raymond. The old baron. Myself. Victor. Yes, Victor has been most impressed."

There they were, the words she had been waiting to hear all of these years, Valerie realized. The tension of thousands of nights of wondering drained out of her.

"He's really alive," she said, unaware that she had actually spoken the words.

"Oh, yes," Claude assured her. "It was Victor, my dear, who finally brought the corporation down. He had made bad business decisions, bought companies that failed to perform, all with funds borrowed from Penn International banks. The loans eventually amounted to more than one thousand percent of the company's assets. And Victor simply couldn't help spending on estates, paintings, furniture, *objets d'art,* and jewelry. When the rumors started to circulate that the FDIC, the IRS, and the Justice Department were on the verge of taking over the entire operation and bringing criminal indictments, Victor had to leave the country to escape prosecution. So I formulated the plan for him. I found, in Argentina, an assassin who would murder the crew of the plane and then bail out. It was child's play for us to provide the authorities with the false dental records to identify the poor fool we had paid to take Victor's place on the plane."

"How did Victor get away?" asked Sid, pouring himself another cognac.

"Oh, he just slipped over the border to Canada, posing as a tourist. When things calmed down a bit, he used his false passport to fly to Singapore. Then it was on to Argentina." He stopped for a minute, shifted in his wheelchair, and rearranged the blanket covering his legs. "Wonderful things, false passports," he mused. "One can pretty much slip in and out of countries at will."

"What about me?" asked Valerie in a small voice. "And the children . . . ?"

"He never considered taking you along, if that's what you mean," said Claude. "Frankly, I was astonished that you held his interest as long as you did. At any rate, he was becoming a bit bored with all of that domestic bliss."

"He left me with nothing. He even took my jewelry."

"Oh, no," Claude corrected her. "Victor didn't even know about the jewels. It was my little joke to clean out the safe-deposit box."

"And you didn't stop there," Valerie said angrily. "You knew every detail of the way we lived. When you took Penny, you knew everything about his classes and his school." She took a deep breath. "Who was it, Claude? Was it Daniel?"

Claude stared into the waning fire, his hands folded on his blanket-covered lap. He turned slowly to look at her, and his expression, Valerie saw, was almost pitying.

"Didn't you ever wonder," he asked finally, "how the Countess di Stefano was able to come up with such treasures to broker?"

Mary, she thought wildly, her hand fluttering at her throat. He was talking about Mary. Her friend. Her dearest friend.

"As soon as she had your wedding presents to sell,

with a chance at a commission on every one of them, she was on the phone to me picking my brain."

"And you picked hers," Valerie said slowly.

"Yes, and I grant you that she may not even have known how much she was telling me," he admitted. "It was all just chitchat, that sort of thing. The dear girl was so anxious to make the company grow. I must say I was stunned when she told me she had put every last cent into it, and cast her lot with you, even before the very competent John O'Farrell appeared on the scene."

"So you knew just where to find Penny, just what time to go to his school. I always thought it was Raymond."

"No, it was Victor." Claude smiled. "I would have done it, of course, but he didn't think little Raymond would come with me."

"But if Victor didn't care about me, what about Max's death? Harry's death?"

"You know how possessive Victor is. Just because he doesn't want something doesn't mean he wants anybody else to have it. Besides, my dear, he was beginning to admire you. He was so concerned that it be done properly that he even attended to the brakes on Max's Maserati himself."

"What about Harry?" she demanded.

"Well, that was a surprise to all of us." Claude chuckled. "I had seen the pictures of the two of you in the London papers, of course, and I had mentioned it to Victor when he telephoned. He was in a fury about it. And then, phone service between England and Argentina being what it is, the lines were down for two entire days. By the time Victor telephoned again, it had already happened."

"I don't think I'm quite following you," said Sid, a puzzled look on his face.

"We didn't have anything to do with Harry Cunningham's death. You see, that really was an attempt on the life of the vice president, and poor Harry Cunningham just happened to get in the way."

"So Victor is in Argentina, and Penny is with him."

"You'll never find them, my dear. They are so well hidden that even with the help of Mr. James and all of his people, it would take you forever."

"I want to see Raymond, Claude."

"I doubt he would be interested, my dear."

"Raymond thought Victor was dead, didn't he?" she asked, remembering the stricken look on Raymond's face at the funeral.

"Yes, at that point there hadn't been any word from Victor. It was only later, when he was safely back in Argentina, that we were sure he was all right."

"You have Raymond's telephone number," Valerie demanded. "Get him on the phone."

"You really have developed a bit of spirit, haven't you? Very well, my dear." He pushed himself to his desk. "You shall have your way."

Sid gave her hand a quick squeeze as they heard Claude murmur softly into the telephone. As Claude wheeled himself back to his place, Valerie steeled herself.

"Raymond is extremely annoyed with me for telling you that he is your father," he said, looking down at the limp hand in his lap. "I knew he would be, of course."

Valerie bit the inside of her lip, feeling a surge of disappointment.

"I don't know what came over me. To betray the

family like this," he mused. "Thank heaven my own father isn't alive to hear about this."

"You didn't do anything wrong," said Valerie, her jaw set. "I'm family, too, Claude."

"Yes, of course you are." He nodded, a bit of color returning to his face. "And it is only right that you are to be reunited with your father."

"You mean Raymond will see me?" she gasped.

"Yes, he'll see you," said Claude, the energy returning to his voice. "It was such a surprise it took me quite off guard." He ran his good hand through his thinning hair, shook his head in wonder. "At any rate, Miss Furst will telephone you at your hotel to make the arrangements. What I wouldn't give to be there for that happy little family reunion, but unfortunately, infirmity forbids."

It had worked, Valerie thought, leaning back against the sofa, exhausted. Raymond was going to see her. Raymond Penn. Her father. She glanced at Claude to see the grayness of fatigue settle over his face.

"There's one more thing," she said hurriedly. "It's going to take me a few days to get your money. You know nobody simply has two million dollars sitting around. I'll have to call Beverly Hills tomorrow and arrange to borrow it from the corporation." She paused, looking into his face, at his slumped shoulders as he sat in the wheelchair. "Will that be all right?"

"Oh, forget it." He smiled. "You know, my dear, I have so much money at this point I couldn't possibly spend it all, not if I live to be a thousand years old." He paused.

"And besides," he added, "I haven't had so much fun in years."

63

Valerie put one tentative hand on the brass knocker, then drew it away again. She glanced down the walk. Through the tall wrought-iron gates she could just glimpse the fender of her limousine, parked at the curb waiting for her.

Raymond Penn. Her father. The thought was almost nonsensical, beyond comprehension.

She remembered the rumors about his life inside the Belgravia mansion. He was a sadist, a masochist, a scholar, a homosexual. A celibate. That he had a torture chamber, where he sacrificed small boys he bought in Africa. And always there had been the rumors about the dolls.

All nonsense, Claude had said dismissively.

Valerie took a deep breath, and firmly hit the knocker three times against its brass plate.

The woman who answered was ancient, dressed in a maid's uniform. Behind her loomed a forbidding entryway.

"You're to come with me," the old woman said brusquely, with a hint of a German accent, as she closed the front door behind Valerie. She plodded down the long, dark hall, where the only light came from tiny spots on ancestral portraits so layered with grime that they were little more than impressions in their heavy frames.

The woman stopped in front of a pair of tall mahogany doors and turned a brass handle.

"Mr. Raymond will see you in here in a few minutes," she said, gesturing for Valerie to enter the room beyond the doors. Valerie hesitated as her heart beat wildly.

"Go in," the woman directed, her manner a bit impatient.

"Thank you," said Valerie, her chin up as she walked past the woman, and heard a click as the woman closed the door behind her.

Valerie's heart raced at the darkness surrounding her. Almost instantly, her eyes adjusted to what light there was: low-wattage, frosted bulbs in wall sconces from the thirties every few feet on either side in an enormous room. This can't be, she thought as she saw the people seated around a massive dining room table. The men were in dinner jackets, the women in evening gowns, though it was only three o'clock in the afternoon. They were still, none of them glancing to see who had come into the room.

The dolls. Raymond Penn's doll collection.

Valerie leaned against the door wishing to God that Sid were with her, wondering if she would ever leave the room alive. Her fear tussled with curiosity and finally she took a few steps toward the table.

At its foot, sitting in an ornate, high-backed chair, was a replica of a woman in her mid-thirties dressed in a mauve velvet evening gown, cut low over large breasts, a shawl over its graceful shoulders. Around its neck was a superb diamond and pearl choker. Diamonds and pearls glittered in its earlobes, and its glass eyes were the same blue as Victor's. The cheekbones were high, the nose slender, aristocratic, the narrow mouth a pale pink. The brown hair—real hair, Valerie saw—was dressed in the pompadour popular during the years of the Second World War.

"That is my mother." Raymond's low voice was behind her. "Your grandmother. Baroness Ingrid von Pentheim. Beautiful, wasn't she?"

"Yes." Valerie looked at him in the pale light. He looked older than when she had last seen him, a trifle more austere. He wore a dark suit and tie, a beautiful hand-tailored shirt, handmade shoes.

"Her family was originally from Austria," he continued. "Vienna. She was quite a gifted pianist when she was a girl. I always thought you must have inherited your talent from her."

"My talent," Valerie repeated, watching Raymond's face, wondering how he was feeling at their first meeting as father and daughter.

"She didn't continue with it. In those days, a girl from a good family didn't have a career." He glanced at Valerie, not quite meeting her eyes, his expression thoughtful and benign.

"You didn't continue either. But I suppose running Victor's many households was a full-time occupation as well."

"I didn't have the dedication." Her voice caught on the words.

"Evidently not. Do you still play? For your own pleasure?"

"Very seldom," she admitted, her cheeks burning. She wondered how, with those few words, Raymond could make her feel like a child who wasn't attending to her music lessons. "The business," she began. "It takes a lot of time. My role in it is very involving."

"That's too bad," he said, glancing at her, something almost shy in his expression. Almost meeting her eyes this time, but she dropped her gaze to the table. It was laid with heavy silver plates and ornate crystal wineglasses that needed dusting. "Mother always played," he concluded. "My father liked her to do so after dinner."

"The way mother looks here," said Raymond, "the dress, the hair, the jewels, was the way she looked in a photograph taken just before we left Germany. Of course, she lived another decade after we moved to Argentina, and she was always very beautiful. More beautiful, in fact, as she grew older. But I always remembered that particular photograph. This was the way she looked when she and my father were going out for the evening, to a dinner party somewhere, or a grand ball. She would come to the nursery to say good night to Victor and me, and I could smell her perfume, touch her furs, as she leaned over my bed to kiss me good night. Yes, that photograph was so like her."

"She's lovely," murmured Valerie.

Raymond's hand was on the back of an empty chair. "This is where I sit when I have dinner in here. The oldest son, on his mother's right, where I always sat."

"Yes, I see." Valerie glanced at the figure to the left of the baroness. She realized with a start that it was a replica of Victor. A bit older than the last time she had seen him, a little more gray at his temples, but the expression in the half-light of the room was perfect. That boyish look, the blue eyes almost alive, almost boring through her. She held on to the high back of the chair in which the figure of the baroness sat.

"Victor. At his mother's left. He was her favorite."

"Claude told me. You don't have Claude here, I see."

"Claude is a servant," he said dismissively.

"Claude told me he is a brother in everything but blood and income."

"He's wrong," replied Raymond with a hint of the contemptuousness that had always made her cringe with fear.

"And an empty chair next to Victor," she noticed, stumbling over his name. "Who sits there? Harry Cunningham when he was here for dinner?"

"Oh, no." He smiled. This time he met her eyes. "When I entertain, it is in the small dining room. I do it so seldom, and there is never more than one other person." He studied her. "This room is for family. That is why I am showing it to you."

Valerie stood still, hypnotized by the pale blue eyes fixed on her own.

"Why don't you sit down next to Victor?" he suggested, seating himself to the right of the baroness. "I've asked Amalie to bring us tea."

"Thank you," she said gratefully, averting her eyes from the replica of Victor as she slipped into the chair. She looked to her right to see a replica of Penny. She inhaled sharply. He was older now, in a dark suit, a dress shirt, a tie. The tilt of his head was proud.

She almost gasped with relief at the tap on the door. At Raymond's command to enter, the old woman shuffled in, pushing a tea tray. Were the dolls to be served tea? Valerie wondered, glancing at the baron, at the head of the table. The woman on his right, she recognized as Cini. A young and glorious Cini, around twenty years old, which would have been the last time Raymond saw her. She was dressed in a low-cut evening gown, showing her magnificent breasts, with a tight waist, a full skirt brushing the floor, and her blond hair coiffed in the style of the mid-fifties. The woman on the baron's left was, she realized, herself. The hair was styled in the same wild blond mane she had combed in the mirror that morning. The figure wore a copy of the unforgettable black dress with the shocking pink poufed skirt she had worn with Harry Cunningham to the gala at Ford's Theater.

As the elderly woman in black poured her tea, Valerie looked from the replica of Cini to the one of herself.

Cini, no more than a girl, right out of the pictures Vicki had scattered over the coffee table in the little apartment in West Hollywood so many years ago.

And Valerie, the age she was now. The international beauty. More slender than Cini, and taller, but her face reprised Cini's.

Anybody seeing the two dolls would think Valerie was Cini's older, more sophisticated sister.

The baron, between them, had a shaven head, a prominent nose, thin lips. The proud tilt of his head was identical to that of the figure of Penny.

"Your father was much older than your mother," she said, sipping her tea.

"Oh, no," Raymond said, glancing at the baron's likeness in its impeccable dinner clothes. "No, they were approximately the same age. But the baron was at his best as you see him there. Sixty years old, he would have been. He started to go bald when he was quite young, and so he always shaved his head. A fine figure of a man, wouldn't you agree?"

"Yes."

"He was a brilliant horseman in his day. Of course, he is much older now, nearing ninety, and very ill." He grimaced as he sipped his tea, replaced the cup in its saucer, and touched the corners of his mouth with his napkin. "It is nice to be able to look at him the way I remember him best, when he was at the height of his intellectual and physical power."

Across from Valerie was the figure of a beautiful prepubescent child in a party dress, with long brown curls falling over her shoulders. Her clear blue eyes looked out at nothing, and around her slender neck was a necklace of pearls. Alexandra, the way she had appeared several years earlier.

"Alexandra is older now," she smiled, motioning toward the figure next to Raymond. "She's no longer a little girl as you have her there."

"Yes, I've mentioned to Miss Furst that she needs to take care of that. She keeps them current, sees that their clothes are replaced."

"Who is Miss Furst?"

"I am afraid I don't understand." A puzzled look crossed Raymond's face as his eyes found hers across the table.

"Who is she to you?" asked Valerie, taking another sip of the lukewarm tea.

"Nobody. She's a servant."

"Does she have a life of her own?" she prodded. "Apart from her work for you, I mean."

"I don't know," he answered, and she could sense his bafflement. "It wouldn't occur to me to ask a servant about his or her life. Why would I care?"

"I'm rather surprised to see my mother," she said, changing the subject. "She was very beautiful, wasn't she?"

"She was a wild girl." His eyes were cold again. "I believe she's dead now. If she weren't, Claude would have found her."

"Found her and killed her."

"She deserved it," said Raymond quietly.

The hurt, the resentment, is still there, Valerie thought. Even now, if Raymond realizes Cini is alive, he'll snuff out her life without a thought.

"She is dead. I found my grandparents. They told me."

"Yes, well, that would have been inevitable," he murmured, his expression bland again.

A replica of Victor as a boy of Penny's age sat to the left of her own likeness. It was somehow different from what she would have imagined Victor to look like as a child. The hair was much lighter than Victor's; the nose wasn't familiar, and there was something different about the mouth.

"There's Victor as a boy," Valerie said, relieved that Raymond's black mood had passed. "Was that from an old photograph, too?"

A frown creased Raymond's brow. He was silent for several minutes. Valerie's heart began to pound in her chest again, and her mouth went dry with fear.

"What is it?" she ventured at last.

"Claude didn't tell you."

"Claude didn't tell me what?"

"He didn't tell you about Victor."

"He told me that Victor is alive," she said. "Oh, yes. He told me."

"But, he didn't tell you about young Victor."

"About young Victor?"

"That is young Victor." He leaned forward to touch the sleeve of the coat worn by the young Victor doll.

"Well, yes," she said doubtfully. "That's why I asked if it was from a favorite photograph. Like your mother, you see."

"This is Victor Penn, Jr." His hand was still on the doll's arm. "He is Victor's son."

Victor's son, she thought wildly. So, Victor had another son. Illegitimate, obviously, and older than Penny. The product of some liaison before he had met her, or perhaps even from the year he was courting her, when he wouldn't touch her. Another, older son. Her fury rose again, bringing angry tears to the corners of her eyes.

"Who is his mother?"

"Why, you are," said Raymond, his eyebrows raised. "You are his mother."

There was a second surrogate, Valerie realized, shock replacing rage. "Who carried him?" she stammered.

"The granddaughter of Amalie, my housekeeper," Raymond said calmly. "She was an eighteen-year-old virgin. We sent her to Gordon Lerner's clinic to be artificially inseminated with four fertilized eggs. All males," Raymond added. "She flew back to Argentina almost immediately. She lived, during the months of pregnancy, in the main house, and our father visited her daily. He felt this was the greatest gift his second son could give him. A grandson, with von Pentheim genes on both sides, for him to enjoy in his latter years."

"What happened to the surrogate afterwards?" asked Valerie, glancing at the young Victor doll, processing its resemblance to the replica of Alexandra next to it.

"Nothing. I suppose she went back home to her parents and married in time. Had children. All of the girls do."

"Victor had the surrogate who bore the twins killed," she said.

"Oh, that's nonsense."

"That's what Claude said," she insisted.

"Claude dramatizes everything. It has always been his greatest failing."

"I want to see my son," Valerie insisted. "I must see Penny."

"Yes, I can understand that," Raymond said, almost indifferent, as he glanced at her across the table.

"Will you take me to him?" She steeled herself for his refusal.

"Victor played a cruel, capricious joke on both of us." Raymond's tone was neutral. "Finding you, bringing you to London, and then waiting all of that time to show you off, to marry you."

"Claude says that if you had found me first, you probably would have had me killed."

"As I said, Claude dramatizes everything."

"But you told him to kill Cini. And you would do the same thing this minute. If she weren't already dead," Valerie added quickly.

"She was a reckless girl," he said noncommittally. He took a sip of his tea. "A very reckless girl."

The old servant entered to ask Raymond if he wanted anything more. Valerie realized, with a sinking feeling in her stomach, that she was about to be dismissed.

"I would like some more tea," she said firmly.

Raymond sighed and nodded.

Valerie sensed his annoyance.

"You haven't answered me," she said, firmly. "I want to see my son. I can't do that without you."

"All right," he said at last.

As he stood to walk her down the long hall, she turned his words over in her mind. "When will we go?" They stood stiffly at the front door, facing each other.

"The end of the week. Miss Furst will call you."

"I'll wait forever. You can't let me down."

He didn't answer. He opened the door, his manner cutting off any last words, even good-bye, and then the door closed soundlessly behind her.

Sid was standing at the window in their suite, looking down at the late afternoon traffic. He started and turned as Valerie opened the door, and smiled broadly to see her standing there.

"I didn't expect you back so soon, buttercup," he said, the relief in his voice palpable. "Come here." He held her tightly, and Valerie realized he wouldn't have been surprised if she had never returned.

Valerie moved out of Sid's arms and removed her linen jacket.

"I didn't even have time to get worried about you." He smiled as she sank into the sofa. "How about a drink?"

"Fine. A double scotch and water. In fact, ask them to bring the bottle."

"So, it was like that." He grinned. He dialed room service and ordered a bottle of scotch, caviar, and smoked salmon. He sat down in the chair next to her and took her hand. "You don't seem to have any bruises."

"No," she agreed, trying for a smile and nearly succeeding. Within moments, there was a tap on the door. Room service. Already. Sid took care of the bill, the tip, poured a couple of drinks the size that Kyle liked, then returned, sat down in the chair next to her again, raised his glass to touch her own in a toast.

He moved to her side on the sofa, his arm around her shoulder. She buried her head in his neck as she told him about the dolls. Victor, Jr. A grandson for the old baron to raise in Argentina. "Penny has to be there, too, Sid. He's being raised with his brother just as Raymond and Victor were raised. Don't you see? A new generation reprising the one before. Never mind about Alexandra. She's female, and obviously females don't matter in their world."

She reached out her hand to Sid, and led him through the door into the bedroom. Slowly, she undressed, hanging up her blouse, her skirt, pulling off her panty hose, removing her pavé diamond and gold earrings.

Sid was already in bed, waiting to take her in his arms. Valerie was the aggressor this time, kissing him first, her hands all over him, grounding herself with his presence. It was dark by the time the room was silent and they lay content in each other's arms.

Sid ordered up a pot of coffee after they had showered together and were sitting in their robes in the suite's drawing room.

Sid watched Valerie as she thought aloud.

"So, after Raymond brings me to Penny," she concluded, "I'll bring him home."

"Does Raymond know that?" he asked.

"No. I told him only that I want to see my son."

"What about Victor, Jr.? Do you plan to bring him home, too?"

"He's Victor's concern, and the old baron's. He has nothing to do with me."

"He does, Valerie. You're his mother."

"Well, I don't know how I feel about it," she said, exasperated. "I'll have to see how it is when I get there. When I meet him. I promised Alexandra that I would bring her brother home, and that's exactly what I plan to do."

"You'll be taking Penny away from his brother."

"I can't help that."

"So Raymond thinks this is just a visit. You'll go down there, spend a few days, and come back. Is that it?"

"That's it."

"I'm going to come with you."

"Don't be ridiculous. Raymond would never agree to that."

"Valerie, you'll never come back." Sid's blue eyes were hard. "You'll be there forever, and you know it. That's the only reason Raymond agreed to take you."

"That's a chance I'll have to take."

"Have you thought about us? Don't we matter?"

"Of course we matter. But, Sid, I want my son back. I have to have my son."

"Valerie." Sid reached over and ran a hand across her shoulder. "Neither of us is a child. We both went into this relationship with our eyes open, after all. When you let me make love to you, you know what it means, no matter how much we kid about it. You've let me tell you I love you. You've told me you love me."

"Yes." Valerie's voice was a whisper. "I do love you."

"Well, I think I deserve to know what this means to you."

"If you think a cottage with a white picket fence, and Valerie at the door in her apron when Sid comes home from the office at six o'clock, you're wrong," she snapped. "It could never be like that. My life is in Beverly Hills. Your life is in New York. I can't believe you ever thought I would give up my life to be with you."

"Don't insult me." She saw from the set of his jaw, the anger in his eyes, that he was furious.

"I'm not insulting you. It's just time for us to talk about the way things are."

"Well, the way things are is that we're in love with each other. We have a commitment to each other, Valerie. We'll just work it out the way other people who live in different places work it out. I'll come to you. You'll come to me. Sounds like pretty hot stuff, in fact," he added, grinning. "Never together long enough to get bored."

"Sid, could you live like that?"

"Of course. You know what a thrill seeker I am. I've fought the same old thing all my life." He ran his hand down her arm again, reached up with a finger and outlined her lips. "You can't go to Argentina, though. You're going to have to assume that Penny is having a wonderful life there with his brother. You're going to have to let it go. For Alexandra. For us."

"Sid, how can there even be an us when I'm still married to Victor? Don't you see? That's got to be resolved, too. We can't be together until he has no more right to me. How would your mother, your brother, and sisters feel if you were living with a woman who was married to someone else? How would *you* feel?"

"You've got a point," he admitted. "I don't see how we can get married until you're divorced. There's just one thing."

"What's that?" she asked warily.

"How do you divorce a man who is legally dead?"

65

Valerie stood in front of the closet in the suite the next morning, realizing she would be needing clothes from home.

She reached Mary in the Beverly Hills office just as she was leaving for the day. "Hello, Mary. It's Valerie." As she said the words, she felt the reservation in Mary's silence on the other end of the line. She knew Mary was remembering the coolness in her own voice the last time they had spoken.

"I'm going on a trip," she continued, "and I don't have the right clothes with me, Mary. I was wondering if you might have the time to run up to the house and pick up some things. I'll need a courier to bring them to me here in London. I'm leaving Friday."

"I'm awfully busy, Valerie," said Mary finally, her voice distant. "Ask your housekeeper to do it. She's paid to give you personal service. I'm not."

"Mary," she replied quietly, "Sid and I went to see Claude Vilgran. He told me he was the one who found for us all of the things you said you had found. He said he did this in exchange for information from you about how I lived.

"It wasn't Claude who kidnapped Penny," she continued. "Victor was the one who did it, but you helped, didn't you? If you hadn't told Claude every detail of our days, Victor wouldn't have known how to go about it.

He was the one who cut the brake cable on Max's car, too."

"I thought Claude had taken him." Mary's voice broke. "I thought it was Claude who had tampered with Max's brakes. Valerie, Claude was someone I had known for years. I didn't know he worked for Victor. I thought he kidnapped Penny because he knew Raymond wanted him. I thought the deal about Penny was just between Claude and Raymond."

Now Valerie was silent.

"All I thought I was doing with Claude was passing along gossip," she continued, close to tears. "Valerie, you've got to believe me. I didn't know I was trading information."

"Claude told me who my father is. It's Raymond." She heard Mary suck in her breath. "I've seen him, Mary. He's taking me to see Victor, who has Penny somewhere in Argentina. That's why I need you to go to my house and pick out some clothes. I'm going to bring Penny home. Finally, I'll have my son back."

Though she sensed Mary's shock, she forged ahead. "There was a second surrogate, too. I have another son in Argentina. He's as much my child as Penny is, and I have to offer him the choice of coming home with us. With Penny and me."

"What if he doesn't want to come home with you?" asked Mary, her voice gentle. "What if Penny doesn't want to come home either?"

"At least they'll have the choice, Mary," said Valerie after a moment. "My children will have the choice. I never did. The choices were all taken away from me."

"And Valerie, what if you don't come home?"

"That's a chance I have to take." Valerie sighed, remembering their years of friendship. "I love you, Mary."

"I love you, too, sweetie," said Mary. She paused for a moment and added with a tense laugh, "Now you're not just telling me that so I'll go by your house and pick out some things for you to wear, are you?"

Valerie laughed with her before she replaced the receiver. An hour later, Mary rang again from the mansion in Beverly Hills.

"I have half your wardrobe lying around," she said, "but it's all going well. Rural, but elegant, right? A bit of the British raj. Dressing for dinner, and pip-pip, right?"

"Mary, you could do all of that in your sleep. What's all this?"

"Well," said Mary, her voice bright, "I thought that as long as there has to be a courier to take this to you, why shouldn't it be Mary di Stefano? After all, I could use a few days away from the office."

"Oh, that's wonderful!" Valerie felt the fine blond hairs rising on her arms as she wondered whether Mary was so worried about her trip that she was coming to London to take one last look at her.

"And even better," Mary added. "When I called John to tell him I would be a little late getting home, and I had decided to take your clothes to London myself, he said he'd come along, too. Won't that be fun, sweetie? John and myself. You and Sid. The four of us, together again."

Perhaps for the last time, Valerie thought.

―――――

It took three of the hotel's bellmen, each with a luggage trolley, to bring all the suitcases to the suite. Valerie and Mary hugged each other while John and Sid shook hands, laughing. "A couple of these are full of presents for the boys," said Mary, gesturing toward the luggage. "I also packed some snapshots of Alexandra so Penny can see how beautiful she's becoming."

Dancing at Annabelle's followed dinner that evening. The next day they visited the National Gallery and the British Museum, and later it was the theater, and a late supper at Langan's.

Everything that needed to be discussed was done in a tacit manner. If Valerie didn't return from South America, the business was in order, and Alexandra would live with John and Mary. As long as none of them verbalized the possibility that Valerie might never come back again, they had a marvelous time.

At night, Sid held her as she lay nude in his arms, touched her hesitantly, studied the contours of her body as if he were committing them to memory. "Valerie, please come home," she heard him whisper as she drifted into sleep the night before her departure.

———

Valerie was dressed, made up, the full-length Russian lynx coat Mary had brought from Beverly Hills over the back of a chair, her luggage already downstairs. Sid, in his robe, kissed her hair. "I have a little something for you to remember me by, buttercup."

He reached in the pocket of his robe and handed her a small, pearl-handled gun and a box of bullets. He explained how it was to be loaded. Where the safety was. How to flick it off. How to aim it.

"You won't be going through security since it's a charter flight. And they won't check your handbag when you land. The only potential problem could be the security on the baron's property itself. They may check everyone who comes in.

"If that happens, you're just going to have to gut it out. Just open those big hazel eyes of yours and blame it on me. Swear that you didn't know it was there, that your boyfriend must have put it in your bag when you were out of the room."

"I love you, Sid."

"I love you, too. If that bastard even looks as if he's going to come near you, aim for his balls."

———

The L-1011 roared down the runway and lifted off into the black, starry night. Made its turn over London, where Valerie saw the lighted Houses of Parliament. Big Ben in its clock tower, the bridges over the Thames, and climbed to cruising altitude on its way to Buenos Aires.

Only then did Valerie ponder the reality of seeing Victor again. She fondled her handbag, thinking about the gun inside, and wondered if she would have the nerve to blow his brains out. Because that was what she had been planning ever since the day her gynecologist confirmed her pregnancy and she realized that every minute, every hour, every day that Victor Penn had been in her life had been a lie.

66

The rotors of the twenty-passenger, jet-powered helicopter were already whirring as Valerie and Raymond hurried across the tarmac to board it. As soon as their luggage was loaded into the cargo area, it lifted off and headed north over Buenos Aires. Below, Valerie saw tall office buildings, apartment houses, ancient cathedrals on wide, tree-lined streets. There were museums, theaters, sports arenas, the homes of the rich, other dwellings, the roofs a sea of corrugated iron. Seagulls hovered over the freighters anchored next to the bustling docks of the Rio de la Plata.

The outskirts of the vast metropolis dissipated into barren terrain dotted with scraggly trees, herds of cattle, and the occasional village. More than an hour later, Valerie looked out the window at the jungle far below. It was dense and impenetrable, punctuated only by an occasional river or waterfall splashing torrents of foam.

Across the aisle, Raymond glanced at his watch and closed his book.

Valerie looked out of the window again. There was no sign of civilization, only the endless green. Her stomach muscles tightened as the helicopter began its descent, straight into the trees.

As it settled in a clearing, a cadre of men in khaki uniforms rushed to open the door and began unloading the luggage into a pair of Land Rovers parked nearby. It was quite an operation, Valerie saw as she looked around. There were a number of hangars housing helicopters in different sizes. Open garages revealed Jeeps, a fleet of trucks. There were vehicles being serviced on racks and at gasoline pumps. A bright red Coca-Cola machine. A radio was playing flamenco music. Somewhere in the jungle a bird screeched and monkeys quarreled in the palm trees.

Valerie realized there were at least fifty men working on the premises, some of them glancing at her as she crawled gingerly out of the helicopter. Raymond nodded to several of them and motioned to Valerie to join him as she was helped into the backseat of the waiting Land Rover. She clutched her fur coat tightly around her against the winter cold as she followed him. Nobody even so much as glanced at her handbag. With a sigh of relief she sank into the backseat of the vehicle.

In moments the Land Rover was crawling along a narrow paved road carved through the jungle. They passed men, women, and children bundled up in heavy vicuna or wool ponchos and wide-brimmed hats, which they tipped toward the vehicle when they realized it was Mr. Raymond Penn in the backseat.

Half an hour later, the driver of the Land Rover turned onto a narrow lane nearly invisible in the foliage. A few minutes later, Valerie saw a low, rambling structure camouflaged by stands of bamboo, great bushes of tropical flowers, palm trees. The main house, she realized. And it was a masterpiece by one of the century's leading architects whose style she recognized at once.

The butler who appeared in the doorway was surrounded by a bevy of maids.

"This is Mrs. Victor Penn," said Raymond. "This is Frederick, who runs the house."

Frederick, who had that air of perfect competence

shared by all good butlers, bowed to her, and the maids, dark-skinned girls in black uniforms, wrestled with Valerie's heavy suitcases.

Valerie walked up the wide stairway to the front door and stepped into a marble hall of purest white shot with pale pink. She noted the clusters of rooms, each opening onto its own courtyard, and the modern pieces of furniture designed by the master architect himself that melded so exquisitely with the more formal French and English antiques.

Valerie followed Frederick to what was apparently her suite, and gasped with surprise as she entered its drawing room. Over the marble chimneypiece was the same Bonnard that had hung in the drawing room of her Beverly Hills suite. It had been one of the first paintings offered by *The Collection of Valerie Penn* after they had been appointed exclusive agents of Victor's properties. Here it was, waiting for her after all this time.

The mirrored drawing room wall reflected a private courtyard outside, and the others were upholstered in white, watered silk. Valerie was struck by the Chinese tortoiseshell-inlaid lacquer cabinet, the concert grand piano, and the superb Louis XV chinoiserie silk screen. Sprays of orchids, their blossoms larger than any she had ever seen, accented the room.

She stepped into the huge bedroom. It, too, was in white. The carpet. The upholstery on the sofas and chairs. The tailored, quilted bedspread, and the bolsters on the king-sized bed.

She heard the maids exclaim over her dresses and furs as they hung them in the enormous closet. Then Frederick knocked politely on the suite's double door.

"Cocktails will be in the drawing room at eight o'clock, madam," Frederick said. "Dinner is at nine.

Dress will be formal unless, of course, you prefer to be more casual after your long flight from London."

"Thank you, Frederick," she murmured. "I'll be dressing."

"Very well, madam." He paused. "We're so pleased you have finally come."

Valerie stared after him as he bowed and closed the door silently behind him. Wandering back into the bedroom, she noticed a familiar sculpture on one of the little tables. It was the little ballerina by Degas, the first gift that Victor had given her.

Valerie heard a soft knock at the door. "Come in," she said. The door opened to reveal Penny, his stance tentative, his expression disbelieving.

He raced into Valerie's open arms, and she knelt, holding him tightly, weak with relief. "Oh, my son, my darling, beautiful boy." She wept, his cheeks wet with her own tears.

In a moment she became aware of a figure in the doorway. It was another boy, standing straight and nearly as tall as Penny. His expression was inscrutable.

"Hello," she said at last.

"Hello," he said, his voice still the thin, piping voice of a boy teetering on the brink of pubescence. He was very good-looking, she saw.

"Why don't you come in and close the door?" she suggested.

"Thank you," he said, closing the door behind him. "I'm so pleased you have finally come."

Slowly, Valerie pulled herself to her feet. She walked over to Victor, Jr., and leaned to kiss his cheek.

"I've brought some presents," she said. "For both of you." She lugged the heavy suitcases through the bedroom.

"One for you, Penny. And one for you, Junior."
Mary had picked out the most incredible things, Valerie
saw as the boys carefully opened each of the packages.
A pair of survival knives, each with a clinometer to esti-
mate elevations and a protractor for map orientation.
Computer games. Videocassettes. Safari hats with built-
in solar-powered breezes. An electronic backgammon
game. A pair of talking chess computers. As each gift was
opened, the boys exclaimed with pleasure.

The *pièce de résistance* was the set of recent snapshots
of Alexandra. She watched Penny examine each of them.
He handed them to Victor, Jr., and waited for his reaction.

"What do you think?" Penny asked carelessly.

"She's the prettiest girl I've ever seen," said Victor,
Jr. Valerie studied his expression again. Was he looking
at his brother with envy? Or regret, perhaps, that Penny
had grown up with her and that he had been alone, with
the old baron, and only the occasional visits from his father and Mr. Raymond Penn, his uncle?

Penny thumbed through the pictures of Alexandra
again, this time with a more critical eye. "She's done
something funny to her hair," he said at last.

"Well, that's the way girls are wearing it now," said
Valerie, smiling at her son, hardly able to believe he was
there.

"When is she coming?" asked Penny.

"What do you mean?"

"Well, she's coming." He looked at her question-
ingly. "Father said she's coming, and we're all going to
be here together from now on."

Valerie's mind was a blank, wiped clean by the
shock of his words.

"She's on vacation," she said lamely after a few minutes. Her sons watched her face.

"Oh, where?" asked Penny.

"With friends," she said vaguely. "It's been planned for a long time. Nearly the whole year."

"Oh, she's at the ranch near Santa Barbara with Jeanine and her family, isn't she?" said Penny. "She's a half-wit, Jeanine," he said, turning to his brother. "One of those dumb girls who giggle all the time."

So that was that, Valerie thought, her hopes fading. If Victor really meant to bring Alexandra to South America so they could all live happily ever after, all he had to do was ask Penny where she was.

Victor, Jr., glanced at his expensive wristwatch. "Raymond, we've got to dress for dinner," he said in a low voice. Both boys stood. Valerie leaned to kiss each of them on the cheek.

"Mother, the presents are really super," said Penny politely. "We'll send some of the servants to collect everything in a few minutes, if you don't mind. If it doesn't interfere with the time you need to dress."

"Of course, that's fine, Penny." She hugged him again.

"Thank you, Mother," he said.

"Thank you, Mother." Victor, Jr., swallowed the words, almost unable to believe he could say them. His mother, Valerie thought. Her son.

67

Valerie had taken her time as she dressed for cocktails and dinner. Soaking in her large marble bathtub, she wondered if there was a road out of the jungle. The children would know.

She sauntered lazily into the dressing room, met her reflection a thousand times as she sat down at the makeup table. In the mirror she saw a woman's face, the eyes intelligent, questioning. A woman's body as well; supple, firm, bursting with good health and energy. No innocence left to be molded, to be exploited.

How Victor would hate me now, she thought, smiling as she pulled panty hose over long, slim legs, over golden pubic hair that was a shield against even the thought of his touch. She dressed in a white satin shell, a cocktail suit of black wool crepe with a long, slim skirt slit to just above the knee. A band of black beads outlined the front of the short, long-sleeved jacket. Around her neck she fastened a choker of marquise diamonds and pearls, then set matching earrings in her ears. She took a long time putting on her makeup, blowing dry her pale blond hair until it was just the way she wanted it to look. Like a pale cloud around her face, her shoulders.

She stood inconspicuously in the doorway of the drawing room as her eyes searched through the crowd of people for Victor. He was standing near the fireplace, talking to a young woman in a long gown who looked raptly into his tanned, handsome face. Raymond was there as well, talking to an older man in dinner clothes. She wondered who all the guests were. They must have invited everybody who lived within five hundred miles to come for dinner and meet her, now that she had finally come. She clutched her black beaded evening bag, and felt the outline of the little gun.

Victor was looking at her now from across the room with an expression she had seen a million times before. Open, charmed, delighted to see her. Valerie met his eyes.

The conversation among the guests died, and she realized that everybody was watching her. Finally, her sons, both in dark suits and ties, hurried over to take her hands, lead her around the room, and introduce her to everybody.

Valerie soon realized the many guests were the boys' private tutors, their doctors, as well as Penn business executives and their assistants, all of whom lived and worked on the estate. She murmured pleasantries as the boys introduced her to each guest. And then she found herself in front of Victor Penn. She looked straight into his clear blue eyes.

"You're looking well, Valerie."

"As are you, Victor," she said, trying to figure out what she was feeling, and realizing that it was nothing, nothing at all.

"Dinner is served," announced the butler. She moved away from Victor as the boys scampered to her side. They sauntered down the wide marble corridor to the dining room, Penny and Junior giving her little glances as if they still couldn't believe she was there.

The dining room was lovely, one of its walls glass with a view of a charming courtyard. Its long table glowed with candlelight, glorious china and silver utensils. The butler held out Valerie's chair at the foot of the table. For one ghastly moment, Valerie had a vision of Raymond and Victor on either side of her. She released a low sigh of relief when Victor, Jr., took his place on her left and Penny settled in on her right. Several places down the table sat Victor, listening intently to a young woman on his right. The fencing mistress, Valerie remembered. She wondered briefly whether Victor was sleeping with her.

The chair at the head of the table was empty. The old baron was apparently too ill to join them this evening. Looking around the table, listening to the chatter, Valerie was grateful that there were so many people there.

She turned to Penny, so happy to see him she wanted to hug him again. She looked into Victor, Jr.'s blue eyes and sensed his awkwardness.

"You must have wondered about a lot of things," she began.

"Oh, not really," he demurred, looking down at his plate. He had very long lashes, she saw, so like her own. "Grandfather wanted to raise me, and so I had to come," he continued, as if it were a dialogue he had had with himself many times. He nodded across the table at Penny. "It had to be one of us, and I was the one."

"Didn't you ever wonder why you never got to visit?" Valerie asked, feeling a wave of tenderness for him.

"No. Whenever I asked, Grandfather said you would be here one of these days. When Father came to live here, he said so, too. Then Raymond came." He gestured toward Penny. "And now you're here. It's just the way everybody said it was going to be, isn't it, Mother?"

"Haven't you ever wondered what it would be like

to see London?" she persisted. "Or Paris? Some of the cities in the United States?"

"Oh, but I've been to all of those places. A lot of others, too. For the theater and the opera. The ballet. The Olympics."

"Who takes you? One of the tutors?"

"Oh, no." He shook his head. "It's usually Uncle Raymond. But Father took me to the Olympics in Los Angeles. It was great fun."

"Do you know that I live there, in Beverly Hills?" she asked carefully.

"Yes, I know. Father had the chauffeur drive by the house where you used to live together. Then we went by the house where you live now. It was too bad you were away on business when Father and I were there," he said earnestly. "It would have been super to visit you and meet my sister." He smiled an open, honest little boy's smile. "She's beautiful, isn't she? I can't wait for her to get here. It'll be smashing."

Valerie glanced at Victor and blinked back furious tears. The impulse to reach into her evening bag and fire at him until he was dead welled up within her. The mass murderer. The monster who had so cruelly manipulated her, her children, and even Raymond. She took several sips of wine, then drew a deep breath, trying to calm herself.

Victor turned his head and his eyes locked with hers. The expression in his gaze was agonized, miserable. Oh, I know that look, she thought bitterly. I know every expression in his repertoire. He can turn them on. He can turn them off. None of them mean a thing.

Valerie excused herself before dessert was served. Penny and Junior walked with her along the marble corridor to her suite, chattering excitedly.

"I've got to get some sleep now." She smiled as she reached down to hug Penny, then Junior. "But we'll have all day tomorrow." She hugged them to her again, together, until each began to pull away.

The old baron's estate was hardly an intellectual desert, Valerie thought, closing the door of her suite behind her, savoring the feeling of holding her sons in her arms. The conversation at the table had been more interesting than that at most of the dinner parties she could remember. The company was first-rate, and so was the food.

"And with our satellite dishes, Mother," Penny had said, "we can get all five television stations from Buenos Aires."

"Do you go to the city often?" Valerie inquired.

"Oh, yes. We've been to the museums there, and the theater, and the opera," said Victor, Jr.

"Sometimes we get to have lunch on the docks and watch the freighters unload," added Penny. "But the best thing is the soccer. It's great fun."

"Or we go in to see a movie," said Victor, Jr. "But we have all the films on videocassette."

"What do you do here?" asked Valerie.

"It's super, Mother!" exclaimed Penny. "We hunt in the jungle, and we can go fishing in the river. And there's a whole string of polo ponies. Have you ever played polo, Mother? We must teach you."

Valerie felt the warm water she was using to remove her makeup trickle through her fingers as she remembered the deference her sons had displayed toward Victor. They so wanted his approval, just the way Victor had wanted his own father's approval. She supposed it was always that way: boys and their fathers. Patting her face dry, she wondered how long it would take for their re-

spect to dissipate if they knew the truth about their father.

Cautiously, she opened the suite's door and looked
into the brightly-lit corridor. A maid popped her head
around a corner.

"Is there anything further madam would like?" she
asked respectfully. Valerie shook her head and slammed
the door shut. Panting, she pushed one of the sofas in
front of it. She was shaking with anger as she switched
off the lights and crawled between the sheets. She took
the little gun from her evening bag and placed it under
her pillow.

68

Valerie slept fitfully that night, reaching for the gun with
trembling hands at every sound. At dawn her eyes
popped open. She threw on a shirt and a pair of trousers,
pushed the sofa away from the door, and stole out into
the marble corridor, where the early morning sun was
already dancing on its polished surface. She wandered
past large and small drawing rooms, dining rooms, librar-
ies, offices, morning rooms, and bedrooms. Maids and
houseboys carrying trays and feather dusters rushed past
her. There must be an indoor staff of forty people, she
calculated, to keep this place in pristine order and the
jungle, only a few hundred feet away, at bay.

She jumped when she heard the quiet voice behind
her.

"Good morning. Did you sleep well?" Turning, she saw Raymond.

"Yes, thank you," she said.

"Come with me. I want you to see my father now." Valerie followed him down a corridor that opened into a suite of several rooms where nurses spoke to each other in hushed tones.

In a large white room, a young doctor leaned over a hospital bed. An oxygen tent covered the top half of the patient's body, and an intravenous tube fed fluid into his arm. Above the bed, Valerie read his heartbeat in the jagged line on the monitor, the jagged line of his brain waves on another. His body, under the white blanket, could not have weighed more than seventy pounds. His bald head was covered by dull gray skin, and his cavernous face was a death mask, the closed eyelids folds of charcoal gray. For a moment, Valerie wondered if they had timed their arrival for the moment of his death.

"How is he?" Raymond asked the doctor, who had finished counting the old baron's pulse and was replacing the claw like hand on top of the white blanket.

"The same."

"Yes, he's always the same," murmured Raymond, satisfied.

"How long has he been like this?" whispered Valerie, her eyes wide.

"A year, two years. I wanted you to see him, you know. See the head of our family.

"I come and sit with him," said Raymond more to himself than to Valerie. "I spend a lot of time with my father. So do your sons. So does their father."

The Land Rover chugged up the long driveway later that morning as Valerie, the boys, and Josie, one of their tutors, waited on the veranda, ready to go on a picnic.

They clambered into the vehicle, and Josie negotiated the treacherous road. Above them, monkeys swung acrobatically from the palm fronds, and Valerie heard an occasional beating of wings as a brightly colored bird took to the air.

The boys, their trousers tucked into high boots and heavy wool ponchos thrown over their shirts, sat in the backseat. Penny grabbed Valerie's shoulder every few seconds to point out birds, monkeys, and what he swore was a jaguar. Both boys, and Josie, wore holstered guns and hunting knives at their belts.

Finally, Josie pulled off the narrow road. They lugged the brimming picnic basket along an overgrown path to a site near a three-hundred-foot waterfall that thundered into the rushing river. A tablecloth was spread, and freshly baked baguettes, two different kinds of pâté, goat cheese, Camembert, Brie, and Jarlsburg were unpacked. The chef had prepared chicken in aspic, a jar of marinated artichoke hearts, crackers, cherry tomatoes, carrot sticks, celery sticks, white and dark chocolate truffles, and fruit tarts the size of a baby's fist. A dozen Cokes for the boys and two bottles of white wine for Valerie and Josie were chilling in a portable refrigerator.

"At first it was funny to go in and sit with grandfather," Penny said at lunch. "I mean, there he was, in the oxygen tent and everything." He pulled off a chunk of one of the baguettes, slathered it with Brie. "But Junior did it all the time, so I would go, too."

"I knew him before, though," Junior said. "He

taught me to play polo. You should have seen him on a horse."

"I got up the nerve to ask the doctor if he knew I was there," Penny continued, "and he said no, he didn't think so. But I keep going anyway. It makes me feel good."

"Father goes all the time," said Junior. "He reads to him."

"He knows he can't hear him," Penny interpolated. "It's because he likes to do it. Well, Grandfather is the head of our family."

"Yes, of course," said Valerie, as she wondered whether the boys would want to leave with her.

It was on the way back to the Land Rover, as they picked their way along the narrow path, that Valerie noticed something unwrap itself from a tree trunk and slide to the ground. She opened her mouth to scream through a barrage of shots. A snake, the longest she had ever seen, seemed to lift in the air before it fell dead before them on the path. The boys ran past her, each claiming it had been his bullet that had killed it.

"What kind was it?" asked Valerie.

"An anaconda," said Josie.

"They're dangerous, aren't they?"

"Very."

"Can you shoot?" asked Valerie.

"Not as well as the boys."

"Maybe they would teach me."

"That's a good idea," said Josie. "The first thing you really have to learn when you come to a place like this is to defend yourself. With all of the interesting people, the wonderful food, it's easy to forget it's dangerous here. But that's the truth. It is dangerous."

"Yes, that's just what I was thinking," said Valerie.

Killing the snake was all the boys could talk about at dinner that night. Valerie nodded, her eyes bright, sharing their triumph. And Victor, at the other end of the table, was telling them how proud he was, trying to catch her eyes. Valerie wouldn't look at him.

"I want Junior to hear you play, Mother," said Penny as they were finishing dessert, a chocolate soufflé. "Would you mind?"

"Well . . ." said Valerie, looking around the table at the expectant faces, inadvertently catching Raymond's eyes. "All right," she said to Penny. "I'll be happy to play."

In the drawing room Valerie played a couple of Strauss waltzes, Chopin's *Polonaise*. As she rose slowly to the ring of applause, she looked at Raymond. His thoughts seemed far away, and she wondered whether he was remembering other evenings in this room when it was his mother at the piano, playing as the old baron liked her to do. Maybe the old baron had heard her just now, she thought, as she realized at the same time that, of course, he hadn't heard her. It would have been fun to play for him, though. To see her grandfather's eyes, approving of her.

———

The next day Valerie stood holding a pistol with both hands, aiming at the target. Missing when she fired. Hitting the outside, the white part.

Penny stood next to her, guiding her arm.

The gun roared.

Bull's-eye.

"Oh, Mother," called Junior from where he was standing, a few feet away. "That's super."

"Thank you," she said, wondering what he would

say if he knew that all she saw when she looked at the target was his father.

A morning later a fleet of Land Rovers was waiting for Valerie, the boys, and Josie when they walked out the front door to begin their tour of the hundreds and hundreds of miles of the old baron's empire. The guides and the cook helped the maids load their luggage into one of them, while others towed the portable kitchen, food and wine, and cases of Coca-Cola for the five-day trip. They were quite an impressive caravan, Valerie saw, as she looked back at the sprawling house receding in the distance.

For the first thirty miles the road was narrow, two lanes, with the jungle encroaching from each side, the driver hitting the horn whenever there was a blind turn. Often, they pulled over to the side, letting trucks pass. The groups of campesinos they passed along the road would stop and watch them, smiling and waving.

Occasionally the road widened and they drove through a settlement, with stores and schools, houses grouped together, vegetable gardens, cows and horses grazing. Chickens and roosters scattered out of their way as the driver gave a couple of beeps on the horn. Two mongrel dogs trotted ahead of them, and children stopped in their tracks to watch them pass, as excited as if they were at a parade. A couple of the settlements even had town squares. Churches. Open stands sold fruit gathered from the jungle, soft drinks, chewing gum. Along the way, they stopped at a bauxite mine, a tin mine, where nearly a thousand men worked and where they were treated like visiting royalty, especially the boys.

At dusk the caravan stopped to set up camp for the night. It seemed to Valerie that the yellow tent she was to share with Josie was erected in a matter of minutes.

Inside, it was capacious, a light powered by a portable generator in place, a table and chairs in its center. Cots on either side of the tent with thin mattresses, sheets, blankets, down pillows, just like home. There was a mirror on one of its walls, a basin, a pitcher of fresh water so big that it took both hands to lift it. Plastic glasses, a giant thermos filled with steaming coffee.

Valerie wore a blouson windbreaker lined with sable over her sweater, trousers tucked into the tops of her high boots, a sable hat that came down over her ears against the biting cold as she, along with Josie, in her fur poncho, stepped through the flaps of the tent. The boys were already waiting for them at the table set up near the blazing fire. They wore furs to their ankles, and their eyes were tearing from the cold. The table was covered with a white linen tablecloth, set with heavy plastic plates, stainless steel utensils. A bottle of wine. The food, prepared in the portable kitchen by the cook and his assistants, was marvelous, unlike anything Valerie had ever tasted. There was thinly sliced beefsteak, called *milensa*, Josie told her, thin, juicy slices of roast pork, both layered onto crisp French rolls and slathered with chimicurri sauce, made with lots of garlic and a dozen other spices. There was a massive platter of fugazzatas, chewy pizza crusts, sliced open and piled with ham and cheese, their tops strewn with mild marinated onions, a sprinkling of herbs. From behind the portable kitchen, they heard raucous laughter from the crew, the buzz of Spanish.

The crew chief appeared, shivering in his wool poncho, opened another bottle of white wine, and splashed it into Valerie's glass, Josie's glass. The wind caught a corner of the tablecloth, whipped it up, while they all grabbed for it. Valerie looked at Penny's face, Junior's face, saw their eyes bright with the excitement of being there.

In the morning the caravan headed south. In a couple of hours, the brush was low and scraggly, the stands of trees stunted. They were on the plains now with great herds of cattle, grazing. A group of gauchos in their leather chaps, their wool ponchos, cantered along beside the Land Rovers, escorting them to the settlement where they were expected. After lunch, the boys rode out on cow ponies, and didn't return until nearly dinner, with the clatter of hoofs, a cloud of dust.

They moved on, stopping to explore areas of interest. To bathe in icy streams. At last, they were heading north again. At a bend in the river there was a logging camp, which harvested the great stands of trees and sent them splashing downstream. It was a large settlement, populated by several hundred people, with dormitories for the single men, single-story apartment complexes for the married couples, a general store, a school. Modern offices where the office manager, an attractive young woman about her own age, approached Valerie and introduced herself.

"I'm Louisa Espinosa," she said, holding out her hand. In back of her were rows of desks where other young women worked at typewriters or short wave radios.

"I'm Valerie Penn," she said, taking the other woman's hand.

"My grandmother works for Mr. Raymond Penn in London," Louisa said, smiling. Pretty teeth in a pretty face. Curling brown hair. Gray eyes.

"Have you ever been there?" asked Valerie, realizing who the woman was. "To London, I mean?"

"Once, long ago," the other woman said. "And

then I went to university in Buenos Aires. The baron paid for it."

"You didn't want to stay? In Buenos Aires, I mean?" Valerie asked, dropping her hand. Not knowing where to look. Not knowing what to say.

"Oh, no," the other woman said. "It's better here. Working for the family."

"Are you married?" asked Valerie.

"Yes, I'm married," she replied. "My husband is the supervisor you met earlier. And we have children. Two little girls so far."

"The boys are here, you know," said Valerie. "They're down below with the men, watching the logs go into the river."

"Yes, I know," she said, nodding. "They're beautiful boys, Mrs. Penn. You must be very proud of them."

"Do you ever see them?" asked Valerie casually.

"Not for a long time," said the other woman. "But I'll always have a special place in my heart for them. For Mr. Victor Penn's son. For both his sons."

And, finally, they were on their way home.

———

They had been traveling for five days, traversing hundreds and hundreds of miles, and they had never left the old baron's estate. There must have been fifteen staff members waiting to welcome them as they pulled up to the entrance of the low, rambling house. One of the maids was already in Valerie's bathroom, drawing her bath. She helped Valerie out of her dusty clothes, whisking them away to be cleaned, pressed, and returned the next morning.

Valerie sank into the bathtub and closed her eyes.

Leaning her head back, she felt the hot water cover her body.

So the surrogate who had carried Victor, Jr., to term was alive and happy. But Engvy Erickson was dead. Valerie shook her head. She also realized the only way to leave the estate with her children was by helicopter. She would need Raymond, or at least his approval. Or Victor's approval, which she would obtain even if she had to take him hostage.

After she had bathed and dried her hair, Valerie lay down on her bed and tried to nap. Tossing, her mind wide awake, she decided that what she really wanted to do was look in on the old baron, see that he was all right. Sit with him for a while. Maybe even tell him about the trip, how impressed she was with the empire he had built. Tell him how much fun the boys had had, riding with the gauchos, exploring. He wouldn't hear what she was saying, of course, but maybe, on some level, he would know somebody was there, sitting beside him. His own flesh and blood. Raymond's daughter.

He looked exactly the same. The jagged lines on the monitors above his hospital bed had not fluctuated. She had been sitting for no more than several minutes when she heard the nurses greet someone else. Deference was evident in their voices.

Victor looked fabulous in a pair of pleated trousers and an open-collared silk shirt. A gold watch flashed on his tanned wrist. His hands were thrust into his pockets. He went pale as he saw Valerie at his father's bed.

"I need to talk to you," she said in a loud whisper.

Victor looked from her to his father, then glanced at the monitors over the bed.

"In fifteen minutes," he said softly. "In my suite."

Valerie nodded. He smiled tightly, turned, and left.

69

Hearing nothing after she tapped on the door to Victor's suite, Valerie pushed it open.

Victor hadn't lost his taste for French and English antiques, she saw, looking around his large, silent drawing room. Drawn curtains along one wall closed off what she assumed was a private courtyard. The old portrait of Valerie with the infant twins in her arms hung above the chimneypiece. It gave her a start to see it there, after so many years.

Around the room in silver frames were photographs. The baron and baroness, she in a gown and jewels, he young and dashing. The two of them in front of a castle in the German countryside, with Victor and Raymond as children. Pictures of Alexandra and Penny. Pictures of Valerie, jeweled, begowned, smiling. Several of Valerie and Victor. Dressed for the Red Cross Ball in Monaco. On the deck of their yacht. In front of the house in France. At the foot of the steps of the Penn International jet, about to board.

There were photographs of Victor, Jr., too. As a baby, in his grandfather's arms. A little older, a toddler holding Victor's hand. Astride a pony. Around four years old, in tennis whites, holding a racket. She thought of all of Junior's years Victor had stolen from her, and her fury at him rose again. What could Junior have thought, seeing the family pictures? Where did he think he fit in that portrait of a happy family? How could she ever explain to him that she hadn't had anything to do with it? That she had known nothing about it?

She wandered into the silence of Victor's bedroom, the muted colors reflecting the master architect's original plan. Bronze mirroring above silk-paneled walls visually extended the pitched ceiling. A magnificent Goya hung over the chimneypiece. There was a Blue Period Picasso. Victor's bow to the twentieth century, she thought wryly. It would probably be moved out in a week or two, another treasure moved in. As Claude said, Victor's attention span was almost as long as a two-year-old child's. If Claude could have produced the ceiling of the Sistine Chapel, da Vinci's Mona Lisa, Michelangelo's David, it still wouldn't be enough for Victor. Nothing was ever enough.

Valerie's eyes lingered on the king-sized bed where, she knew, Victor always slept alone. He wouldn't have changed that much. Whichever woman he was sexually involved with would wait for him, as she had waited. In her own quarters, until the mood was upon him. She sauntered into his dressing room area, a room nearly as large as his bedroom. Mirrored closets concealed his hundreds of suits and as many pairs of handmade shoes. All made especially for him. Like so many of the things in his life. Like Valerie Hemion Penn. Created practically from sugar and spice, everything nice, a hank of hair and a bag of bones, by Lady Anne Hallowell. A virgin, too. Satisfaction guaranteed.

At a tap on the door, she hurried into the drawing room. It was Frederick, the butler, showing no surprise to find her there. The lady of the house where she should be, at long last. Valerie motioned toward a parquetry-inlaid table where he was to set the things for tea. Victor entered the room a moment later.

"Please sit down. I'm sorry I'm late. There were problems in the communications room. The lines to Buenos Aires are down, the usual sort of thing." He avoided her eyes as he poured their tea. "So, how was your trip with the boys? Did you have a good time?"

"Oh, yes. It was wonderful. The boys are the most intelligent, attractive children I have ever seen." She paused. "But they are laboring under a misapprehension." She sipped her tea. "They seem to think I'm here to stay. They told me you're going to send for Alexandra, too. And that from now on, we'll all live here together. Just like one big, happy family." She paused. "Perhaps you thought I would just give up my life, everything I've built, the people I love, and come running," she continued. "Of course, it wouldn't be the first time, would it, Victor? You have precedent on your side. Bringing me to England for the music scholarship. Getting rid of the Hemions so I wouldn't have any option but to stay where I was."

"That was my responsibility." Victor's voice was soft, his gaze lowered. "You were Raymond's daughter. A member of our family."

"Wouldn't it have made sense to mention it to Raymond? After all, I was his concern. Not yours."

"You can't really mean that," he said, still not looking at her.

"Why not?" she persisted.

"Because I didn't know what Raymond's reaction would be," he said, finally meeting her eyes. "Well, maybe I did know, and that wasn't what I wanted to have happen. But you were the only member of the family left. The end of the line. I felt I had to protect you."

"The Hemions were my family," she flared.

"Claude said you were so thrilled when he got them out of the country, you gave him van Gogh's *Hyacinths*."

"Van Gogh's *Hyacinths*?" His expression was disbelieving. "You mean Claude has *Hyacinths*?"

"He certainly does."

"So, Claude has van Gogh's *Hyacinths*," said Victor almost to himself, a laugh in his voice. "Why, that sly old fox. I've been trying to buy that painting for twenty years, and he's had it all along." He shook his head, amused.

Valerie sat back in her chair, watching Victor, the smile on his face. She knew from the finessing she had done in business and that others had tried on her, that Victor was telling the truth. Her hand shook as she sipped her tea.

"He kept telling you that you should meet me," she said quietly.

"Yes." Victor remembered, smiling. "He kept telling me how pretty you were, how charming. How talented."

"He also said you insisted that he introduce you to Maria. You wanted to have an affair with her."

Victor threw back his head and laughed until tears came.

"Excuse me," he said finally. "Yes, yes. It was something like that. But he was the one who wanted me to meet Maria." He gazed at Valerie, his blue eyes dancing, a smile on his face. " 'But, Claude,' I said, 'she's the most notorious lesbian in Europe.' And he said, 'Oh, just now and then, dear boy. Give it a try. You're a man of the world.' "

"And so you did."

"And so I did," agreed Victor, grinning.

"And it was a fiasco."

"It was, indeed," he said, starting to laugh again.

"But you gave her diamonds and rubies," said Valerie.

"That's true," he said, his voice gentle. "Whenever Maria needed anything, I was there for her. She is a great artist. That's the sort of thing one does for the great artists of the world, if one is able. And I was certainly able."

"She said it was so she would keep quiet about your sexual failure. So it wouldn't be all around London that you couldn't perform with her."

"But she didn't keep quiet about it," Victor laughed. "It was all over London twenty minutes after we got back to town. There isn't a man alive who can perform with every woman, darling. Everybody has his failures. And failing with Maria, well, that got me quite a bit of commiseration from the other chaps. Quite a bit of respect, too, that I would ever have attempted to climb that particular mountain."

Darling. Valerie felt a shock at the word.

"Finally, you decided to meet me," she prompted.

"And I decided you were the most exquisite creature I had ever met. Like a wood sprite. Almost unearthly.

"I invited you and Lady Anne for supper and an evening of bridge at Regent's Park," he recalled. "I wanted you to see the house, to show off for you. But really it was so Raymond could meet you and see how lovely you were, what a lady you had become."

"You knew Raymond would know who I was, that I was Cini's daughter. His daughter."

"I thought he would be happy. His daughter. Our own flesh and blood. I was amazed at his reaction." Victor's voice was almost a whisper as he recalled Raymond's fury and scorn.

"Well, Lady Anne was happy," said Valerie bitterly. "She was beginning to put it all together by that time. That her real job had been to raise a proper wife for you. To see that I arrived in our marriage bed a virgin."

"What are you talking about?" He stared at her.

"She was almost out of her mind by that time," said Valerie.

"My exquisite girl—"

"Don't call me that," she snapped.

"Valerie." He flushed, shaking his head. "I didn't know any of this. My only instructions to Claude were to see that you were happy. That you had everything you wanted."

The evening had drifted into night now, the sunlight in the room fading into gray. Valerie watched Victor as he rose, walked across the room, and flipped on the lights. She wondered again who he was.

70

"By the way, I met Louisa Espinosa," said Valerie conversationally. Her hands on her lap covered her handbag, the loaded gun inside.

Victor was across the room, leaning against the mantelpiece, every word she spoke draining a few more drops of blood out of his face.

"She was certainly happy to see the boys. Especially Junior. She told me she'll always have a special place in her heart for him."

"It had to be that way," said Victor reflectively.

"Oh, really? What way was that, Victor?"

"I need a drink to talk about this," he muttered, walking over to the phone, hitting the intercom, giving a rapid order that she couldn't quite hear. In a minute, maybe less, there was a tap on the door and Frederick was there with a silver ice bucket and an unopened bottle of Roederer Cristal was being set on the table in front of her.

Victor uncorked the champagne, filled her glass, then his own. There was a faint ring of crystal as he touched his glass to hers. He ran his hand through his hair.

"Raymond was very upset when I told him I wanted to marry you," he said in a low voice, looking away from her. "He seemed to think that all I wanted to do was get at him in some way by making you my wife. But it wasn't that way. I wanted to marry you because I loved you, because I wanted to spend the rest of my life with you. The drawback, that we might have a deformed child, well, that wasn't possible. My sperm count was so low that the chances that I could ever impregnate you were about a million to one."

"How did you know that?"

"Oh, in my wilder days there had been a couple of incidents." He grinned. "Women whose attorneys had contacted mine, threatening to bring paternity suits. I had the results of my tests."

"And you put me through that charade, Victor, telling me it was my fault I couldn't get pregnant."

"That was unfair," he said, his eyes down, "but that was the masculine thing to do, I guess. You thought I was perfect. I could see that every time you looked at me. For me to admit that it was my fault, well, I just couldn't. I thought I could make you so happy that the two of us together would be enough. But I knew you wanted a child. And my father wanted a grandchild, too.''

"And because of Gordon Lerner you told the baron there might be a way," she prompted.

"Yes, I explained the procedure to him after I sat down with Lerner and had it explained to me. He told me the hormones you would be taking could produce as many as twelve eggs, and that it was only safe to inseminate the surrogate with four of them. My father asked me what would happen to the rest of the eggs, and I said that I supposed they just disposed 'of them. Well, he wouldn't hear of that. He would send a girl from here. She could be inseminated with the other eggs, and he would have his own grandson to raise here on the estate. He loved the notion.''

"And you went along."

"I never thought it would work. I thought, Oh, well, let him have his way. It isn't going to hurt anything. I couldn't believe it when he told me Louisa was pregnant, and that the doctor here had assured him she would deliver a fine, healthy baby boy.''

"You never told me about Louisa."

"How could I?" he asked helplessly. "What would I have said to you, Valerie? That you were my niece, and that my father insisted that a woman in Argentina be inseminated with our child? When you were in Switzerland with Engvy, waiting out the birth of the twins? You must see I couldn't have done that.''

It would have been impossible, she realized. Yes, she could see that.

"God, that was a terrible time," he murmured. "The pressure from my father. My failure that I saw in your eyes every time I looked at you. And then after it all started, the procedure, with you taking those hormones. All I wanted to do was make love to you, feel your legs closing around my back, those long, beautiful, white legs. Feel you engulf me, lose myself in you. Become you."

Valerie shook her head, wondering if she was really hearing these words.

"Instead," he said, his smile almost shy, "I was doing what Gordon Lerner had told me to do. Harvesting the sperm, as they euphemistically call it." He smiled ruefully. "Gordon Lerner must have had about three gallons of the stuff to work with by the time I was through."

"Engvy . . . she died," Valerie said.

"I couldn't tell you," he whispered, shaking his head. "I knew how much you loved her. How grateful you were to her for giving us our babies. And then, that terrible, terrible accident. It was so unfair. So grotesquely unfair."

"Claude told me you had her killed so she couldn't say anything."

"Did he?" He smiled. "Did he really say that?"

He hadn't, Valerie realized. He had only implied it when he mentioned the terrible accident.

"But you had all the passengers on the Penn International jet killed."

"Claude didn't say that," he said, his tone brusque.

"He didn't have to."

"Look, Valerie," he said, standing again, pacing. "There are a lot of sins that have rightfully been laid at my door. Yes, the crash of the Penn International empire. I made bad business decisions. Many of them. I committed to expanding the business into America, and it turned out to be overexpansion. I compromised the banks and their assets."

"Laundering drug money, millions that terrorists all over the world had been paid in ransom," she enumerated quietly.

"Those were strictly my father's policies."

"Didn't that bother you?" She searched his face. "A little, maybe?"

"If you examine the origins of many major businesses, you'll find they were far worse," he said coldly, leaning against the wall while looking across the room at her. "We didn't sell the drugs, and we didn't kidnap anybody. We just dealt with the money."

"But you did go along with Claude when he told you that he had come up with a plan to cover your escape."

"He said he had a plan he thought might work," he corrected her. "I told him to go ahead with it. I didn't know what it was." He pulled open the curtains covering the glass wall. A million stars gleamed in the dark sky, a full moon silhouetted the trees, the flowers, the fountains in the courtyard.

"You didn't want to know what it was."

"Valerie," he said impatiently, "all I did was slip across the border into Canada, get on a plane a few days later to Singapore, come back here." He walked back to the table and poured himself another glass of champagne. "When I read about what Claude had done, I was appalled. It was overkill. A waste."

So what if he hadn't actually dirtied his hands, she thought. He had certainly given the final approval. Said something like, "Good work, Claude."

"And you never considered taking me along," she murmured.

"I couldn't do that to you," he said with a dismissive, angry gesture of his hand. "I couldn't put you through the disgrace. It would have been unthinkable to ask you to share a fugitive's life with me. Unthinkable."

"Claude said you didn't take me along because you were getting bored with me," she said, remembering her pain at Claude's words. "You were tired of me gazing at you, adoring you. You only stayed with me to annoy Raymond."

Victor's face was grim, flushed with annoyance. He locked his eyes with hers and gestured toward the bedroom.

"If you want to find out just how bored I am with you, let's go in there, and I'll show you right now."

"You left me with nothing," she said savagely.

"Well, that's not quite true," he said, sitting down again in the chair across from her. "I left you with Alexandra."

"Why didn't you take her, too?" She fought back angry tears. "It almost killed her when you took Penny."

"I couldn't take her." He shook his head. "I couldn't do that to you. Leave you without a child." He sighed, exasperated over arguments evidently resolved in his own mind long ago. "It was what the baron wanted. As soon as he saw that picture of you with Max in the *New York Times* and read that the two of you were going to be married, the baron told me to get Claude to pick up the children as soon as possible and bring them here. You see, he wasn't going to have his grandchildren raised by outsiders.

"But I said to him that I wouldn't take both of them. It was ghastly enough that you were destitute, that I couldn't do anything about it because the FDIC and the IRS were watching you. They would have known in a second if I was getting money to you somehow, known that I was alive." He paused. "It was the only time in my life that I stood up to him," he finished quietly.

She gazed at him, the handsome face, the bright blue eyes, wondering if she had ever really felt that he was her life. She shrugged; blamed it on her youth.

"It was bad enough that Raymond refused to funnel my money to you, to see that you were financially secure," he continued. "I literally got down on my knees and begged him. Finally, the baron said that it would be all right to just bring the boy. He had thought it over, and he had decided that a girl should be with her mother."

"And what did Raymond think?"

"He wanted to bring them both. Right after I had gotten here. Even before they went home to Beverly Hills, to you."

"Claude said it was you," she mused.

"You believe a man like Claude Vilgran." He shook his head in disbelief.

"He said you killed Max."

"That's absurd," snorted Victor contemptuously. "You lived with me for twelve years, Valerie, and you know I needed my valet even to put on my cuff links. Now you're telling me I suddenly developed the mechanical skill to tamper with the brakes on a car? To be able to calculate what to do with them so they would last ten miles, twenty miles, whatever it was?" He looked at her angrily. "Listen to yourself. You can't believe what you're saying."

She drew in a deep breath. "Victor, I'm going to take the boys back to Beverly Hills with me when I leave. That's why I wanted to see you. To tell you that I'm going to take them."

Victor toyed with the stem of his champagne flute. "I had hoped you would want to stay."

"I have my own life."

"You're my wife," he said quietly.

"I'm a different person now."

"Of course," he conceded. "A beautiful woman now, instead of a girl. Competent. Wealthy in your own right. Every man who sees you wants you, wants to take you to bed and touch you. Make love to you." His gaze swept across her face and met her eyes. "How I hated them."

"You hated them so much you killed Max, or had him killed," she muttered. "You would have had Harry Cunningham killed, too, if somebody hadn't beaten you to it."

"Did you get pregnant?" he asked. "Was it Harry?"

"Yes." She sighed.

"And you had an abortion."

"Yes, I had an abortion. And yes, I've been to bed with other men. But they weren't criminals, or murderers, or fugitives." Her whole body was shaking now, her voice trembling with fury. "Don't you see why I have to take the boys out of here? To see that they have the chance to lead decent lives?"

"You're not extending the same generosity to me that I extended to you. I left you Alexandra."

"Look, Victor, this isn't about dividing up the prizes. I'm taking my sons out of here."

"What if they don't want to go?" he asked mildly. "After all, they're royalty here. And Victor, Jr., has never lived anywhere else. This is his home."

"Oh, they'll want to go," she said with a bitter laugh. "If it comes to it—and believe me, Victor, I pray it doesn't—I'll tell them the truth. You see, I have that."

Victor sat silently, so still in his chair that Valerie had to strain to see that he was breathing. Finally he sighed, glanced at his watch, and stood up.

"All right," he said finally. "I'll go along with anything they want to do. If they want to leave, I won't try to stop them."

"Oh, thank you, Victor," she stuttered, tears of relief flooding her eyes.

"But telling them about the *in vitro* fertilization, and the surrogates, isn't going to convince them," he said. "They already know."

"What?" she asked blankly.

"Of course, they don't know about Raymond. I haven't told them yet that he's your father. That I married my niece. No, they're still a little young for that. I don't think they would be able to understand the passion a man can feel for a woman when he loves her, wants her so much, he'll do anything to have her. Anything." He paused. "Do you intend to tell them that? That Raymond is your father? Their grandfather?"

"No," she whispered, shaking her head, both of her hands clutching her handbag under the table.

She felt his hand on her shoulder. "It's getting late," he said softly.

"Yes, of course," she murmured, pushing back her chair, starting to rise.

He was standing in front of her, politely moving aside to let her pass.

"What did they say?" she asked. "When you told them about it, I mean."

"Oh, they thought it was wonderful." He grinned. "I told them what a pregnancy does to a woman. About how it stretches her skin, destroys her body. How a fetus sucks what it needs from her, depletes her." He walked toward the door and placed his hand on the knob. His smile broadened. "They were horrified. Neither of them wanted his mother to have gone through anything like that. Especially since it was so easy to pay somebody else to do the hard part."

"Was that your reason, too?" she asked, her voice a whisper. "You didn't want me to be in pain, to be frightened?"

"No, not at all." He shook his head. "My reason was just what you probably assumed it was. I wanted your body to be slim, lithe, with high, firm breasts. Pale pink nipples. I wanted your stomach to be flat under my touch, your hips narrow, your legs slender and white. I wanted to know that all you were thinking of was me. I used to sit on the plane, in meetings, thinking of you nude under your dress, always ready for me. I couldn't get enough of you."

"You had them drug me after the twins were born," she said, her breath coming in little gasps. "So I wouldn't know it when they inserted the ring."

"That's right."

"And later you would drug me yourself, you'd watch me while I screamed, begged you to take me . . ."

He reached toward her face, and, with a finger, traced the outline of her jaw.

"And you loved it," he said in that soft voice that was like a caress.

"Yes," she whispered. "I loved it."

71

Valerie stumbled into the marble corridor, every vestige of poise stripped away. Back in her suite, she rushed to her bed and threw herself down, burying her face in the pillow. Put her arms around herself, trying to pull herself together.

After a long time, she rose wearily and walked over to the glass wall leading onto the courtyard, watching the fountain spray over the sculpture in its center.

Amazing, that he could still get to her that way, she thought, looking at her shaking hands. It was just that he'd pushed the button on some old tape, though, she reassured herself. It was about who she had been, not who she was now.

It had been different between them, she knew, as she thought back over the afternoon. Very different. Victor had spoken to her as an equal. He had addressed her by name, Valerie. It had been straightforward.

Yet whose version of their relationship was the truth? If Claude's version was the truth, Victor would have been at Raymond all the time, taunting him, keeping the game with her going because, without Raymond's daughter, any other game between him and Raymond wouldn't be nearly as much fun.

Or, Victor really cared for her, loved her to distraction, felt a passion he couldn't begin to describe. A passion so intense that he had to marry his brother's daughter to assuage it.

Her step was firmer as she walked across the room, stood in front of her closet trying to decide what to wear to dinner. If Victor loved anybody, it was the Valerie of long ago. He didn't know the woman she had become. He couldn't even begin to know her.

And clearly she had never known whether he was even capable of love. Never known him. As she strode toward the drawing room with its chatter of voices, she wondered if their encounter that evening had been just another inning in the game he had played with Raymond since boyhood.

That evening at dinner, Victor treated her with the same polite charm he showed everybody. She slept fitfully, his face floating in her mind. Just before dawn, she woke with a start. In the jungle, an animal roared.

I've accomplished what I came for, she told herself, fingering the little gun. I can leave. I can take my sons. In time, Victor, all of it, will just be a memory. She drifted off to sleep.

———

She heard the handle of the door turn in the next room, the door open and softly close.

"Who's there?" she said, already knowing. She sat bolt upright in her bed, holding the gun in front of her with both hands.

"Are you going to shoot me?" asked an amused voice.

"What do you want?" She was shaking now.

"Well, I was thinking, way back in a corner of my mind, that we had a date. You were going to meet me at the plane, and we would go back to the house. Close the door of your suite. Make love for a long, long time." He walked slowly toward her, his watch glinting in the moonlight for a fleeting second before he took another step and passed into the shadows.

She looked up at him, her heart beating wildly in her chest.

"And that's rude," he said, sitting down on the bed. "It isn't nice to make a date with a lady and then not keep it. Especially if the lady is your wife."

"You're out of your mind, Victor," she said hoarsely, holding the gun limply in one hand. She closed her eyes and turned away from him.

"Of course, if you're not interested, just say so, darling," he said, his fingers splaying an inch or two above her face. "Tell me to leave, my sweet girl, and I will. You know that."

She was speechless as his fingertips touched her cheek. Turning her head, and looking into Victor's eyes, she was helpless against the impulse to brush his cheekbone with her palm, run her fingers in the thick graying hair at his temples. A sob escaped from her throat as he took her in his arms, brushed his lips against hers, and kissed her, licking her lips, his tongue entering her mouth. She clung to him, held him as if she couldn't get enough of the feel of him against her.

"Do you want to touch me, darling? Here, unbutton my shirt and you can put your hand on my chest." Her hands trembling, she touched the buttons. Victor moved her fingers for her until her hand was against his chest, and she felt his heart beat, his breath, the familiar tangle of hair. His hand was on her shoulder, pushing down the sheet she held weakly against her chest. He fingered the lacy straps of her nightgown, the curve of her collarbone.

"I love you, darling," he whispered, his lips soft against hers. "Oh, how I've missed you. Looking into your face. Hearing your voice. Touching you." He held her tightly, his chest pressed against her breasts. Rocking her in his arms. He kissed her forehead, her cheeks, ran his tongue along her nose. He pushed the sheet to the floor and stared at her in her nightgown for a moment. Unable to let him go that long, unable to stop touching him, she kneaded his shoulders with her hands, she pulled his face down to cover it with kisses. Knowing all the time that she shouldn't be touching him at all.

Victor was touching her, ripping off her nightgown, his mouth on her breasts, his tongue pushing into her navel. His hands stroked the soft pubic hair between her legs as he somehow struggled out of his own clothes at the same time. He whispered urgent words of love to her as she frantically kissed his mouth, his body, not wanting to stop long enough to tell him how much she loved him, how she had missed him, how she had longed for this moment.

But no, the man I missed, longed for, was the husband I trusted, she thought, as she felt his mouth on one of her nipples, biting it. That man never existed.

And this man?

He was getting back at his brother. Taking her here, in this house where they grew up, would prove once and for all which of them was stronger. And it would be all the sweeter for Victor because she was part of the game now. She knew who she was.

I'm not going to do this, she thought wildly, trying to wiggle out of his grasp, her hand searching the sheets, trying to find the gun. I won't be your ultimate conquest, you monster.

She was panting, her body soaked with perspiration, tendrils of hair wet against her neck. Victor was on his knees between her legs, triumphant, lifting each slim ankle into the air, as she struggled against him. She looked up, saw his chest, glistening with perspiration, his head thrown back, his eyes closed in ecstasy. Felt his penis touch the mouth of her vagina, as she felt hard metal in her hand.

"Victor." She gasped, as the room flooded with light.

Raymond stood in the doorway, a gun in his hand, aimed at Victor's back.

"Daddy, no! Don't shoot him! Please!"

There was a sharp crack as Raymond pulled the trigger. Victor slumped on top of her, the blood splattering over her breasts, her face, her hair.

Raymond stood over her, his expression icy with contempt, his face white, as he grabbed the shoulder of Victor's body. He rolled him off her onto the floor, where he lay obscenely sprawled, his chest matted with blood.

Valerie cowered on the bed, the bloody sheet pulled over her breasts. Looking up into Raymond's pale blue eyes, she realized he was going to kill her, too. She closed her eyes tightly, wondering if she would hear the sound of the gun firing before the bullet smashed through her skull.

Something warm and wet stroked her face. As Valerie slowly opened her eyes, she saw that Raymond was awkwardly dabbing her face with a wet towel.

"I didn't have anything to say about what he did to you in the first place," he murmured to himself, "but I wasn't going to let it happen to you again. It isn't right. It never was.

"I saw him wrap Mother around his little finger, too. He just had a way with women, that was all. But my daughter? Well, I couldn't have that."

He glanced at Victor's lifeless body.

"I realized . . ." Valerie gasped, touching his hand. "I wasn't going . . ."

"Yes, well, you'd better get into the shower, get cleaned up," he said gruffly, pulling away. "We're leaving. The boys are packing, and a helicopter is waiting to take us to the airport in Buenos Aires. The plane will take us back to London."

He rose, looked down at her.

"You had better hurry, dear," he said.

Valerie's legs were trembling as she stood up. After she had taken a couple of steps she stopped and braced herself with a hand on the table where the little Degas sculpture stood. Tentatively, she touched it, remembering.

As she stepped into the shower and felt the hot water rushing over her body, she thought about Raymond and what she had called him. Daddy.

He had called her his daughter. And a pet name, too. Dear.

Imagine.

She wondered what Sid would say when she told him.

She was hurrying now.

She didn't want to keep her sons waiting.

Or her father.

Barbara Wilkins is the former Los Angeles bureau chief of *People* magazine. She lives in Beverly Hills. *Elements of Chance* is her first novel.